The Cadet Corporal

The Army Cadets

C.R. Cummings

Also By
CHRISTOPHER CUMMINGS

The Boy and the Battleship
The Green Idol of Kanaka Creek
Ross River Fever
Train to Kuranda
The Mudskipper Cup
Davey Jones's Locker
Air Cadet
Below Bartle Frere
Bowling Green Bay
Airship Over Atherton
Cockatoo
**The Cadet Corporal*
Stannary Hills
Coasts of Cape York
Kylie and the Kelly Gang
Beyond the Barrier Reef
Behind Mt. Baldy
The Cadet Sergeant Major
Cooktown Christmas
Secret in the Clouds
Mischief at Mingela
The Word of God
The Cadet Under-Officer
Through the Devil's Eye
Barbara in the Bush
The Smiley People
Barbara at her Best
Barbara's Bivouac

The Cadet Corporal

The Army Cadets

C.R. Cummings

Second Revised Edition Published 2021 by DoctorZed Publishing

DoctorZed Publishing books may be ordered through booksellers or by contacting:

DoctorZed Publishing
10 Vista Ave
Skye, South Australia 5072
www.doctorzed.com

ISBN: 978-0-6450656-5-7 (hc)
ISBN: 978-0-6450656-6-4 (sc)
ISBN: 978-0-6450656-9-5 (ebk)

National Library of Australia Cataloguing-in-Publication entry

Author: Cummings, C. R., author.

Title: The Cadet Corporal/ Christopher Cummings.

ISBN: 978-0-6450656-5-7 (hardcover)

Series: Cummings, C. R. The army cadets.

Target Audience: For young adults.

Subjects: Adventure stories, Australian.

Military cadets--Queensland--Fiction.

Printed in Australia, UK & USA

DoctorZed Publishing rev. date: 21/03/2021

Special Thanks

This book is dedicated to Captain 'Dibbo' Duncan and the Officers of Cadets of the Cairns State High School Cadet Unit (1961-1962) with fondest regards and gratitude for providing that life-altering experience.

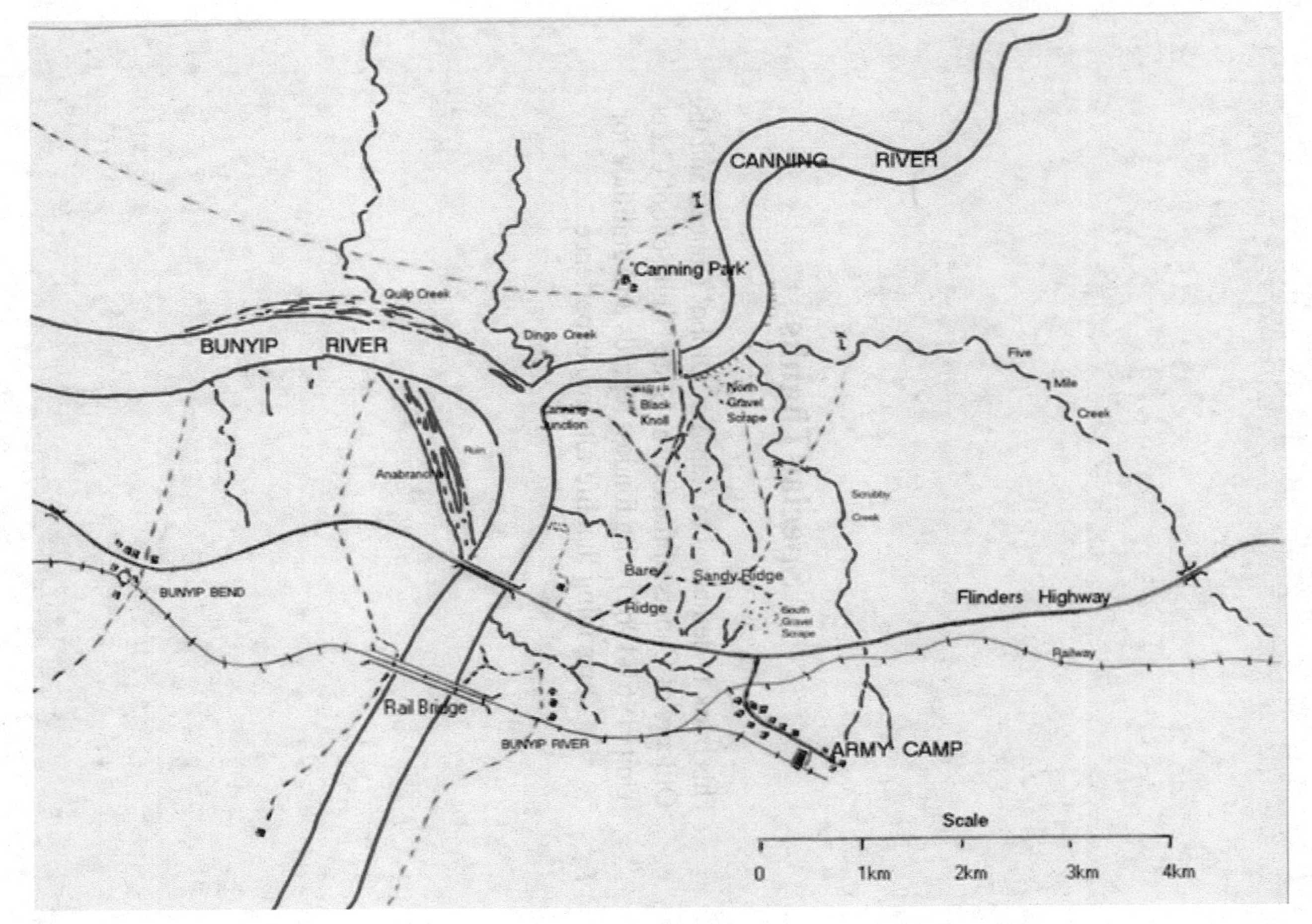
CANNING RIVER
'Canning Park'
Quilp Creek
Dingo Creek
BUNYIP RIVER
Black Knoll
North Gravel Scrape
Five Mile Creek
Ruin
Anabranch
Scrubby Creek
Bare Ridge
Sandy Ridge
South Gravel Scrape
BUNYIP BEND
Flinders Highway
Railway
Rail Bridge
BUNYIP RIVER
ARMY CAMP
Scale
0
1km
2km
3km
4km

Chapter 1

COWARD!

"You're a coward Kirk. Yer' gutless!"

The jeering insult bit deep, and 15-year-old Army Cadet Corporal Graham Kirk turned to face his accuser, the heat of his anger mixing with the chill of fear. He blinked to clear the sweat from his eyes while his mind raced in an attempt to find an easy way out of the crisis which had suddenly erupted. 5 paces away stood the bane of his life: Cadet 'Pigsy' Pike. Behind and beside Pigsy stood his cronies: Waters, Franks and Moynihan. On the ground lay a cadet they were bullying.

Pigsy sneered and bunched his fists onto his hips. "Well? Come on ya gutless wonder. Whatcha gunna do then eh?"

Graham stared at Pigsy with a mixture of fear and distaste. His rational mind tried to tell him that theoretically the situation was simple to resolve. He was a corporal with two stripes on his sleeve and Pigsy was only a cadet with none. But he knew with gut-wrenching certainty that it was far from that simple. To start with they were only part-time army cadets, still at school and not covered by any sort of military law regulations to give him effective power. On top of that both boys were the same age and went to the same high school, as did the other bullies. Any confrontation would carry on long after the camp and could, Graham knew from bitter experience, make life a misery for months.

Besides, Pigsy was considerably bigger, a hulking brute whose physical appearance matched his nickname: pale blue eyes close together, a scowling jowl, pug nose and close-cropped hair behind a receding forehead. Pigsy's arms hung down like those of a gorilla and he had huge hands and feet. The feet looked even bigger, encased as they were in army boots. Graham had seen him use them to kick a person.

I could threaten to call the officers, Graham thought anxiously, glancing sideways to check that the object of the bullies' attention, Cadet David Carnes, had regained his feet.

Another glance flickered around the tops of the surrounding gully in the hope that one of the officers, or even a sergeant, might arrive.

The confrontation was taking place in a shallow, gentle sided re-entrant among dry savannah bush. Only a hundred metres away were a whole company of cadets. The company was busy setting up camp, but none were visible.

By this time Graham regretted he had ever walked down into the gully looking for a place to do a pee out of sight of the girls in the unit. Here he had come upon Pigsy and his toadies busy teasing and tripping Cadet Carnes. Carnes was only a new recruit and was a Year 8 student while Pigsy and his mates were, like Graham, Year 10s. It was obvious why Pigsy and Co. were there; they were a work party sent to dig the male latrine. Franks, who was a lance corporal, was obviously supposed to be in command. Equally obviously he wasn't as he held a pick and had been digging when Graham had walked over the crest. Pigsy, needless to say, had no tool in his hands.

Graham breathed deeply and tried to calm his heart rate. He wiped perspiration from his lips and blinked.

Blast! he thought. *Why did this have to happen?*

They had only arrived at the camp site half an hour earlier and he had been really looking forward to the camp. Once again he looked hopefully back to see if anyone of senior rank was visible.

Pigsy clearly divined his thoughts. He gave an ugly laugh and said, "Hoping some officer will come along and save you are you, you snivelling little crawler?"

At that Graham mentally winced. He knew that he could threaten to tell the officers but equally knew that, if he did, the gang would make his life hell in various ways. Instead he turned to the white-faced and crying Carnes. "Get back to your platoon Cadet Carnes," he ordered, trying to keep the quaver of uncertainty out of his voice.

"Stay here Carnes," Pigsy countered.

Carnes glanced fearfully from one to the other, uncertainty on every line of his face. Graham became exasperated. "Get going Cadet Carnes. That is an order."

"And I'm tellin' you to stay here," Pigsy growled.

"Go!" Graham cried. "I'm the corporal. Do as I say." Even as he said this Graham knew it would enrage Pigsy. Both he and Pigsy were 'Second Year' cadets but Graham had been chosen to go on the promotion course the previous December while Pigsy and his friends had not. That had caused festering resentment and many snide comments about 'crawling', 'boot-licking' and 'being the officer's bum boy'.

His heart now hammering with anxiety Graham stepped closer to Carnes and pointed up the gully. "Get moving!"

"You go and I'll pulp ya!" Pigsy threatened. He also moved a pace closer.

Graham moved to stand between Pigsy and Carnes. He had a horrible sinking feeling that the whole situation was getting out of control and that he would have to do something. To his intense relief he heard Carnes go hurrying away up the slope, his boots rustling the tufts of dry grass and dead leaves that gave sparse covering to the ground.

"You want a fight Kirk?" Pigsy asked, his eyes glittering with the challenge.

"No," Graham replied. He had trouble keeping his voice steady and his vision seemed to narrow down to just Pigsy.

"That's 'cause you are gutless!" Pigsy taunted. "You are just a weakling; a gutless lump of shit."

Graham swallowed and wondered what to say. He had been in plenty of fights over the last few years and had even been suspended from school over it. Whatever else he wanted he didn't want any more trouble like that. As well, he had been steadily absorbing the leadership ethos of the Australian Army and that did not include the use of physical violence to compel obedience. In fact it was specifically forbidden.

Feeling very much caught in a cleft stick Graham tried to stare Pigsy down. The situation was not helped by Waters jeering and calling, "Smack him about Pigsy!"

Graham knew that any comment about reporting them if they struck an NCO would lead to real aggravation as Pigsy had many lackeys who would do what he ordered. Instead Graham turned on his heel and strode away. It took an effort not to run and at every step he half-expected to be grabbed or hit.

It was insults and jibes that followed. "Coward!", "Gutless turd!", "Officer's pet!" they called.

It hurt but Graham tried to rationalise his retreat as the best tactic in the circumstances. Even so he flamed with shame and wondered if he really was a coward.

What will I do when things really come to the crunch? he thought.

At that moment a person appeared among the spindly, black-trunked ironbarks at the head of the re-entrant. It was the company sergeant major, Cadet Warrant Officer Cleland. The CSM pointed down the gully and shouted, "Hoy! You lot, get up here on the double!"

Pigsy shouted back, his tone insolent. "We gotta dig a dunny."

"Dig a dunny SIR you mean Cadet Pike," CSM Cleland snapped. "You can get that finished after the OC has done his briefing, now get up here."

By now Graham was halfway up the side of the gully. Relief had swept over him to such an extent he felt ashamed of himself.

Am I really a coward? he wondered again.

Also, his original problem still remained: the need to relieve himself. It was now becoming physically urgent. They had been travelling for nearly two hours after leaving the rifle range at Townsville earlier that morning and he was busting. So urgent did his need become when he thought about it that pains shot through him. He cast about for some cover, a gully or bushes.

I can't wait till after the OC has finished his safety brief, he thought.

From experience he knew that would take half an hour or more. Equally, there was no way he wanted to try to do the pee in sight of Pigsy and Co. They would, he knew, tease him mercilessly.

Over to his right was a small dip with several clumps of the small, spiky bushes which grew in the sandy soil. It wasn't much cover but would have to do. He turned towards the bushes. That drew an instant comment from CSM Cleland. "Where are you going Cpl Kirk? Get back to your section and get them on parade."

"I need a leak CSM," Graham replied, blushing with embarrassment.

"Humpf! Get a move on!" CSM Cleland snorted. He turned and strode away.

By now Graham was so far up the slope that he could see the hutchies of the nearest platoon. These were only about 25 metres away but no-one was visible. Reaching the bushes he glanced around to check on Pigsy. The bullies were still 50 paces away and just visible. They had begun strolling in his direction.

By this time Graham could not wait. As quickly as he could he undid his fly and started. Not wanting to allow Pigsy and Co to see it, and thus make insulting comments Graham half turned away from them.

The approach of Pigsy and Co provided the incentive to make all the effort he could to finish. Already Graham could see them looking in his direction and it was obvious from the cruel grins that they had guessed what he was doing. Blushing with embarrassment he looked down and urged his body to complete its business.

A giggle from the other direction attracted his attention. To his dismay, he saw two heads emerging from the top of the next gully—two female heads. Even as he saw them he recognised them. Both were girls in his own section: Kirsty Weldon and Lucy Hind. It was also very obvious they could see what he was doing. Burning with shame he quickly turned away from them. That brought him into full view of Pike.

"Don't point that little thing at us, Kirk!" Pike called.

Hot and flustered Graham forced himself to stop and stuffed his member back into his trousers. With his back to the two girls, who had now walked up out of the gully, he did up his fly, then set off at a fast walk towards the platoon area. As he did, Pike called again.

"Bloody flasher! He was showing it off to the girls. Hey you sheilas, don't look. You'll die laughing!"

Hot with shame Graham hurried on, sick with fear in case the girls complained to the officers. But there was annoyance too because the girls should not have been there. They had been told to go the other way to go to the toilet.

Graham was now up on the flat, open ridge the unit was camping on. Sandy Ridge they nicknamed it because it was more sand than dry grass. The ridge was so wide and flat it extended for hundreds of metres in every direction. In the central area there were only a few trees and under the largest of these, a huge Ironbark, the company was assembling. Around the edges of the ridge were clumps of trees, mostly thin eucalypts. Among these was where the cadets were to camp.

By the time Graham arrived at the big tree most of the company was already there. By then he was perspiring from the effort. He saw that his own platoon, 2 Platoon, was just arriving. As quickly as he could he reported to Sgt Grenfell, then looked to check how many of his section were there. A quick check showed five of them, including his 2ic (and close friend) Lance Corporal Roger Dunning. It was apparent that Roger had acted in his absence and had the section organised. The only ones not seated were the two girls walking across the flat behind him.

Shameful memories made Graham fluster, but he knew he had to act. He went to the back of the section and met the girls as they arrived. "Please don't tell! I'm sorry. I didn't know you were there," he pleaded.

The previous year he had got into real trouble over misbehaving with a girl and he did not want a repetition of that. On that occasion he had not even been in the cadets and the incident had been instrumental in his joining. Now being a cadet was so important to him that he was desperately anxious not to get into any more trouble. His heart was set on becoming a sergeant but he knew he had a real reputation to overcome.

To his relief both girls smiled and giggled. "That's alright," Kirsty replied. "We didn't really see."

In his relief Graham had to bite back a cheeky reply. Kirsty was only a new recruit, a Year 8 girl who had joined three weeks before. She was a slender blonde with no obvious female shape. Now, for the first time Graham really saw her. He noted the sparkling blue eyes full of mischief, the dimples, and the freckles which spotted the plain face and pale white skin. There was no way he would have described her as a beauty, unlike her companion Lucy. Lucy was another blonde, but had a 'peaches and cream' complexion and heart-stopping prettiness.

The two girls were seated at the back of the section and Graham made his way to the front. As he turned to seat himself, he met Kirsty's eye and she gave him an impish smile. That sent his heart skipping, and his anxiety soaring. He knew he was a sucker for a pretty face and that women were his greatest weakness. He hoped they would not be his downfall. Knowing the strict rules in the cadets against 'fraternisation' and relationships, especially across the rank levels, he tried to cool the fire of optimistic speculation which had blazed up.

Seeing the three bullies approaching helped. Before he sat down Graham glanced across to 3 Section and saw Cadet Carnes. Carnes was a thin, pasty-faced cadet who looked miserable most of the time. For a second Carnes met Graham's gaze, then lowered his head so that all Graham could see was the top of his hat.

Poor bugger! he thought. *He looks as though he invites bullying.*

When he was seated at the front of 4 Section Graham tried to relax as CSM Cleland checked with the sergeants that all the cadets were present. The company was seated in section lines behind their corporals so that the whole unit fitted into a very small area and it was easy for the

CSM and sergeants to check if everyone was there. When this was done CSM Cleland turned and strode off in the direction of a clump of trees a hundred metres to the left front. Four vehicles were parked there and a group of people stood in the shade talking: the Officers of Cadets and Cadet Under-Officers.

The OC, Capt Conkey, a tubby, middle-aged man who was also Graham's History and Geography teacher, walked back with the CSM. He was followed by the four Cadet Under-Officers. The CUOs were cadets who had reached the highest rank they could and they were the cadet equivalent of a 2nd lieutenant. All were 17 and were in Year 12 at school.

Graham made himself comfortable, knowing what was coming. It was done at the start of every weekend bivouac and camp: a Ground Orientation and Safety Brief. The only difference was that, at the end of the briefing Capt Conkey got every new cadet to come out the front and promise personally to him that they would do the right thing and behave.

As they did Graham had several sharp flashbacks to doing the same thing the previous year when he had joined cadets. Shame at the memory of breaking his promise now made him silently vow to try even harder to keep it.

Capt Conkey gave me a second chance, he thought. *The best I can do is repay him by not causing trouble.*

That this might turn out to be more difficult than he had supposed became evident even as he thought it. One of the new cadets was Kirsty and as she walked back after making her promise to Capt Conkey she looked at Graham and smiled. It had a very unsettling effect. *Surely she isn't giving me the eye?* he thought. In his patchy experience of females he had suffered so many rebuffs that it did not seem likely. Even so it was food for 'perhaps' thoughts.

After the briefing the OC and CUOs walked away and CSM Cleland ordered the sergeants to 'carry on'. As the cadets in 1 Platoon stood to move off there was a chorus of comments. These were a mixture of amazement and disgust. CSM Cleland called, "What's going on in One Platoon?"

"Carnes has pissed himself!" Cadet 'Puddles' Rundle cried.

"You'd know all about that," added Cadet Grey from 1 Section. Puddles was a notorious bed-wetter.

Graham turned and looked. The front of Carnes' trousers was soaked. Carnes hung his head, a look of utter misery on his face. *Poor bugger!* Graham thought. He knew what had happened. Like himself Carnes had gone down into the gully to have a pee but had been caught by the bullies and had not done it. Then he had been unable to hold it any longer.

Above the babble of comments and jeering cries cut CSM Cleland's voice. "Silence in the ranks! Sergeant Sherry, move them away without all this talking. And stop the teasing."

The noise dropped immediately. Graham looked at CSM Cleland with admiration. The CSM was a stocky Year 12. He looked tough and had a reputation for being hard on people who gave trouble. It took only one more warning from him to ensure complete silence except for the commands of the sergeants. Graham knew that the CSM, although lower in rank than the CUOs, was the cadet with the most responsible and powerful position in the company. The job needed a tough person and Cleland certainly looked tough as he stood there with his hands on his hips in the swirling dust.

Having run foul of CSM Cleland several times, Graham had no desire to incur his displeasure again so he screwed his head around and glared at his section to keep them silent. When it was their turn to move Graham added 'Keep quiet!' as they stood. Sgt Grenfell then marched them back to their platoon area. This was on the south side of the ridge beyond HQ and the officer's area. 2 Platoon was to bivouac among a stand of tall, thin gum trees. As usual the corporals were at the front of the platoon as it marched. This put Cpl Gwen Copeland on Graham's left and his friend Cpl Stephen Bell beyond her.

As soon as the section was fallen out after returning to its area Graham said, "Okay, carry on putting up your hutchies."

He then walked over to where he and Roger were erecting theirs. The cadets did not have tents but were issued with the camouflaged plastic sheets named 'Shelters, Individual'. These were put up by clipping two together along one edge, then tying cord from the joins to two trees and then pegging down the four corners. The result was nicknamed a 'hootchie' or 'hutchie' by the cadets.

As they set to work, Kirsty smiled at Graham and cooed. "Will you help me put up my shelter Graham?" she asked.

The use of his first name annoyed Graham and he knew he should correct her and insist on her calling him by his rank. However. he decided not to. *I will tell her not to later so she isn't embarrassed,* he thought, then despised himself for being a weakling.

"Who are you sharing with?" he asked.

"I don't know," Kirsty replied.

"Who would you like to share with?" Graham asked.

"You," Kirsty answered cheekily.

Graham could not believe his ears. He heard the others snicker and blushed. "You can't. Unit policy is that only people of the same sex can share a hutchie. You will have to share with the other girls."

Kirsty made a face. "Oh poo! I don't like girls. Besides, there are three of us."

That was a problem. There were eight cadets in the section, including three girls. Graham and Roger, having been mates for years had automatically paired off and so had Pat Sheehan and Gary Andrews. Dianne Williams and Lucy Hind were also together. That left one boy and one girl: Jack Halyday and Kirsty.

Kirsty glanced at Halyday and wrinkled her nose. "I don't want to share with him! Besides, you said boys and girls can't share."

"You could go in with the other girls," Graham suggested, looking hopefully at them. The frozen smiles on their faces indicated they were not keen on this idea.

Kirsty looked at them hopefully but Dianne shook her head. "Be too crowded," she said.

"Kirsty smells anyway," Halyday commented.

"Shut up, Halyday!" Kirsty retorted. She and Halyday were both in the same Year 8 class and often made barbed comments to each other.

"You will have to hutchie up on your own then," Graham suggested.

Kirsty nodded. "I will do that."

Graham looked around for two trees she could use. The nearest were almost in line with his own hutchie and a few metres off. "What about these?" he suggested, walking over to them.

Kirsty again nodded. Graham added, "You will only have one side, a lean-to. That won't give you much privacy."

"That will be alright," Kirsty replied, giving Graham what he took to be a meaningful look.

That unsettled him some more. *Is she giving me the "come on"?*

As he turned to go, Kirsty asked, "Will you help me put it up please?"

Graham didn't want to encourage her but she smiled so appealingly that he gave in. "Oh alright!" he answered.

For the next ten minutes he helped teach her how to tie a slip knot and then put up the hutchie. As she was fumbling to tie the knot at one end he reached forward in exasperation to take the cord from her. In doing so their hands touched. He instantly pulled back, but their eyes met.

Heavens! They are pretty eyes, he thought.

For the first time he noted tiny flecks of gold in the blue of her irises. For a long moment they held each other's gaze. She smiled and Graham felt his heart rate shoot up.

Then he looked down in flustered amazement. *Maybe?* he thought. *I might be in luck here.* Then he shook his head. *Don't be silly boy! Be strong!*

But oh! What a temptation!

Chapter 2

FIRST TESTS

By the time the sun began to go down Graham was in a state of indecision he found very unsettling. Doubts and hopes warred with each other. The result was a nagging feeling of dissatisfaction and uneasiness.

Damn! he thought. *I really wanted to enjoy this camp.*

Until the company had arrived in the field training area at Bunyip River, he had been enjoying it. It was already the end of the second day of a nine-day annual camp and he did not want to think about how soon it would all be over. The unit came from Cairns and had travelled to Townsville in coaches the previous morning. The afternoon had been spent at Lavarack Barracks doing weapon training with the Steyr rifle, something Graham had really enjoyed. The cadets had then been given the opportunity to practise in the electronic range, the Weapon Training Simulator. Graham had done very well at this, his shooting being only bettered by Capt Conkey and CSM Cleland.

The previous night had been spent in the barracks, allowing them a taste of army life which Graham had found very enjoyable as he was seriously beginning to consider an army career when he left school. That morning the cadets had been put over the obstacle course by army instructors and had then gone to the range to actually fire live ammunition from the Steyr. Once again Graham had gained an excellent score, being third best shot, beaten by Sgt Grenfell and CSM Cleland.

Graham didn't particularly mind that as he respected and admired both. *Anyway,* he consoled himself, *Capt Conkey has always said that the CSM should be the best soldier in the company.*

It was only when they had arrived in the bush a few hours earlier that life seemed to become complicated. It wasn't the roughing it he minded. That was something he loved. With his friends Roger, Stephen and Peter he spent nearly every second weekend in the bush on hikes. The friends did this so often they called themselves 'The Hiking Team'. However some of the new cadets plainly found the conditions a bit of a shock.

Once the camp was set up the corporals and CUOs were called to HQ Platoon to be issued with radios. This was done by Peter Bronsky, the signals corporal and Graham's friend. The radios were small hand-held 'Citizen Band' UHF radios with a range of about 3 or 4 kilometres and powered by three AA batteries. Each CUO and NCO got the same radio issued all year and Graham signed for his and looped the light green cord around his neck and hung the radio on his shirt. Then he did a radio check which Peter answered. The unit also had half a dozen army radios and seven larger CB pack radios for safety and control.

The evening meal had been routine; a hot, fresh meal prepared by army cooks in the kitchen of the small army camp located a kilometre away on the other side of the highway. This was delivered by army Land Rover in 'hot boxes'. The platoons had filed past one at a time to get their food. The food was ladled into their mess tins. After that the cadets had seated themselves on the ground in platoon areas to eat. There had been no problem with that as the weather was fine and likely to remain so. In this part of North Queensland in September rain was a rarity. The weather was usually dry and fairly hot (Fairly being a relative term, as they came from Cairns, which was even closer to the equator. To them temperatures of 30 degrees C were not considered anything unusual).

The place was familiar to Graham as he had done a ten-day promotion course at the Bunyip River Army Camp the previous December. Part of this course had included navigation exercises during which he had walked through the area they were now bivouacked in. Thus, as he prepared his section for a night navigation exercise, he at least had no worries about getting lost.

But it quickly became apparent that some of his cadets were feeling a bit stressed. The first real sign was when Cadet Andrews mumbled that he was feeling sick. "It must be the heat," he moaned. "Can I stay here?"

"No," Graham replied.

"But I'm sick," Andrews moaned.

That threw Graham a bit. He did not want to lose members of his section from any activity, so he cast around for some convincing argument. Finding none he could only suggest that Andrews go and see Sgt Grenfell. To his surprise Dianne then said she wasn't feeling very well either.

Both were taken to Sgt Grenfell who questioned them. Only then did it begin to dawn on Graham that the real problem was that it was getting dark and they were in the bush. Sgt Grenfell wasn't very sympathetic but commented in a scornful voice that if they wanted to they could go to see the officers, "if you really are sick."

Neither did. It was when they were walking back to the section area in the gathering dusk that Graham noted Dianne glancing anxiously from side to side.

"What's wrong?" he asked as gently as he could.

"I... it... I... it's very dark isn't it," Dianne replied.

They were back at the hutchies by then and Graham looked around in the gloom. He could see quite well, and several torches were flickering around the area. "It will be alright. The moon will come up later," he said. But he said it without conviction as he wasn't sure what time moonrise was.

"But there are no lights," Dianne wailed.

Graham realised that Kirsty had moved to stand close beside him. "You don't need lights," he said, trying to sound confident. "Your eyes will adjust to the dark as you get your night vision."

"But we are miles from anywhere!" Andrews cried.

"We are not!" Graham replied. He pointed to where several lights could be seen through the trees. "The army camp is just over there."

As he said this a car went past along the Flinders Highway, its headlights flickering through the trees. "And there is the main road," he added.

"But what if we stand on a snake?" Lucy asked.

Now that got him. The mention of snakes brought to the surface of Graham's consciousness his one great fear. Three years earlier he had been bitten by a King Brown and it had left him very scared of the reptiles. He had no idea what types of snakes lived in this dry country but that only added to his uncertainty.

He was saved by a vulgar comment by Halyday. "The only sort of snakes you need to worry about," Halyday said to Lucy, "are one-eyed trouser snakes."

"Don't be crude Cadet Halyday!" Graham snapped, his own fear adding to his growing irritation.

"But what if we get lost?" Andrews persisted.

That again saved Graham. If there was one thing he really prided himself on it was his navigation in the bush. "We won't," he snapped. "I've been here before and I know where to go. Just stick close to me."

As he said this, he felt Kirsty gently touch his side and arm. He wasn't sure if it was an accident, a joke, or a 'come on'. This time he was saved by CSM Cleland. The CSM was over near the big tree and began calling loudly for the platoons to move in. Sgt Grenfell at once called on the platoon to form up. To Graham's relief Kirsty moved away.

"Make sure you have your webbing," he called as he hurried to his own hutchie. Now he began to fluster. All the time spent with Andrews and Williams meant he was not ready. For one thing he had not refilled all his water bottles. A quick check showed he had one full one. *It will have to do,* he decided. As quickly as he could, and spurred on by Sgt Grenfell's calls to form up, he made sure he had all the things he needed: compass, protractor, pencil, map, torch. In his haste he kept catching himself on things and became all hot and sweaty.

Oh strewth! I hope I have everything, he thought as he hurried back to where the platoon was starting to assemble.

"Hurry up 4 Section!" he called, noting that only Roger and Pat had so far arrived. Next to them stood all of Gwen Copeland's Number 5 Section. Up till then Graham had considered he was lucky to have good kids in his section; no real troublemakers, but now he wasn't so sure. "Hurry up Cadet Halyday!" he shouted angrily.

Kirsty, Lucy and Dianne joined them but Halyday and Andrews were still in their hutchie. Sgt Grenfell called to ask if all of Graham's section were there. "Not yet sergeant," Graham replied, blushing hot with annoyance and shame.

"What about you Five Section?" Sgt Grenfell asked Gwen.

"All here sergeant."

"Cpl Bell?"

Stephen replied that all of 6 Section were there. That made Graham even more agitated. It also made him worry that his section might get a bad reputation. He shouted angrily to Halyday and Andrews. "Get here! Now!"

"I haven't filled my water bottles," Andrews cried.

"Tough! You had plenty of time. Form up," Graham snapped. Even as he said this he knew it was the wrong answer. Andrews could easily get heat exhaustion, even at night, if he was dehydrated from the day. The air temperature was still quite high. The dilemma made Graham angry with himself for not checking earlier.

With some muttering and grumbling Andrews and Halyday joined them. "All here now sergeant," Graham reported.

"About bloody time! I hope you weren't aiming to win 'Best Section' in the section competition this year," Sgt Grenfell retorted. Graham found that a very worrying and hurtful comment but could only silently fume.

I'd better get this mob better organised, he told himself.

The platoon was marched over to where the company was being seated in section lines. With a hundred and twenty cadets all milling around in the dark it seemed like bedlam but CSM Cleland used his voice and authority to quickly impose order, calling the platoons one at a time and directing the sergeants where to seat their people. That done he did a check on who was present.

During that Graham discovered that all the other platoons had one or two 'sick' who had been sent to where the officers had a fire. That made him feel better but also raised his anxiety lest one of his cadets even now opt to go there. To his relief, none did. CSM Cleland handed over to Capt Conkey, who then sent the CUOs and sergeants over to the fire. They were to provide the check points and were to be briefed by the unit 2ic, Lt Mel Maclaren.

After another safety brief, during which the cadets squirmed and fidgeted a lot, Capt Conkey began to give detailed instructions for the night navex. Graham took out his map, notebook and pencil. Then he dug out a pocket torch and turned to the cadet behind him.

"Hold this torch for me," he whispered.

It was Kirsty. She turned it on then moved to lean over his shoulder to shine the torch beam on his notebook. In doing so she pressed herself against him.

That has got to be deliberate, Graham told himself as he tried to concentrate on what Capt Conkey was saying.

As the whole unit had been given a briefing on sexual harassment and related subjects only the previous afternoon, he knew that Kirsty was not acting out of ignorance. Her behaviour annoyed him, but he was also disturbed by it. To his added annoyance he started to get aroused.

I hope Capt Conkey doesn't notice Kirsty leaning on me, he thought anxiously. That would do his promotion chances no good at all, and having determined to try to make sergeant at the end of the year, it made him worry. But it was hard to keep his mind on the job!

Capt Conkey gave each corporal a different Grid Reference to go to on their first leg. The section commanders then had to work out the magnetic compass bearing and calculate the distance in paces. As he started working these out an idea came to Graham. "Cadet Andrews, go and fill your water bottles while I do this," he said.

It took him only seven minutes to do the calculation. Kirsty helped by kneeling beside him to hold the torch. As soon as he had the bearing and distance worked out Graham went to Capt Conkey to let him check it. He noted that he was the second corporal to finish the calculation. Only his friend Peter had beaten him.

That's Okay, he told himself. *Pete's a brain.*

"Very good Cpl Kirk," Capt Conkey complimented him. The praise made Graham glow and he felt good. If there was one person on earth he wanted to impress it was Capt Conkey.

I owe that man a lot, he reminded himself.

As he moved away, Graham found his path blocked by Cpl Bannister from 4 Platoon. "Bloody sniveller!" Bannister hissed. "Always sucking up to the officers."

Graham was so surprised he made no reply. In hurt silence he moved away, wondering what he had done to offend Bannister. Then it came to him. *Bannister is Pigsy Pike's section commander!* Then he shook his head. *Poor bugger! I'm bloody glad I don't have mongrels like Pike in my section.*

But the taunt still annoyed him because he thought he was just trying hard and doing the right thing, not crawling. With a shake of his head he dismissed the incident and went to collect his section. "4 Section, move out here," he called.

In the darkness they moved out to one side of what was rapidly becoming a milling throng. After checking that Cadet Andrews was back Graham asked Capt Conkey if he could go.

Having received permission to start the course Graham did a radio check then set the compass and handed it to Cadet Sheehan. Pat had been in cadets all year and had done four weekend bivouacs so was quite experienced for a 'First Year'. Without hesitation he led off.

Their first leg took them close past the officer's fire. As they walked past the fire Graham noted Lt Standish, a lady teacher, sitting there with five cadets. That surprised him and he wondered if they were all 'sick' the way Andrews and Dianne had said they were. Then he noted Carnes sitting staring unhappily into the flames. At that Graham shook his head.

Poor bugger! I wonder why he joined the Cadets?

Then the section passed out of the circle of firelight and almost at once the fears closed in. First the snakes! Graham found he was staring hard at the ground, even though he could barely see it in the darkness. Then he had the thought that it was good that Cadet Sheehan was leading.

He will scare the snakes away, he reasoned.

Then a saying he had heard somewhere slipped into his mind to gnaw at his confidence: that the first person woke the snake up and enraged it and it bit the second person!

Trying to reassure himself on this count Graham forced himself to walk steadily forward. The other members of the section trampled noisily along behind him. They passed by the edge of the 3 Platoon bivouac area and headed towards an old gravel scrape in the direction of the army camp. Suddenly a torch came on behind him.

Angrily Graham swung his head to look. It was Dianne. "Turn that torch off! We are not to use torches except in a safety emergency," he ordered.

Reluctantly she obeyed, but only for about 50 paces. Then it clicked on again. Graham opened his mouth to tell her to turn it off but before he could CUO McAlistair's voice rang out from a hundred metres ahead: "Turn that torch off!"

"Turn it off!" Graham snarled angrily, stung by the reproof.

Within 10 paces a torch again flickered behind him. "Turn it off Cadet Williams!" Graham snapped.

"It's not me. It's Halyday!" Dianne replied hotly.

"Halyday, turn the torch off!" Graham yelled.

Even as he did, he knew he wasn't handling things well. *I shouldn't be losing my temper so easily,* he told himself, *and I should always call people by their ranks.* To help regain control he stopped them.

"Listen," he said, "This is not just to train you to navigate at night. It is to build up your confidence, to show you that you can walk through the bush in the dark."

"But why?" Dianne asked.

"Because if you turn on a torch and the enemy are watching they could kill you, or your mates," Graham replied.

"But we aren't in the army," Lucy replied.

"And how would they hit you if it is dark?" Halyday added.

"They have night sights on their rifles that allow them to see in the dark," Graham replied.

"So, if they can see in the dark what difference does it make if we use a torch?" Andrews retorted.

For a moment Graham was unable to reply, stung both by the fact that he had talked himself into a stupid contradiction, and also by Halyday's tone of voice. It took him a moment to think of what to say, hotly conscious that with every minute he hesitated his credibility and leadership were going down. At last it came to him. "Because you can only see a few hundred metres with a night sight whereas a white light, a torch or match or something, can be seen from kilometres away."

There was mumbling but no more protests. Feeling that he had things under control again Graham gave the word to Pat to keep going. As he did, Andrews called out from the back in a quavering voice.

"I want to go back to the fire."

Graham silently cursed and went back to him. The glow of the fire was clearly visible only about 200 metres away. "Don't be silly. We are nearly finished the first leg," he said.

"I want to go back," Andrews repeated.

"No. Not unless you have hurt yourself, or are really sick," Graham replied. He was getting annoyed and short tempered again. "Are you sick?"

Andrews snuffled and shook his head. "Not really, but I want to go back."

"I heard you. We are going on. Get moving Pat," he called.

Pat began moving and Graham set off after him. However he had only gone 10 paces when Roger called from the back, "Wait for us Graham. Andrew's won't move."

"Oh blast!" Graham thought, angry that Roger had used his first name, and that he now had a problem he didn't know how to solve.

Chapter 3

IN THE DARK

"Come on Cadet Andrews, get moving!" Graham ordered.

"No. I want to go back to the fire," Andrews replied.

"Start walking, that's an order!" Graham growled. He knew that everyone else in the section was intently following the struggle of wills. Panic at not being able to get his cadets to obey began to well up in Graham. Fear of failure gripped him.

Andrews shook his head. "No. I'm not going on."

"I said start marching," Graham grated angrily. He moved close to Andrews and added, "I am a corporal and I'm giving you a direct order."

"I'm not going!" Andrews replied, his voice rising and cracking.

Exasperation and embarrassment both assailed Graham. He gestured angrily at his sleeve. "Listen you, see these stripes? They mean I can give you orders and I'm telling you to start walking."

"No! I want to go back to the fire," Andrews replied stubbornly

The situation began to overwhelm Graham. His temper flared. He shook his fist in front of Andrews' face. "Listen you disobedient little bugger, get moving or... or..."

Even as he began to say it Graham had just enough sense and self-control to stop making a direct physical threat. Even that amount of restraint nearly gave way when Andrews again refused to move. For a minute Graham stood in a lather of indecision.

What will the officers think if I can't even get one little 'First Year' to do what I say? They will think I am very weak, he thought. *So much for wanting to be a sergeant!*

He then tried another tack. Knowing that time was getting on he said to the others, "We will leave him here. Come on."

With that he started walking towards the check point at the gravel pit, hoping that Andrews wouldn't call his bluff and just walk back to the fire. To his relief the others started walking. He heard Roger say quietly, "Come on Andrews, stay with us," but Andrews didn't. When Graham glanced back he saw him standing silhouetted against the distant fire.

By now Graham was almost in a blind panic. *He is not going to follow,* he thought. *What can I do?*

He knew he could not leave a cadet in the dark without getting a roasting from the OC. By then he had only walked 20 paces and was about to stop and admit defeat when a loud wail came from Andrews.

"Wait! Don't leave me! Don't leave me!"

At that Graham did stop. "Then catch up and stay with us," he called back.

Andrews didn't move. Even from 30 paces away Graham could hear the boy crying. With a snort of exasperation he snapped to the others, "Wait here!" and strode back to where Andrews stood. The boy was now sobbing loudly and crying, "Don't leave me! Help! Help me!"

"What's wrong?" Graham cried as he got closer.

"I'm scared!" Andrews wailed.

By then Graham was back with him. The boy's answer came as such a relief he felt like laughing. It was on the tip of his tongue to jeer and deride the boy's fears, but he managed to restrain himself. In a flash of insight he remembered a similar episode the previous year. It also made him very aware that all of his cadets were only 13 years' old.

He stepped close to Andrews and very quietly said, "I'm here. You can calm down. You are quite safe."

To Graham's relief, Andrews stopped his loud wails and stood sniffling and sobbing. Graham now spoke softly so that the other cadets could not hear. "It's alright. What are you scared of?"

"I don't know! The dark?" Andrews sobbed. Then he went on, "Snakes, spiders, th... things."

"What things?" Graham asked.

"D... d... d... drop... drop bears and b... bunyips," Andrews sobbed.

In a flash Graham realised that the older cadets had been practising on the credulity of the new recruits. He shook his head with relief. "Have you ever been camping before?" he asked.

"N... no," Andrews replied. He was now calming down.

"So you have never been in the bush at night?"

"No, and I'm scared," Andrews replied, his voice low but full of real terror.

"Okay, I understand that," Graham said. "Now, think about this. There are no such things as drop bears or bunyips."

"They said there are," Andrews replied, "And Yowies."

"Who said?" Graham asked.

"4 Platoon guys," Andrews replied.

At that Graham swore softly. *Bloody Pigsy Pike and Co!* he thought. He said, "They are just having you on. Look, if these things really existed wouldn't you have learned about them at a school? Wouldn't there be some in the zoo?"

Andrews was silent for a while. Then he sniffled and said, "What about the Yowie Men? They have been seen."

"Only by truck drivers who have taken too many pills!" Graham replied sarcastically.

"Pigsy said he's seen 'em around here before," Andrews replied.

"He is just saying that to scare you," Graham answered. "Look, if there was real danger do you really think the officers would send us out to walk around? It would be more than their jobs are worth."

That seemed to sink in. Andrews was silent for a while. Then he said quietly, "What about snakes and spiders?"

"I don't know about spiders but there are sure to be snakes," Graham replied. "Just remember what the OC said: the snakes will hear us coming and get out of the way. It is when we run and startle them they strike, but only in self-defence."

"I'm scared of snakes," Andrews persisted.

"So am I!" Graham replied with feeling. "And I've been bitten by one."

"You have not!"

"I have so!" Graham replied. "By a King Brown, when I was eleven. You ask Roger. He was there. And I'm still alive."

Then another idea came to Graham. From where he stood he could clearly see the lights of the army camp. As he stood looking the headlights of a car went past along the highway. "Look, see that car? It is on the Flinders Highway. If you get bitten, we will have you in a car in a few minutes and it is only twenty minutes or half an hour to the hospital at Charters Towers."

By this time Andrews had calmed down. Graham said, "Have a drink, then stay with me. And we won't mention this to anyone."

"But I'm still scared," Andrews replied, but he began taking out his water bottle.

"Of course! That's normal. We all are. But this is one of those real challenges life throws at you. If you back out you escape the fear for a few minutes but then you will despise yourself for being a coward. Worse still, other kids will look down on you and tease you. Much better to face up to it. So come on, we will keep you safe in the middle."

Graham waited till Andrews had had a drink and replaced his water bottle in his webbing, then murmured 'come on' and started slowly walking. To his enormous relief Anderson walked with him. When they reached the others, who still stood in a line waiting, he said quietly, "Cadet Andrews is a bit worried because he has never been in the bush at night. So we are all going to help him. And I want you all to promise not to tease him, or to tell anyone from another section about this. 4 Section helps each other, alright?"

To his relief the others all nodded or murmured yes. Roger patted Andrews on the shoulder and said, "Good on you!"

Kirsty also put her hand on Andrews' arm and said, "I'm glad. You can help keep me safe."

At that Graham told Pat to lead on and the section continued with the compass march. It was only a hundred metres down to where CUO McAlistair and Sgt Sheila Sherry, the 1 Platoon staff, were seated on a mound of earth in the old gravel pit but Graham barely noticed as he was so relieved to have overcome the crisis.

"What was all that talking back there?" CUO McAlistair asked as they arrived.

"Just one of the cadets not feeling well sir," Graham replied.

To Graham's consternation CUO McAlistair replied, "They can stay here at the check point in that case."

"I think he is OK now," Graham answered quickly, hoping that none of the cadets suddenly opted for this 'out'.

To his relief none said anything. CUO McAlistair told Graham to get out his notebook and torch and then gave him the Grid Reference of the next check point. Roger stood and held his torch while Graham wrote, and Kirsty stood close on the other side. Graham then crouched and unfolded his map. A moment's work gave him the location, a dry creek about 500 metres to the west. As quickly as he could he drew a pencil line across the map through the two points and placed his protractor on it. He was so self-conscious of being watched by a CUO, sergeant and half his section that he became quite flustered and all 'thumbs and fingers' but he got the bearing at last, then did the calculation to convert it from Grid to Magnetic on his notebook.

"Two hundred and thirty-six degrees magnetic, sir," he said. "And about seven hundred paces."

"That sounds about right," CUO McAlistair replied. "You should find CSM Cleland and Sgt Gayney there."

"Thanks sir," Graham said. He adjusted the compass and then stood up. "Shine the torch in the top to improve the luminous Roger," Graham said.

He instantly regretted not calling Roger Lance Corporal Dunning in front of the others, but no-one seemed to notice. What he was really trying to do was gain some time while he decided who should take the compass for the next leg. *I could ask for volunteers,* he considered. *No. That will make me look weak and indecisive.*

He said, "You are next Cadet Hind. Here is the compass."

Lucy muttered a few 'Oh noes!' but took the compass. Graham then stood close to check she was holding it the right way and that she had the luminous north pointer lined up between the two luminous dots. Satisfied she had it right, he told her to start walking.

"Cadet Andrews and Cadet Weldon, you both count paces," he added.

As they started slowly moving Graham was relieved to note that all of the section followed, even Andrews. He also took comfort from the fact that they would be moving on a course which converged with the highway. *If we get really lost we can just go to the road,* he told himself. The lights of the army camp were now behind his left shoulder and he noted that the glow of the officer's campfire was hidden by a rise.

Their course took them down a gentle slope into a tangle of small gullies and small bushes. The only real guidance other than the compass was the flicker of car headlights over to their left whenever a vehicle went past along the highway. There were so many bushes and small washouts that Graham completely forgot to worry about snakes. So, apparently, did Andrews as he made no further comment. After five minutes of shuffling along, they reached the edge of a larger gully. In the starlight Graham could see it was only a couple of metres wide, but it looked to have steep sides.

"Take your time going across this," he cautioned.

To no avail. Andrews slid down with a sharp thud and a cascade of sand and pebbles. "Ow! Aargh! I think I've broken my leg," he cried.

Graham had been just about to climb out the other side. A stab of alarm made him spin around. He whipped out his torch and turned it on. Andrews was half lying, half crouching in the bottom amid a cloud of fine dust. "Which leg?" Graham asked anxiously.

"Uh! I dunno," Andrews replied. He squirmed and struggled to his feet and looked down at both legs.

"Neither," Graham said, relief adding an edge of sarcasm to his voice.

"I could have!" Andrews grumbled in an injured tone. He rubbed his right leg but had no difficulty climbing out of the washout. This time Graham kept the torch on till everyone had safely crossed. Then he turned it off and told them to have a drink while they recovered their night vision.

The compass march was resumed. The section went up over a wide gentle ridge through very open bush. The soil was sandy and almost devoid of grass. Up to his right Graham saw the glow of the officer's fire. *This is the ridge which comes down from our bivouac area to the highway,* he thought, relieved to be sure of where they were.

A hundred paces on, just as they were starting to go down the long gentle slope on the western side of the spur, Dianne suddenly said, "I need to go to the toilet. Can we go back to camp please?"

Graham gave a short laugh he was so surprised. "We are in the middle of an exercise. We can't go all the way back just so you can go to the dunny."

"But I really need to go. It is urgent," Dianne wailed.

"If you'd mentioned it when we were back at that gully you could have gone easily," Graham said. "The girl's latrine was just near there."

"But I need to go! Can we go back please?" Dianne persisted.

"No! Just go over behind a bush somewhere. We will wait here," Graham replied.

Dianne was plainly appalled. "I can't just go out here! Not in the bush! Not in the dark! I need a toilet."

With an effort Graham bit back a sarcastic retort asking why she was different from other girls. "It's dark," he said. "No-one will see."

"Nothing much to bloody see anyway!" Halyday added.

"Shut up Halyday!" Graham snapped. "Look Dianne, take Kirsty and use your torch. Find a clear spot and then turn the torch off till you want to come back," he said, exasperated at all the song and dance about what he thought was such a trivial thing.

"But something might be there!" Dianne wailed.

"A big snake might bite you on the bum," Halyday said, then snickered.

"Shut up Halyday! Oh hurry up!" Graham cried. He knew time was slipping away.

Kirsty took out her torch and switched it on, and said, "Come on Di."

To Graham's relief, Dianne followed Kirsty off into a fold on the ground behind a bush. *I wonder how the time is going?* he thought. To his dismay, he saw it was already 2040. He knew that there were seven legs in the course and he had to get around in 120 minutes. That allowed about 15 minutes for each leg; to do the calculation and then walk the half kilometre or so.

We should have covered three or four legs, he thought anxiously. *We need to speed up. We are already twenty minutes behind!*

To his added embarrassment Andrews and Halyday both snickered and made comments about the girls. "Shut up you two grots!" Graham snapped. "Hurry up you girls! We are late."

To his ears came the trampling of boots and the mutter of voices. Another section was heading their way from the opposite direction. That did not surprise Graham as he knew from experience that the officers usually sent one section each way around a course. "Hurry up," he called to Dianne, "There is another section coming."

From in the dip he heard a gasp of alarm and noises of talking and hasty movement. Then Dianne and Kirsty hurried back to them, their torches flashing. This drew torch beams from the approaching section.

"Who's that?" called Cpl Crane from 3 Platoon.

"4 Section," Graham replied. To Dianne and Kirsty he snapped, "Turn those torches off!"

Crane wanted to stop and chat, but Graham shook his head impatiently. "We are late. No time to talk, sorry. Start going Lucy."

For the next few minutes they walked steadily west through open bush. As they did the cadets kept chattering to each other, despite Graham several times telling them to stop talking and to be quiet. At the next check point CSM Cleland was waiting. "What was all that noise and those torches about?" he enquired. "This is supposed to be a field exercise, not a nature ramble!"

"Yes sir," Graham replied, but he gave no explanation, just burned with shame.

Instead he got ready to work out the next leg. Once again Roger held the torch and Graham worked as fast as he could, well aware of the minutes slipping by. While he worked another section came trampling in out of the darkness. It was Gwen Copeland's. That sent a stab of anxiety through Graham.

Gwen is probably the section from our platoon on the opposite course and she has only two legs to go and we have five. I had better get a move on if I want to get around in time.

As Graham completed his calculations a cadet came and stood close to him. "Hi Graham. How's it going?"

Graham looked up. It was Barbara Brassington, a lovely red-headed Year 9 girl. Graham had helped rescue her from two prison escapees a few weeks earlier and he had a special affection for her.

"Good," he replied, then found he was tongue-tied. All he could do was gesture and then blush. To save himself he completed the calculation, hotly aware that Barbara was watching.

"That was quick!" Barbara cried as Graham finished the sum.

Kirsty reached down and took the compass from Graham's hand and placed it in the beam of Roger's torch. "Two ninety-eight degrees is it?" she said, twisting the milled vane to set the compass for the next leg. "I'll take the compass this leg," she added.

Graham looked up in surprise, just in time to catch a glimpse of Kirsty giving Barbara a hard stare. *Oh dear!* he thought. *Is this what I think it is?* His ego easily allowed him to accept the thought that Kirsty might like him, but that she was jealous of Barbara was altogether more unsettling.

"See you later," Graham said to Barbara, then instantly regretted it as Kirsty flashed him a look. To divert the conversation he asked CSM Cleland who was at the next check point.

"Lt Hamilton with a safety vehicle," CSM Cleland replied.

"Thanks CSM. Come on 4 Section. We'd better move or we won't make it in time," he said.

Chapter 4

NIGHT NAVEX

CSM Cleland's checkpoint was in the dry bed of a small creek. From there the section walked northwest across a grassy flat, across another small dry creek, then up a long, gentle slope that was bare of trees. A sparse covering of grass on sandy soil offered smooth walking. By now their eyes had adjusted to the starlight and visibility was quite good. The dark shapes of a few scattered trees in the distance were the only vegetation. Graham quickly realised that a tree on the crestline ahead of them was their next objective, but he resisted the temptation to point this out to Kirsty.

She obviously worked it out for herself, particularly when the flicker of a torch showed under the tree. "That big tree is the next check point," she said.

Graham agreed and they walked quickly on. He was pleased when they covered the distance in only five minutes, and no-one caused any problems. Lt Hamilton, the unit QM, was there with the Company Quartermaster Sergeant, Coralie Bates. Also, there was 2 Section, Cpl Costigan. They were departing as 4 Section arrived.

"Who's that?" Costigan called.

"4 Section," Graham replied.

"Huh! Late and lost probably!" Costigan replied in a sneering tone.

The fact that they were late caused Graham to flush with shame and annoyance. With an effort he ignored the comment and went over to Lt Hamilton. Lt Hamilton was a slim officer in his late twenties. He had a moustache which he continually stroked; a gesture Graham found irritating. 'Fancies himself with the ladies,' was the rumour.

As quickly as he could Graham worked out the next leg. Lt Hamilton added a spur by saying, "You had better get a move on. It is nearly twenty-one hundred. It is only fifteen minutes to the cut-off time."

That sent Graham's heart rate soaring with anxiety. *This is only the third checkpoint,* he thought. With feverish haste he worked out the next leg and showed his sums to Lt Hamilton.

The OOC nodded and said they could go.

"Let's go, 4 Section," Graham said, while setting the compass.

"I'm tired. I want to stay here," Andrews replied.

"No way, not unless you are really sick," Graham snapped back.

"I am sick," Andrews replied.

Sgt Bates stepped forward. "No you aren't Cadet Andrews. You just want a ride back in the Land Rover. Get moving."

Andrews grumbled but he moved. Graham handed the compass to him. "Your turn, now get moving."

There were more grumbles, but Andrews took the compass, lined it up and, to Graham's intense relief, started walking. "Thanks," he whispered to Sgt Bates.

The next leg took them north across the gravel Canning Road and on over the wide, flat top of Bare Ridge. As they crested the rise Graham noted a bright cluster of distant lights. So did the others.

"Oooh!" Lucy cried. "What are those lights?"

"Charters Towers," Graham replied, naming the town.

"Is it far?" Kirsty asked.

"Twenty or thirty kilometres," Graham replied.

"Oh, as far as that?" Dianne said, the disappointment clear in her voice.

"I wish I was there," Lucy added.

"Me too!" Halyday cried.

"Never mind gaping at the bright lights of the big city," Graham said, "We are late, so keep walking."

"I'm tired," Dianne replied.

"And I'm getting a blister," Andrews added.

"So walk fast and we will get home quicker," Graham said.

With a steady flow of grumbling the section continued on over the crest to a gully where they found the 3 Platoon staff, CUO Mitrovitch and Sgt Yeldham. A glance at his watch told Graham it was 2107hrs.

Only eight minutes to the cut-off time, he thought anxiously.

Even so CUO Mitrovitch gave him the next leg to do. Graham set rapidly to work. This time it only took Graham three minutes to do the calculation. As he showed it to CUO Mitrovitch she nodded with approval. "Very good, that is the quickest so far, and you even got it right."

Before Graham could answer her Kirsty bumped against him and said, “That’s 4 Section Ma’am, the best!”

That led to some good-natured teasing while Graham gave the compass to Roger. “Go flat out Roger,” he said. “We have three legs to go and only about twenty minutes.”

They set off up the slope out of the gully. This led them through a stand of gum trees. The bare ground was covered with small stones and dry leaves and sticks so their progress was quite noisy. So was that of another section heading towards them.

The other section appeared as dark shapes among the trees.

“Who are you mob?” called a voice.

Graham’s heart sank. Cpl Bannister, Pigsy’s section.

“4 Section,” Graham replied.

At once Pigsy called back, “Kirk, the gutless wonder! I’m surprised you were even game to leave the fire in case a Yowie Man got ya!”

Andrews replied to that. “There aren’t any such things as Yowie Men, or Drop Bears!”

Jeering, mocking laughter erupted from the other group. “Might not be Drop Bears but the Yowie Men are out there,” Pigsy said. “They will get ya if ya ain’t careful.”

“Shut up Pike and stop making up stories to frighten the new cadets,” Graham retorted. To his added annoyance both groups had stopped walking and were now about 10 paces apart.

“Oh yeah, who’s gunna make me?” Pike replied in a sneering tone.

“Me,” Graham answered. He found he was trembling and that his lips had gone dry.

“Huh, you and what army?” Pigsy taunted.

Roger spoke up for the first time. “This army.”

That caused more cruel laughter and Moynihan’s voice called back, “If it isn’t the fat little fag!”

That hurt. Graham knew there had been a few rumours about Roger over the years and he also knew Roger was very sensitive about his weight. To end the confrontation he said, “Keep moving Roger. We want to finish.”

Roger growled but obeyed. As they began to move Waters called out a crude comment. To which Pigsy added an even cruder one. That embarrassed Graham. He hated crude talk in the hearing of girls.

He called angrily back, "That's enough of that sort of talk. There are girls here."

"You are all sooky girls in that section!" Moynihan jeered.

The sexist comment and crude swearing really stung Graham. He shouted angrily, "Why don't you control your section Cpl Bannister?"

It was Pigsy who replied. "Shut up Kirk and mind your own business or I'll smash you to pulp. Now clear out, you pack of mincing queers."

Rather than aggravate the situation Graham made no reply. The section walked quickly on through the bush. To Graham's relief, he heard the other section go trampling off in the opposite direction. "Sorry about that," he said to the section.

"That's alright," Kirsty replied. "Wasn't your fault. Anyway, we've heard worse."

"They are gross animals," Lucy added.

Suddenly Pat tripped. The section had come out into an area that had once been scraped for gravel and there were several small erosion rills. As Graham turned Pat struggled to his feet, muttering and swearing. He rubbed his knee.

Graham helped him keep his balance. "You OK Pat?"

"Yeah, push on. We want to finish this. If we move, we will still do it," Pat answered.

"Yes, we can," Roger agreed. "And I reckon Pigsy's mob won't because they probably have three legs still to go."

Graham turned this over in his mind but could not decide. He knew each section went a different route, with zig zags all over the area from check point to check point. But it was worth trying.

The group hurried on, although Andrews still grumbled about blisters. Two minutes later they came to a road junction. From the map Graham knew that the road to the left went to the junction of two rivers, the Canning and the Bunyip. The other road ran north to the Canning and crossed it to a cattle station on the north bank. At the road junction was a Land Rover and two OOCs: Lt Maclaren, the unit 2ic, and Lt McEwen, a pretty lady teacher in her twenties.

Lt Maclaren shone a torch on them as they arrived. "You people are out of time. You had better just walk home along the road," he said.

Graham looked at his watch. It was 2118hrs, 3 minutes past the cut-off time. His heart sank but he made an effort to win. "We only have two more legs to go sir and one of them takes us home. Can we please go on?"

"There might not be any at the check point when you get there," Lt Maclaren replied.

"Can you find out sir, please?" Graham asked. It now seemed very important to him to get right around the course and, even more, to beat Pigsy's section.

Lt Maclaren studied the exercise plan and the said, "I will try. You're next checkpoint is 'Foxtrot' and the OC is there. I'll see if he will wait." He picked up a radio handset and called. To Graham's relief, Checkpoint 'F' replied at once. Lt Maclaren said, "Sunray, I've got Corporal Kirk's section here and they want to come home through your check point, over."

There was a pause and then he heard the OC's voice. "Yes, if he is quick. He only has one more leg after us. Send him on and tell him to be here in ten minutes, over."

By then Graham had his notebook and map out. Roger clicked on his torch and Lt Maclaren read out the Grid Reference. "It is a power pole on top of a rise," he added.

Graham found it and made a mark on his map. "About four hundred metres," he said. As quickly as he could he drew the pencil line and got to work with his protractor. As he did, Kirsty pressed against him, but he barely noticed. In two more minutes he had the bearing. "Eighty-seven degrees." He stood up, adjusting the compass. "Who hasn't had a go?"

"Dianne," Roger told him.

"Here, quick," Graham cried. He passed the compass to Dianne and then leaned close to check she was holding it correctly. As he did, so he fretted at the time. 2125! Where did the minutes go? As soon as it looked like Dianne was facing the right way Graham gave her a push to start walking.

"I'm staying here," Andrews then said.

"No you aren't," Graham replied. "Come on. We are on the way home now."

"But I've got blisters!" Andrews moaned.

To Graham's relief, Roger, Pat and Kirsty all chipped in. "Oh make the effort please. We want to get around as a section," Kirsty asked.

Andrews grumbled but started walking. Graham heaved a big sigh and then concentrated on the navigation. The course was through another area of dry open bush which was easy to walk through and it was only as they crossed a small dry creek bed that he realised he hadn't even thought about snakes for most of the time. Nor had Andrews made any further comment about being scared.

Within five minutes the section was up on another low ridge and came out into a powerline clearing. Graham looked left and right to see if he could see the people at the check point. "Left," he said, walking quickly that way.

Capt Conkey was waiting at the pole with two other people. To his mild dismay Graham saw they were his own platoon staff: CUO Masters and Sgt Grenfell.

"Okay Cpl Kirk," Capt Conkey said, "It is right on 2130 and I want to be back at camp by 2140. Take us home."

The thought of having to work out navigation in front of the OC, his platoon commander and sergeant, sent Graham's stomach into a flutter of nerves. He took out map and notebook. Now teamwork helped. Roger held the torch and Graham studied the map. Once again Kirsty crouched beside him and pressed against him.

That is very nice, he thought, *but I wish she wouldn't do it in front of the OC!*

A study of the map showed Graham that if he just walked south he would come to Sandy Ridge. He also noted that the ridge they were on led up between two creeks to a vehicle track which led to Sandy Ridge.

It will be easier going if we walk a dog-leg, he thought, but he wasn't sure if that was what the OC wanted. *I'll risk it,* he decided. *Be easier than struggling across the head of those gullies in the dark.* He remembered seeing the top ends of the gullies and noting they were quite steep and rocky.

He did not even bother to do the sums to calculate a magnetic bearing, just estimated. *It won't matter. It is only about 300 metres and we must come to that other track anyway,* he reasoned. He set the compass on 75 degrees and handed it to Halyday.

"Your turn. Do you remember how to use it?" he asked.

"Think so," Halyday replied. He turned to face what he thought was the right way, but Graham saw that he was actually facing north. Feeling very conscious of all the important eyes on him Graham got Halyday to turn the right way. "Now keep the north pointer between those two dots. Okay, let's go."

Graham was sweating now, anxious not to muck it up in front of the OC and CUO Masters. The group set off up the grassy spur. *Only six minutes to go!* Graham thought anxiously.

He tried to hurry Halyday, walking beside him and constantly peering at the compass to check he wasn't going off course. After about a hundred metres he realised they were walking along a cattle pad which seemed to follow the very crest of the gentle spur uphill. He was tempted to tell Halyday to just follow the cattle pad but resisted that.

Better not, not with the OC watching, he reasoned.

It took four stressful minutes to reach the vehicle track. By then Graham was becoming anxious because they were angling slowly towards the slope leading down into a gully on the right and they were meeting small outcrops of rock which slowed them down. Perspiring with effort and anxiety he strained his eyes in the starlight to see. Just as he was wondering if the track no longer existed, he noted two faint wheel ruts through the grass. Once again he sighed with relief.

"Okay Halyday, just turn right and follow the track," he said.

"What track?" Halyday asked.

Graham could not believe that Halyday could not see the lines in the starlight. He pointed. "These two-wheel ruts."

"Oh yeah! Now I see them," Halyday replied. They set off along the track which wound slightly through the bush and up a very gentle slope. Behind him Graham heard the OC grunt and make some comment to CUO Masters but whether it was approval or not he did not know.

Within a hundred paces they came to 4 Platoon's hutchies. At that Graham felt very relieved. *One minute to spare!* he thought.

From ahead, out at the big ironbark, came the sound of many voices and Graham saw torches flickering. Then the glow of the officer's fire became visible on his left front and he knew he had done it. His sense of satisfaction was added to when Capt Conkey said, "Well done Cpl Kirk. Take your section over to the company and sit them in line."

Graham did so. Sgt Grenfell followed and took over 2 Platoon. Almost the whole company was seated there in section lines, the sergeants standing at the back. Finding the correct place Graham seated his section and then sat down next to Gwen.

"You took your time," Gwen commented as Graham sat down.

The comment rankled but Graham only half heard it because he was very aware that Kirsty was pressing her knees against his back. *Is she doing that deliberately, or is it just crowded back there?* he wondered. Unsure, he decided he didn't mind and said nothing.

Two Land Rovers came driving back along the track which led in from the Canning Road along the top of Sandy Ridge. Several groups of CUOs and sergeants walked in out of the bush and reported to the OC at the fire then joined the company. After a few minutes CSM Cleland arrived and bellowed for silence. After the cadets had stopped talking the CSM called for reports, a platoon at a time. At 4 Platoon, Sgt White answered, "Two sections still missing CSM."

There was a ripple of snickering and comments. Graham experienced a spurt of satisfaction which turned to positive glee when he heard that one was Bannister's section. The other was 12 Section, Cpl David Doyle.

"Bloody 'Dimbo' Doyle!" muttered a dozen voices.

"Who else!"

"What else could you expect?" asked Stephen.

Graham could only silently agree. Dimbo's navigation, or lack of it, was now legendary. It had been an error on his part in the exercise near Bowen in August that had put him five kilometres outside the exercise area because he had marched along a Back Bearing. That this had fortuitously placed him in a position to help rescue Barbara, Gwen and two other girls was another thing.

While CSM Cleland was checking if both groups from HQ were back a section came walking in from near the officer's fire.

"Which section is that?" CSM Cleland called.

"Eleven Section Sir," replied Cpl Bannister.

"Lost and late!" called someone.

"Silence in the ranks!" CSM Cleland roared. His torch swept over 2 Platoon where the comment had come from. "Platoon sergeants, control your troops."

When 11 Section was seated CSM Cleland sent a runner over to the OC. Capt Conkey and the officers walked over and stood in the circle of light from a lantern. When CSM Cleland reported that the only people missing were Cpl Doyle's section Graham noted that the expression on Capt Conkey's face did not change.

"Thank you CSM. We will look for them in a moment. These people can be dismissed first."

Capt Conkey then took a sheet of paper from Lt Standish, who then shone a torch on it while the captain read. "Well, we had fourteen sections go out on the Navex and it appears that only five have managed to get right around in time. They are 1 Section, 4 Section, 5 Section, 6 Section and 9 Section."

There was a buzz of conversation, quelled by the CSM as Capt Conkey went on. "That means that all of 2 Platoons sections made it, and they took all their cadets with them. Well done 2 Platoon."

Yes! Graham thought, even as he was aware of some jeering and unkind muttering from other platoons. Now he was pleased.

Capt Conkey then turned to CSM Cleland and said, "It is nearly 2200. They can stay up for another twenty minutes or so, but I want them all in bed by 2230. The sergeants are to stay with the platoons, but I want all CUOs to help the officers find Cpl Doyle's section. Carry on CSM."

As the OC walked away CSM Cleland told the sergeants to move their platoons back to their areas and get them ready for bed.

"Will the canteen be open?" called Cadet Rundle from 1 Platoon.

"You address me as 'Sir', Cadet Rundle," CSM Cleland replied. "And no. The officers have to find Cpl Doyle. Now get moving sergeants."

"Bugger Doyle!" was the muttered consensus as the cadets stood and dusted themselves before moving off in platoon lots. Graham shook his head and silently thanked his lucky stars. *Boy, am I glad we didn't get lost!* he thought. That sort of public humiliation did not appeal at all. To rub this in his radio came to life as the OC called Dimbo's call sign.

Sgt Grenfell marched 2 Platoon straight back to their area, then fell them out. As he did, Graham called out, "4 Section, stay here!"

"Oh, what for!" cried Andrews in exasperation.

"Yeah, hurry up, I'm busting for a leak," added Halyday.

Graham was too but he managed to suppress the surge of annoyance at their grumbling. "I just wanted to say well done. You did a great job. It was a great team effort. Thanks. That's all, off you go." he said.

That mollified them. As they dispersed with an outburst of chatter Graham walked beside Andrews. "Particularly you Cadet Andrews. Because you had the guts to try you helped the whole section."

Andrews made no reply, but Graham could tell he was pleased.

Graham walked to his hutchie and dropped his webbing with a sigh of relief.

"What about a cup of coffee?" Roger suggested.

"Good idea," Graham agreed. "We still have fifteen minutes."

He dragged his pack out and sat on it beside Roger. As he dug out his hexamine stove, he heard a below from Sgt Grenfell and saw a torch beam light up two boy's backs. Graham recognised Andrews and Halyday.

Sgt Grenfell roared angrily, "Hoy! You dirty little toads! Don't you do a pee there! You walk to the latrine."

Graham blushed with shame. *Little grubs!* he thought in exasperation.

He watched to see that they did actually walk off towards the latrine. He was annoyed they had been caught as he had often been guilty of just using the nearest bit of dark bush himself.

Stephen came and joined them as Roger lit his hexamine. Gwen and Barbara then sat opposite and also began organising their 'supper'. As they lit stoves and began heating water the two Land Rovers drove off out to the Canning Road and a group of CUOs led by Capt Conkey went past heading out into the night. Every few minutes the OC called Dimbo on the radio but got no response.

"Dimbo won't be very popular," Graham commented.

"Again!" Stephen added.

They all laughed, but as Graham looked up he met Barbara's eyes and he could tell she was reliving that ghastly experience. She said softly, "He saved my life, so don't tease him please."

Graham felt embarrassed and nodded. Barbara held his gaze for a second longer, making him wonder if she was sending him some sort of invitation. *She is an extraordinarily beautiful girl,* he thought, watching the firelight shimmer on her copper red hair. When he had rescued her, she had been naked and he had been granted more than a good eyeful. Now images of her nude shape flooded his mind and fired his thoughts. *I wonder?* he began to speculate. It went no further. Deep down he sensed she probably wasn't the girl for him. *A bit too much strong will and fire there I think,* he thought.

That got him thinking about girls and girl friends and his thoughts wandered onto Kirsty. *Might be possibilities in that direction,* he mused.

But that gave him twinges of guilt. Not only was Kirsty one of his cadets, but he knew that there was a girl back in Cairns who loved him deeply. That was Margaret Lake, a Year 8 student at his school. She was also his sister Kylie's best friend. Margaret had openly adored him for years and he wavered between loving her and being attracted to other, prettier girls.

Poor little Margaret. She's a nice kid but she can't compare with Barbara, or Lucy, he thought, picturing Margaret's cheerful, freckled face and chubby build.

At that moment, a piercing scream of pure terror sounded. It came from the darkness over beyond 4 Platoon.

Chapter 5

'HUTCHIE MEN'!

"Bloody hell!" cried Stephen in alarm. His head jerked up so that the firelight reflected on his glasses.

"At the boy's latrine," Graham said, scrambling to his feet.

More distant screams sounded, almost lost in the babble of voices that arose around the company area. Then quite distinctly Graham heard Halyday's voice. "No! Stop it! Let me go! Help! Help!"

"Halyday," Graham cried. He set off at a run.

As he ran, Sgt Grenfell yelled, "Stand fast 2 Platoon. Stay here!"

Graham stopped, his agitation rising as more shrieks and screams sounded in the night. "But sergeant, that's Halyday. One of my cadets."

Sgt Grenfell nodded, then rapped out orders. "Keep going Cpl Kirk. Cpl Bell, get a torch and follow. Cpl Copeland you are in command. Put the platoon to bed if I'm not back in time. Cadets, stay here!"

By then Graham was running hard across the grassy flat past HQ. As he crossed the vehicle track CSM Cleland's voice roared out, "Stop that running! All you cadets go back to your platoons."

Sgt Grenfell and Stephen were now pounding along close behind Graham. Once again the CSM's shout came. "Stop running I said!"

At that Graham and the others slowed to a fast walk. Graham knew that one of the unit's 'Standing Orders' was 'no running in the dark' but he found it very hard to obey as more shouts and screams sounded.

From the male latrine at the head of the gullies near 4 Platoon came a loud, deep bellowing, "Yowieeee! Yowieee! Ooohoo! Yowieee!"

Another voice shouted deep, ape-like grunts. Mixed among these Graham detected other voices: Andrews', Halyday's and... was it Carnes'?

Andrews screamed, "Stop it! Leave us alone. Aargh! Stop it!"

As Graham trotted past the big ironbark his eyes detected dark shapes running towards the latrine from 4 Platoon's bivouac area and also more figures flitting about among the trees on top of the slope where the latrine was located. Shouts of laughter sounded over at 4 Platoon and more deep "Hoo! Hoo! Hoos!" over at the latrine.

Two figures came running towards Graham, ignoring more orders by the CSM to stop running. As they got closer, Graham identified them by their voices: Andrews and Halyday.

"What's going on?" Graham yelled as they approached.

"Yowie men! Yowie men!" Andrews screamed.

"Wait! Stop!" Graham shouted as the cadets reached him, but they kept on going. Graham did not wait. He had suspicions and wanted to confirm them. As he broke into a run he heard Sgt Grenfell ordering Halyday and Andrews to stop.

By now the noise had died down at the latrine. Graham thought he saw a couple of dark figures flitting amongst the trees on top of the gully but when he arrived at the Hessian screen strung between the trees there was no sign of them. He was about to run past to look into the gully when sounds of scuffling and sobbing stopped him.

A cadet was squirming on the ground and crying. *Carnes!* Graham thought. *Must have been those bloody bullies!*

As Graham moved towards Carnes the cadet began to scrabble away from him. "Stay away! Leave me alone!" Carnes shrieked, fear making his voice crack.

Graham halted, shocked by the boy's distress. "It's me, Cpl Kirk," he called back.

Stephen arrived at that moment and turned his torch on. When the beam swept over Carnes Graham sucked in his breath in shock. Carnes had his trousers and underpants around his ankles and Graham could see his buttocks and half his back. He also noticed that Carnes' clothing and skin appeared to be stained or smeared with something.

"Turn the torch off Steve," Graham called. "Go and see if there is anyone in the gully."

Stephen did so. Graham moved closer to Carnes, who had now stopped screaming. The boy lay in a shuddering huddle, sobbing uncontrollably. CSM Cleland and Sgt Grenfell arrived simultaneously.

"What the hell's going on here? What are you up to Cpl Kirk?" CSM Cleland snapped.

To be thought one of the troublemakers instantly sparked Graham's ire but he was saved by Sgt Grenfell who said, "I told Cpl Kirk to come here CSM. He is with me. He had nothing to do with it."

"What the devil is going on?" CSM Cleland demanded.

"I think someone's been playing silly pranks CSM," Graham replied. "They have frightened the wits out of poor little Cadet Carnes here."

CSM Cleland clicked on a powerful torch. The beam transfixed the cringing, huddled form of Carnes. "What's going on Cadet Carnes? What's happened to you?"

Carnes made no reply. He shielded his eyes from the beam and hunched into a tighter ball. In the light Graham had his suspicions confirmed: the stains on Carnes' skin and clothing were shit. *Poor little bugger!* he thought.

Seeing Cadet Carnes undressed state CSM Cleland swung his torch beam around, picking out Stephen. "Can you see anything Cpl Bell?"

"No-one here CSM," Stephen replied. He walked back to join them.

Other people now began arriving. CSM Cleland turned his torch on them. Most were just cadets rushing to see the spectacle but Sgt White and Sgt Gayney were among them. "You people go back to your platoons," CSM Cleland yelled. "Cpl Bell, keep people away."

The cadets were shooed away but not before a few had peeked around the Hessian. Reluctantly the cadets withdrew, their voices a babble of speculation and snickering. From over at the 4 Platoon camp a loud, cruel laugh sounded.

Pike! Graham thought. *I'll bet he was in on this.*

By now Carnes had calmed down a bit. He still lay in a shivering huddle, but his sobs had died to sniffles. CSM Cleland walked over to him. "What happened Cadet Carnes?"

Graham said, "I'd watch where you step CSM."

The smell was now making itself felt. CSM Cleland flicked his torch onto the ground and Graham saw that turds and used toilet paper were scattered and smeared around the ground. He also noted that Carnes had shit smeared all over his right buttock. Sand adhered to it. Worse still there was a large turd inside Carnes' underpants and trousers.

"What happened Cadet Carnes? Who did this to you?" CSM Cleland asked again.

"Y... Ya... Yow... sniff... Yowie Men," Carnes sobbed.

"Crap!" CSM Cleland snorted.

Not well chosen that word! Graham thought.

CSM Cleland went on, "There are no such thing as Yowies. It was cadets dressed up. Who were they and what did they do?"

"I d... d... don't... sniff... don't kn... know... sniff... wh... who they w... wu... were," Carnes replied.

"What did they do?" CSM Cleland asked.

"They came up out of the gully (sob) while I was doing... doing a... a... a poo. They screamed and (sniffle) pushed me into the hole," he said. At that Carnes burst into tears again.

Lt Standish joined them, a teacher in her thirties and, Graham thought, a lovely person. She now confirmed that, as well as demonstrating she could handle a crisis. "What happened CSM?" she asked.

As CSM Cleland began to tell her what he knew Carnes began to whimper and pull at his clothing. "Go away! I'm not dressed!" Carnes shrieked.

Cruel laughter sounded from over at 4 Platoon. Graham said, "I'll bet Pigsy Pike and his scaly mates know something about this."

Lt Standish spoke softly to Carnes. "It's alright David, I'm a mother you know. I've got three boys about your age. Don't worry. Just lie still." She turned to the CSM. "What's wrong with him CSM?"

"He's all covered in... in... er... er." CSM Cleland stammered. Graham had to sympathise with him as he struggled to find a word suitable to say to a teacher.

"Shit you mean?" Lt Standish said.

"Er... yes Ma'am. It's all over his clothes. They pushed him into the hole."

"And they used the shovel to dump more on me!" Carnes cried.

"Who were they?" Lt Standish asked.

"Don't know Miss."

"How many?"

"Two of them," Carnes replied. "They had horrible faces and big shaggy heads and were huge."

A suspicion formed in Graham's mind and he asked, "Was it Halyday and Andrews?"

Carnes sobbed. "N... no. They had just arrived and were doing a pee when the Yowie Men ran out of the gully," Carnes said.

"Halyday and Andrews might know something," Lt Standish said. "CSM, you and Sgt Grenfell go and question them while I clean up here."

"4 Platoon I reckon," Graham insisted.

Stephen agreed. "I thought I heard 'Porno's' voice."

Lt Standish gestured. "Get some proof and don't make accusations Cpl Kirk. Go on CSM. Cpl Bell, you keep people away. Cpl Kirk, you stay here to help me."

Graham didn't want to stay but had no choice. Lt Standish sent him to collect a jerrycan of water. "And don't say anything to any cadet," she added as he walked away.

Although 4 Platoon area was closest, Graham went instead to HQ and got a jerrycan from the row beside the vehicle track. He lugged the jerry back, puffing and perspiring with effort. When he arrived back, Lt Standish was standing well away from the latrine, with her back to a naked Carnes who was busy washing himself using the washbasin and soap kept at the toilet for hygiene. In the starlight Graham could just see Carnes' pale skin. The boy had his back to them and was still sobbing.

"Put the jerrycan next to Cadet Carnes please Cpl Kirk, then go to his platoon and get his section commander to bring his kitbag," Lt Standish ordered.

"Yes Ma'am," Graham replied.

"What section are you in Cadet Carnes?" Lt Standish asked.

"3 Section, Cpl Brown, Miss," Carnes replied, misery in every syllable.

"Then we can't get your platoon sergeant here," Lt Standish commented.

As 1 Platoon sergeant was a girl, Sheila Sherry, Graham could only quietly chuckle as he strode across to where 1 Platoon was camped. He felt sorry for Carnes but thought his reaction a bit overdone.

The mongrels would regret it if they tried to do that to me, he told himself.

With that came the thought that maybe he had better be careful when and where he went to the toilet. He was uncomfortably aware that he had no friends in 4 Platoon.

Five minutes later Graham walked back with Cpl Brown, who carried Carnes' kitbag. As they arrived at the latrine Graham saw that Carnes, still naked, was now crouched in a shivering ball behind a tree. "There are prickles Miss!" Carnes moaned.

"Won't be long now,"Lt Standish told him.

As she did, the headlights of the two Land Rovers appeared out at the Canning Road. "Here comes the OC. Cpl Kirk, go and find the CSM and have him report to Capt Conkey. Cpl Brown, you stay here and keep watch for Cadet Carnes."

By the time the two Land Rovers had parked at the officer's fire Graham saw that his mission was wasted. CSM Cleland was already walking that way. Curious to know what Halyday and Andrews might have said Graham continued on. Lt Standish walked beside him, and they arrived at the fire just after the CSM had informed Capt Conkey of the outrage. While he was doing this the other officers and the four CUOs all climbed out of the vehicles and joined the group around the fire.

In the firelight Graham saw Capt Conkey's lips press together and his eyes harden. When the outline of the story had been given, he asked, "Do we know who did it?"

CSM Cleland answered. "No sir. Sgt Grenfell and I have questioned Cadets Halyday and Andrews but they either don't know, or won't say. All they could tell me was that they were big and that they had hutchies wrapped around them which they wore like cloaks. Apparently when they ran forward they spread these like bat's wings. They wore some sort of rubber masks, those horrible things you see in the novelty shops, and they had wigs made of scrim."

"Hutchies!" Capt Conkey cried in astonishment. "I'll give them bloody hutchies if I catch them. So there are no suspects?"

"It was suggested that 4 Platoon were involved sir," CSM Cleland replied, gesturing in Graham's direction.

At that CUO Grey scowled at Graham. "You got any proof Kirk?"

Graham swallowed and wished he hadn't spoken. He replied, "I heard their voices afterwards, and they thought it was very funny."

"Whose voices?" asked Capt Conkey as he glanced quickly at Graham.

CSM Cleland answered. "Someone said they thought they heard Porno's voice sir."

"Porno eh?" Capt Conkey replied, rubbing his chin thoughtfully. Cpl Pornosittipol was a huge Thai, a Year 12 student who had been passed over for promotion. Along with two others he had been placed in what was called the 'Control Group', but more usually 'the Enemy', because that was the role they normally filled on exercises. The unit policy was that, if a cadet NCO was not promoted, they were moved sideways onto an unofficial part of the establishment table, though still being enrolled and counted as a Cadet for official returns. This allowed more cadets to have a chance of being promoted.

"Has he got an alibi?" Capt Conkey asked. Graham knew that Porno was a notorious practical joker and mischief maker.

CSM Cleland nodded. "He claims he was with 4 Platoon all the time and Sgt White and Cpl Bannister back that up," he replied. He sounded annoyed.

"What about Pigsy Pike?" Graham interjected.

"Be quiet Cpl Kirk! Speak when you are asked," Capt Conkey rapped back. He turned to the CSM. "Well?"

"He says he was with 4 Platoon too sir. Others backed his story."

Capt Conkey frowned. "Do you think they are telling the truth?" he asked.

CSM Cleland shook his head. "No sir."

At that CUO Grey became indignant. "Oh sir! That's not fair, to blame my platoon without any evidence. We get blamed for everything." He flashed Graham another venomous look, making him wish he had stayed away.

"That's because it usually is 4 Platoon," Capt Conkey replied.

"We might be able to find something if we looked sir," CSM Cleland suggested.

At that Lt Maclaren chuckled. "We could rush the shovel to the police and have it checked for fingerprints."

Capt Conkey shook his head. "This is potentially serious Mel. If Carnes complains and we do nothing, then it will look bad."

"From the quantity of shit thrown around a sniffer dog might be more use than fingerprints," Lt Standish said, her face forming an impish smile. Graham was astounded.

I didn't know she had a sense of humour! he thought.

"Hmmm. I wonder if a kit search would reveal anything?" Capt Conkey mused. He checked his watch. "2310hrs. Bit late, but I think we had better look into this business of the Hutchie Men straight away. It will settle the issue about 4 Platoon's guilt or innocence. Now, what are we going to do about Cadet Carnes?"

Lt Standish said, "I will take Cadet Carnes over to the army camp. He can use the shower while I put all his clothes through the wash. We will be an hour or so."

"That's a good idea Jill. okay, off you go," Capt Conkey replied.

"Did you find Cpl Doyle's section?" Lt Standish asked.

Capt Conkey snorted. "Yes, we did. They were just waiting beside the road down at the Highway turn-off."

"How the hell did they get there?" CSM Cleland asked. Then he shook his head.

Graham chuckled. "This is Dimbo we are talking about," he said.

At that Capt Conkey turned on him. "That's enough of that talk! You are only a corporal too! Now you get back to your section Cpl Kirk."

Abashed, Graham fled. *Bloody drongo!* he told himself. *Learn to keep your mouth shut!*

As he walked away Graham heard Lt McEwen ask why Dimbo hadn't answered his radio. Lt Maclaren answered. "He didn't have it turned on!"

The officers groaned and Graham shook his head. He made his way back to his platoon Graham heard movement and voices and saw a line of cadets come walking in along Sandy Track- Dimbo's 'Lost patrol'.

Some unhappy cadets there too, he thought.

As he arrived back at the section hutchies Graham found Sgt Grenfell, Stephen and Roger standing to one side in the darkness. Naturally they wanted to know the outcome. As Graham arrived Gwen got up from her hutchie and joined them. Graham then related all that had passed, with the injunction not to talk about it.

Stephen chuckled. "Hutchie Men! I like that. I'll bet it was Porno and Ziggy."

"I'll bet it was too," Graham replied, "and I'll bet it was Pigsy who put them up to it."

"It certainly scared the crap out of Halyday and Andrews," Roger said.

They all laughed at that but then Sgt Grenfell got serious. "This is no good. We might have a problem if the little cadets aren't game to go to the dunny for fear of the Hutchie Men."

Stephen gave another chuckle. "We will know after a few days when they look very full in the face."

Sgt Grenfell laughed with the others but then said, "It wasn't constipation I was worrying about. The little buggers might just start to crap anywhere and then we will have a hygiene problem."

CUO Masters came over to join them from the fire. "What are you lot talking about?"

"The dreaded Hutchie Men sir," Sgt Grenfell replied.

"Then keep it quiet. Lt McEwen can hear you from there. In fact get to bed, it's nearly midnight."

They moved off to their hutchies. Roger crawled straight in but Graham realised he now needed a pee. He looked in the direction of the latrine and felt a distinct reluctance to go back there. He told himself the Hutchie Men would not be there because the distant sound of voices indicated that 4 Platoon was being searched by the officers. But it was still a long way in the dark.

One little leak won't matter, he rationalised. *I'll just nip into the gully.*

Even so he went carefully, worried about snakes more than Hutchie Men. Thus, when the bushes in front of him suddenly erupted he leapt back, heart hammering, and let out a cry of fright. Then he swore. "Bloody wallaby!" he muttered.

Glancing around to check he was out of sight of the hutchies he stopped and did a pee, then walked quickly back up to the camp. As he passed Kirsty's hutchie, he got another fright when she sat up and spoke to him.

"Did the Hutchie Men give you a scare then, Graham?" she asked, giving a chuckle.

He meant to rebuke her for not calling him Corporal Kirk, but didn't. *We are alone*, he rationalised, even as he named his weakness for what it was. Instead, he stopped and knelt down. In the starlight he saw white skin extending down from her face to her neck, and then on down past her shoulders. *Holy Mackerel!* he thought. *Is she wearing anything?*

By staring hard, he was reassured that she had her sleeping bag held across her chest. Then he whispered, "How do you know about the Hutchie Men?"

"I could hear you talking just now," she replied.

"Well don't say anything to the other cadets about it," Graham replied, feeling guilty at having done so himself. "And don't you get a chill," he added.

"It's not cold," she said, shrugging her shoulders. "Now tell me what happened?"

"I can't tell you," Graham relied.

"Oh, spoil sport. I won't tell!"

Graham snorted. "Humpf! That's what all the girls say!"

"Do they?" Kirsty asked. Graham wasn't sure if it was because she was whispering or not, but he thought her voice sounded very sultry and sexy. He began to get aroused.

Sgt Grenfell's voice ended any speculation on his chances. "What are you two doing?" he called from his own hutchie.

"Just telling Kirsty about the Hutchie Men," Graham answered.

"Well don't! And get to bed," Sgt Grenfell called back.

Kirsty smiled and giggled. "I'd like a man in my hutchie," she whispered. Graham's heart began to hammer rapidly, and his mind raced with possibilities and hope.

Maybe? he thought. *Is she giving me the 'come on'?*

For several seconds he stayed, looking into her eyes. He noted that they seemed to sparkle with the reflection of the stars and that her lips were slightly parted. She was breathing rapidly. The temptation to ask for a kiss was almost overpowering but, fearing a rejection and not trusting his senses, he stood up.

I might be reading the signs wrong, he thought. *Then I will be in real trouble when she complains.*

Regretfully he said, "Good night," and walked away.

As he did, Kirsty smiled again. "Sweet dreams," she murmured.

Oh bloody hell! he told himself. *Don't be tempted. Be strong!*

He crawled into his hutchie, hoping Roger hadn't noticed any of that. To Graham's relief, he hadn't. He was lying on his side asleep. Graham unrolled his bedding, his gaze continually diverting to Kirsty's hutchie. From the end of his bed, he could just see the top of her head. As he looked, he saw her twist around to look at him. Then she turned away and let the sleeping bag drop so that Graham was granted a fleeting glimpse of white skin in the starlight. That set his imagination working and he became almost instantly aroused. She fidgeted a bit, apparently adjusting her bed then slid down into her sleeping bag.

Graham took off his boots and stretched out fully clothed, feet towards Kirsty. He was very conscious of his aroused state, and of her. From where he was lying he could only see the top of her head and part of her shoulders but it was enough for his adolescent imagination to seize on.

Oh hell! he mentally screamed. Then a terrible temptation rose to torment him. *Will I risk sneaking back over to ask her for a little kiss and a cuddle?*

Even as he thought this, he saw her roll over and twist her head around to look at him.

Does she want me to? he wondered, his heart hammering frantically and his mouth dry with lust and excitement. *Do I dare?*

Chapter 6

TEMPTATION

Graham stared from the shadows of his hutchie at Kirsty. He could see she was looking in his direction but still wasn't sure if it was an invitation.

She said she wanted a man in her hutchie. That must mean she wants it? he reasoned.

Voices over at the officer's fire caught Graham's attention and he moved to poke his head out to look. He saw that Capt Conkey, the officers and CSM Cleland were standing in a group deep in conversation. Movement from Kirsty's hutchie attracted his attention. She half sat up and looked toward the officers. As she did, Graham thought her sleeping bag would slip off her front but she held it on. Then she turned her head to look at him and he saw her lips move.

What is she saying? he wondered, although he thought he knew. *No,* he decided. Too many years of not succeeding with girls made him shake his head in disbelief. *No, it is too good to be true,* he told himself. *She's not offering surely?* But she did seem to be giving him a smile. Graham smiled back and felt his desire press harder. *I could just creep over and ask her what she wants,* he thought.

But that took real courage, and he found his mouth dry and his palms sweaty. His breath came in gasps as though he had run a race. He had only really misbehaved with a girl once in his life and been caught in the act. As a result, he had got into terrible trouble. That memory now flooded his consciousness to further confuse him.

Ooh it was wonderful! he remembered. But not what followed! *Come on coward,* his naughty imp urged him. *Faint heart never won fair lady! Opportunity knocks but once.*

The urge to go was now strong in him and he felt his pulses racing. With a tiny sob he plucked up the courage and moved to the end of the hutchie. As he went to stand up, a noise nearby caused him to freeze in fright. Someone was coming! As quietly as he could Graham hunched back inside his hutchie as the footsteps came closer.

It was CUO Masters. He walked through the gap between the two hutchies and on towards the officer's fire. Graham sank back onto his sleeping bag, his heart thudding.

Bloody hell, that was close! he thought.

He saw that Kirsty had also subsided into her bed. After CUO Masters had gone she again raised her head and looked towards Graham. He crept to the entrance and put his head out and shook it.

Too risky, he mouthed.

Kirsty made a face but nodded. She then lay down, seeming to toss her hair in annoyance. Graham also lay back, his mind and emotions racing.

Is she just teasing me, or does she mean it? he wondered.

He lay there in frustration, wondering and fantasising while his mind roved over Kirsty's possibilities. It was a terribly tempted and torn young man who slipped into sleep.

* * *

"Wake up! Out of bed! Boots and hat! Check Parade!" called Sgt Grenfell.

Graham groaned and opened sleep-gummed eyes. Then he realised it was daylight. Rubbing his eyes, he sat up. As he did, he noticed that Kirsty was sitting up buttoning her shirt. She had her back to him, but he broke into a sweat of anxiety over what to do about her.

As quickly as he could, Graham hauled on his boots and then found his hat. Urged on by more calls by Sgt Grenfell, Graham crawled out and stood up. As he did, Kirsty turned and their eyes met. Graham forced a smile. To his relief she smiled back but she looked tired and grumpy.

At another bellow from Sgt Grenfell, Graham went to ensure the remainder of his section were all awake and moving. Dianne and Lucy were, and Graham was careful not to look into their shelter in case they thought he was perving. Instead, he walked on to roust Andrews and Halyday out. He saw with satisfaction that Pat was already up.

"Come on you pair! Get up and out," Graham snapped irritably. He was very conscious that Gwen's section all seemed to be lined up already. Stephen went past with several of his cadets to join the platoon.

"Mob of dozy slugs," Stephen commented with a grin as he did.

Graham was not amused. He grunted a greeting, then turned and snapped angrily at Andrews and Halyday. "Get a move on you pair! We are last now."

He looked in and saw that Andrews was lacing his boots up and that Halyday was trying to pull on a sock. At that he exploded. "Don't waste time putting on socks Halyday! Just get your boots on; and don't lace them up. Just shove the laces inside so you don't trip on them!"

Sgt Grenfell added to Graham's discomfiture by calling, "Hurry up 4 Section! We don't want to be the last platoon on parade."

Urged on by a shamed Graham the two cadets crawled grumbling out and made their way to join the ranks. It was apparent that all of 5 Section and 6 Section were already there. A quick head count assured Graham that all members of his section were now present.

"All here Cpl Kirk?" Sgt Grenfell queried.

"Yes sergeant," Graham replied, hotly aware that CUO Masters was looking towards them as he walked past towards the officer's fire.

The platoon was then marched over past HQ to line up along the vehicle track. Despite the delay they were not last on check parade. 3 Platoon was. As they arrived CSM Cleland muttered his annoyance, then called the company to attention, right dressed them and stood them at ease. "Platoon sergeants, call the roll!" he ordered.

That done CSM Cleland called for reports. Next, he told them when to be ready for work and which platoon would be first for breakfast. The sergeants were then told to 'carry on'. Sgt Grenfell marched the platoon back to their bivouac area and fell them out.

Needing a pee urgently Graham immediately made his way towards the latrine in the gully beyond 3 Platoon, reasoning that he did not want to go to the one near 4 Platoon where the Hutchie Men had struck. On the way he passed close to 3 Platoon and called hello to several cadets he knew.

As soon as he topped the rise at the head of the gully, Graham realised he had made a mistake. Down in the dip were a dozen male cadets including Corporals Crane and Costigan, and Cadets Moynihan, Rundle, Waters and Franks. They were smoking, something which was strictly forbidden, both by State Law and the Cadet Regulations.

For a second Graham considered veering away, pretending he was going somewhere else but by then he had seen their eyes on him. *If I don't keep going, they will think I am scared of them,* he thought. The nub of the situation was that he was feeling scared of them. Despite this he continued walking down into the dip.

Waters spoke first. "Well, if it isn't little Mister Brown Nose himself! Did ya shit yerself last night Kirk?"

Graham wanted to ignore Waters but managed to meet his eye and shake his head, even though his heart had begun to hammer hard. For a moment he thought Waters and Moynihan were going to block his path, but he managed to keep walking and went past within arm's reach.

As he did, Costigan snarled at him, "Don't you bloody well dob on us Kirk."

At that Graham gave a wry smile. "Don't worry, I won't. You aren't in my section. It's your conscience."

"Conscience!" jeered Cpl Crane. "Bloody 'goody-goody' weakling."

Graham flamed at the insults but held his tongue. There were a couple of cadets from 3 Platoon at the urinal, but they left as he arrived, so he was now alone with the gang standing 20 paces behind him. Feeling very self-conscious and afraid Graham stood with his back to them to urinate. Then the emotional turmoil made it hard for him to start and he burned with shame.

As he tried, Waters called out, "Kirk can't find his dick!"

"That's 'cause it's so tiny!" Moynihan added, his voice full of contempt.

To Graham's relief, Franks said, "How do you know, Lew? Have you been looking?"

"Get stuffed!" Moynihan snarled.

By then Graham had managed to get started. Even so he feared the gang would do something to him while he was so vulnerable. To his relief they did not. After zipping up his trousers, he turned and walked back past them.

Once again, Costigan glared at him and said, "You tell on us and you'll regret it."

Graham made no reply but walked on up out of the dip. By the time he reached the top his heart was once again hammering as though he had run a race. Almost immediately he was presented with a dilemma. Not 20 paces away was the 3 Platoon sergeant, Sgt Yeldham.

I could tell him, he thought.

But he shook his head and tried to tell himself that the smokers were none of his business. That left a sour taste in his mouth and he walked on back to his own platoon area wondering if he really was a coward.

The business of getting himself and his section ready at once claimed all Graham's attention and he had no more time to worry about troublemakers in other platoons until breakfast time. During the mess parade Graham found Kirsty behind him in the line and she seated herself next to him when he took his food to the area allocated to the platoon.

She must like me, he mused as he walked over to the table where the bread and cereal were placed.

After collecting some cereal and milk he went to his platoon area. Kirsty came with him and sat beside him. The main topic of conversation in the platoon was the 'Hutchie Men' and Graham was asked several times to give his account of what happened.

"They reckon Carnes was rolled in his own shit," Bert Lacey said.

Graham just grunted and pretended to have a mouthful of food.

"Carnes is a useless idiot!" Cadet Lucas observed.

At that Graham reacted. "Leave the poor bugger alone!" he cried. "He's on his first camp and is being bullied by Pike and his slimy mates. He doesn't need us picking on him as well." That effectively ended that conversation, but Graham sensed he wasn't very popular for shaming them into silence.

The next half hour went by in a rush for Graham. He had to get himself ready and at the same time ensure the section was as well. Adding to his feeling of tension was the need to go to the latrine to do a crap but he put this off.

I'll go later when I've got time, he told himself, then doubted whether he was just trying to rationalise his own fears. *Am I coward?* he wondered. *Am I actually scared of the Hutchie Men?*

In the end he did not have time as both Andrews and Halyday were not ready for inspection at 0730hrs. Nor were Dianne and Lucy anywhere to be seen. Both had gone to the toilet and only returned after Sgt Grenfell had been waiting five minutes to inspect. Sweating with anxiety and annoyance Graham snapped at the late cadets to get a move on. To add to his feelings of poor performance his section was then left till last. This was because both Stephen's and Gwen's sections were lined up ready.

"See what you've done!" Graham fumed.

"Aw keep yer shirt on Kirky," Halyday retorted.

"Don't back answer me Cadet Halyday; and call me corporal. This is the Army Cadets!" Graham snapped. He glanced around and saw that his outburst had drawn a frown from CUO Masters, who had just begun inspecting Gwen's section. That made Graham feel even worse.

I'm not handling this very well, he thought unhappily.

Aware of rebellious muttering by Halyday, Graham ordered the section lined up with their mess gear laid out on their packs. Halyday kept giving him sulky looks but Graham pretended to ignore this. To ensure everything was ready he went along and inspected them himself. While doing this he found himself looking into Kirsty's eyes.

It was as though they just grew in size and somehow drew him in. *They are pretty eyes!* he thought, marvelling again at the tiny flecks of gold in the blue of her irises. *I wonder?*

She smiled and he tried not to smile back, and failed. Then his eyes travelled down over the front of her shirt. *Not a lot in there,* he thought with regret. He really liked larger bosoms. Then he blushed at his own thoughts and hastily looked on down at her boots and then her mess gear.

A few minutes later CUO Masters and Sgt Grenfell came over to inspect and Graham was sure it was a disaster. CUO Masters found a dozen things wrong which Graham had not noticed.

He said, "This section needs to lift its standards Cpl Kirk."

That left Graham burning with shame and he glowered at the line of cadets, who stood and sullenly glowered back. It was a relief to be called on parade.

During the company parade CSM Cleland handed over to Capt Conkey. Capt Conkey then ordered the platoon commanders to 'fall in'. Once they had done so he proceeded to lecture them about the previous night.

"If I find out who these Hutchie Men are they are in for a miserable camp," he threatened. "Now stop the bullying and teasing and get on with making the camp work smoothly."

After that, the company was seated in the shade of the big ironbark. The CUOs and sergeants went over to the officer's fire for a briefing while Capt Conkey gave the remainder their instructions for a day navigation exercise. This was to be a slightly longer version of the night exercise they had done, but all sections following a different route from the previous exercise.

By the time the briefing was over Graham was feeling quite uncomfortable. He now badly needed to go to the toilet but was absorbed in calculating his first 'leg'. As he did, the OOCs, CUOs and Sgts moved off with vehicles and radios to set up the check points. With an effort Graham kept his bowels under control and concentrated on the mathematics.

Satisfied he was correct he stood in line behind Cpl Bannister. Bannister showed his workings to Capt Conkey and was told to go away and check them. At that Bannister scowled at Graham as he stalked off. Heart fluttering with anxiety Graham stepped forward to present his calculations.

Capt Conkey scanned them then nodded. "That's fine Cpl Kirk. Off you go."

That earned Graham another scowl from Bannister, who had stopped to talk to Cpl Brown. Graham ignored them and called 4 Section to join him. He undid the compass.

"You first, Kirsty," he said, holding it out.

Chapter 7

DAY NAVEX

The first 'leg' went southwest for 400 metres, past 1 Platoon's hutchies and down the gentle slope, then across a small gully to the flat outcrop of rocks at the head of the shallow valley between the camp and Bare Ridge. Kirsty had no trouble using the compass and took them directly to the spot. Sgt Yeldham was there. He gave Graham the next leg, which was even easier- on across the valley for another 400 metres to the Burdekin Plum tree beside the road on Bare Ridge.

The tree was plainly visible from the rocks, but Graham insisted that Pat use the compass correctly. The section walked across to find Lt Hamilton there again, his Land Rover parked nearby. As Graham worked on the navigation his attention was distracted by the sound of a train. He looked up and saw the train off to the south. It was about a kilometre beyond the highway. From where they were the highway was clearly visible, but the railway was partly hidden by trees and long grass. As Graham watched it, the big diesel locomotive went out of sight behind a cluster of houses that the map named as 'Bunyip Bridge'.

Graham looked down to continue with his calculations but an abrupt change in the sound of the train, from a noisy sort of vibration to a distinct roar, made him look up. For the first time he noticed the railway bridge. At a glance he could see that it wasn't just an ordinary rail bridge. This one was huge. A long, grassy embankment led across the plain to the nearest end. The first section of the bridge, over the last part of the high bank, was steel-sided. After that it was a massive steel girder construction set on top of colossal concrete pylons. As Graham watched the train it was swallowed by the criss-crossing steel girders, the noise changing to an even deeper roar.

Through truss, Graham told himself. Being a keen model railway builder, he was interested in such things. He noted that the girders were mostly a dull reddish colour. The train, a long 'goods', passed through with a continual flickering effect. *Bloody big bridge,* Graham thought, estimating the length at over half a kilometre. It was marked on his map, so he now studied it carefully and then revised his estimate. *Nearly a kilometre long! That is a big bridge,* he thought.

The train had gone by then, so he resumed his mathematics. Two minutes of work gave him the next leg. It was also very easy. They had been there the night before and could see the check point from where they were. It was in the dry creek which ran down from 1 Platoon's hutchies to the highway. Halyday took the lead with the compass and they walked the distance in five minutes.

CSM Cleland was there. As Graham's section arrived from the west No 9 Section (Cpl Gallagher) came in from the east. There was a fair amount of good-natured teasing and chatter between the sections while the two corporals worked out their next leg. Graham liked Gallagher and was happy to compare notes and to check his sums.

After that, 4 Section went on eastwards over the low ridge which ran down from 2 Platoon to the Highway. Andrews was the cadet with the compass.

"We are now going backwards around the same course as last night," Roger said as they puffed up the slope from the gullies to the South Gravel Pit.

"So far," Graham agreed.

After that, the course changed. Sgt Sherry was at the South Gravel Scrape and she told them to move to a Grid Reference over towards Scrubby Creek. That pleased Graham as he was finding the exercise too easy. Even the next leg was no real challenge. Dianne did the compass work but as the route went across the gullies where the other boy's latrine was Graham knew exactly where he was most of the time.

Checkpoint 'S' was at a track junction and was staffed by Capt Conkey and CUO McAlistair. The CUO gave them a cheerful greeting and told them to move to another grid reference, a gravel scrape further north.

"There's a fence you need to go through," he cautioned. "But don't cross the Canning River."

Very conscious that Capt Conkey was watching, Graham studied his map and noted that the left-hand track went north to the North Gravel Scrape while the right-hand track went to a windpump called 'Quiglys Mill' beside Scrubby Creek. That made the navigation simple, but he decided he had better work out the exact magnetic bearing with Capt

Conkey there. Otherwise, he would have just walked along the vehicle track.

The OC's presence made Graham anxious, but he quickly did the calculation. He showed this to CUO McAlistair, who nodded. The next person to navigate was Lucy so Graham gave the compass to her and they set off. It was easy going through more open savannah, heading down a long, gentle ridge. However, the navigation was not Graham's only problem. Leadership soon came to dominate as Andrews and Halyday both began to complain. Andrews said it was too hot and Halyday moaned of sore feet. Dianne also muttered that she needed to go to the toilet. That made Graham conscious of his own needs, but he insisted they get to the next check point first.

As they walked along Graham saw Peter's section go past a hundred metres away and he gave his friend a wave. After that Graham began to fret about the time. The exercise was due to end by 11:30 and he saw with alarm that it was almost 11:00 already. He hurried the section along, encouraging and growling at Halyday and Andrews in turn. The fence was encountered and they rolled under, several cadets objecting because the sand was now quite hot.

On the other side they paused for a drink and Graham wiped sweat off his face. The sun was now blazing down from a clear blue sky and there was no breeze to cool them. *I'd better watch out no-one gets heat exhaustion,* he thought, noting the red, sweaty faces.

Two hundred metres of walking along a gentle, open slope brought them to a stand of timber. Beyond that was the harsh, bare redness of the North Gravel Scrape. The checkpoint was under the last of the trees beside a vehicle track which led in from the Canning Road. No 1 Section, Cpl Rankin, was there already. Manning the checkpoint was the CQ, Sergeant Coralie Bates, a tall thin girl with fair hair and a freckled face. With her were two of the 'Control Group': Cpl 'Porno' Pornosittipol and Cpl 'Ziggy' Zeiglitz.

Graham could not resist. As he arrived, he said loudly, "Well, well, if it isn't the famous Hutchie Men!"

Porno gave an evil grin and called back, "And if it isn't Mister Crap-in-pants- Kirk."

The unjust jibe hurt but Graham noted that neither denied being Hutchie Men.

Halyday said, "Jeez, you blokes scared the crap out of me last night!"

Both Hutchie Men laughed and Ziggy nodded. "We sure scared the shit out of Carnes too."

That annoyed Graham. He stood over them and said angrily, "You shouldn't pick on the poor bugger. He doesn't deserve it."

Porno had the grace to look embarrassed, but Ziggy sneered. "Huh! He's just a bloody weakling!"

"All the more reason not to pick on him!" Graham flared.

"Yeah, yeah, alright," Ziggy agreed. "We'll leave him alone in future."

"Good!" Graham said.

"But we won't stop picking on you," Ziggy added, giving Graham a challenging stare as he said it.

Graham felt his stomach turn over with anxiety (He did not want to name it as fear), but he managed to keep a bold face. "I look forward to it," he retorted. Even as he did, he was uncomfortably aware that he still hadn't managed to have his morning crap and the need was becoming insistent.

So, on the next leg, which took them down to a fair-sized dry creek towards the Canning Road, he halted the section and told them to wait. "Just sit under this tree," he said, "I'll only be a few minutes." He was embarrassed at having to admit to bodily needs in front of the girls, particularly Kirsty, but he knew he could not hold on any longer.

Dianne pointed up the creek. "We will go the other way," she said. "Come with me, Kirsty, to keep watch."

Graham walked away, burning with embarrassment. As quickly as he could he found a spot hidden from the others. This was around the bend and behind some small bushes. After scraping a hole with the heel of his boot he dropped his trousers and proceeded to relieve himself.

In the middle of this Graham heard a peculiar scuffling noise and looked anxiously around. His first thought was that the Hutchie Men had followed him but no-one was visible. Then he heard what sounded like a sniffle, or a sob.

"Definitely someone crying," he muttered anxiously. As quickly as he could, Graham finished his business and dressed then walked up to some bushes nearer to the Canning Road to investigate.

It was David Carnes. He was sitting hunched up, tears streaming down his cheeks. At the sound of Graham's footsteps, he looked around, fear all over his face.

"It's only me, Cadet Carnes," Graham said. "Are you alright? What's happened? What are you doing here?"

"They keep teasing me!" Carnes cried, as more tears flowed.

"You should tell your corporal," Graham replied, somewhat uneasily.

"Brown! He's the worst! He puts me down all the time. I hate it! I'm going to run away!" Carnes sobbed. Graham saw that he was very red in the face and looked utterly miserable.

"Where is your section?" Graham asked, looking in all directions.

"They wouldn't stop so I walked away. I don't know where they are," Carnes replied. His chest heaved and his lower jaw quivered as he sobbed.

"You mean they left you?" Graham asked. He was astonished. One of the unit's strict safety rules was that no-one was ever left in the bush.

"I don't know," Carnes admitted between sniffles.

"Why didn't you just walk back to camp?" Graham asked.

More tears flooded Carnes' eyes. "I don't know the way. I'm lost!"

Graham shook his head in amazement. From where he stood, he could see both the red scar of the North Gravel Scrape and the tin shed beside the Canning Road. "You'd better come with us," he said.

Carnes didn't want to, but Graham insisted. "You can't bloody well stay here! You'll get heat exhaustion," he snapped. He made Carnes have a drink and wash his face, then led him back to rejoin the section.

As Graham and Carnes walked down into the dry creek bed to rejoin the section Andrews curled his lip and called out, "Well, look what the cat dragged in!"

Graham was in no mood for any more nonsense. He was hot, tired and angry. "Shut up Cadet Andrews! If you've got nothing good to say, then say nothing. Come on, get up! Let's go!"

Andrews looked sulky and moaned about the heat and feeling tired but the group began moving. Lucy did the compass work. They crossed a bare, sandy flat through scattered trees and then crossed another sandy creek bed. Graham saw on his map that it was the one which had it's beginnings up near the 4 Platoon latrine. A fifty metre climb up a bare slope brought them to the Canning Road opposite the tin shed.

To his surprise and dismay Graham saw that Capt Conkey had just arrived there and was talking to Lt McEwen. *Oh no! I hope he doesn't notice Carnes,* Graham thought. But even as they walked across to the two officers Graham saw Capt Conkey's gaze rove along the section. A frown wrinkled his brow.

"What is Cadet Carnes doing with your section Cpl Kirk?" he asked.

Graham did not want to answer, knowing it would just lead to more ill will and trouble, but he could not think of any sensible excuse. He stopped in front of Capt Conkey and gestured back towards the creek. "We... he... we... er, we found him back there sir."

"Found him! What the devil does that mean?" Capt Conkey cried.

"He wasn't with his section sir, so I told him to come with us," Graham explained, knowing as he said it that his explanation sounded lame.

"Not with his section! What on earth?" Capt Conkey exploded. His gaze shifted to Carnes, who burst into tears again.

"They left me, sir!" Carnes shrieked. "They tease me and call me names all the time, and they hit me."

"Who, the people in your section? Doesn't Cpl Brown stop it?" Capt Conkey asked angrily.

"N... n... no sir. He teases me too," Carnes sobbed. He then burst into tears and howled. "I hate this! I want to go home!"

Capt Conkey looked grim. He turned to Graham. "You keep going Cpl Kirk. We will deal with this. Cadet Carnes will stay here with us." He indicated that Graham should go to Lt McEwen and turned back to comfort the distressed boy.

Graham did as he was told, but with a sinking heart. *Bloody Brown will give me a hard time now,* he thought unhappily.

Nor was he wrong. After getting the final leg (back to camp) from Lt McEwen, Graham worked out the bearing, gave the compass to Roger, and then urged his grumbling and protesting band into motion. They trudged up the bed of the dry creek until they reached Sandy Ridge. After reporting to Lt Standish, Graham led the section back to the platoon area and fell them out. Half an hour later Brown arrived, furiously angry.

Graham was lying in the shade of his hutchie resting. Brown kicked his boots and snarled at him. "You bloody dobber, Kirk! You bastard! Now you've gotten me in the shit!"

Half expecting to be struck as he did so, Graham crawled out of his hutchie and stood up. "I did not. We found Carnes and took him with us. Capt Conkey saw him and asked what he was doing with us."

"Bull! You're always suckin' up to the OC. You just want another stripe, ya boot-licking turd!" Brown shouted. He had his balled fists on his hips and it took all of Graham's resolve to stand his ground.

I don't want a fight, he thought. *That could get me into real trouble.* But his pride was hurt and he stood his ground. "You shouldn't have left him in the bush," he said as calmly as he could.

"We didn't! The moaning little mummy's boy just walked off," Brown snapped. "He's bloody lucky I didn't thump him one, the things he called me!"

"You shouldn't call him names," Graham replied as levelly as his anxiety allowed. He was now breathing very fast and resigning himself to a fight and all the unpleasantness that would follow.

"I didn't!" Brown yelled angrily.

Graham noted that his face was very red and his eyes glaring dislike. It made his stomach turn over and he trembled. "Your section does though," he retorted. "You should stop them."

At that Brown's anger really flared. "Don't you lecture me on how to run my section! Who the hell do you think you are! You don't outrank me!"

Graham braced himself, determined not to throw a punch until it was obvious self-defence. He was dimly aware that a crowd was gathering. Brown raised his fists.

"That's enough!" shouted a voice: CSM Cleland. He walked in between them. "Don't Cpl Brown," he snapped. "I'm warning you."

"So am I!" cut in another voice: Lt Hamilton's.

Graham glanced away from Brown's angry eyes and saw that both Lt Hamilton and Lt Maclaren had arrived. CUO Masters and Sgt Grenfell also appeared.

CSM Cleland stood facing Brown. "Cpl Brown, go back to your platoon area. Get your section and move them to the big ironbark for a roll call. That applies to 2 Platoon as well Sgt Grenfell."

That defused the situation. Brown glared at Graham, and his face twisted in animosity, but he lowered his fists and walked away. Graham stood and heaved a huge sigh, then shook from head to toe with emotion. Roger clapped him on the back, "Well done mate!" he said.

Graham was now all a-fluster with emotions, not least because he noted Kirsty giving him an adoring look. Again, he was saved by Sgt Grenfell calling on the section commanders to move their people to the big ironbark. Stephen was curious to know what it was about, but Graham told him he would tell him later. Still trembling with reaction, he led 4 Section across to the tree.

On arrival he caught the eye of several people in 4 Platoon and he felt sick inside at the sneers and hissed threats they offered. CSM Cleland took control and seated the company in their sections, then silenced them while he called on the platoon sergeants for a roll check. There was only one section missing: Dimbo Doyle's. It seemed so inevitable that the company gave a collective sigh and burst into laughter and comments.

"Silence!" thundered CSM Cleland. He was so obviously in a bad mood he got it instantly. "Sergeants, take your people back to their areas and get ready for lunch."

Poor old Dimbo. He led his section in halfway through lunch, to a rising tide of jeering comments and laughter. With him came CUO Grey and CUO Mitrovitch, who had found them down in the bed of the Canning. Graham sat among his section and shook his head.

Poor bugger! he thought. He vowed never to get lost if he could possibly help it.

After eating lunch and washing up Graham felt the need to do another pee. The climate was so dry that he was drinking a lot and he really needed to go. He looked towards the 4 Platoon latrine and bit his lip.

Don't be a bloody coward, he told himself. *Don't let them scare you.*

He at once amended that to, *Don't let them think they've got you scared!* But he knew he was. For a minute he hesitated, wondering if he could ask Stephen to come with him. Then he shook his head. *You are being stupid, and gutless! Just go!*

So he did, and walked straight into more trouble!

Chapter 8

FIELDCRAFT

In a small depression near the head of the gully sat a group of cadets. From the way their heads turned, Graham at once deduced they were guilty about something. The furtive hand movements gave it away as they tried to hide cigarettes. With a sinking heart Graham noted Waters, LCpl Franks and Poschalk, another 4 Platoon cadet. Then, to his dismay, he realised that one of the other cadets smoking was Andrews. A couple of cadets from 1 Platoon also sat there.

But for Andrews, Graham would have walked away in disgust. Smoking was one of those things that was considered an acid test in the unit. While not particularly important in itself, Capt Conkey had made it quite clear that, in his opinion, it was critical in such things as trust. It angered Graham that Andrews, who had only promised the day before to behave, was letting the section down.

Bracing himself for the aggravation he knew must follow, Graham strode angrily across to the group. As he did, he saw the sneers and snide asides being cast by Waters and Co. It made him feel ill inside, but he kept on.

Waters spoke first, "Piss off Kirk, you bloody sniveller."

Graham ignored him. He looked down at Andrews, who was looking quite guilty and was hiding the cigarette in his hand. "Get rid of the cigarette, Cadet Andrews, and get back to the platoon area," he said, trying to keep the anxiety out of his voice.

"Why should I?" Andrews queried, but nervously.

"Because I am your corporal and I've just given you an order."

That drew jeers and insults from the 4 Platoon cadets. "Don't do it Andrews, tell the moron where to go," Waters called, glaring dislike and defiance at Graham.

That made Graham shiver inside but also annoyed him. "Get up and get moving, Cadet Andrews!" he snapped.

"He doesn't have to. It's lunch time," Watts said. He deliberately put his cigarette in his mouth and took a puff.

Graham tried to ignore him but felt very anxious, aware that things could quickly go wrong. "Get moving Andrews, or else," he threatened.

"Or else what?" Franks queried. "Will little Mister Weakling run to the CSM with tales? That's about all you are good for Kirk, you bloody boot licker!"

Graham glared back at him, his heart rate rising as his fear and anger grew. He was blushing and knew it and that did not help. Now he was regretting making an issue of the situation but felt he had to go on.

"Move Andrews!"

Andrews looked worried. "What ya gunna do?" he asked, anxiety evident in his voice. "Are you gunna tell on me to Sgt Grenfell?"

"No I'm not. I'll deal with you myself," Graham replied. "From now on you win every dirty job that the section gets."

That drew more jeers from the others. "Don't believe him Andrews," Waters cried. "He hasn't got the guts to do anything without one of the officers standing nearby."

Andrews looked anxiously around. Then, to Graham's intense relief, stubbed out his cigarette and stood up. The others all jeered him and called him a wuss and a weaky, making him blush with resentment.

Waters called at Graham, "What about us Mister Goody Goody? Aren't you going to boss us around too to show how tough you are with two stripes?"

"You aren't in my section or I would," Graham retorted. But inside he felt bad. He knew it was not the right answer.

If I did the right thing I would. A corporal can give orders to any cadet, he told himself.

But he just wanted to resolve the situation with some dignity left. His answer drew derisive jeers and sneering laughter. Graham turned and told Andrews to start walking.

As he did, Waters called after him, "You better not dob us in Kirk or you'll bloody well regret it!"

"Yeah!" Franks added. "If ya do, we'll get ya!"

Graham ignored them and started walking. As he and Andrews made their way up out of the hollow, a stone went skittering past through the grass beside Graham. He felt a wave of cold, then hot resentment but kept walking without changing pace or looking back.

"Don't dob, Kirk!" called Waters as another stone went flying past.

Andrews ducked and looked scared, but Graham managed to pretend he was not affected.

With relief, Graham led Andrews away from the area. Once they were safely past the 3 Platoon hutchies Graham stopped and so did Andrews. "You shouldn't be smoking Cadet Andrews," he said.

"Why not?" challenged Andrews. "My dad smokes. Why shouldn't I?"

All sorts of medical reasons like lung cancer and so forth rushed through Graham's mind. He managed to bite back a comment on how stupid it was. Instead, he said, "Because it is against the law, and specifically forbidden in the cadet regulations."

"So?"

"So you made a promise to Capt Conkey to behave!" Graham flared.

Andrews shrugged. "So who'll know if you don't tell him?"

"You'll know! Where's your self-respect?" Graham cried. "Isn't your word worth anything?"

Andrews had the grace to blush and he mumbled. Graham kept on, "And you are letting down the section and the platoon. If you don't want to be with us, then ask for a transfer to another platoon."

At that Andrews shrugged, but he made no reply and Graham thought he had gained his point. He led Andrews back to the platoon area, then realised he still hadn't had his pee. Nor did he get a chance as Sgt Grenfell called him over and told him to get his section ready for training.

"Make sure all their water bottles are full. It's going to be very hot this afternoon," he added.

For the first lesson the entire company was moved to sit in the shade of the Burdekin Plum tree on Bare Ridge. To get there they walked the 500 metres cross-country, going down along the dry creek from 1 Platoon's bivouac, then across the shallow valley. They were then seated in sections as part of a company group. By then Graham's need was very urgent. As they were still waiting for 3 Platoon to arrive Graham went to Sgt Grenfell and asked permission.

Sgt Grenfell frowned. "Hurry up! You should have bloody gone at lunch time," he growled.

Graham hurried away, walking west over the Canning Road and across the crest of Bare Ridge. The ridge turned out to be just that- bare. It was also much flatter and wider than it looked so he had to walk over a hundred metres to get over the curve out of sight of the officers on the road. Moving to a clump of thorn bushes he thankfully relieved himself. As he did, he noted that the ground dropped gently away to a flat plain on which cattle were grazing in a paddock. In the distance an old farmhouse stood beside a dirt road that came in from the Flinders Highway. A few hundred metres beyond the farm was the line of the river.

The Bunyip came around from the northwest in a mighty curve, then went off southwards. In the bend Graham could see sunlight glinting on water but most of the riverbed appeared to be dry sand and trees with a few clumps of rocks. On the outside of the curve another line of trees came in from the right to join the river.

Canning River, Graham thought, recalling the map. The Canning came from behind a tree-covered hill on Graham's right. *And that is Black Knoll, where that shed is,* he told himself.

Looking directly to his front Graham could see gently undulating, tree-covered country as far west as the eye could see. A couple of small hills broke the monotony on the horizon. To his left was the highway bridge. A kilometre further downstream was the massive rail bridge. Once again Graham admired its sheer size and marvelled that such a huge construction could be in such a middle-of-nowhere place.

Hurrying back over the crest he saw that he was not late. 3 Platoon was still marching across the shallow valley, spurred on by CSM Cleland calling on Sgt Yeldham to speed them up. Feeling much better Graham resumed his seat at the front of his section.

"Feeling better?" Kirsty asked, giving him an impish grin as she did.

Graham blushed but nodded. "A bean's a bean but a pee's a relief," he quoted.

Kirsty giggled and blushed. She opened her mouth to say something but CSM Cleland called for silence as the last of 3 Platoon were seated. Lt Hamilton then took over and gave a lesson on 'Why things are seen'. This was part of the unit's fieldcraft training. Graham had been taught this both as a First Year cadet and on his Corporals Course but he still made himself pay attention.

The lesson covered the usual shape, shine, shadow, silhouette, spacing, etc. Senior NCOs and the Control Group provided the demonstrations. This led to an outburst of laughter and cheering when, on Lt Hamilton's command, the Control Group stood up along the small dry creek 200 metres away. They wore their 'Yowie' suits- strips of Hessian (scrim) and pieces of camouflage net all made into a shapeless, shaggy outer garment. As soon as they were visible, someone cried, "Hutchie men!"

The cry was taken up by virtually the whole company. "Hutchie Men! Hutchie Men!" they chanted.

The Hutchie Men responded by striking victory poses, causing another outburst of shouts, laughter and cheering. It took a minute or so for Lt Hamilton and CSM Cleland to restore quiet. Graham took the opportunity to look around to see how Carnes was reacting to this. However, he could see no sign of him.

I wonder where he is? he thought. With a shrug he decided he was probably still back at camp.

The Hutchie Men were moved to do more demos. Other displays were put on by the CQ and HQ Sergeant and by a couple of HQ NCOs . Graham found the lesson interesting, but he did watch the Hutchie Men make their way back towards camp with mixed emotions.

If I muck up that might be my fate next year, he thought soberly.

His heart was now set on being one of the eight corporals selected for the Sergeants Course at the end of the year. As there were 16 corporals in the unit, that meant he had to do better than half of them.

The next lesson was to be in platoon groups back near the camp. Before the platoon moved Sgt Grenfell ordered them all to have a big drink. Then they marched across the valley and up the shallow dip beyond to be again seated in the shade of trees near 1 Platoon's camp. Here they were given a First Aid lesson on treatment of snake bites and stings by Lt McEwen.

Graham thought she was a lovely person. She was in her early twenties and had a pretty face and brown curly hair. She taught the lesson very well and had everyone in the platoon carry out the practical exercise of putting on a constrictive bandage.

At the end of the lesson they were told to drink again. Some of the girls asked if they could go to the toilet, which was just over the low ridge behind them. Barbara was one of these. She and Gwen Copeland had only walked 20 paces when Barbara suddenly cried out and pointed.

"Snake!"

The cadets scrambled to their feet and half the platoon hurried over to where Barbara and Gwen were standing. It was a snake alright, a big, golden-coloured one which slithered slowly along through the short grass. Graham stared at it, both fascinated and afraid simultaneously.

Bloody hell! he thought, noting that the reptile was over a metre long. *This is where we walked last night on the Navex!*

He found Kirsty beside him and she gripped his arm. "Oooh! Look how big it is!" she cried.

That caused a ripple of laughter and several comments based on jokes about size not being important. Lt McEwen was not amused. "Stop that sort of talk!" she snapped.

As the snake slid closer, apparently ignoring the cadets, Kirsty backed against Graham and clung to his arm, pressing herself against him as she did. "What sort is it?" she asked.

"Don't know," Graham had to admit. He liked to pride himself on being a snake 'expert' but was coming to realise that most could not be identified easily, at least not by their looks. "Might be a Western Taipan, or maybe a King Brown," he suggested.

"That's what bit you, wasn't it?" Kirsty asked.

Graham nodded. He began to step backwards as the snake slid even closer. To him it looked like the very essence of liquid evil, but it also held a fearful fascination and beauty.

Lt McEwen now took charge. "Move away you people. Get back here!" she ordered, her voice full of anxiety.

"It's alright, Miss," Halyday called. "We know how to treat snake bites now!"

"Don't be cheeky Cadet Halyday!" Lt McEwen snapped. "Now get back here this instant."

They did as they were told. By then the snake had vanished into an incredibly tiny bush. Roger gave a short laugh and said, "He is late for the lesson Miss. You needed him at the start."

"Yeah, he could have bitten you," Andrews called.

"Bite your bum Andrews," Roger retorted.

"That will do you boys," Lt McEwen called. "Where did it go?"

"Into that bush Miss," they chorused.

So the platoon was moved away and the girls made a big detour to go to the toilet and back. When they returned Sgt Grenfell again ordered them all to drink. It was now very hot and sweaty, and again with no breeze so they did so. CUO Masters arrived and also ordered them to drink. "Lt Maclaren just told me that the Heat Monitor says it is thirty-four degrees," he said. "That is three or four degrees hotter than it usually is in September, so drink. We don't want anyone getting heat exhaustion."

They all did as they were told, then moved for the next lesson. This was taught by the section corporals. It was on personal camouflage and concealment. Graham was prepared for this. Fieldcraft was something he really enjoyed, and he prided himself on being good at it. For the next half hour he had them all 'cammed up', and then took them to demonstrate places to hide and to explain 'dead ground'. The girls were reluctant to apply camouflage cream to their faces and so, surprisingly, was Halyday.

"I don't want to!" he protested.

Graham insisted so he reluctantly did so, applying only the bare minimum. Then he did not want to lie down on the ground to practice hiding. "What if there's another snake?" he asked anxiously.

"You gave us the answer yourself," Graham replied. "We have just learned how to treat snake bites."

The section all laughed. Halyday scowled. "Oh very funny!" he retorted. With the minimum of enthusiasm he took cover near a bush.

During the lesson, the Hutchie Men came around to show the cadets their Yowie suits and to demonstrate once again how they were almost impossible to see if they lay still, even out in short grass. They then moved off up to where 1 Platoon was training.

At the end of the lesson Sgt Grenfell called them in and made them drink again. All were hot and sweaty and a few were starting to show the effects of the heat. By this Graham had drunk so much he needed to go to the toilet again. As most of the section needed to refill their water bottles, he led them back to the bivouac area and then headed quickly for the 4 Platoon toilet while they did this.

There was no-one at the toilet and Graham stood facing towards where he could see 4 Platoon training over near the track to Scrubby Creek while he did another pee. Thus, he was able to look over the top of the Hessian screen and see that no-one was near. He relaxed. No-one from 4 Platoon could get close without him knowing.

All of a sudden, his senses prickled and he heard a noise behind him. Unable to stop peeing he could only glance over his shoulder. What he saw made his heart palpitate in fright. Two huge, hairy forms had risen up from the head of the gully behind him and were walking towards him, arms uplifted.

Hutchie Men!

"Ooh hoo! Gotcha Kirk!" cried Ziggy.

Graham tried to pretend he wasn't scared and kept on peeing as they ran over to him hooting and shouting. Porno came and stood on one side of him and Ziggy on the other. Graham could not see their faces but knew who it was by the voices. He braced himself for some sort of indignity or assault, but they just stood beside him and looked down. Now he came under another sort of pressure, male pride.

To Graham's dismay, from not being able to stop he now found fear was shrivelling him and drying up the flow. With an effort of will he forced himself to keep pumping.

"What a tiny dick!" Ziggy sneered.

Stung by the insult, Graham retorted. "Do you go around looking, do you?"

"Get stuffed!" Ziggy snarled.

But Graham could tell his jibe had gone home. For a second he thought he was going to be attacked as Ziggy shouldered him. However, he stood his ground and kept going. Next to him Porno heaved his Yowie suit to one side and unzipped his trousers.

As he started to pee, he said, "Scared you then, Mister Dobber Corporal!"

Graham felt really hurt by that, but he tried to stay calm. To try to defuse the situation he said as calmly as he could, "What are you blokes doing next?"

"We are just about to head off on a recon patrol over to the army camp," Ziggy replied.

"What for?" Graham asked, surprised by the statement.

"That Heatley Cadet Unit is due to arrive at 1600hrs and Capt Conkey wants to keep an eye on them," Ziggy explained.

"Bloody Heatley! They think they are just too good!" Graham commented. The army cadet unit based at Heatley in Townsville was famous throughout North Queensland both for the tough exercises it did, and for nearly always winning some of the prizes on the promotion courses.

"We'll show them who's best!" Ziggy replied.

By then Graham was finished so he hurried back to his section. He had another big drink, refilled his own water bottles, then joined the platoon under the big ironbark for the next lesson. This was on stretcher drill and the improvised movement of casualties. Lt Hamilton was again the instructor. HQ and the CUOs provided the demo squad. It was a very practical lesson with various drags, arm carries and lifts practised. During it Graham noted the Hutchie Men, plus Cadet James (a sig from HQ), being briefed by Capt Conkey. Peter was there as well and he was also carrying an army radio.

The patrol headed off, sparking envy in Graham. He badly wanted to lead a patrol against 'the enemy' to earn glory. Peter did not go but instead moved the radio under a shelter near the officer's fire. He was joined there by Sgt Gayney and Cpl Forman, the black-haired girl who was the Intelligence Corporal.

The cadets were all told to have another drink and then moved over to near the shelter. Capt Conkey then briefed them, explaining that the shelter was the 'Command Post' or CP. He then talked them through the procedure the unit would follow in case of a serious accident or snake bite. Lt Maclaren acted as Duty Officer and followed a check list to assemble a First Aid party with all the things they needed while, at the same time, informing all the people who needed to know, such as the army commander in the camp, the OC, the driver of the safety vehicle, and the Charters Towers ambulance. The First Aid party then headed off into the bush to collect the Cpl Storeman, Brookes, who was pretending to be injured.

At the end of the demo, Capt Conkey reminded all of them on what to do in an emergency, then sent them back to their platoon areas for a short break. Sgt Grenfell made them all drink again, after which CUO Masters led the platoon off along the track to Scrubby Creek past 4 Platoon's bivouac area.

The last lesson of the day was to be on stalking and movement. Once again, the corporals were to teach it. Graham led his section a hundred paces further on, going down into a shallow dip towards Scrubby Creek. The other sections also spread out and training was commenced. Graham stood the section in a line in the shade.

"This lesson is on movement," he said, "On the various ways you can creep and crawl when you are stalking the enemy."

Andrews guffawed and said to Roger, "You'll be good at that."

"Good at what?" Roger asked.

"Crawling!"

"Get knotted Andrews!" Roger retorted, anger mottling his face.

Graham glared at Andrews. "Be quiet so we can get on with the lesson," he snapped. He then proceeded to explain when they would need to use such fieldcraft. To conclude he said, "There is to be an exercise against other cadet units later in the camp and stalking will be an important part of it."

Again Andrews guffawed, but this time he turned to Dianne and said, "Storking! You'll like that, Williams."

It took Dianne a few moments to get the crude innuendo. Then her temper flared, and she moved to slap Andrews. "Keep your filthy comments to yourself!" she cried angrily.

"That's enough! Andrews, apologise to her," Graham ordered.

Lucy then interrupted, "And to me! I was offended too!"

Graham nodded and insisted. With bad grace Andrews mumbled an apology. It wasn't much but Graham felt he could not push the issue and was worrying that he was losing control of his lesson. He could see CUO Masters and Sgt Grenfell standing on top of the slope a hundred paces away and became anxious they might be able to see this.

To get the lesson moving he demonstrated and explained 'The Walk', then got them all to practise this. That went easily enough, and he began to recover his confidence. Then he went on to show them how to do a 'Monkey Run'. This did not work as well because the cadets were reluctant to get down.

"The sand is hot!" Lucy complained.

"It's only your hands and knees!" Graham cried in exasperation. "Have a go for a few seconds."

Reluctantly they did this. Then Graham got down to demonstrate the 'Leopard Crawl'. The sand was hot, he had to admit, but he kept on with it.

Dusting his hands, he stood up. "Okay, your go. Get down and do that," he said.

Again there were mumbles and complaints, but Graham insisted. The only one who wouldn't get down was Halyday. "Get down Cadet Halyday. It's not that hot," Graham ordered.

Halyday looked askance at Roger and Pat, both of whom were down on their stomachs. “I don’t want to get dirty,” he muttered.

Graham was astonished. “What rot! Surely you expected to do this sort of thing when you joined the army cadets?”

Halyday shook his head. “No. I thought there’d be a lot of drill, marching and stuff, but I didn’t think I’d have to crawl around like an animal.”

Graham shook his head in amazement and struggled to think of a policy that might work. In the end he said, “Either get down and practice or go up to CUO Masters and tell him you want a transfer from this section.”

Halyday glanced to where CUO Masters stood, gave Graham a sulky look, then very reluctantly knelt down and lowered himself onto his stomach. Graham heaved a silent sigh of relief and talked them through the actions. As the cadets stood up at the end of their practise, Halyday made a big show of wrinkling his nose with distaste and of brushing off the sand and dust. As they were all sweating heavily in the heat there was plenty of this stuck to their skin.

Getting Halyday down to practice the ‘Hunger or Kitten’ crawl was even harder. After more threats Graham managed to get him down but he hardly moved at all when he was. Exasperated and bemused, Graham moved the section to a nearby dry creek bed. This was only a metre or so wide and was little more than a knee-deep rill.

“The next part of the lesson is about selecting lines of advance when you are stalking,” he said. “This is where you need a good eye for ground. You need to be able to pick out ‘dead ground’ and ‘covered routes’.”

“What sort of roots?” Andrews asked with a snicker.

The double meaning at once annoyed and embarrassed Graham. His eyes briefly met Kirsty’s and it was obvious she was thinking the same thing, and wasn’t shocked. He hastily looked away. The dilemma of how to cope with this caused him a momentary fluster.

Do I just ignore it, or make a big deal of it? he wondered. He decided to pretend he had not understood the double entendre.

“Covered routes Cadet Andrews,” he grated. “It means a... a... (he groped for some other word than route) a way of getting from one place to another under cover and without being seen by the enemy.”

He then quickly went on to talk about how to read the ground and got them to consider how they would move across the area. The half hour was almost up by then and he found that he was both very thirsty and again needed a pee.

"Sit in the shade and have a drink," he ordered.

Then he looked around, wondering where to go. Up the slope to his right seemed to be the closest and best so he walked quickly that way. Behind him the section sprawled on the ground and broke into chatter. Knowing that they all guessed what he was going to do made Graham feel very self-conscious and he felt himself to be walking in a jerky, awkward manner.

Thankfully, he reached the crest and went out of sight. The track to Scrubby Creek and the North Gravel Scrape ran along there and he paused on it to look around. No other sections were visible, so he quickly walked a few more paces and stopped beside a small tree. Before he started, he had another careful look in all directions. Even though he knew the Hutchie Men should be many kilometres away he still had an irrational fear they would catch him. Seeing nobody he did a pee. As he finished, he again looked around. There was still no sign of any one close, but he saw that 5 Section was a couple of hundred paces away.

They won't see me from there, he thought.

Then his gaze registered on two hats moving towards him up a gully about 50 metres away. As quickly as he could, he turned away and zipped up his trousers. He began walking quickly back towards his section. As he did, he glanced back and saw two cadets climb up out of the gully. With a shock he realised they were not just cadets but girl cadets!

Oh no! I hope they didn't see me, he thought.

Chapter 9

STRUGGLE OF WILLS

Graham was aghast. *It is Harriet Harris and Fiona Davies!* he thought. Harriet was a tall, slender girl who was a corporal in 3 Platoon and Fiona was a Year 9 girl in her section. Shame and embarrassment scorched through him as he wondered what to do.

If they saw me and they complain I could be chucked out of the cadets! he thought.

Vague notions of legal complications to do with indecent exposure and unpleasant thoughts about the police and courts and things like that almost paralysed him.

To apologise seemed the best course, so he turned and walked back towards them. As he did, his mind raced and he stared at them in dismay. It was obvious from their camouflage that they were doing the same sort of fieldcraft training as his own section. His tongue then seemed to stick to the roof of his mouth.

Fiona spoke first. "Hi Graham!" she said. "What are you doing here?"

From her words and facial expression Graham decided that the girls had not seen him but doubt and anxiety remained. "Going to the toilet," he explained, his voice almost breaking with anxiety. "Sorry, I didn't know you were there. I didn't mean to offend you."

Cpl Harris shrugged. "We didn't see that. We aren't offended. It's okay," she replied.

Graham began to relax slightly. "Where is your section?" he asked.

"Back around the bend in that gully. We have to find a place to hide and they are going to look for us. They will be along in a minute or so," Cpl Harris explained.

"I'll get back to my section then and get out of your way," Graham answered, feeling sure now that things would be alright.

Then Harriet's words sank in and the horrible thought came to him: what if her whole section was watching. He glanced anxiously down the gully and noted that he might have been seen. Hot with embarrassment, he turned and walked away.

Back with his own section, he still flushed with shame and hoped they would not notice his embarrassment or hear about it. It was time to begin the last 30-minute lesson for the afternoon, which covered the same movements but adapted to night. Once again Graham had trouble getting Halyday to get down and he made the minimum effort, then stood and watched.

Towards the end of the lesson, Graham saw 6 Section training nearby and had the idea to try to creep up on them. He pointed them out to the section and then got down and urged them to follow him. To his annoyance Halyday only half got down and then just sat in the grass on the bank of the small gully.

Graham led the others down the gully until they were close to Stephen's section, then suddenly jumped up and yelled, "Bang! Bang! Gotcha!"

Stephen quickly rallied his section and the two groups had a short, high-spirited pretend battle that ended in laughter. Graham ended up standing next to a grinning and laughing Stephen who stopped to wipe his glasses clean.

"Bloody glasses keep fogging up in the heat," Stephen grumbled.

"Oh, any excuse!" Graham cried. "We caught you then."

Stephen put his glasses back on and then pointed down the gully. "Look, here come some of 4 Platoon. Let's ambush them."

Graham looked and saw figures appearing on the edge of the trees along Scrubby Creek. Ordinarily the idea would have appealed but the thought of provoking 4 Platoon made him feel anxious. However, he did not dare let Stephen suspect this so he nodded and called on his section to get under cover and to follow him. At that point the small creek was about waist deep and had a sandy bed with bends every ten or twenty metres.

A glance showed Graham that they would need to get further down the creek quickly if they were to have any chance of catching 4 Platoon. With that in mind, he set off down the creek doing a monkey run. His cadets followed, with Stephen's section also piling into the creek and joining in. It was hot and sultry in the ditch, but Graham was excited now and he hurried along, ignoring the sand and dust which stuck to his perspiring arms, face and hands.

It was just too far and they weren't in the right place when Graham realised they must act if they were to achieve anything at all. By then they had scurried a good 50 paces down the creek and were all gasping for breath. To check on the situation Graham cautiously raised his head, just in time to see Pigsy pointing towards him from fifty metres away.

Damn! He's seen me, Graham cursed.

But then he noted the direction of Pigsy's arm and that made him glance behind him. It was Halyday. He had followed but had only walked along the creek and now, much too late, lowered himself down out of sight.

While the cadets recovered their breath, Graham signalled Stephen to crawl up to join him so they could discuss what to do CUO Grey acted. He signalled and waved his arms and 4 Platoon suddenly changed direction from single file to extended line and came charging towards them.

There seemed only one thing left to do, so Graham did it. He stuck his head up and yelled, "Bang! Bang!"

Shouting and screaming broke out on both sides. The Second Years came charging towards them at such a speed that Graham felt his heart rate shoot up with anxiety. 4 Platoon shrieked a piercing 'rebel yell' as they ran and Graham knew they would not stop. He was also aware that the older cadets had a huge moral advantage over the First Years. To put it bluntly, they were scared of them.

This showed at once. Andrews sprang up and began running. Dianne and Lucy both stood up and put their hands up. Only Pat and Roger stayed down pretending to fire at the 'enemy'. Kirsty went down out of sight. Graham screamed for them to fight but by then it was too late. The attackers swept over them. At the last moment Graham realised that Pigsy and Waters were both running straight towards him. He was not unduly worried as one of the unit's strict rules was: 'No physical contact on exercises'.

Pigsy yelled threats and swear words as he ran and his eyes met Graham's. Only at the last instant did Graham realise he was in trouble. By then it was too late to jump up. All he could do was duck. A boot slammed into the middle of his back, hammering him down into the sand as Pigsy stamped on him. Then Graham received a kick to the head as Waters followed him. Luckily, it was only a glancing blow, but even so Graham's head exploded in lights and stars. He tried to get up but Pigsy had stopped and now stood on his back, forcing him down face first into the sand.

Graham screamed in genuine alarm and anger but he had to spit sand to do it. As he did, Pigsy jumped off. A boot thudded into Graham's ribs-Waters. Suddenly, Pigsy called out loudly, "Oh sorry Kirky! Didn't see you there, mate."

Graham rolled over and scrambled up, furious at being assaulted. By then both Pigsy and Waters had run on. Graham saw CUO Grey running past, giving him a suspicious look. The CUO obviously knew something had happened but Graham saw no point in appealing to the 'enemy' commander. He stood up and dusted himself, then winced at the pain in his side and back.

Are the others alright? he wondered.

Stephen appeared to be and so did Pat, but Roger had obviously been bowled over and was shaking sand out of his shirt and hair. Kirsty came up from her hidey-hole looking scared. 4 Platoon ran on up the creek, screaming threats and bangs. Graham saw Halyday suddenly spring up from cover, then get knocked over and trampled by Pigsy and Moynihan. That caused his temper to boil over and he set off running after them, shouting angrily.

It was to no avail. 4 Platoon ran on and did not stop till they reached the track on the crest of the ridge. Here they engaged Gwen's section till CUO Masters and Sgt Grenfell arrived and the two platoon commanders ended the 'battle'. By then Graham had reached Halyday, who was crying and had a big bruise showing on his forehead.

"They hit me!" he whimpered.

"Yeah well, you deserve it!" Graham snapped. "If you had been under cover we could have ambushed them. It was you they saw first. And if you'd stayed with us you wouldn't have been on your own."

"But they knocked me over!" Halyday wailed.

"And me!" Graham retorted angrily. He was now really feeling the kicks to his head and side.

"They aren't allowed to do that!" Halyday wailed. "I'm going to tell one of the teachers."

Graham was torn. He didn't really want to make a big issue of it but he also knew that if he tried to prevent a cadet complaining it could come back on him. Reluctantly, he said, "You can if you really want to."

"I do!" Halyday cried. Tears began streaming down his face.

Graham looked around and saw CUO Masters looking their way. Still hoping that Halyday would forget it Graham told him to wash his face. Instead Halyday turned and walked towards the CUO. Reluctantly Graham followed, knowing he was being a coward and mentally scourging himself.

By the time they got up to CUO Masters, however, 4 Platoon had marched away towards camp. CUO Masters listened and looked worried. An assault charge could be serious trouble and he took out his notebook and wrote down the names of all involved and the time.

"I will tell the OC," he said. "Now round your section up and take them back to camp Cpl Kirk. You actually did well to get them that close to the other platoon unseen. I was watching from up the hill."

Still feeling very anxious and unhappy, Graham did as he was told. As they walked back past where 4 Platoon were now sitting at their hutchies, Graham met Pigsy's eye and received an angry, challenging stare, coupled to a sneer, in return. Back at 2 Platoon's camp Graham fell the section out and arranged to get some washbasins and a jerrycan of water so they could rinse off the sand.

"I want a bath!" Lucy moaned.

"You smell like you do," Andrews commented.

"Shut up Andrews!" Lucy spat back.

Graham had to calm the situation, even as he watched CUO Masters talking to Capt Conkey over at the officer's camp. Then CUO Masters headed towards him.

Oh no, Graham thought, his heart sinking.

CUO Masters moved both Graham's section and Stephen's over to near the officer's camp. While they were seating themselves, Graham saw Lt Maclaren walk over to 4 Platoon. Then the questioning began. It was only about Halyday.

Graham glanced at Roger and whispered, "Do you want to complain?"

Roger looked unhappy but shook his head. "No. What's the point?"

That was how Graham felt but, once started, the official process could not be stopped. Twenty minutes went by, making Halyday very unpopular with the others in the platoon. Finally everyone but Graham and Halyday were told they could return to the bivouac area. Capt Conkey led CUO Masters, Graham and Halyday over to where Lt Maclaren, CUO Grey and CSM Cleland stood with Pigsy, Waters, and Moynihan. The three bullies looked very hostile and resentful and that did nothing to calm Graham's anxiety.

Capt Conkey told Pigsy and Moynihan that they had to apologize to Halyday. They did so reluctantly, all the while flashing daggers at Graham. Graham and Halyday were then told to go. As they walked away, Graham overheard Capt Conkey cautioning the three bullies. He said that, if there were any more incidents like it, he would consider discharging them and sending them home.

It was a very unhappy Graham who took his section to their evening meal. As he was collecting his food Pigsy walked by and 'accidentally' bumped him. Some of Graham's custard spilled onto the ground. Pigsy hissed, "We will get you Kirk!"

That made Graham even more upset, but he tried to hide it. He also noted Waters snarling at Halyday, who looked very pale and anxious.

Damn! Graham thought. *I really wanted to enjoy this camp and do well. This is spoiling it.*

Kirsty was sympathetic and sat next to him while he ate. Stephen and Roger also sat with them. As he was eating Graham looked around. Several times he saw one of the bullies but each time he looked hastily away, then flushed with shame for being a coward.

Later, when he went to do his washing up, Graham found himself next to Peter. The two friends chatted about the camp and Graham told him about the problems with the bullies, and also how the bullies had been picking on Carnes. Peter said he'd also clashed with Pigsy and Co. He then hurried away, reminding Graham they had a night exercise to prepare for. After washing up Graham also hurried back towards his hutchie.

On the way he was joined by Kirsty, who had been washing up nearby. She grinned and flirted in such a friendly way that Graham's hopes went shooting up. He flirted back with what he thought were witty comments. Then they arrived back at the platoon area and had to end the conversation but by then Graham was feeling quite aroused and was amazed at how his mouth had gone dry and how fast his heart was beating.

Maybe? he thought, exciting fantasies flitting through his mind.

However, the need to get the section ready for the night exercise drove these thoughts aside and he walked around urging the cadets to ensure they had their water bottles full.

"Where are Andrews and Halyday?" he asked.

"They walked off along the track towards the road," Pat replied.

Drat! Graham thought, remembering Andrew's earlier crime. *I hope the little toads haven't snuck off to have a smoke.*

Dusk was setting in by then and Graham saw that there were only 15 minutes left before training began. *I'd better go and get them,* he thought.

He set off walking quickly along the crest of Sandy Ridge past 1 Platoon and the meal area until he reached the vehicle track. There was no sign of anyone further along the ridge towards the Canning Road, so he hurried on. A hundred paces further along the ridge the track skirted the very top of the gullies, which led northwards to the Canning.

It was an obvious place for smokers to lurk, so Graham moved off the track to look down the gullies. It was getting dark by then but even so he detected movement behind a big ironbark near the top of the next gully. A leg and a boot were sticking out. Mentally preparing himself to blast Halyday and Andrews if they were doing the wrong thing, Graham strode angrily over to the tree. As he got closer the leg withdrew and a pale face peeked around the trunk, then vanished.

Graham reached the tree and stopped, looking down in surprise. It was Carnes. The boy was huddled in a ball against the tree, staring up at him with a look of fear. He wore uniform but no hat and next to him was his kitbag.

"What are you doing here, Cadet Carnes?" Graham asked, still looking around.

"Nothing," Carnes mumbled.

"You haven't seen Halyday and Andrews have you?" Graham asked.

"No."

"Have those bullies been giving you a hard time again?"

"Yes. And Corporal Brown," Carnes sniffled. He appeared to relax slightly and lowered his head.

Graham looked around in the gathering gloom. *Where have those little ratbags got to?* he wondered. Then he turned back to Carnes.

"You should tell your platoon commander."

Carnes shook his head. "Then the bullies will just wait and get back at me later," he replied, his voice heavy with misery.

"You must. Anyway, it is nearly time to start training. You had better get back to your platoon."

Carnes shook his head. "No. I'm not going."

"You have to. You can't stay here," Graham replied. He didn't really want to get involved with Carnes' problems. His priority was to get his own section ready in time.

"Not going," Carnes replied stubbornly.

"You have to. Now get up and go!" Graham snapped testily. He was annoyed by the boy's manner and attitude.

"No! You can't make me. I want to go home," Carnes replied.

"Then tell Capt Conkey," Graham said. "Now get up and get back to your platoon."

As he said this, the possible significance of the kitbag dawned on him. He said, "Are you planning to run away?"

Carnes said nothing but hunched into a tighter ball and looked down.

That got Graham even more exasperated and annoyed. "Don't be so unfair. That would cause a lot of other people a lot of trouble. Now go back to your platoon."

"Don't care!"

"Don't be so selfish! Get up and go! I am giving you an order!"

"No!"

Graham felt his anger surge. His next impulse was to threaten the miserable boy. He had to restrain himself from reaching down to physically drag him to his feet. For half a minute he seethed with impotent rage while trying to decide what to do. He knew he couldn't just walk away.

Should I go and tell Capt Conkey? he wondered. Whatever else he was determined that Carnes would not cause Capt Conkey a lot of grief by sneaking away.

To gain time he asked, "Were you going to hitch hike along the highway?"

Carnes made no answer, but Graham deduced by the way he hunched that his guess was correct. "That would be very dangerous and cause the officers a lot of trouble," he said.

"I don't care. They don't help me," Carnes replied.

"They probably don't know you need it," Graham replied. "If you don't tell them they can't help."

Again, Carnes made no reply. Graham again cast around for an argument to get him to obey. To his dismay, he heard CSM Cleland start calling for the sergeants to move the platoons in for the night exercise.

Damn! Now I will be late, he thought angrily. It was quite dark by this so Graham could only hear the company stirring into activity.

"Come on please," he asked. "If my section is late, I will get into trouble."

"You can go," Carnes replied.

"No, I can't. I can't leave you and you aren't running away," Graham answered. He reached down and grabbed the kitbag.

"No!" Carnes shrieked. He scrambled to his feet. "Let it go! Let go!"

"Don't be stupid!" Graham snapped. He could now hear Sgt Grenfell calling his name.

"Let go! Let go!" Carnes yelled. He began to hit at Graham.

The blows weren't very skilful or well directed but they enraged Graham. He had to step back so as not to retaliate, but he kept hold of the bag.

"Stop it Cadet Carnes. Don't get yourself into trouble by hitting a corporal."

Carnes hit him several more times, but Graham now just felt sorry for him and ignored the blows. Suddenly Carnes let go and turned to run off into the night. At that, Graham lost his temper as he could still hear Sgt Grenfell's angry voice calling his name. He tossed the bag aside and sprinted after the boy. Carnes didn't get far. He was no runner and not used to the bush in the dark. Within 20 paces he had tripped on something and fallen.

Graham stopped and stood over him then realised Carnes was sobbing. "Are you alright Cadet Carnes? Did you hurt yourself?"

Carnes made no reply. All he did was lie there and howl. Graham felt his anger evaporate. "Oh, you poor bugger!" he muttered. Instead of reefing Carnes to his feet he reached down and patted his shoulder.

Carnes kept crying but the sobs eased after a few minutes. All that while Graham could hear sergeants shouting as they moved their platoons in to join the company. When Graham heard CSM Cleland call for silence and then for reports his distress mounted.

Now I am in trouble, he thought.

He patted Carnes again then said, "Please, Cadet Carnes. I am now late for parade and I will get into trouble. I'm not leaving you so you may as well come with me."

Carnes sniffled but then struggled to his feet. Graham helped him up and then heaved a silent sigh of relief when Carnes turned and began walking back towards the camp.

Chapter 10

LANTERN STALK

As they walked back towards where the company was now seated in the dark, Carnes began to deviate towards the 1 Platoon bivouac area.

"Not that way, Cadet Carnes. The CSM knows we aren't there. We must report to him."

"No. You do it. I'm not going near them," Carnes replied.

Blast! Graham thought. He did not feel like another battle of wills. "Alright then, go to the officer's fire and sit there and I will tell the CSM," he said.

To Graham's relief, Carnes turned and headed for the fire. Satisfied that he was actually going there, Graham walked across to where the company waited in a murmuring dark mass. CSM Cleland was standing out the front.

"Who is that?" the CSM asked.

"Cpl Kirk, CSM."

"Where the devil have you been? We have had people searching high and low for you! Have you seen Cadet Carnes?"

"Yes, CSM. There he is over there." Graham pointed to where Carnes could just be seen against the glow of the fire. "He is going to the fire."

"Why? Is he sick?"

"It's a long story, CSM."

"Then tell me later. We are already ten minutes late and Capt Conkey will be spitting chips," CSM Cleland replied. "Now join your platoon."

"I was looking for Halyday and Andrews CSM. That is how I found Carnes. Are those two here?" Graham asked.

"Yes, they are, now sit down," CSM Cleland replied.

"Can I dump Carnes' gear and get my webbing sir?" Graham asked, indicating the kitbag slung on his shoulder.

"Gear? What? Oh, blast your webbing. You go to the fire as well. We can't wait."

At that Graham felt quite hurt. He had been looking forward to the lantern stalk and to be excluded and not be with his section really stung. However, he sensed that the CSM was in no mood to argue so he quickly moved away. As he did, CSM Cleland told Sgt Sherry to start 1 Platoon moving. There was a stir as the cadets all stood up and adjusted their webbing and dusted themselves.

First Graham hurried to his hutchie to collect his webbing. By then the whole company had started moving off, walking west along the track towards the Canning Road. Graham found his throat was very dry, so he had a big drink. A strong temptation to disobey the CSM and to just follow the company and quietly find his section caused him to pause. Then he shook his head.

I'd better check that Carnes actually did go to the fire, he thought.

So he walked towards the fire, feeling distinctly annoyed and dejected. As he did, two Land Rovers started up and drove off in the wake of the company.

At the fire Graham was relieved to see Carnes sitting staring into the flames. Lt Standish was there as well, plus five other cadets including Beverly Berry from Stephen's section. Mrs Standish looked surprised when Graham walked into the firelight.

"Are you sick, Graham?" she asked.

"No, Miss. I was just bringing Cadet Carnes' gear over," he replied.

"His gear?" Mrs Standish queried, giving Carnes a quizzical glance.

"Can I explain in private please, Ma'am?" Graham asked.

Mrs Standish stood and walked away from the fire into the darkness. Once they were out of earshot of the cadets, she asked Graham what the problem was. Graham told her the story and handed her the kitbag.

"I don't think he will run off now Ma'am, but he is a miserable poor bugger. Something must be done to help him."

Mrs Standish was very thoughtful, then nodded. "Yes, you are right. Thank you for that."

"Can I catch up with the company now please Ma'am?" Graham asked.

He had noted one of the vehicles stop out at the junction with the Canning Road where it turned its lights off. What made him anxious was the unit rule that nobody should be walking around the bush on their own, particularly at night.

"Do you know where to go?"

Graham nodded. "Out on the Canning Road Ma'am."

"What if you get lost? Or hurt yourself?" she asked.

"Oh Miss! I can see one safety vehicle from here and I will just walk along the road to the other one. And I've got my radio," Graham replied. His pride in bushcraft and navigation were both slighted by the comment and he could not keep the annoyance out of his tone.

"Oh, alright. But you stay on the road," she replied.

"Thank you, Miss," Graham said. He turned and started walking as fast as he could.

It took him five minutes to reach the vehicle at the Canning Road. Lt Maclaren was there and shone a powerful torch on him, then directed him left along the road on Bare Ridge. Another five minutes of fast walking had Graham at the company. They were easy to find. He could hear them talking and Lt Hamilton's Land Rover was again parked near the big tree.

Instead of reporting to CSM Cleland, Graham sought out Sgt Grenfell and told him he was there. By the time he had found his section CSM Cleland had called for silence and Capt Conkey had started briefing them. Graham found Roger at the head of 4 Section and quietly squeezed in next to him.

Capt Conkey explained that they were now going to practise what they had been taught during the day. "This is a fieldcraft exercise," he said. "It's individual training and you may do it on your own or in groups. It is to get you ready for a major inter-unit exercise in four days' time."

That sounded very interesting to Graham and he wanted to know more but Capt Conkey went on to explain that the lantern (dimly visible through the trees) was both the objective and a navigation aid. The lantern was located on the gentle ridge running down from 2 Platoon's camp to the highway. To reach it they had to cross the shallow valley and the two small dry creeks.

"The guards are there to make you do the right thing," Capt Conkey explained. "If you are trying to use proper fieldcraft and they see you they have been told to let you go past. If not, they will send you back. There are no guards within fifty metres of the lantern. Good creeping and crawling is what is needed for this exercise. I will now show you where the guards are."

Capt Conkey turned and called on his radio. Immediately about twenty torches came on across the valley. They flashed back and forth.

There seemed to be an awful lot, but Graham noted they were in three quite distinct lines, the first near the bottom of the valley, the next beyond the second creek and the last back near the lantern.

Capt Conkey then explained the safety rules and the fact that there was to be no running in the dark and no physical contact or throwing things. He also pointed out the boundaries: the Flinders Highway, Canning Road, Sandy Ridge vehicle track, and the 2 Platoon ridge. He then sent CSM Cleland off to join the 'defenders'.

During the short wait Graham had another drink. As he was putting his water bottle away, Roger nudged him. "What happened?" he asked. "Where did you get to?"

"I went looking for Halyday and Andrews and found Carnes hiding in a gully," Graham whispered back. "I'll tell you the details later."

Capt Conkey then gave the order to start. There was an immediate rush of running figures which drew an angry bellow from Capt Conkey. "This isn't a bloody race! There's no need to have a stampede! Slow down and creep. You have an hour and a half."

The running stopped but not the talking. As the cadets moved away there was continual discussion on which was the best way to go and whether to move in groups or not. Graham would have preferred to do the exercise on his own, but he found Roger beside him and three others trailing along behind. Lucy and Dianne vanished with Pat. Kirsty moved up to walk on Graham's other side. That both pleased and peeved him.

The other two were Halyday and Andrews. Graham stopped and hissed at them, "Where did you two get to after tea?"

"Just over to 4 Platoon," Halyday answered, but to Graham he sounded defensive.

"You weren't smoking I hope," he said.

"No. We were just telling jokes and listening to the Hutchie Men," Andrews replied.

"What were they doing?" Graham asked.

"They had just come back from their patrol to watch the other units arrive," Halyday replied.

Roger asked, "Did they see them?"

"Yeah. They are camped over the other side of the army camp in the bush. Ziggy thinks one lot went further over to some airfield," Halyday said.

He began to embellish the tale with the exploits of the Hutchie Men. Graham cut him short as a torch was flashed in their direction from the first creek.

"Okay, tell me about it later. Let's see if we can creep right up to the lantern without being caught."

Having said that Graham continued on. The others followed in a bunch till he hissed at them to spread out. Now he was sweating with anxiety. On his own he would have enjoyed the exercise but with most of the section following he felt real pressure.

I'd better pick the best covered route, he thought.

He soon stopped and lay down to try to detect the weakest part of the defender's line. The others lay down with him. There was almost no grass or cover of any sort and Graham could see the black silhouettes of dozens of cadets crawling forward ahead of him. There were more on both sides. The defenders were now starting to shine their torches on the faster, less careful ones.

"The sergeants are the front line of defenders," Roger whispered.

Graham nodded. He could tell that by their voices. He watched the pattern for another two minutes then decided.

"Down closer to the road I reckon," he replied.

Roger nodded so Graham got up and began to ghost walk forward, aiming for a gap in the groups of torches. *Yeldham and White,* he identified, *and Bates and Brookes down near the highway.*

Several times he dropped flat as torches came closer, but the group was able to reach the first creek and drop into its dry bed without being detected. Graham then began a process of crawling and walking to get across the flat to the second creek. Luckily, there were a couple of big trees, some bushes and a log which he could use for cover. The others followed one at a time, moving from cover to cover as the guards moved away, then hiding as they came back.

The gap was just big enough and Graham reached the second creek without being seen, although dozens of other cadets on either side were spotted and ordered back. As soon as Roger joined him Graham headed up a small dry gully which led up into the next ridge. They were well past the first line of defenders by then and Graham began watching the torches ahead through the trees, trying to pick out who it was and what patrol pattern they were using.

Headquarters, he decided. Then he heard Lt McEwen call out to his right front. *And some of the officers.*

Someone crawled up beside him: Kirsty. Graham didn't know whether to be annoyed or pleased. Halyday and Anderson followed.

"Spread out more and don't make so much noise," Graham ordered.

"Is this where we saw that big golden snake today?" Halyday asked.

A chill of fear gripped Graham. He had quite forgotten about snakes and he was crouched in the dry gully near some tree roots which could easily harbour one of the reptiles. However, he tried to reassure them.

"No. That was in another gully a hundred metres over to our left," he replied.

With that he continued on. Much of the time he walked at a crouch until they got closer to the head of the gully. Then they used a monkey run. As they moved closer to the next line of defenders, Graham saw torches moving to cross their front and told those with him to get down and wait. He lay flat in a small washout and felt Kirsty squash in against him. That got him anxious and he raised his head to see where the others had gone but could only just make out a huddle in a small side washout to his left.

Kirsty pressed so close that her hair touched Graham's face. It felt very nice but was also quite alarming. *If that is Lt McEwen coming she might get the wrong idea,* he thought.

But he didn't know how to ask Kirsty to move away. By then it was too late. The torch beam swept over them and settled on a group of figures Graham had not seen about 20 paces ahead. It was Cpl Rankin and the two notorious unit tarts: Magda Mollwitz and Erika Goltz.

They were ordered back and came grumbling past to vanish somewhere near the second dry creek. Lt McEwen and Sgt Gayney then turned and headed back towards the highway. Even so Graham remained under cover as two other torches were now heading across from the left. There was a scuffling of people hurrying up the gully behind Graham and the new arrivals dropped down beside them.

It was Pigsy, Waters and Moynihan. "Who's that?" Pigsy hissed. "Oh, it's you Kirk. Who's that with ya? Kirsty Weldon eh? Is she well done yet?"

Graham flushed with anger and embarrassment and felt Kirsty stiffen and press closer. He made no answer, which annoyed Pigsy.

"What's wrong, sook? Did we interrupt your little cuddle session? Move aside you useless dork and let us have a go. She might appreciate real men."

"Don't be crude!" Graham retorted angrily. As he did, a torch beam from the left began questing about the area.

"Move over and let us into that gully," Waters snarled. He was too late. The torch beam swept over them. Graham and Kirsty lay flat while Pigsy and his mates got up and started running.

"Stop that running!" shouted CSM Cleland. His torch beam transfixed the trio, who reluctantly stopped. "Go back to the creek and try again," CSM Cleland ordered.

Pigsy and his mates all grumbled and swore but CSM Cleland was adamant. The three bullies came walking back. As they got closer, Graham braced himself in case they deliberately stepped on him or kicked him. Instead, they just called crude insults.

"Sniveller Kirk! We'll get ya, and we'll tell the officers we seen ya pashin' your little girlfriend too," Waters said.

Anger seethed in Graham at the unjust accusation and he flamed with embarrassment. He was about to speak to Kirsty when there was a thud and Moynihan cried out in pain.

"Hoy! That hurt!"

"What?" Pigsy replied.

"Some bastard hit me with a rock," Moynihan said.

"Bloody Kirk for sure," Pigsy said. "Let's sort him out."

To Graham's dismay the three bullies turned and came walking back. So as not to be kicked he quickly stood up and told Kirsty to get up as well. Just as the bullies arrived, there were more thuds and the sound of a stone hitting a tree trunk, then a cry of pain from Waters.

"That came from over there, to the left," Pigsy cried.

At that two figures sprang up and raced off down towards the creek. Pigsy shouted, "After them!" and the three bullies dashed off in pursuit, Moynihan tripping and falling in the process.

Andrews and Halyday, Graham thought.

He wondered whether he should join the pursuit to help his two cadets but then decided the three bullies weren't likely to catch them. At that moment, a torch beam swung their way.

"Down!" he hissed, dragging at Kirsty's sleeve.

They dropped into the shallow washout and huddled low. In the process Kirsty again pressed hard against Graham's right side. *She is doing that deliberately,* he decided. That idea got him interested and excited. Her hair was in his nostrils and it smelt a lovely 'girl' aroma.

To his relief, the torches turned and went away. Graham raised his head to watch and found himself looking into Kirsty's eyes at very close range. The reflections from the torches made them glisten.

Gosh, she's pretty! Graham thought. Without conscious will he found his head moving closer to hers. She closed her eyes and parted her lips. *She wants a kiss!* he thought, both astonished and afraid.

Natural desire got his heart thudding and his body tingling, and he moved to lean across to kiss her. But even as he moistened his lips his racing mind told him not to do it. *It will be nice but could lead to disaster,* he thought.

So he hesitated and glanced anxiously around, looking at the same moment for a way out of the situation that would not set her against him and to check if anyone could see.

Kirsty opened her eyes and gave him a quizzical but friendly look. Then she whispered, "You are nice."

"I think you are nice too," Graham murmured. But he resisted his urges.

Again, he battled with desire and by an effort of willpower he held back. By then he was quite aroused and really struggling to control himself. Then a shout nearby made him look up in alarm. By swivelling his head around he could make out running figures 50 paces to his left rear and torches flashing near them. Then he received another shock when he saw a person lying in the gully 10 paces away. It was Roger.

Strewth! I hope he hasn't seen us, Graham thought.

But that concern melted into insignificance within seconds as two powerful torches came on 20 paces to his right front. Their beams swept towards him as he and Kirsty both ducked. Then Graham heard Lt McEwen's voice just as he became aware that the torches were now fixed on them.

Oh no! What will she think? Graham thought.

"Who is that there?" Lt McEwen called, walking towards them.

Chapter 11

FRICTION

Graham froze in fright, very conscious of closeness to Kirsty. Apprehension at the probability of being disciplined caused his emotions to surge and he felt panic and embarrassment. In anticipation of the worst, he tried to think up some reasonable explanation. But he knew it would sound hollow and he felt sick.

Then, as Lt McEwen strode in his direction, her torch beam moved on. "Who is that there?" she called.

Graham was about to answer when he was surprised to hear Roger's voice. "Lance Corporal Dunning, Ma'am."

"You need to keep down more," Lt McEwen said.

There were scuffling noises further down the gully and the distinct sound of breaking sticks. Then someone fell. Graham raised his head and, as he did, slid away from Kirsty. He saw that Lt McEwen now had her torch beam aimed at three more cadets: Pigsy, Waters and Moynihan.

"You three go back out of sight and get down," she ordered.

There was muttering and grumbling from the three bullies, but they did as they were told. Graham then expected Lt McEwen to moved closer to him but, to his relief, she moved on down the gully 20 paces then was distracted by more cadets further over.

"Now's our chance," he whispered to Kirsty.

"What for?" she replied mischievously.

"To get away from here. Come on," Graham replied.

He stood up and began to walk as quietly as he could, glancing back continually to check on where Lt McEwen and her companion were. Both Kirsty and Roger followed. Graham found he was both relieved and irritated by Roger's presence.

At least I can't misbehave if he is there, he thought. But it was with sharp regret and he knew that he really wanted to kiss Kirsty.

After 50 paces Graham stopped. His heart was still beating fast, but with excitement rather than lust. The scare had ended his arousal. Now he concentrated his efforts on the fieldcraft. Ahead were two more groups of two torches, CUO Grey and CUO Mitrovitch in the group on his right front and CUO Masters and CUO McAlistair in the other. They were the last guards before the lantern.

It was 2035hrs by then. "Twenty-five minutes to go," Graham said. "And about a hundred metres. I think we should crawl."

With that he got down and began inching forward, sometimes on hands and knees but mostly on his stomach using toes and elbows. It was, hard slow work but they drew steadily closer to the lantern and the pattern of the CUO's patrolling became clear. There were other cadets crawling forward on both sides and more behind. In the light of a torch Graham recognised Halyday and Andrews twenty metres to his left. He was amazed. Halyday had even blackened his face and was right down crawling properly.

There were noises behind as a group of cadets came hurrying forward. A torch swung towards them. Graham lay flat behind a small log. The group kept on hurrying forward and out of the corner of his eye Graham recognised Pigsy. As he went striding past Pigsy swerved and gave Graham a good kick in the thigh. It happened so fast that Graham was unable to react and it took an effort not to call out.

CUO Masters did though. His torch picked out the three bullies, who had gone running on ahead. "Stop running and go back you three!" he ordered.

Pigsy and Co at first disobeyed but CUO Masters raced over to them and repeated the order. With bad grace and much muttering they did as they were told, CUO Masters and CUO McAlistair walking back down the slope with them. In doing so they passed 15 metres to Graham's right.

This is our chance, he thought.

There was now no-one between him and the lantern. He rose to his hands and knees and gestured to Kirsty and Roger to follow. Quickly but quietly he crawled quickly up the slope, his head swivelling to keep track of CUO Masters, and also of CUO Grey and CUO Mitrovitch, who were again approaching from the right. But he and his friends were now past them. Over on Graham's left were Halyday and Andrews. They also crawled quickly forward.

At 2115hrs they stood up near the light. Graham was surprised to find Capt Conkey standing behind it controlling a dozen cadets who had already arrived and were seated in the darkness beyond.

"Who is that?" Capt Conkey asked.

"Cpl Kirk, and 4 Section, sir," Graham replied.

Capt Conkey shone his torch on them all and then grunted with approval, "Good. Sit over there." His torch showed where. Graham walked past the lantern with a real feeling of achievement. As he told the others to sit, he said, "Very well done 4 Section. Well done Cadet Halyday."

He then sat at the front of the group and talked about the exercise. What he really wanted to know was whether Pigsy and Co had caught Halyday and Andrews. "It was you chucking rocks at them wasn't it?" he asked.

"Yeah," Andrews replied. "We wanted to get them back for teasing us."

"Did they catch you or see you?"

"No fear! We ran faster than them," Andrews replied.

As they talked, Graham was uncomfortably aware that he needed to do another pee. A check of his watch showed five minutes to go. *If I don't go now, I might not get a chance for a while,* he thought.

Without saying anything he stood up and walked back past the waiting cadets into the darkness. After 20 paces he turned and headed down the ridge towards the highway, his eyes questing for a good piece of cover. Finding a big ironbark, he stopped close to it and looked carefully in all directions.

I don't want to get sprung by Pigsy and his slimy mates, or by any of the girls, he thought.

Satisfied no-one was near, he relieved himself. All the while he glanced anxiously in all directions, not wishing to be caught again.

As Graham walked back to the lantern, CSM Cleland began bellowing that the exercise was over and that they were all to move to the lantern. He hurried back and, in the resulting commotion, sat without anyone noticing.

Once CSM Cleland had checked they were all present and Capt Conkey had debriefed them, they were sent back to their platoon areas. This was only a hundred paces for 2 Platoon. They still had 30 minutes to bed and Graham wondered if he should light his stove and heat some water for coffee. It was the third night of camp and he was feeling very tired. He also felt very dirty.

Nor was he the only one. Dianne came and asked if she could have a wash.

Graham shook his head doubtfully. "We are having a shower at the army camp tomorrow."

"But I've got sand and dirt everywhere!" Dianne wailed.

"Then get a washbasin from the Q," Graham replied.

"Good idea. Come on Lucy, Kirsty," Dianne replied.

"Be quick. You have to be in bed in twenty minutes," Graham called after the three girls.

As they walked away, he thought about that. *A quick wash would be nice,* he thought. What was really on his mind was the knowledge that he was really sweaty and chafed between his thighs and the armpits. *I don't want to stink if Kirsty gives me a kiss,* he thought. He knew he shouldn't be thinking like that, but he was aroused with desire and hope.

With that he strode off after them and arrived at the Q area just as they were trying to pick up a jerrycan of water.

"It's too heavy!" Lucy wailed.

"I'll carry it for you, if one of you will carry a wash basin for me," Graham said.

"Oooh! Are you going to have a bath too?" Kirsty asked, her voice alive with interest.

Graham picked up the jerrycan and laughed, "Just a little wash."

"You can't bath with us," Lucy said.

"Why not? It's dark," Graham teased.

The girls squealed and Dianne snapped, "You cannot!"

"I was only joking," Graham replied.

It was on the tip of his tongue to say other things he thought witty and sexy but managed to stop himself. Instead, he carried the jerrycan down past the platoon area towards the female latrine. When he was 50 paces past the last hutchie he put it down and retreated back to his hutchie feeling very aroused and with his mind full of delicious fantasies about the girls.

At his hutchie he unrolled his bedding and sat down to unlace his boots. Roger was already lying down. The two friends talked for a while, mostly about Pigsy and his mates and what to do about them. As they talked, Graham heard occasional girlish laughter and he imagined the girls washing themselves.

The next thing he knew, Sgt Grenfell was calling to the girls to get to bed. When they told him they had no clothes on he sent Gwen Copeland to round them up. Graham pulled his boots on and stood up to ensure that the others were in bed. They were, so Graham went and stood with Sgt Grenfell and explained that he had allowed the girls to have a wash. Sgt Grenfell grumbled but nodded so Graham said he would like a few minutes to have a quick rinse himself.

"After all your cadets are in bed," Sgt Grenfell replied.

He went off to quieten Stephen's section. They were all laughing at some joke. A few minutes later the girls came back with Gwen. They had lugged the now almost empty jerrycan back.

"Get to bed," Graham ordered.

He then stood and supervised as they crawled into their hutchies. Kirsty sat down under her half hutchie and pulled off her boots then looked at him in the starlight. That got him wondering and anxious.

Is she hinting she wants a kiss?

Now he wished he had washed as he was sure he stank. After a glance to check that no-one was near, he walked over to her, hoping at the same time Roger wasn't listening.

With beating heart, he bent down. "I am just going to have a quick wash," he whispered.

He could see Kirsty's eyes glistening in the starlight. She nodded and she whispered back, "I could scrub your back. Would you like that?"

That got Graham's mind racing with erotic hopes and fantasies, but he shook his head. "I'd love you to but Sgt Grenfell or CSM Cleland might catch us. So, no."

Graham knew he shouldn't be talking like this, but he was now very aroused and the prospect of even a little cuddle with Kirsty was something he badly wanted. He crawled back into his own hutchie to get his toilet gear and towel.

Roger was awake and caused him some anxiety by asking, "What was all that about?"

"Just Kirsty flirting," Graham replied offhandedly.

"You be careful," Roger warned.

"I will be," Graham replied. "I'm just going to have a quick wash."

With that he stood up. As he collected the washbasin and jerrycan, Graham looked towards Kirsty and saw she was now lying down. She was looking his way and for a moment he was tempted to go over and make more suggestive comments.

With Roger's warning in mind, he resisted this and walked down into the gully 25 metres away. By now he was breathing fast and was very aroused. He stood behind some bushes where he could see whether anyone was coming and from where he was sure no-one could see him. There was no sign of anyone, so he quickly stripped off. That felt very nice and he gripped himself and groaned with frustration.

After pouring some water into the basin he crouched and quickly splashed water on his skin and soaped himself. By this time the camp had settled down and he was very conscious of the water splashes, so he tried to wash as silently as possible. The sting of the soap on his chafe helped calm him but he was still gripped by lust and temptation. After washing he cleaned his teeth, just in case.

When he was finished washing Graham pulled on his trousers, tugged on his boots, then loosely pulled his shirt on. Slinging the towel over his shoulders he picked up the washbasin and jerrycan and walked back up the slope. He dearly wanted to go to Kirsty's hutchie, and he was sure she was still awake watching, but he first went to his own hutchie and crawled in.

After taking off his boots and packing his toilet gear Graham had a drink, then lay back, wondering if Roger was awake but not daring to speak in case he was. Instead, he lay on his side and peered towards Kirsty. All he could see was the top of her head, but that was enough to spur his imagination. Time passed and he became very drowsy. The only sounds were the occasional mournful cry of a curlew, and the wind in the trees. Then he noted the sound he wanted to hear: Roger snoring.

For another ten minutes he lay there fantasising and trying to pluck up the courage. At last he sat up and crawled to the end of the hutchie. He tried to do it silently but made some noise. Kirsty moved and he saw her face swivel in his direction. In the starlight he could see she was smiling.

Come on coward, he told himself.

He knew he would be taking a fearful risk but was now driven by urgent desire. After taking a deep breath he crawled out and stood up.

For a minute he stood looking in all directions and listening. The loudest noise seemed to be his own heart and he knew he was fearfully aroused and being stupid. His skin seemed to flush hot and cold and he had trouble steadying his breathing. Licking lips, which had gone dry from fear and lust he stepped quietly over to Kirsty's shelter.

She looked up as he reached her and he saw she was smiling. He knelt, again licking his lips. Then fear and caution gripped his mind. After a false start he managed to get out a hoarse whisper, "You should be asleep."

Kirsty smiled and nodded. "I know, but I am wide awake."

Graham knelt there in the starlight and battled with temptation. Through his mind raced all the fantasies and all the fears of what could go wrong if he gave in. He stared at her and a great shuddering tremor wracked his body.

No. I must not give in, he told himself. With an effort he said, "It is late. We had better try to sleep."

Kirsty grunted and did not reply. Graham was confused and knew he was scared. To end the situation, he said, "See you in the morning."

She was disappointed. Even in the dark he could tell that. But she just nodded and lay down. Graham stood and walked back to his hutchie. As he did, he was torn by both desire and shame.

Am I really a coward? he agonised as he crawled into his shelter.

For the next hour he lay engulfed by passion, regret and doubt, waves of heat sweeping over him. He was so aroused he could not sleep. Feverish fantasies kept him awake and aroused until he at last slid into a deep sleep.

* * *

"Wake up Cpl Kirk," Sgt Grenfell called.

Through a muzz of sleep Graham heard him. He opened his eyes but everything was dark. Then he realised it was cold, wet plastic he could feel. He groped and shook his head to clear his thoughts.

Hutchie must have fallen down, he thought.

As it was deliberately tied up with slip knots, he knew that was quite possible. Still half asleep he struggled to push the hutchie away from his face. Next to him Roger also began squirming and groaning.

Suddenly the hutchie was dragged aside. Graham saw it was light and Sgt Grenfell was the person doing it. Then a look of astonishment crossed Sgt Grenfell's face and he shook his head.

"You'd better get up and clean up," he said.

"What? What do you mean?" Graham asked, his mind still groping to wake up.

Then he looked at Roger as he sat up and the reason became clear. Roger's face was covered with some sort of black slime.

Mongrels! he thought angrily. *We've been greased!*

Chapter 12

FRICTION

As Graham rolled over to stand up, he saw Roger looking at him from his sleeping bag. Roger's face registered astonishment and then, amusement.

"You should see your face," Roger said.

"You should see your own!" Graham retorted.

He could see Sgt Grenfell grinning and that annoyed him. It was just getting light and the rest of the platoon were still in bed. Obviously CSM Cleland had just roused Sgt Grenfell so he could get ready early for check parade and he had seen the hutchie down.

"Bloody Pigsy!" Graham added.

"We don't know that for certain," Roger said, sitting up and wiping his face. He grimaced with disgust at the smear of black slime that came off onto his fingers.

"Oh, who else would it be?" Graham cried as he tugged on his socks.

Sgt Grenfell answered that. "Pigsy isn't the only person who doesn't like you."

That was a hurtful comment, but Graham could not dispute the truth of it. What really burned was the idea that anyone would not like him as he thought he was a good person. Sgt Grenfell said, "Anyway, get cleaned up. Check parade is in five minutes."

Graham pulled on his boots and looked for the washbasin and jerrycan he had left nearby the night before. Picking up the jerry, he filled the washbasin and then moved to dig his soap out of his webbing. As he did, Kirsty snuffled and stretched, then moved her head and opened her eyes. She turned to look in his direction. For a moment her eyes met Graham's and he saw puzzlement, then amusement, cross her face.

"What happened?" she asked, sitting up.

"Someone greased us," Graham replied gruffly. He did not enjoy being humiliated.

Kirsty giggled but then saw his expression and shook her head. "Sorry, but it does look funny."

"Humpf!" grunted Graham.

He splashed water on his face and began to soap it. Roger moved to join him. A couple of minute's vigorous rubbing made some improvement, but the mixture of boot polish and toothpaste would not yield easily. By looking at Roger's face Graham could check on his own. He shook his head angrily, noting the smears of black on his sleeping bag and clothing. By using his towel, he made a better job of it.

By then Sgt Grenfell was calling out for the platoon to get out for check parade. Graham rinsed his face again and began rubbing hard. As soon as he was satisfied he had the worst of the greasing off, he turned and strode over to hurry Halyday and Andrews as both were still apparently in bed. Sgt Grenfell's angry shouts then hurried them all to get on parade. Check Parade led to more irritation. As 2 Platoon marched across past 1 Platoon, there were snickers and grins and someone distinctly said the word 'greased'.

How do they now? Graham wondered. He was sure his face was now reasonably clean. Doubts about who might have been the perpetrators began.

The doubts were reinforced at breakfast when Graham was standing at the condiments table spreading lemon spread on his bread. Cpl Brown sidled up beside him and hissed, "Bugger you Kirk, you mongrel! You got me in trouble with Capt Conkey."

"How did I do that?" Graham asked, genuinely surprised.

"By dobbing about bloody Carnes," Brown replied.

Then it became clear. Carnes was in Brown's section. "So what happened to him?" Graham asked.

"The useless little turd has been moved to headquarters platoon," Brown replied, "and bloody good riddance. If you give me any more grief I will snot you, so keep clear!"

The threat annoyed Graham but he thought it was just bluster so he shrugged and went on smoothing the spread on his bread. Brown stalked off and Graham walked back to the platoon eating area feeling aggrieved and upset.

I didn't mean to get the bugger in trouble, he thought with annoyance. *Anyway, he should have stopped the bullying.*

He sat down and was even more relieved when Kirsty came and sat beside him, sitting close enough for her knee to touch his. For the next twenty minutes he ate and happily flirted with Kirsty, sending her 'meaningful' messages with his eyes- until he noted CUO Masters looking thoughtfully at them. *Uh oh! I hope he doesn't suspect anything,* Graham thought. *I'd better be more careful.*

After quickly eating his breakfast Graham washed up, then made a point of walking back to his hutchie with Roger. The friends then re-erected their hutchie- the work of minutes- and set about cleaning up for morning inspection. When he had as much ready as he could Graham decided to quickly visit the toilet. It then occurred to him that choosing which latrine to use had now become a high stress decision. So which latrine: the one near 3 Platoon or the one near 4 Platoon? The 4 Platoon latrine was closer and it was more open. Berating himself for being a coward he marched over to it.

To his relief, there was no-one else there and Pigsy and Co were over near their hutchies. But they saw him and Pigsy jeered and called, "Jerk! Hear you got greased. Do you good, you boot-licking crawler."

Graham ignored him and strode back towards his own platoon. On the way he went between HQ and 1 Platoon. At HQ he found Peter. Next to him was Carnes. Both were busy putting on camouflage.

"What are you doing?" Graham asked Peter.

"We are setting up an OP down near the highway just in case that mob from Townsville try to send any recon patrols over to spy on us," Peter replied.

That sounded like a good idea to Graham and he nodded. He then looked at Carnes. "How are you, Cadet Carnes?"

Carnes scowled. "Rotten. I just want to go home."

"Oh well, the camp is half over," Graham said. "Hang in there."

No wanting to become involved in a debate, Graham said he had to get ready for inspection, which was true anyway, and hurried off, wishing Peter good luck as he did. As he walked towards his own platoon, Graham was suddenly struck by a stone. It was so unexpected and hurt so much that he stopped and then spun round.

Brown. For sure! he thought, seeing Brown's face with malicious satisfaction written all over it.

Brown was about 30 paces away, standing beside his hutchie, but Graham was positive he had thrown the stone. As anger flared, he strode over, clenched fists on hips.

"Don't throw stones at me, Brown," he grated.

Brown glared back. "Or what, big man?"

"Or I'll flatten you," Graham replied.

"Oh yeah? You ain't good enough. You're all talk, you gutless sniveller," Brown retorted.

The words really stung. *Is that what people think I really am, a coward and a crawler?* Graham wondered. But now his pride was badly hurt and he put up his fists.

"Anytime buster," he challenged.

"Oh yeah!" Brown relied with a sneer.

He clenched his fists and began to shape up, but Graham sensed he wasn't very keen. By now other cadets had begun to form an audience.

CUO McAlistair's voice cut over the babble. "What the hell is going on here? You two put your fists down!" He shoved in between Graham and Brown.

Graham did so. After a moment Brown did likewise. CUO McAlistair looked from one to the other. "What the devil is this all about?" he said.

"Brown hit me with a stone," Graham said.

"Did not!" Brown replied hotly.

"Did so!" Graham cried angrily.

"Prove it," Brown snapped.

"That will do!" CUO McAlistair ordered. "Both of you be quiet. Speak when you are asked to. Now, Cpl Kirk, what happened?"

Graham described what had happened. Brown denied it, adding, "He's just trying to get me into trouble, sir."

"Why would he do that?" CUO McAlistair asked.

"Because he's a crawler who wants to be a sergeant and he's jealous," Brown replied. "He wants to make himself look good by making the rest of us look bad."

The accusation really stung Graham and he strongly denied it, although he knew he did badly want to be selected to be a sergeant the following year. CUO McAlistair could not decide so told them both to stop their nonsense and then ordered Graham back to his own platoon.

Graham went, seething with the apparent injustice, only to find he was now late and in trouble with CUO Masters and Sgt Grenfell. The platoon inspection was under way. Roger had the rest of the section lined up but Graham had to try to justify his absence to an irritated CUO and sceptical sergeant. He then stood at attention at the end of his section, his emotions seething.

Damn! If I keep getting into trouble, I will never get to be a sergeant, he thought unhappily. Once again, the statistics haunted him: half the corporals would miss out. He did not want to be one of the unlucky ones.

As soon as they were fallen out to get ready for company parade, Graham turned to Roger and thanked him.

"That's okay," Roger replied. "Besides, they were all ready on time this morning, so it was no problem," he replied.

Graham looked at the others, noting Halyday's cheeky grin, and thanked them too. He then had to explain to Roger what the incident at 1 Platoon had been about. By the time he had done this it was time for parade. As the platoon marched across to parade Graham noted the Hutchie Men, again dressed in their Yowie Suits. They were heading off from the officer's fire in the direction of the army camp. Obviously, they were going to keep an eye on the rival units again.

Good old Capt Conkey, Graham thought.

After the company parade the unit was organised for training. The whole day was devoted to individual fieldcraft training for the junior platoons. HQ had three tasks: signals and medical training, plus maintaining the OP to warn of any other unit trying to send patrols across the highway. 4 Platoon were to act as 'enemy' for the juniors while the Hutchie Men were to do recons of the other cadet units.

For 2 Platoon the morning was taken up by two observation activities, rotating with 1 Platoon. The first activity was a moving observation. This was set up by the officers along the small dry creek that ran down from 1 Platoon's area to the highway. Along about 500 metres of the creek were placed 25 items such as pieces of webbing, tins, trip wires, pretend land mines, clothing and small objects. Cadets were sent along this one at a time, 3 minutes apart. They had to try to locate all the objects and note their sequence.

CUO Masters went along first and Sgt Grenfell went last. He timed the cadets. In each section the corporal went first and the 2ic last. While they waited for their turn the cadets sat under the trees near 1 Platoon. 4 Section went first so Graham led the way. He had done several similar exercises and knew what to do. He enjoyed this one and only missed one item along the way.

At the other end, Graham was sent across to the second small creek and sat in the shade of a Burdekin Plum tree while waiting for the remainder of his section. Kirsty was next to arrive, so he then had a few minutes to sit and talk to her alone. The first thing he did was test how she felt about him.

"You are really nice," he said. "I'm glad you were with me during the lantern stalk last night."

Kirsty shook her head and smiled. "It was good fun," she replied.

Graham hesitated over saying what was on his mind, knowing in his heart that it was wrong. But he was now driven by the urgent desire of lust and badly wanted to be with Kirsty (Or, he was honest enough to admit to himself, with any girl who would let him). So he moistened suddenly dry lips and asked, "Would you mind if I kissed you?"

She smiled. "I'd like that."

Graham felt a surge of joy that was almost immediately replaced by worry about things going too far so he again hinted that they behave. He also did not want to incur her wrath, so he said, "I want getting to know you to be really special, so I'd like to wait till we are home after camp."

She went all doe-ey eyed at that, and said, "You are really sweet."

He wasn't sure if she accepted this, but they had no further chance to talk because Pat finished the course and joined them. Pat and Kirsty struck up a conversation, so Graham lay back and tried to sleep. The ants and the heat made this ambition difficult to achieve and he was only drowsy when Roger arrived and CUO Masters told Graham to take his section up to Lt McEwen at the flat rocks near the head of the valley.

This was only 500 metres and the rocks were visible, so they just walked up the shallow valley beside the second creek. Lt McEwen told them to sit in the shade near the members of 1 Platoon who still had to complete that activity. Mostly these were 1 and 2 Sections. Graham had no particular friends in either section, but Roger struck up a conversation with LCpl Lofty Ward. Once again Graham thought it would be a good opportunity to catch up on his sleep, so he lay back and pulled his hat over his eyes.

As he lay there, he thought hard about Kirsty and whether she really liked him. *What if she is just having a bit of fun?* he worried. *I don't mind getting into trouble for true love,* he thought. But to go down over some silly crush did not appeal at all. *But how do I know?* he wondered. It was a whole new realm of uncertainty and he looked at Kirsty with new eyes. *Does she like me, or is she just playing with me?*

By her manner she really liked him. She smiled and flirted and Graham was moved to flirt back. There was a lot of eye contact and frequent secret smiles and once he was moved to hand her a tiny flower he plucked from the dry grass. As he did, she went all coy and lowered her eyelids but smiled. Graham then realised that Lt McEwen was standing watching and he felt a rush of anxiety. Blushing with guilt he looked away and began talking to Pat.

I hope Lt McEwen didn't notice, he thought.

The activity Lt McEwen was running was a static observation. Cadets were moved one at a time to the other side of the rocks where they stood and looked. 25 items were placed within 25 metres and they had 3 minutes to spot them all and point them out to the OOC or CUO. Graham got 24 of them, failing to notice a shiny brass cartridge case right near his feet. He then went up the gully to another tree to sit in another waiting area. Here he lay down again and this time, heat and ants notwithstanding, he did go to sleep.

It was a mistake though. When Sgt Grenfell woke him up half an hour later, he felt sweaty and even tireder. His mouth had a horrible taste and his eyes felt dry and scratchy. It was 1200hrs by then and the platoon had all completed the activity. CUO Masters led them back to their platoon area and they were fallen out to wait for lunch.

Lunch was cold meat and salad which Graham did not particularly like, but he drank two big cups of cold lemon cordial as it was now very hot and he was very thirsty. After that he went and lay down in his hutchie to get some more rest. He did not succeed.

Roger joined him and said, "You should go to sleep earlier at night."

That really twitched Graham's guilty conscience. *Did Roger see me talking to Kirsty last night?* he wondered. But he did not dare ask so he just grunted and kept his eyes closed until they were called out for the afternoon training.

That was an individual observation and contact course along the creeks towards the Canning and 4 Platoon acted as the enemy. Graham suspected he might have a few problems but was unprepared for quite how many.

The exercise developed into a major drama which he really regretted.

Chapter 13

OBSERVATION COURSE

The afternoon exercise was conducted in the creeks and gullies running north from Sandy Ridge to the Canning River. Both creeks, which were used, had their beginnings near the camp and came together down near the North Gravel Scrape. Two observation courses were laid out. One went down the creek that led off to the left from beside the Scrubby Creek track. This went all the way to the junction of the two creeks. From there the second course led back up the creek that ended near 1 Platoon's bivouac area.

Along each course cadets from 4 Platoon were positioned, along with trip wires and pretend land mines. Cadets were sent along each course singly, depending on their good observation to detect and avoid the problems. The time between each cadet was 5 minutes. 1 Platoon was sent to the junction of the two creeks via the Canning Road. They were to work their way up, then cross to the other creek and go down it. At the same time 2 Platoon and some of HQ were to start down at the creek junction and then come back up the other creek. They would then move over to use the course 2 Platoon was starting on.

Graham's section was led across to the start point on the Scrubby Creek track by CUO Masters and CUO Grey. His section was then told to sit in the shade. They were told they would be moving after HQ. Graham was surprised to find Peter there.

"I thought you were out on some sort of guard patrol," Graham said.

"I was. Corporal Forman is out there now with two others."

"See anything?"

"Not a sausage," Peter replied.

Noting Carnes lying in the shade nearby Graham gestured with his head towards him. "How did Carnes go?"

"Just sat there feeling sorry for himself," Peter answered.

"Do you know what his problem is?" Graham asked.

Peter shook his head. "No. Didn't ask him. I'm not pleased he got stuck in my section."

At that moment CUO Grey called on the first HQ person. That was Peter. He stood up and moved off. "Good luck," Graham called after him.

"I prefer to use skill," Peter quipped. He gave a grin and added, "It is only 4 Platoon we are fighting, and they aren't nearly as good as they think they are." With that he walked off and vanished into the head of the gully.

4 Platoon! Graham thought. The idea made him feel distinctly anxious and he wished he didn't feel the need to go to the toilet. *It's just all that cordial reaching the bottom of the plumbing,* he tried to rationalise. However, after a moment's reflection, he decided that a nervous pee before action might be a good idea.

But where? He stood up and looked around. The vehicle track ran along the crest of a very gentle ridge covered with sparse grass and scattered ironbarks. The nearest privacy appeared to be about fifty metres away across the track, where several small gullies led down towards Scrubby Creek. These were the same gullies where he and Roger had been kicked by Pigsy and Co.

No chance of anyone being there now, he decided. 1 Platoon was down near the North Gravel Scrape and 3 Platoon and the rest of HQ were doing the observation courses he had done during the morning.

With that in mind Graham started walking off through the bush. He had only gone 20 paces when he heard boots in the grass behind him. He glanced back and saw that it was Kirsty. *Oh blast!* he thought. That caused him to cast a guilty look back to where the platoon lay or sat in the grass. No-one seemed to be taking any notice.

"Where are you going, Graham?" Kirsty called.

"You should call me Corporal Kirk," he replied.

At that Kirsty poked her tongue. "Oh poo! No-one can hear. Where are you going?"

"To have a leak, so go back to the others please," Graham replied.

"Oh! Do I have to? I want to be with you."

At that Graham's heart rate shot up and he remembered previous conversations. "I don't want to offend you and I don't want to get into trouble. Please go back."

Kirsty pouted but stopped. But Graham was now both interested and aroused. By then they were well down the slope and out of sight of the others. He said, "Wait there. I will be back in a minute."

With that he continued walking for another 20 paces and went down into the head of a gully so that he was sure Kirsty could only see his head. Graham stopped and looked back towards the track and then scanned the open country out between where he was and Scrubby Creek. There was no-one in sight. His heart was now hammering fast and he was amazed at how dry his mouth felt and at the sweat which had broken out on his hands. After another quick glance around he undid his fly and began to pee.

Footsteps behind him made him glance back. It was Kirsty. She was walking closer and out to one side. "Kirsty! Stay back," he cried.

"But I've never seen it," Kirsty answered, but she stopped walking.

Graham was astonished. "You must have," he answered.

"Oh, only little boys," Kirsty said. "I've never seen a man do it."

Man! thought Graham. It was balm to his male ego and he was sorely tempted to let her look. But fear of getting into trouble joined to anxiety at not being able to physically perform and he shook his head. "No."

"I won't tell," Kirsty replied. Her face was now alive with interest.

"That's what they all say!" Graham answered.

Kirsty took a few more paces towards him and Graham felt a surge of anxiety that all but dried up the flow. "I won't tell, truly," she said, her voice earnest.

"Promise?"

"Yes, promise," Kirsty said with a nod.

It was that word that decided Graham. Already he was being torn by savage memories of how just such a situation as this had gotten him into terrible trouble a year earlier. He had been in trouble with his parents, her parents and the school. One consequence was him being given the choice of joining the cadets or being expelled from the school.

Capt Conkey had faith in me and has saved me, he thought. *And I promised to behave.*

So he stopped and shook his head. "No, please go back," he said as firmly as he could. Kirsty pouted and looked unhappy and tried to argue. "Oh, please," she said. She increased the pressure by stepping closer and craning to look. Graham felt his determination waver and he was about to say yes when a movement in the gully 20 metres away caught his eye.

Oh hell! Who is that? he wondered as near panic surged through him.

It had been a face, a camouflaged face under a scrim net, but a face all the same. *Yowie men,* was his first thought. That brought waves of scorching shame as he imagined the teasing and blackmail he would have to endure from his enemies as the word inevitably spread.

"There's someone in that creek bed," Graham cried.

He quickly did up his trousers. At the same time, he stepped behind a tree. As he did, he distinctly saw another camouflaged head move up behind a clump of grass.

Kirsty gasped and went pale. Graham walked 5 paces sideways up the slope so he could get a better view down the gully. That brought into his view four shaggy bundles of scrim but also some details such as legs and army boots: cadets in camouflage and Yowie Suits. By then Graham felt so ill he wanted to just faint. Then his eyes detected a yellow epaulet.

Not ours! Heatley or St Michaels, he thought.

That changed things a bit. *Maybe they didn't see?* he thought in desperation. He grabbed Kirsty's arm. "An enemy patrol, from Heatley. Quick, back up the slope before they capture us."

They turned and ran. As they did Graham got another shock. Walking along the vehicle track down from camp were Capt Conkey and Lt Maclaren! And even as Graham noted them both officers turned their heads to look. Graham's heart turned over with a sickening lurch, but he tried to act as though nothing unusual was going on.

"Sir! Sir! There's a recon patrol from Townsville just down there in the gully," he cried.

Capt Conkey frowned. "What are you two doing down there?"

What do I say? Graham wondered, flustering in panic. Instead of answering he called, "Four enemy, sir, in the little creek just there."

Capt Conkey frowned even more. "Where is your platoon?"

Oh bloody hell! I'm sunk! Graham thought. He pointed, "Just there, sir."

And to his relief they were. He could see their heads above the grass. As he spoke CUO Masters and Sgt Grenfell stood up and looked towards them. By then Graham and Kirsty had reached Capt Conkey. To Graham's intense relief Capt Conkey called CUO Masters over.

"Quickly CUO Masters, get your platoon lined up in extended line along the track and sweep east towards Scrubby Creek," he ordered. "There is a Heatley recon patrol in the gully just there."

In the rush of orders Graham took the opportunity to run off and get

4 Section lined up as far from Capt Conkey as he could. While he was still urging the section to spread out in extended line, he heard a shout from Stephen: "There they go!"

Graham looked and saw four shaggy creatures running off across the flat to the right. They vanished around the end of a low spur while CUO Masters shouted for 2 Platoon to run. It was good fun, but they had no hope of catching the four intruders. The platoon had to change direction and the sections became mixed up. The less fit and the unenthusiastic fell quickly behind and after a hundred metres CUO Masters called a halt. Graham had to shout three times to get Halyday to stop. By then the four intruders had vanished into the thick cover along Scrubby Creek.

Capt Conkey called the platoon to come back. By then he was busy on the radio directing the HQ OP to move to watch the way the intruders had been last seen. The platoon walked slowly back, most talking rapidly with excitement and discussing the incident. Not so Graham. He walked in a sick fog of apprehension wondering what story to tell.

I will have to lie to protect Kirsty, he thought miserably.

But he was spared that. Capt Conkey was taken up with directing the Hutchie Men to try to intercept their opposite numbers and appeared to have forgotten about him and Kirsty. Perspiring from effort and anxiety Graham sat in the shade and had a big drink. Kirsty moved to sit with him but he gave her a shake of the head and she nodded and sat well away from him. Minutes dragged by and still Capt Conkey did not come and ask what they had been doing. He seemed to be engrossed in directing the patrols.

The fieldcraft exercise went on. The last of HQ went down the gully, a reluctant Carnes, then CUO Masters. Graham was next as the section commanders were to go first and 2ics last. He found it a relief of sorts to move into the gully out of sight of Capt Conkey, but that was tempered by anxiety about how he might fare at the hands of 4 Platoon.

He soon found out.

The first problem was a trip wire, which he spotted, then four dummy land mines. Ahead on the right was a clump of rocks that looked like a probable sniper position, and it was.

Cpl Bannister suddenly shouted, "Bang! Gotya Kirk! Ha ha!"

Graham had been expecting it but was too slow. That hurt his pride and he blushed with shame and gritted his teeth with determination to beat the next one. He did. It was Cadet Norris and he was easy to spot and too slow.

Feeling better Graham crept on down the dry gully, which was getting slowly deeper all the time. Another trip wire was avoided and he kept switching his gaze from side to side, then ahead. He found it stressful but enjoyable, until a rock came hurtling out of a side gully he had already looked up and started to pass. The rock struck him a glancing blow on the right side and went skittering off.

Graham dived for cover and saw Moynihan's grinning face. "Bang!" Graham shouted. Moynihan just jeered back. "Ya drongo Kirk! I just blew you up with a grenade."

Graham knew that Moynihan was well aware that unit standing safety orders banned throwing things. Equally he knew it was pointless to say anything. *I wouldn't be able to prove it,* he thought.

Angered and even more on guard he moved on, crouched and ready. Somewhere ahead were Waters and Pigsy and he expected worse from them. He got it. First he negotiated a trip wire at a fallen tree, then spotted movement up on the bank to his left. He dashed for cover and pretended to fire up the side gully. It was Waters and Graham's move caught him off-guard.

"Bang!" Graham shouted, then, "Ouch!"

A rock had slammed into the small of his back. As he spun around, he saw Pigsy with his arm raised to toss another stone. Graham was able to dodge this but then Waters threw one from the other side and it struck him a painful blow on the hip. Anxious that his eyes did not get injured Graham shouted back and dived into the creek bed out of sight.

"Stop it you buggers!" he shouted.

"Don't call me a bugger Kirk!" Pigsy yelled.

He ran down and threw another stone. This struck Graham on the webbing. Waters also threw more but kept back. One of these grazed Graham's cheek. "Stop throwing stones you bloody idiots!" he shouted. He realised that trying to take cover in the creek bed had just made him more of a target. Fear and anger both forced his adrenaline to surge.

Without really thinking about it, he sprang up and charged at Pigsy. Pigsy threw the stone he had in his hand, which struck Graham a glancing blow on the shoulder, then bent to pick up another. By then Graham was so close Pigsy gave that up and straightened up. For a fleeting second fear flitted across his face and he ran back a few paces. Pigsy then stopped and raised his fists. Waters meanwhile had thrown two more stones, one of which hit Graham on the back.

Ignoring Waters, Graham confronted Pigsy. "Stop it Pigsy or I'll smash you to pulp!" he shouted angrily.

"You ain't good enough!" Pigsy replied with a sneer but Graham thought he detected anxiety in the bully's eyes. *He's all bluff and bluster,* he thought. He stepped closer and raised his fists.

At that moment, Lt Hamilton's voice cut across his consciousness. "What's going on here?"

Graham turned his head and saw Lt Hamilton and Lt Standish on top of the bank. He pointed at Pigsy and said, "Sir, they are throwing stones at me!"

"We are not, sir!" Pigsy called back, his voice all injured innocence. "He threw stones at us."

The blatant lie left Graham speechless for a second, then his anger flared. "Oh, you bloody liar, Pigsy!" he shouted.

"That will do!" Lt Hamilton ordered. "Cpl Kirk, just get on with the exercise."

"But sir! They hit me and it hurt!" Graham cried, the injustice of it inflaming his temper.

"Don't you back answer me or argue, Cpl Kirk!" Lt Hamilton shouted in reply.

With an effort Graham bit back a sharp retort and stood to attention, chest heaving and close to tears. *You drongo!* he berated himself. *Arguing with the officers is no way to get promoted.* He took several deep breaths.

"Yes, sir. Sorry, sir," he said.

With that he turned and walked on down the gully. What really stung was seeing what he thought was a glint of malicious glee in Pigsy's eye. *Mongrel! I'll get him,* he told himself.

The remainder of the course was simple after that, merely a test of skill. Graham was so stirred up that he seemed to have unnaturally heightened perception and was able to detect every single incident in time to react. He was particularly pleased to find that Capt Conkey was watching at the point where the fence crossed the gully. Graham went under the fence halfway up the bank and managed to avoid some mines and another lurking cadet.

On reaching the junction of the two creeks Graham was directed by CUO Grey to go back up the other creek. By now he was really enjoying himself, despite the heat. He battled his way up and again managed to detect all but one of the hidden opponents in time. The second creek he liked even better.

That was fun! he thought as he reached the head of the gully at the Sandy Ridge track near 1 Platoon's bivouac.

He then sat in the shade of the big ironbark where he had found Carnes and waited till the rest of his section arrived. Kirsty was the first to arrive but CUO Masters was also there with Sgt White so there was no chance to talk privately. This was just as well as Capt Conkey and Lt Maclaren arrived soon after and stood talking.

Roger was last to arrive and Graham could tell he was upset. "What's wrong," he asked, although he had a good idea what the problem might be.

This was confirmed when Roger replied, "Bloody Pigsy and his mates. They teased me and threw rocks."

"Me too," Graham answered. Roger did not say what the bullies had called him, but Graham could guess. "Do you want to complain?" he asked.

"What would be the use? It would be my word against theirs," Roger replied with an unhappy shrug.

The friends left it at that and changed the subject, but Graham knew that he really should be taking some sort of action to help his friend.

Maybe I am a coward? he wondered.

Chapter 14

'DON'T DROP THE SOAP!'

As the platoon walked back to their bivouac area, Graham saw that he had another problem. Even from a hundred metres away he could see that his hutchie was down and that gear was strewn around.

Bloody Pigsy! he thought, then felt a flush of shame as he knew he had no proof and that it could just as easily have been Brown.

Sgt Grenfell halted the platoon near their hutchies and looked first at the downed hutchie, then at Graham and Roger. "You had better get that cleaned up quickly," he said. "We want to be moving in fifteen minutes. We don't want to be last through the shower and miss the hot water."

Graham shook his head and gritted his teeth as a spasm of intense anger seized him. "If I knew who did this, I'd pulp him!" he muttered.

Roger was more philosophical and just shrugged, then gestured towards the camouflaged CP at HQ. "They might have seen something."

That sent Graham striding over to the CP. Inside were two girls: Cpl Forman and LCPL O'Brien. Both looked surprised and shook their heads. "No. Sorry. Didn't see anyone there, not in the last hour," Cpl Forman replied.

She looked sympathetic and Graham believed her. For a minute he stood there gripped by anger, grinding his teeth and looking around for clues. However, he was also acutely aware he did not have time to waste so he strode back to his hutchie and set to work scooping up his scattered clothing and tossing it into his kit bag.

By then Sgt Grenfell was calling on them to line up in their sections. Muttering swear words Graham snatched up his laundry bag, stuffed a clean uniform, underwear and socks into it, then shook his towel to flick off as much dust and grass as he could and added it to the bundle. Then he began to chivvy the others to hurry.

"Come on! Hurry up! One Platoon is already lining up," he called to Andrews and Halyday.

They kept digging in their kitbags till Graham wanted to scream at them but they at last came out and stood in line. For once 4 Section was not last. One of Stephen's cadets held them up. By then 1 Platoon had begun moving but CUO Masters arrived, pack on back, and said, "Follow me."

He led the platoon in single file down across the head of the gully near the officer's hutchies while 1 Platoon took the longer route around along the track. That gave 2 Platoon a 50-metre lead. By cracking on the pace, they maintained this down through the South Gravel Scrape. By then the highway was clearly visible. So was their destination, the army camp. The roofs of the large store sheds stuck up above the sea of gum trees, visible for many kilometres.

The fence along the highway increased their lead over 1 Platoon by another 50 paces because CUO Masters ordered each section to use a different panel and to roll under the bottom strand of the barbed wire while 1 Platoon all climbed through a single point where their CUO and sergeant held two wires apart. By then 4 Platoon and HQ could both be seen heading down the slope through the gravel scrape.

It was 1630hrs when the platoon crossed the highway near the turn-off to the army camp, the whole platoon at once in extended line. They then reformed in single file and marched along the side road. This led across the railway and into the camp. By then all were sweating and some of the smaller cadets were complaining of blisters and sore muscles. It was very hot and Graham badly wanted a drink.

As they marched up the approach road to the boom gate at the entrance to the camp Lt Hamilton went past in his Land Rover. From the back grinning faces of members of HQ teased the marching cadets.

"Mob of bludgers! How come they get to ride in the rover?" Andrews grumbled.

"Because they have to work in the kitchen," Graham replied. He was now feeling happier. The army camp was one place he liked. The ten days he had spent there the previous December had been one of the watershed events in his life and he knew it. The Corporals Course had been very demanding, physically, emotionally and intellectually, and he was proud to have survived and passed. From 0600hrs in the morning till 2130hrs at night they had been on the go; 13 periods of lessons, parades, inspections and being assessed.

The camp itself was spread over nearly a kilometre of bush on a wide, flat ridge. It dated from World War 2 and was now only used for storage.

A bitumen road wound its way along the crest of the ridge through the trees and buildings. The buildings were widely scattered, most being 50 to 100m apart. Some were now gone and only concrete slabs and drains marked their former locations. The trees were mostly ironbarks and were also widely scattered, the short grass under them giving a park-like appearance.

Two houses for regular army staff flanked the entrance gate. There was then a small wooden guard house with a front veranda. The civilian caretaker leaned on the railings of this and grinned as they trudged past. A dozen large steel sheds were scattered well back on either side of the road. As the road curved slowly left it passed two more sheds on the left, then a truly massive 'igloo' style shed on their right. Bitumen roads went along each side of this shed and even through the huge double doors near each end. A railway line ran through the far end of the shed.

As he marched past the big shed, Graham gave a wry smile, remembering a foolish prank which he and Stephen had indulged in and which had nearly had them chucked off the course. On a dare they had climbed right up over the shed. It had turned out to be a real test of courage as the shed was very much higher than it looked and the only grip on the downslope had been the heads of the nails holding on the sheets of corrugated iron.

Silly buggers we were, he thought, shaking his head at the memory.

Beyond the shed were more memories, but of a different type of stress. It was in the limited shade of the straggly ironbarks there that he had taught his first lessons to a squad. The main road ran straight for 200 metres to more buildings. On the way it passed a grass parade ground which lay between the road and railway, then a huge concrete slab which had once been the base of a second giant shed. It had been burned down by a disgruntled soldier, or so Graham had been told by one of the storemen.

On the far side of this were a small lawn with two trees on it, two small wooden buildings, a circular 'ring road' around a tennis court and ablution block. Three other buildings and a water tower and treatment works completed the camp. The buildings were the kitchen and dining areas and accommodation huts. When Graham had been here on his course there had been rows and rows of tents and hundreds of cadets and staff. It all now seemed very quiet and deserted.

A couple of vehicles were parked near the kitchen and only a few people were visible. However, the sight of one group of people caused a murmur of annoyance. Seated in a line were four Cairns cadets in camouflage suits. Standing around them were half a dozen strange cadets, who were obviously guarding them.

"Looks like one of our patrols has been captured," Graham said to CUO Masters.

"Yes, by Heatley," CUO Masters replied. "The OC won't be very happy with that."

Graham now saw that the four Cairns cadets were from 4 Platoon: Cpl 'Dimbo' Doyle, LCpl Laidley and Cadets Shearer and Duncan.

As 2 Platoon passed the first small building a Land Rover came from behind and they moved off the road to let it past. It was Capt Conkey with CSM Cleland and Lt McEwen. Capt Conkey parked the Land Rover and they got out. As he walked across to where the four prisoners sat on a low concrete wall beside a deep drain two officers came out of the other small building, their faces covered with grins.

A tubby major called loudly, "These are yours I believe Cyril?"

Capt Conkey grinned back and went to shake the major's hand. Graham could not tell if he was annoyed or not, but the sight of the gloating Heatley cadet's faces certainly irritated him. However, he had no time to worry about it as CSM Cleland called to them and led them across onto the lawn beyond the tennis courts and ablution block. They were allocated an area of lawn where the sections were placed in lines and told to get through the shower a quickly as possible.

It was a real relief to stop marching and to slump down on the grass. Graham sat and began unlacing his boots. "Boots off and thongs on," he ordered. He knew how things had to be organised to get a large number through a shower in a short time.

Dianne pointed to the small, corrugated iron building. "What's that?"

"The showers," Graham replied.

"Where do we go?" she asked.

"In the showers I suppose," he replied. He meant to say after the boys had finished but Stephen now piped up.

"We all go in together, and there are no partitions. This is an old-fashioned army shower with just a row of six shower roses set in the wall."

At that Lucy blanched and stared at the building in horror. “Oh, we do not!” she cried.

“Yes, we do, all together,” Stephen insisted.

Kirsty met Graham’s eye. “Do we really?”

Impishly Graham nodded. “Yes, why not?”

“That’s right,” Stephen added. “Anyway, as my mum says: If you haven’t seen it, it is educational; and if you have it doesn’t matter!”

“Well, I’m not going in!” Lucy cried in a shrill voice.

Gwen now called out, “You stop teasing the girls, Stephen Bell! You girls do not go in there. We go over to that building and we have individual showers there.” Gwen pointed to the first accommodation building where Lt McEwen stood on the veranda. She was talking to a strange female lieutenant.

“Oh, spoil sport!” Stephen replied with a laugh.

Lucy poked her tongue at him, and she and Dianne scooped up their clothes and towels and headed after Gwen. Kirsty leaned over close to Graham and whispered, “It would have been really interesting.”

That got him speculating, and as she walked after the others he could not help fantasising about that. To his dismay, he began to get aroused as he lined up at the door under Sgt Grenfell’s direction. By then 1 Platoon and 4 Platoon had also arrived and seated themselves on the area of lawn allocated to each. CSM Cleland called to Sgt Grenfell to get 2 Platoon moving through the shower, 2 minutes per person.

“In you go,” Sgt Grenfell ordered.

Feeling very anxious and shy Graham led the way in, followed by Stephen and Roger. The other male cadets began filing in. A queue formed, leading back out the door. As Graham knew, there were only six showers, then a long wooden bench, a plywood partition and beyond that a urinal and row of toilet cubicles. As he tossed his gear onto the wooden bench, he felt very stressed and he deliberately took his time undressing.

By the time he had, Stephen, Halyday, Andrews, and ‘Thomo’ Thomson had all stripped off and were adjusting the water flow. Roger was rather self-consciously undressing and Graham was left with the shower nearest the door. Half the platoon stood there staring in at him. That got him really anxious. He had often swum naked on hikes with Stephen, Roger and Peter, and even with little Margaret, but to strip in front of his subordinates was a new and embarrassing experience.

Part of the problem was that he did not want to them to suspect he was in any way anxious. Nor did he want to endure looks of mocking pity or smirks.

I don't know why I am worrying, he thought *I am quite normal. Get on with it,* he told himself.

Pretending it was of no consequence he 'casually' peeled off his trousers and underpants and stepped over to the shower, hotly aware that a dozen pairs of eyes were critically evaluating his manhood. Turning his back on them he turned the water on and began adjusting it.

He had just started soaping himself when he heard Sgt Grenfell saying loudly at the door, "Hey! Where are you 4 Platoon blokes going?"

"Just going to the dunny," Graham heard Pigsy reply.

Damn! Graham thought anxiously.

Pigsy, Waters and Moynihan came pushing past the cadets at the door. "Get out of the way you warts," Pigsy ordered.

Then Graham saw his leering face appear. Pigsy guffawed and called to his cronies, "Well well! Look at this. Bum buddies bath time. Hey Dunning, don't drop the soap!"

"Piss off, Pigsy!" Stephen called back. He was busy lathering his hair and obviously had trouble seeing because he did not have his glasses on and had soap in his eyes.

"You watch out yerself, Bell, ya dork," Pigsy retorted. "You want to watch out for Dunning here, or he will catch you unawares!"

At that the other bullies and several members of 2 Platoon laughed. Waters sneered and called, "Three bloody queers all together in the shower."

Graham could see that Roger was blushing self-consciously. His own temper was rising and he now turned to face their tormentors. "You three must be the deviates," he snapped. "Why did you come in here? Do you creep in to watch boys in the shower?"

At that an ugly scowl crossed Pigsy's face. "Watch what you say, Tiny!" he snarled.

"You're the queer!" Graham retorted. "You spend all your time lurking around dunnies to peek at the boys."

Pigsy's face suffused with anger and he stepped forward. Graham felt his own heart rate shoot up, but he gritted his teeth and stepped out of the shower and squared up, fists raised.

"Come on you bloody bully, fight me," he challenged.

He was uncomfortably aware of his nakedness and saw Pigsy's eyes flick down to his genitals. Fear of being kicked in the testicles caused Graham to half turn but he did not back down. Rather he took another step towards Pigsy. Now that the showdown had come he was unconcerned with his nudity, at least from the perspective of self-consciousness.

For just a second he saw fear flicker in Pigsy's eyes. *He's scared of me!* Graham thought in surprise. *If he didn't have his cronies to back him up he wouldn't even try it on.*

It was a comforting revelation. That caused him to take another step and he lowered his fists and put them on his hips. Standing feet apart, exposed, and only an arm's length from his enemies Graham suddenly sensed that his nakedness was a weapon, discomforting them. He was also aware that both Roger and Stephen had now moved to back him up.

Pigsy sneered and said to his mates, "Come on. Let's get away from this pack of fags."

To Graham's relief, Pigsy turned and walked on into the toilet area. Waters and Moynihan both sneered but followed. Feeling intensely relieved Graham breathed out and went back to his shower.

"Thanks," he said to his friends.

"It wasn't you they were scared of, Kirky," Halyday called. "It was that bloody ugly-looking thing Steve pointed at 'em."

Flustered and embarrassed, Graham snapped at Halyday, "Corporal Kirk to you, Cadet Halyday, not Kirky!"

"Yes, Kirky," Halyday replied.

Graham shook his head and resumed washing himself, leaving Steve to deal with the situation. Sgt Grenfell ended it by walking in. "What's the delay? Come on you people, get a move on. There are a hundred boys waiting out there."

At that moment, Pigsy came walking back from the urinal. "Kirk would like that, the sissy!" he called, but he kept going, hurried on by Sgt Grenfell.

Waters and Moynihan followed him. That eased the situation and Graham hurried to rinse the soap off. He quickly dried himself while ordering the next cadet to take his place under the shower. Two minutes later he was dressed and seated out on the grass outside drying his feet.

CUO Masters then inspected his feet and told him to get his boots on. Stephen and Roger came back out and joined him, also having their feet inspected. Dressing himself, and organising the section kept Graham busy for the next fifteen minutes. During that time the long line of boys slowly edged into the shower and the girls began returning in ones and twos. Kirsty came back, all smiles. She sat and began to brush her hair, something Graham found very appealing and erotic.

A group of Heatley cadets had come to talk and tease. Graham recognised two corporals who had been in his section on promotion course. "How are you blokes?" he asked. He found it very interesting to see cadets from other units, and to watch how they did things.

They chatted cheerfully and Graham learned how the Cairns recon patrol had been captured. Apparently after watching from under cover for an hour or so Cadet Duncan had stuck his head up over the top of a big pile of boxes over at the end of the railway. His head had been skylined and a Heatley cadet had spotted the movement. A quick sweep by their 4 Platoon had netted the prisoners. Graham found he was really vexed by the 'defeat'.

By then all of 2 Platoon had been through the shower and CUO Masters finished inspecting their feet. He then went in for his shower, as did Sgt Grenfell. Graham took the opportunity to elbow into the small laundry in the room at the end of the ablutions to wash his dirty shirt and socks. The wet washing was shoved into his laundry bag with his towel and he went back to where his webbing lay on the lawn, to find his back-pack open.

Chapter 15

TROUBLE

As soon as he saw his open webbing ugly suspicions crowded through Graham's mind. He quickly crouched and looked. His worst fears were soon confirmed. His mess tins, knife, fork and spoon set, and the tea towel they were wrapped in to stop them rattling, were all gone.

I've been robbed! he thought.

All around him were other cadets talking, dressing and resting. "Has anyone been in my webbing?" he asked Pat, who was next to him.

Pat shook his head. "Haven't seen anyone."

Graham asked Andrews and Halyday and then Kirsty, but none had seen anything. The theft was not just annoying, it really jolted Graham. He was sure it wasn't just a random act and the thought that he had a secret enemy who wished him ill so upset him that his stomach churned. He looked around, eyes seeking Pigsy and Co. They were over at 4 Platoon and Pigsy was busy telling a joke. The 4 Platoon people all burst out laughing but none glanced in Graham's direction, so he didn't know if they were laughing at him or not.

Tears began to prickle in the corners of Graham's eyes. So that nobody would see them he stood up and walked quickly away to be on his own. He went off past the end of the ablution block and stopped under a big ironbark.

Oh, damn it, he cursed. *I really wanted to enjoy this camp and it is now just one horrible thing after another.*

For a minute he stood staring at where the sun had now gone down behind the big shed. The sunset was bathing the western sky in a blaze of red and gold. Ordinarily he would have savoured the beauty of it but now he was too upset.

Footsteps made him quickly wipe away a tear which had trickled down his cheek. It was Kirsty. She stopped beside him and put her hand on his arm. "It will be alright Graham, you can use one of my mess tins," she said.

Graham nodded. "Thanks," he muttered.

As he talked to Kirsty, he looked across towards the big shed through the chicken wire surrounding the tennis court, and got a shock. Standing on the other side were four officers: Capt Conkey, and three tubby majors. One was Major Wickham, the OC of Heatley. The others were Major Snodgrass, OC of St Michael's at Broadsound, and the other, the one thumbing his moustache, was Major Ross, the army cadet battalion commander. To add to Graham's distress and concern, he noted that Capt Conkey was glancing in his direction and frowning.

"Kirsty, take your hand off my arm," he said. "Capt Conkey is watching us and we don't want him to get the wrong idea."

Kirsty did but she pouted. "The right idea you mean," she replied, sending his hopes and heart rate soaring.

That really prickled his conscience. He shook his head. "No, not at camp. We promised to behave."

"Oh! He won't know," she replied. "Anyway, what's wrong with a bit of a kiss and a cuddle?"

Unknowingly Kirsty had said the worst possible thing. All of Graham's concepts of integrity and honesty were thus challenged. "I will know," he replied. Then he realised how abrupt he must have sounded. A bit of his father's advice flitted through his mind: 'Hell hath no fury like a woman scorned!' He looked at her and managed a smile. "And one little thing leads to another," he added.

She smiled at that and said impishly, "It looked pretty big to me."

"Kirsty!" Graham cried. Lust and desire surged in him to weaken his resolve. "Come on. Let's go back to the others. Those officers are watching us and it must look suspicious."

Kirsty looked at the three OCs. "Who are they?" she asked. While walking slowly back towards the others Graham named them. Kirsty nodded and asked, "Where is Broadsound?"

"Down past Mackay somewhere," Graham replied.

"How do you know them?"

Graham described the promotion course and how they met cadets and OOCs from a dozen units on it. By then they had re-joined the others and Graham resumed trying to locate his missing mess gear. By then Sgt Grenfell had finished his shower and dressed and CSM Cleland came striding over to tell him to get 2 Platoon lined up by 1800hrs for mess parade.

Twilight was setting in by then and the temperature had at last begun to drop so that it was now quite pleasant. In an attempt to get another set of 'eating irons' Graham sought out Sergeant Bates, but she just shook her head.

"None here," she said. "You will have to wait till we get back to camp."

That made him late as by the time he returned Sgt Grenfell was calling on the platoon to line up and rebuked him. "Don't go wandering off Cpl Kirk."

"But someone has stolen my mess gear sergeant," he replied.

"You need to be more careful," Sgt Grenfell answered.

"But what will I do?"

"Borrow. Ask the cook," he replied.

CSM Cleland's voice cut across the hubbub. "Sergeant Grenfell! Get 2 Platoon moving!"

They marched across to the end door of the dining area and filed in to where the army cooks and four cadets from HQ were standing in line behind a serving bench. Graham spoke to one of the cooks who produced two plates and some cutlery from the kitchen storeroom.

"I want it back," he added.

Graham nodded with relief. It was a good meal: roast pork, baked potatoes, peas and gravy, with fruit and custard for dessert. He carried it through into a smaller annexe where eight tables with benches were set up. One each table were bowls of fruit and bottles of sauce and jam. All of 4 Section squashed around one table, Kirsty pressing against Graham's side. Feeling somewhat better, Graham began to eat.

Gwen's section took up the next table and then Stephen's at the third. 4 Platoon then began filing in. To Graham's irritation, Pigsy and Co ended up at the table diagonally opposite. As they sat down, Pigsy sneered at him.

"What are you looking at Kirk?"

Graham had actually been studying the mess gear of Pigsy and his cronies, but he just shook his head and went on eating. Suddenly a piece of soggy bread struck the side of his face. He looked up in surprise and was struck right between the eyes by several peas. Waters had flicked them and the bullies burst into laughter.

Graham sprang up. "Stop that!" he shouted.

In reply, Moynihan picked up another piece of bread and dipped it into his custard, then moved to throw it. Graham raised his arm to protect himself. As he did, he saw CSM Cleland come in from the kitchen. Hastily he pulled his arm down but as he did an orange flew past from behind him, striking Waters full in the face.

"Stop that! What the devil is going on here?" CSM Cleland bellowed.

Waters sprang up and pointed. "Sir, Kirk is throwing food at us!"

The blatant lie stunned Graham speechless for a moment. CSM Cleland glared around, then snapped, "Stop it! Corporal Kirk to you Cadet Waters. Corporal Kirk, you keep control of this mob; and your section can clean up the mess hall after the company has eaten."

"But, sir! That's not fair! I didn't do anything," Graham cried.

"Don't you argue with me, Corporal Kirk. I saw that orange come from over here. Even if you didn't throw it, one of your cadets did. You control them, and stop causing trouble," CSM Cleland snapped.

It seemed so unjust to Graham that he had to struggle to control his tongue. "Yes, sir," he replied between clenched teeth.

The smirks on the bullies' faces did nothing to ease his emotions. At that moment Sgt Grenfell and CUO Masters came in from the kitchen. Sgt Grenfell raised an eyebrow but CSM Cleland just grunted that it was sorted and stamped out. Both CUO Masters and Sgt Grenfell gave Graham calculating looks as they passed to seat themselves at one of the spare tables. For a moment Graham considered appealing to them for justice but then shook his head and sat down.

"Who threw the orange?" he hissed, looking around his section. Andrews shamefacedly owned up. Graham glared at him "Good, you can do all the dirty jobs then!" He turned back to his food. As he ate, CUO Grey and Sgt White came in and joined CUO Masters and Sgt Grenfell at their table.

The situation was further eased when Cpl Doyle's section came in. As Dimbo sat opposite Stephen's section, Stephen called out to the room, "What are those reasons why things are seen? Let me see; there's shape, spacing, shine, surface, shadow, and silhouette. Oh, and don't forget movement!"

The room erupted in laughter and Dimbo scowled and his cadets blushed. Cadet Duncan tried to make excuses and was laughed at and teased till he shut up. A discussion of the recon patrol and how it got caught broke out. Graham ignored this, just feeling the hurt to the unit's pride.

CSM Cleland had Cpl Rankin's section from 1 Platoon sent in to eat at the last vacant table. Among them were Erika Goltz and Magda Mollwitz. The two girls made smart comments to 4 Platoon, who all called back and made suggestive comments till CUO Masters snapped at them to behave. Erika then stopped to talk to Sgt White.

Bloody flirt! Graham thought sourly. *Tonight is a free night,* he thought. *Is she setting up Sgt White?* But what could he do about it? *I don't have any proof, and who could I tell?* Not the CSM at the moment, he decided. *He would just think I was getting back at someone.*

Graham blushed with private shame as he knew he was being a hypocrite. At the back of his mind was still the idea of having at least a bit with Kirsty. It all seemed very difficult, so he concentrated on eating, then hurried the section to finish so they could start working. That was an unpleasant hour, wiping tables, mopping the floor, and having scraps and rubbish picked up. Supervising kept him moving from room to room in a lather of sweat and anxiety, very conscious that CSM Cleland and all the officers were still eating and were watching.

It was 1930hrs and dark by the time the job was done to CSM Cleland's satisfaction. By then everyone else except 9 Section, who were cleaning the ablution block, had set off back. Lt Hamilton had arrived in his Land Cruiser with the piquet who had stayed to guard the camp. They were joined at the meal table by the Hutchie Men who filed quietly in out of the night after stashing their Yowie suits, webbing and radio in a corner.

Graham stood and pointed to them, then asked CSM Cleland, "Do we have to wait till they finish, CSM?"

"Yes, so relax."

A grumpy half hour followed with 4 Section bickering and blaming each other. At last the meals were all eaten and the last tables could be cleaned. The Hutchie Men were briefed by Capt Conkey and went to collect their gear. They vanished into the night again. Capt Conkey turned and told Graham to wait till he had inspected. He and CSM Cleland then walked around from building to building.

"Looks okay. Right, 4 Section, wait here till Lt Hamilton comes back. 9 Section and CSM get into the Land Cruiser."

"Oh, bloody hell!" Andrews muttered. "More waiting!"

"Your fault Andrews, so shut up!" Graham snapped.

The section sat outside the kitchen and waited. Their mood was disgruntled to say the least, knowing everyone else was back at camp having a good time, well, not everyone. Suddenly, loud yelling sounded from off to the south side of the camp. Graham knew that Heatley were camped there in the bush along a creek line half a kilometre away. The noises came from there.

Then he made sense of the sounds. The loud 'Hoo! Hoo! Hoos!' and bellows of 'Hutchie Men!' made it clear who was responsible for the uproar. "The bloody Hutchie Men are scaring the crap out of Heatley!" he cried with delight.

It was some recompense for the shame of the captured recon patrol. More loud yells punctuated by screams of fright caused the section to grin at each other and to burst out laughing.

As they were laughing, two of the cooks came out to listen. "What's going on?" one asked.

"The Hutchie Men have struck," Graham replied. Then he burst into laughter as another scream split the night. Angry officers and NCOs could be heard yelling.

The cooks laughed as well. After a minute, the noises died down. "What are you blokes doing here still?" the cook asked.

"Waiting for a vehicle to pick us up," Graham replied.

"Would you cadets like some ice cream?"

They did like, and it had strawberry topping. On top of the Hutchie Men episode that restored morale in the section, and they were laughing and joking by the time Lt Hamilton returned. He then insisted on having ice cream too, so they waited another ten minutes, amusing him with the story of the Hutchie Men. The group then climbed into the vehicle and ten minutes later were back at camp.

As he reached the bivouac area, Graham's restored good mood almost evaporated when he discovered his hutchie once again lying in the dirt. Then he shrugged. It wasn't important really. He quickly tied a rope between two trees and hung up his wet clothes and put away his gear then stood and looked around.

No lessons or exercises had been scheduled for the evening. Each platoon had lit its own campfire, except for HQ, and cadets were allowed to roam and visit. For a minute Graham stood looking around at the glow of the fires which made distinct 'islands' of light in the darkness.

Will I go anywhere, or go to bed? he wondered.

Kirsty decided that for him. She came and stood beside him. "Come to the fire," she said.

May as well, he thought, reasoning that he would be safer from Kirsty there.

They walked across to the 2 Platoon fire and sat down, to be joined by Roger and Pat. Halyday and Andrews appeared for a few minutes then walked off into the night, as did Dianne and Lucy.

Kirsty sat so close that her knee touched his. This set his body working. It also got him worrying as CUO Masters was there. So were Gwen and Barbara. Barbara gave Graham a few odd glances that got him wondering.

Is she trying to hint she likes me, or is she warning me not to misbehave? he thought. He tried to edge away from Kirsty, but she stayed right next to him, her touch getting him aroused.

Stephen arrived and began telling jokes. The story of the Hutchie Men's latest exploit was retailed, and the atmosphere improved. Sgt Grenfell arrived and CUO Masters left. Stephen gestured into the night.

"Let's go and see what is happening at the other platoons," he said.

This was agreed to and half a dozen people stood up, including Graham and Kirsty. With Stephen and Roger beside him and Barbara, Gwen and Pat following they strolled off into the darkness. Stephen suggested they see how Peter was getting on, so they detoured to HQ. HQ did not have a fire, but they found the CP manned and Peter sitting there with Cpl Parnell.

"Whatcha doin' Pete?" Stephen asked.

"Radio piquet," Peter replied.

"Why?"

"Because we have an OP down near the highway and the Hutchie Men are still out," Peter replied.

That led to another description of the Hutchie Men's latest exploit. Peter nodded. "I know. They told us that they have struck again since then. They reckon they just chased a group of Heatley girls who were walking to the dunny."

The group burst into laughter and, after talking for a few more minutes, wandered on to where 1 Platoon was camped. All the way Kirsty kept bumping against Graham, keeping him aroused. 1 Platoon campfire was even sadder than 2's. Sgt Sherry was there with half a dozen cadets but there were no jokes or acts so the visitors only stayed a few minutes before wandering back the other way along the vehicle track towards 3 Platoon where it sounded like there was more life.

On the way they met a group coming the other way. It was Harriet and Fiona and a couple of other junior cadets. The two groups stopped to yarn, and Graham stood behind Kirsty. To his delight she moved back so that she pressed against his front. That got him very excited and he glanced anxiously around to make sure no-one else could see. Even though it was dark, it wasn't that dark.

When the group continued walking, she leaned over and whispered, "I wish we could get away on our own."

"I might get out of control then," he whispered back.

"Good," she replied in a husky voice that set his pulses racing even more. The idea of actually being alone with Kirsty set him on fire, but also increased his anxiety enormously.

Fears of all the things that could go wrong began crowding into his mind: thrown out of cadets in disgrace, or if they went too far, Kirsty pregnant, or him catching some horrible rotting disease, or going to jail because she was under age.

We will just play a bit, he decided, hoping he could control both himself and the situation should the opportunity arise.

It didn't. To his annoyance, Barbara came and walked on his other side. The group arrived at 3 Platoon's fire to find an act in progress. Jokes followed. To Graham's relief, Barbara and Gwen were drawn into another group with Lofty and some cadets from HQ. CUO Masters arrived and began talking to Barbara. CUO MacAlistair and Sgt White also arrived, then more cadets. Pat joined another group.

Now, if Steve and Roger will just leave us for a few minutes we can get away on our own, Graham thought.

Over on the other side of the campfire there was a commotion and then a shout went up: "The Hutchie Men!"

Graham saw the three Hutchie Men come walking into the firelight, their camouflage pulled clear of their grinning faces. All the cadets present began cheering and calling out: "Hutchie Men! Hutchie Men!"

The Hutchie Men gave victory salutes and bowed to the applause. They then trekked on towards the 4 Platoon fire. More cadets arrived to see what the commotion was. The group followed them into the darkness. Along the way they met Magda and Stephen at once proceeded to flirt with her. At some of his suggestive comments Graham scorched with embarrassment. He also knew he was being a total hypocrite as he wanted to do exactly the same thing with Kirsty. Having Kirsty pressing against him did not help and he was aware that he was now very aroused.

Magda then nudged Stephen and said, "Come on, Steve. They don't want us here."

Stephen leered and replied, "Graham doesn't mind."

That caused Graham to blush even more fiercely. To his relief Stephen and Magda walked off into the night. *I hope Steve isn't going to be silly,* he thought. But he was in the grip of lust himself. Kirsty snuggled against him and said, "What about us?"

Graham felt his desire surge and knew he was in danger of losing control. But she was there and willing! Anxiously he looked around, wondering where Roger was. Seeing no sign of him and knowing they were now alone he took Kirsty's hand.

Without a word they set off into the dark bush.

Chapter 16

HEATED

As he and Kirsty walked hand in hand into the darkness, Graham was torn by strong emotions. He sensed that he was facing one of those crisis points that could affect his whole life and he wanted, with a feeling of quiet desperation, to get it right. The strongest force was sheer physical lust. Here was a girl who apparently wanted him to make love to her. Against that were all the fears, and his now tormented conscience.

That raised the whole issue of his promise to Capt Conkey. The dilemma filled him with misery which went a long way towards dampening his heated condition. But then Kirsty stoked the fires again by stopping and embracing him. Her mouth sought his and her body pressed eagerly against his own. Oh, it felt so good! And he wanted it so badly!

Unable to help himself he responded. All the while his mind raced, trying to find a way out that kept Kirsty happy, and which eased his conscience. She then increased the pressure and forced him into a mental corner.

"Where will we go?" she murmured.

At that Graham eased himself back and swallowed. He was now so upset he felt like he wanted to throw up. "Back to the campfire," he managed to croak. It was such an effort that he found his heart was racing and his breath came in rapid gasps.

"Oh! Spoil sport! I am just starting to enjoy myself," Kirsty said. Even in the starlight he could see she was pouting.

Graham gulped and said, "We shouldn't be here doing this. We promised not to misbehave."

"Oh, don't be such a scaredy cat! No-one is going to find out. I won't tell," Kirsty replied, petulance and frustration now clear in her voice.

"That's not the point. I promised. After camp I will do anything you want, but not now," Graham replied. Now he had said no he found it much easier.

They separated, still holding hands. Graham felt his lust draining away as the misery seeped in. *I've spoilt it now,* he thought.

"Don't you like me?" Kirsty asked, her voice quavering with emotion.

"I like you enormously. That's why I don't want us to do the wrong thing at the wrong time. Love should be wonderful and special, not dirty and sneaky," he replied.

"Oh well!" she cried, plainly exasperated. For a minute they stood in silence and Graham feared she was going to tell him to go to the devil.

He was saved from that by the beam of a powerful torch. CSM Cleland's voice called out, "What are you two doing over there?"

Transfixed by the light Graham was stunned into silence for a moment. Then he mastered the shock. He released Kirsty's hands. "Just talking, sir," he called back.

Thank God we weren't kissing! he thought. It had been a very close call.

"Go back to one of the campfires and do your talking there," CSM Cleland called, "And don't go sneaking off into the dark."

That burned at Graham's self-respect and he at once started walking. To his relief Kirsty moved with him. "That was close!" she said with a giggle as the torch was switched off.

"Too bloody close! No more of that, Kirsty," he replied.

"Not even a little kiss and cuddle?" Kirsty asked. She seemed to have recovered and accepted the situation.

If she really wants to, she can find plenty of willing partners in 4 Platoon, he mused.

They were now walking past the top of the gully leading to the 3 Platoon male latrine and were heading towards 4 Platoon's camp. Graham did not really want to go there, and he had just begun to turn left when a peculiar, strangled cry sounded out in the darkness to his right. He stopped.

"What was that?" he asked.

"What?" Kirsty said, also stopping.

The cry came again, a muffled groan and plea. Suspicion flooded Graham's mind. He started walking quickly that way. As he did, the groans came again, then the sound of hitting.

"No! Please!" gasped a voice.

Carnes! Graham thought. Instantly he broke into a run.

About 50 paces away he saw a group of figures struggling in the dark. Carnes pleaded again and again Graham heard blows and then a sharp cry of pain.

"Hoy! Stop that!" Graham shouted as he raced towards them.

By then he could see that there were at least four people. Three were struggling to hold down the fourth. At Graham's shout the group dissolved. Two fled and one sprang up and lunged at Graham. As he did, Graham noted that all three wore black balaclavas. Before Graham realised his own danger, the person had cannoned hard into him, using his shoulder and a stiff-arm to strike at him.

The blows hurt and he went down hard, clutching at the person as he did. He managed to grab a sleeve, but the person grunted savagely and lashed out with a boot, knocking Graham flat. Another punched him and then raised his boot to kick at him. Another figure arrived at the run and crashed into the kicker, knocking him over.

It was Roger. He immediately turned on Graham's first attacker. The attacker then turned and fled into the night. A torch beam briefly illuminated his running figure before it vanished into the nearest gully. Graham rolled over and got to his feet, momentarily undecided which way to go.

Groans and wails of pain from Carnes decided him. Carnes was doubled up on the ground and whimpered loudly, "Oh it hurts! It stings! It hurts!"

Graham went to him as other people came running through the dark. First to arrive was Kirsty, followed closely by Roger. Then CSM Cleland arrived, his torch lighting up the scene. In its light Graham saw that Carnes' shirt had been ripped open and his trousers and jocks had been reefed down to his boots. The boy was lying on his side clutching his genitals and crying in pain.

"What the hell is going on?" CSM Cleland demanded, sweeping the beam of his torch across Carnes, then up onto Graham and Kirsty.

"Someone has greased Carnes," Graham replied. "Three blokes. They scattered." He pointed into the darkness.

CSM Cleland at once swung his torch beam around. "Right, you two stay here and keep other people away. Lance Corporal Dunning, get one of the officers, quickly!"

Kirsty had moved to kneel beside Carnes, but Graham moved to her. "Go back, Kirsty. He will only be more embarrassed."

"What have they done?" she asked, plainly upset by Carnes' cries.

"Put something on his private parts that stings," Graham replied, "Now go back."

From the smell Graham suspected the concoction used to grease Carnes included toothpaste and insect repellent. Which, he knew from experience, had a ferocious sting on tender skin, and testicles definitely fell into the tender category. He knelt and patted Carnes' shoulder.

"I know it hurts," he said. "Just hang in there. The officers are coming." He could feel Carnes shuddering with agony as he touched him and it was obvious it was no act. The boy was in real pain.

CSM Cleland and Kirsty had meanwhile stemmed the rush of the curious and sent them back to their campfires. Graham heard a vehicle start up and a few seconds later headlights came on. The Land Cruiser came rushing across to them. It was Lt Hamilton and Lt Standish.

"What happened?" Lt Standish asked. She had a First Aid kit.

Graham quickly explained what he knew, then added, "I reckon soap and water might help Miss."

"Right. Get a washbasin and jerrycan," Lt Standish ordered.

Graham raced down to the 3 Platoon male latrine and snatched up the washbasin, soap and jerrycan there and hurried back with them. By the time he got there Capt Conkey and Lt Maclaren had also arrived. By then Carnes was nearly hysterical with pain and was shivering with violent spasms.

Lt Standish at once set to work with the soap and water, easing Carnes' hands away and soothing his trembling and agonised cries. By then Graham was feeling quite upset himself. Capt Conkey concentrated on attending to Carnes. After the initial washing Carnes began to calm down, his body still twitching as he sobbed uncontrollably.

"Hospital for him," Capt Conkey ordered. "Get him in the vehicle and get going. I will phone and warn them."

Graham was ordered, along with Roger, to help lift Carnes into the back seat of the vehicle. In the process they tried to cover him as well as they could with his clothes. Lt Standish then climbed in and held him while Lt Hamilton sprang into the driver's seat. Within a minute the vehicle was moving. As it drove off Capt Conkey used his mobile phone to call the hospital, then rang the army camp to tell the staff major of the incident. Graham could tell that he was furiously angry.

Capt Conkey snapped his phone shut and snapped at the group, "Well? What happened? Who did this?"

CSM Cleland answered. "Cpl Kirk was first here sir."

"Kirk eh? Well Cpl Kirk, what happened?" Capt Conkey demanded.

He suspects I was involved! Graham thought with dismay. He swallowed and said, "We heard screams and I ran over to find three blokes in balaclavas greasing Carnes. They ran away when I arrived."

"You weren't involved? You've got some of the grease on your hands," Capt Conkey said.

CSM Cleland's torch was shone on him. Graham glanced at his hands in sick surprise. There was black muck smeared on both. "I didn't do it, sir. I grappled with one of them and he knocked me down. Then I helped Carnes. I must have gotten it on me then."

"Oh, yeah? What were you doing out here in the darkness?" Capt Conkey demanded to know.

Graham's heart seemed to stop and give a sickening lurch. *No point lying,* he thought. *CSM Cleland saw Kirsty and me.* He said, "I was trying to get Kirsty to give me a kiss, sir."

At that Kirsty let out a cry and said, "Oh sir! That's not true! It was my fault. I asked Graham to walk with me in the dark. I wanted the kiss."

Capt Conkey shook his head. "I don't care who wanted a kiss! I will deal with that later. I want to know who greased Cadet Carnes. CSM, what did you see?"

"Sir, it wasn't Cpl Kirk or Cadet Weldon. They were further away and just talking. I told them to go back to the campfire and they were on their way when we heard the cries," CSM Cleland replied.

At that Graham felt a huge wave of relief. Capt Conkey then questioned him minutely about the three attackers. All Graham could say was that they were big male cadets wearing black balaclavas. None had spoken a word and he could not identify any of them positively. He also pulled up his shirt to show the livid bruise that had now formed where he had been kicked. By then Lt Maclaren had arrived and confirmed that the prime suspects: the Hutchie Men, and Pigsy's gang, all had strong alibis.

"I was talking to the Hutchie Men when it happened," Lt Maclaren said.

"What about Cadet Pike and his friends?" Capt Conkey asked.

Graham was sure it hadn't been any of the three bullies, or at least not Pigsy himself. Besides, he had seen Pigsy and Co only minutes before so he said, "No, sir. I saw Pigsy over at 3 Platoon." But now his mind was working. If it wasn't Pigsy, or the Hutchie Men then Carnes obviously had some secret enemy who really wanted to hurt him, but who?

Capt Conkey was very worried. "This becomes criminal assault if Carnes makes an official complaint. That will make it a matter for the civil police. Oh blast! Just what we don't need in the middle of a camp!"

Hearing that made Graham feel sorry for the captain and officers. He silently vowed to try to find out who had done it. Capt Conkey turned to the group and said, "You cadets had better come back to HQ and we will get some written statements just in case this has to be formally investigated."

CSM Cleland shone his torch on the jerrycan, soap and washbasin. "Cpl Kirk, you and LCpl Dunning take these back to the latrine on the way please."

Graham and Roger did as they were told, then set off for HQ. As they walked up the slope from the latrine Graham asked the question that had been nagging at him.

"Where were you Roger?"

"About to stop you being silly," Roger replied. That sent a rush of shame through Graham, but he was also peeved. "You don't have to be a Peeping Tom you know!"

"Maybe not, but I thought you might have needed a bit of help to stay on the straight and narrow," Roger replied.

"You mean with Kirsty?" Graham asked, appalled that his intentions were so transparently obvious.

"And with any other nice little bit that takes your fancy," Roger replied.

"Thanks very much!" Graham cried indignantly. "But I don't need you to be my conscience. Anyway, we were only talking."

"Funny way of talking," Roger replied equably. "So I thought I'd better save you from yourself."

"Mind your own bloody business!" Graham cried in outrage.

"No. I will not. I am your friend, and I know your weaknesses, so I will help look out for you," Roger replied calmly.

Roger's good intentions and strong sense of purpose quite deflated Graham's anger. "Is it that obvious?" he asked.

"You may as well carry a bloody sign," Roger replied.

Strewth! I'd better be much more circumspect in future, Graham thought with dismay. He then felt a real rush of affection for his friend.

"Thanks mate," he muttered.

By then they had arrived at the officer's fire. CUO Masters was there as well. Capt Conkey ordered them to sit separately, then began questioning them one at a time, writing down their answers. It took over an hour to do and by then Graham's bruises were throbbing. Headlights appeared along the track but the vehicle was an army staff car. The staff major responsible for all cadets in North Queensland came over to the fire.

Capt Conkey turned to the cadets. "You people can go back to your areas now. Thanks for your help."

The group walked back to 2 Platoon's camp in relative silence.

"A cup of coffee is what I need now," Roger said.

To this Graham agreed, so he and Roger collected their webbing when they reached their hutchie. The campfire there was still going but only a couple of people were sitting around it. The friends seated themselves and set about heating water. Kirsty came and sat beside Graham and then Stephen and Gwen appeared and wanted to know what had happened.

For a while they discussed the greasing and its possible outcomes. "Capt Conkey is really angry," Graham commented.

"Yeah, but Carnes is a real dope," Stephen replied.

"Maybe, but that was over the top. It was straight out vicious bullying," Graham replied. "And it will now harm the rest of us."

Sgt Grenfell appeared. "Come on you people, time for bed."

The friends packed up and moved back to their hutchies, still talking. On the way Kirsty brushed against Graham. "What do you want?" he whispered.

"Just a good night hug," she replied.

"Fair go Kirsty! We were lucky tonight," he replied. He glanced around to see where Roger was and could see no sign of him.

"Oh poo!" she muttered. Then she gestured to where two dark figures could just be seen standing at the end of a hutchie. "There's Thomo giving Krissy a good smooch."

"When everyone's asleep then," Graham replied. Secretly he was hoping she would go to sleep and he would be safe.

"Oh, alright then," Kirsty replied. She went off to her hutchie and knelt down to unroll her bedding. Graham crawled into his and did likewise. Then he sat to unlace his boots, watching Kirsty do the same. Roger returned and crawled in. The two friends then gossiped as they took off their boots and prepared for bed.

Sgt Grenfell walked around shining his torch and urging people to bed, and then to be quiet. Graham was happy to lie back in silence and try to relax. He found, to his frustration, that he couldn't stop thinking about Kirsty and that kept him very aroused. Roger just seemed to roll on his side and go to sleep but Graham found he could not drop off. Frustrated he lay and let his thoughts wander between fantasising and brooding. Determined on sleep he undid his waistband then stretched out to relax. Still sleep would not come.

An hour went by and the camp settled into silence. At 2315hrs a vehicle came driving in so Graham sat up to look. It was the Land Cruiser returning from Charters Towers hospital. People got out and Graham heard voices but could not tell if Carnes had come back with them or not. Curious to know he got up and crouched to look out. While he was peering out of the end of his hutchie he saw movement in Kirsty's and her head turned to look at him.

Oh bugger! he thought. *She's awake and she's seen me.*

Kirsty first sat up, then moved into a crouch facing him. He wanted to move back out of sight but could see that she was looking at him. *I won't go to her*, he told himself. *Be strong Kirk! Stay here.*

To his consternation, she got up and padded across to him. She bent over close to him and whispered, "I'm scared. Come and sit with me please."

Near panic and disbelief warred in Graham. So did lust, which surged in his veins. *Does she mean that or is it a ploy?* he wondered. In a feeble attempt to stop himself giving in he whispered, "What are you scared of?"

"The Hutchie Men, and things. I keep seeing things out in the bush," she replied.

Graham got anxious then lest Heatley have a raiding party sneaking in. *Or the Hutchie Men might be up to mischief,* he thought.

Unsure and very anxious he crawled out and stood up next to her. Not wanting Roger to see them together he moved to the side of the hutchie. For a minute or so they stood in silence and he stared into the dark bush down in the gully and then around the bivouac. But he could not see or hear anything other than the normal night noises of the bush. "I don't think there is anything," he replied.

To his delight and surprise, she moved to touch him, their arms rubbing together. That sent his heart rate shooting up and he looked around in alarm. *I hope nobody is looking,* he thought.

Graham fervently hoped Roger was sound asleep. He also listened very carefully for sounds that might indicate that Sgt Grenfell of CUO Masters could still be awake. He found it hard to hear because his heart was now thudding so loudly the blood seemed to swash in his skull.

Hearing nothing and now impelled by powerful physical forces he stood while desire and fear battled for control. He badly wanted physical contact with her and thought she would not object if he tried to kiss her. But there were those gnawing doubts. *If I do and she objects I am done for,* he thought.

Just as frightening was what might develop if she did not object and let him do other things. Self-knowledge of his own strong passions and urges warned him that once he started it would be difficult to stop. That they might lose control and go too far was a strong possibility. Legal, moral and medical consequences rose to cool his enthusiasm and to help him keep control.

But how to end it without upsetting her? Graham decided to play along with the scared story but even as he thought this he was disgusted with himself for being such a coward. *What a weakling you are!* he told himself.

In a last desperate effort to regain control and to do the right thing he stepped away from her.

"What's wrong" she whispered huskily.

"We shouldn't be doing this. You should go to bed," he croaked back.

Kirsty pouted. "But I want to be with you."

As Graham opened his mouth to reply a powerful torch came on, its beam slashing through the trees. Capt Conkey's voice called out.

Chapter 17

CAPTAIN CONKEY GETS ANGRY

Graham felt a rush of pure fear as the torch beam stabbed the night. Then he saw that it was aimed at two other people. Transfixed by the light were Cadet Mal Thompson and Cadet Krissy Dunstan. Both were standing near Krissy's hutchie, arms around each other. Krissy appeared to be wearing only a shirt, her white legs glowing in the torch beam.

"Stop that and get to bed, you pair!" Capt Conkey snarled, his voice tense with anger.

By then Graham had recovered from the initial shock. *He hasn't seen us!* he thought. With that he ducked down, hauling Kirsty down with him.

"Back to your hutchie," he hissed, giving her a push.

At any moment he expected to hear Capt Conkey get really mad at Mal and Kristy but all he heard was another growl to 'get to bed, your own bed, and behave yourselves or I will phone your parents and send you home tomorrow!'

As quickly but quietly as he could, Graham crawled around the far end of his hutchie, keeping it between himself and Capt Conkey, who he could hear walking towards him. Kirsty did the same thing, scuttling across to her bed and sliding onto it. With his heart hammering rapidly and his mouth dry with fear Graham slid into his hutchie and onto his sleeping bag. Trembling with anxiety, he tried to drag it over him.

Mal and Kristy might have gotten away with it, he thought but he felt sure that if Capt Conkey caught him and Kirsty he would be very angry. *They are the same rank, but I am a corporal and Kirsty is only a cadet. At the very least I could lose my stripes,* he thought anxiously.

By then Capt Conkey was very close and Graham froze. At every second he expected to be called out, or to have the torch shone on him. Neither happened and Capt Conkey walked on towards the officer's camp. It took a while for Graham to accept that he had not been seen and wasn't in trouble. Then he lay back and sighed, closing his eyes and feeling his heart still hammering.

After that he did not dare budge. He wriggled into his sleeping bag.

As he lay there and tried to relax, he could only shake his head at the closeness of the escape.

Sleep came in a mix of emotions and doubts.

* * *

Day 5 began as usual with a check parade. Graham woke up feeling lightheaded and alert. He was surprised he didn't feel tired, but noted that Kirsty looked a wreck: hair all messed up and eyes puffy and bleary. Unsure if she regretted their actions the night before, he anxiously met her eye and forced a smile. To his relief, she smiled back.

Sgt Grenfell bellowed to get out on parade, so Graham hurried, unable to meet Roger's eye because of his guilty conscience. To hide this, Graham went and roused at Halyday and Andrews to hurry them out. This time 4 Section was the first ready. Stephen's was last. He heard Stephen calling, "Hurry up Cadet Dunstan!"

Krissy called back, "I can't find my pants."

"Ask Thomo!" called LCpl Lucas.

That caused a ripple of laughter from the rest of the section, quelled by Sgt Grenfell's angry bellow. Graham met Kirsty's eye and blushed fiercely with guilt. To his annoyance, she smiled. At last Krissy found some trousers and the platoon marched to the parade area.

CSM Cleland was in a savage mood too. He barked his orders and bawled out anyone who made mistakes. This got them all doing good drill very quickly. When he called for reports CSM Cleland even rebuked Sgt White for poor drill. That was so unusual that Graham stared in surprise. He knew the CSM should not correct the sergeants in front of the troops. CSM Cleland then called, "Cadet Thompson, Cadet Dunstan, after parade report to the OC."

They are in trouble for fraternising, Graham thought.

From behind him Stephen whispered, "Storms today!"

Gwen replied, "After last night I'm not surprised."

"Silence in the ranks!" growled Sgt Grenfell out of the side of his mouth.

When the sergeants gave their reports Graham listened intently, curious to know what had become of Carnes. He heard Sgt Gayney say, "Posted strength eleven, on parade ten, one sick."

Does that mean Carnes isn't in hospital? he wondered.

CSM Cleland then reminded the company that they were moving that day and were to have everything packed by 0730hrs. He then handed back to the sergeants. As they marched back to their area past HQ, Graham noted a person lying in a hutchie. It was Carnes.

He's still here, poor bugger! He should be sent home.

After being fallen out Graham strode straight over to the 4 Platoon latrine for a pee. He was in such a mood that he did not care who was there. In fact, he met LCpl Telford who told him that the Hutchie Men were about to head off on patrol as soon as they had eaten breakfast.

Mess parade followed. Kirsty stood behind Graham and then sat next to him while they ate but she looked tired and did very little talking. Afterwards they walked back to the hutchies in relative silence. Roger walked with them so there was no chance for a private conversation. The next thing was to pack up. Graham and Roger dropped their hutchie and dragged it aside, then folded it. Next the bedding was rolled up into their packs and everything needed for three days transferred from their kit bags to their packs. Graham was then kept busy walking around the section ensuring they were packing the right things in the correct places.

By 0730hrs the section's packs were placed in a neat line and the section was busy filling water bottles. While they did, they saw Thomo and Krissy come walking back from a meeting with the OC and CSM. Both looked unhappy. Roger pointed and said, "What did they do?"

Before he thought about it, Graham answered, "The OC caught them kissing after lights out."

Roger gave Graham a very sharp look. "How do you know that?"

Graham realised he had made a mistake, but he decided not to lie to his friend. "Because I saw it. I was talking to Kirsty."

Roger shook his head. "You be careful, or you will be demoted and spend the rest of the camp digging dunnies."

"I will be careful! We didn't do anything," Graham replied. But he blushed and thought of the classic excuse of 'We were only talking' and knew it was not what he had been thinking of doing.

Roger just made a face and shook his head, then went to ask Thomo what had happened. He then told Graham. The pair had been reprimanded, reminded of the rules and been given the job of digging latrines or filling them in for the next two days.

After that, the platoon was moved on parade. As they did Graham noted a miserable looking Carnes sitting in the CP beside an army radio. CSM Cleland 'right dressed' the company and checked the number on parade, then handed over to a grim-faced Capt Conkey.

That Capt Conkey was deeply angry was evident from both his body language and the tone of his words. And he did not mince them. "Last night," he shouted, "Three cowardly bullies attacked and greased Cadet Carnes. He was so badly burned by the liquids they used that he had to be taken to hospital for treatment."

He paused, glared and pointed, then bellowed, "Wipe that smirk off your face Cadet Poschalk! If you think it is funny, then go and get your bags and we will send you home now! And that goes for any of you. I have spoken to Cadet Carnes' parents and they are considering asking the police to investigate. That could mean criminal charges of assault! I am really angry about this. There has been too much nonsense already but this is just cowardly and stupid."

He paused and ran his eyes over the company. The anger in them made Graham feel like flinching, even though he was innocent. Capt Conkey went on, "Worse still we have had to report the incident to Cadet HQ in Townsville, and they have reported it to AAC HQ in Canberra. The whole affair makes the unit look very bad. When we find out who carried out this attack, I will give them a dishonourable discharge and send them packing within the hour, and I will pass their name to both the army and the police."

There was a shudder of dismay through the ranks and Graham shook his head but then nodded it in agreement. Capt Conkey waited to give time for his words to sink in, then said, "And I warn you, if there is any more of that sort of harmful nonsense the persons involved will also be chucked out of cadets. I will not have the good name of this unit destroyed by malicious fools! Remember that the officers have given up their holidays to be here so don't make things harder. And remember you have all promised to me personally to behave."

Graham flushed with shame at that and felt sure that Capt Conkey had been staring straight at him when he had said these words. He berated himself for being so weak and resolved to do better in future.

Capt Conkey then handed back to the CSM and told him to sit the company in section lines. When that was done new photocopied maps of the area were handed to the corporals and Capt Conkey organised and briefed them for the orienteering exercise. This was run as a 'treasure hunt' and the results counted as part of the annual section competition. Graham had not thought much about the section competition and realised with a jolt that he probably had a lot of leeway to make up.

If I want to get to be a sergeant it might help to have the best section, he thought.

The treasure hunt was also a race that required a team effort because all the clues were in some sort of code. Capt Conkey handed out code sheets and an Instruction sheet explaining the various codes used. That made Graham anxious as he knew he was competing with Peter.

He is a whiz at this sort of thing, he thought unhappily.

What made it difficult was that there were a dozen messages to decode but at least seven of them all appeared the same: letters in groups of three as 'Trigrams' but all arranged by different methods.

Having handed out all the necessary stores Capt Conkey then nominated a CUO or sergeant to each section. These came from a different platoon and were there for fairness and safety. The rules also insisted that sections move together and that no work could begin on a new clue until every member of a section was there. The 'DS' for 4 Section was Sgt Yeldham. That did not please Graham because he did not particularly like him.

By the time Capt Conkey read out the first clue in the Phonetic Alphabet Graham was sweating with anxiety. It was also becoming warm and promised to be another hot day. Certainly, there wasn't a cloud in the sky. As soon as he had the message copied down Graham called on the section to get up and follow him. He moved them 25 metres away and then sat them down.

"Take out your notebooks and copy this down," he ordered.

"I haven't got a notebook," replied Andrews.

"Nor have I," added Dianne.

"Why not? You were told to bring one to camp," Graham replied.

Then he realised he was wasting time. He tore several pages out of his own notebook and passed his spare pencil to Dianne. Roger gave Andrews a pencil. The message was letters in Trigrams and Graham now read them out. To his annoyance he found that neither Andrews nor Halyday understood what he meant.

As quickly as he could he explained, then said, "Now, Roger, you do the 'Alternate letters' method. Pat, you do the 'every second letter' method. Kirsty, you use the Trigram sheet. Lucy, you use the codewheel. Dianne, you try the 'writing normally but grouping' method. Halyday, you try 'writing backwards'."

"But I can't write backwards," Halyday cried.

"Can't write at all!" teased Andrews.

"Stop the teasing Cadet Andrews!" Graham snapped. He shook his head in exasperation and turned to Halyday. "You don't write backwards. You take the last letter and put it first, then the second last and put it second, and so on till you see if it makes a word."

"What about me?" Andrews asked.

"Help Halyday," Graham cried. He then set to work writing out two alphabets along the edges of two pages. These he was then able to slide them up and down beside each other, in the same manner as the code wheel worked. Very quickly he realised that one of the alphabets needed to be double. While he was doing this, he was dismayed to see that Gwen's section had cracked the message and was on the move.

The direction they went in at least gave a clue to the sorts of words to look for. Graham set to work moving the letters one to the right so that A became B and so on. As he wrote, his alarm was increased when Bannister's section set off, followed almost immediately by Peter's.

"Keep working!" Graham called, seeing that Andrews had stopped to watch.

Then Harriet's section moved away, followed by Stephen's. That irked Graham and he broke into a sweat. *It must be easy to work out,* he thought. He hadn't seen any of the people in the other sections using their codewheel or code sheet, so he stopped and thought. *I will try backwards,* he decided.

As quickly as he could, he began to copy the message placing the last letter first and then reversing each letter's place. Almost at once a word began to appear. A wave of exhilaration swept through Graham.

"Backwards! That is the method."

"So why am I being made to do it if you are too?" Andrews asked.

Graham did not answer. Instead, he rapidly decoded the message, then sprang up and showed it to Sgt Yeldham. Sgt Yeldham shook his head. "You have to write it out neatly so I can read it."

Graham opened his mouth to protest, then gritted his teeth and quickly re-wrote the message. This time Yeldham nodded and Graham said, "Come on 4 Section! Get up and move! Let's go!"

Andrews and Halyday muttered and grumbled and were last up. Roger helped urge them all along. They set off at a fast walk across the top of Sandy Ridge. Almost at once Cpl Gallagher called on his section to get up and move. As quickly as he could walk Graham hurried his section down into the hollow where Lt McEwen had conducted the static observation and on up to the flat tongue of rocks. There were already five sections there and, to Graham's dismay, he saw Gwen's section get up and head off on the second leg even before he had arrived.

After copying the message, Graham got the whole section to copy it.

"Don't see why I should bother," Andrews grumbled. "If you are going to do it too."

"Oh, please co-operate," Graham said. He didn't want a bickering match to bring the teamwork unstuck.

By then Peter's section was also on the move, followed within a minute by Bannister's. *Oh, come on!* Graham thought anxiously.

This time he concentrated on checking whether the alphabet had been moved on to the right or left and allowed the others to work at the tasks he had given them. Most of his energy was then used up in keeping Andrews, Lucy and Kirsty at their tasks. Kirsty looked very tired and was in a bad mood. He did not dare annoy her by trying to urge her to work faster.

Crane's section arrived. Harriet's and then Stephen's left. Then Gallagher's also moved, passing Graham's. "Oh, come on!" he urged. "Just try the first four or five letters. If it isn't working, try something else!"

Then Kirsty spoke up. "It's this Trigram sheet."

That annoyed Graham a bit because, when he looked at it, it was both obvious and easy. As quickly as possible he copied the message neatly, aware that Crane had overheard Kirsty and was also now decoding the message. Worse still, two more sections were hurrying across the dip towards them: Rankin's and Cpl Parnell's.

4 Section set off with Crane's hot on their heels. The route led them north on a compass bearing to a creek junction in the gullies leading down from Sandy Ridge. On the way they hurried past the odd formation

looking like a railway embankment washed out by floods. Graham could not decide whether it was a natural 'dyke' or an old dam constructed by miners in the 19th Century.

By the time they reached the next clue Gwen's section had already left and Capt Conkey was visible hurrying after them. Peter's section set off as Graham arrived. That all made him feel very anxious and flustered. Once again, he quickly copied the message, then got the section to make copies.

"Stop talking and concentrate on your own task!" he cried as Dianne and Lucy began talking.

As they did Graham's impatience increased as first Bannister's, then Stephen's and Harriet's sections all got up and hurried on ahead. As they did Graham felt his hopes of doing well sinking. Then Roger handed him a neatly printed message.

"Alternate letters," Roger explained. "That is the complete message."

"Good on you Roger!" Graham cried. He sprang up and showed it to Sgt Yeldham who was busy talking to Sgt White and did not seem inclined to hurry.

The section set off down the dry creek and angled across the hillslope on a compass bearing to end up at the junction of the road to Canning Junction. Lt Maclaren was there with a safety vehicle and water jerries so Graham told his cadets to refill their water bottles as they were all perspiring in the heat. While they did that he copied the message, noting with satisfaction that all the sections ahead of them were still there.

"Must be a hard one," he muttered, then focused on getting them all to work at their allotted task.

Then Gwen's section got up and moved, causing the sinking failure feeling to seep in again. Soon afterwards Peter's section set off. Minutes ticked by and Graham determined that the message was not in any of the easy methods.

"It isn't backwards, or grouping, or every second letter, or alternate letters, and it isn't the Trigrams so it must be the code wheel," he said.

He had already tried moving A to B and A to Z so now he concentrated on working around the Alphabet on the code wheel. He did C while Lucy and Dianne did D on the codewheel. Then he tried five letters of E and Lucy started on F.

"It's 'F'," Lucy said delightedly. Graham at once set his two

Alphabets to F and began working on the second half of the message while Roger wrote it down. "Kirsty, start making a neat copy while we decode," Graham ordered.

By teamwork the message was cracked but not before both Stephen's and Gallagher's sections had moved off. Graham showed Sgt Yeldham and then got the section moving. It was a compass bearing and distance, but he did not need it as the other 2 Sections were walking ahead of them. They hurried after them, with Andrews and Lucy starting to trail behind and mumble about blisters and heat.

The leg took them only 500m, back across the same dry creek to a big Burdekin Plum tree. The next message was coloured naval flags drawn on a sheet of paper and Graham was able to decode it in seconds. Unfortunately, so had all the sections ahead of them and they had all gone by the time he showed it to Sgt Yeldham. By then Harriet's and Bannister's sections were arriving.

"Come on, we have moved up from sixth to fifth," Graham urged.

He now badly wanted to stay in the front half of the company but could see two more sections hurrying across from Lt Maclaren's vehicle. The next leg was only 150 metres: across the flat, down over the dry creek and up to the shed where Graham had handed Carnes over to Capt Conkey during the Navex. The shed was visible from the tree, so they just puffed up the slope without navigating.

By then the first 4 Sections had already moved off. *Must be easy,* Graham reasoned, and it was. The message was in 'pig pen' code and only took 2 minutes to decode. By then both Harriet's and Bannister's had arrived, and Brown's and Crane's could be seen coming up the slope.

The message took them north along the road for 500 metres to the Canning River. It was a hot walk and the section strung out in the heat and it took all of Graham's urging to encourage them. He had to resist the impulse to shout angrily at them. The road curved around the base of the large, low hill nicknamed 'Black Knoll' and Graham glimpsed the actual 'knoll' of black rocks on top amid the scattered ironbarks.

The Canning was a pleasant surprise. The river was about 200 metres wide and the steep banks were lined with a dense growth of trees and rubber vines. Most of the riverbed was dry, white sand which was almost blinding in the sunlight but the ten metres closest to their bank was water. The water was crystal clear and only about knee deep. The road crossed the riverbed on a long, low concrete causeway which had a trickle of water flowing over it.

The message was in Morse Code, but even so Gwen, Peter and Stephen had already gone on the next leg and Gallagher left while Graham was still copying the message. This turned out to be a very frustrating and disheartening stop because the message just would not seem to come out, at least not to Sgt Yeldham's satisfaction, and Bannister moved ahead of Graham again. Worse still, Harriet, Brown and Crane were all there before Graham finally realised he had made a mistake in his copying of the dots and dashes. Blushing at the mistake and feeling angry and ashamed he quickly corrected the message and set off.

The route led up a winding narrow gully which was in fact the lower end of the dry creeks flowing down from Sandy Ridge. This section of the gully was deep, and the banks had a thick tangle of rubber vines on them as far up as the junction which had been the half-way point on the observation course the previous day. It was stiflingly hot in the gully and Graham found he was very thirsty. Both Kirsty and Lucy looked very red in the face and he insisted they drink.

The next message was taped to a rock in the creek bed. It was in Trigram code and this time Kirsty recognised it in seconds and they hurried on, the sections still in the same order. The leg was only a hundred metres, up onto the bare top of the North Gravel Scrape. To Graham's surprise Gwen and Peter were only just leaving and the other sections were all still there. Lt Hamilton had a safety vehicle there with more water, so Graham told the section to refill their water bottles and to have a big drink while he copied the message.

By the time that was done Stephen's and Gallagher's sections were on the move, but this time Dianne worked out the method was grouping and they managed to move off ahead of Bannister's section.

We are now fifth again, Graham thought. *Maybe we are in with a chance?*

Chapter 18

HOT GOING

The ninth leg led up a long, gentle and open ridge to a gate in the fence that ran east-west across the area. Along the way the heat was reflected up from the sand and bare earth so fiercely that Graham found himself parched. He wiped sweat from his face and drained his second last water bottle. Grumbling became endemic in the section but Roger helped to urge them to keep on trying. Concern about heat exhaustion kept Graham glancing at the others. Lucy worried him the most as she seemed to be very pale. She was still perspiring so he hoped she wasn't getting sick.

At the next clue, Graham found only Stephen's and Gallagher's sections. Gwen's and Peter's had already moved on. *We won't catch them,* he thought ruefully. The message was a long one in Trigrams and that discouraged Graham as well. He copied it and sat the section in the shade of a tree, then started them working.

Three more sections arrived: Harriet's, Bannister's, and Rankin's. Rankin's was a real surprise as Graham had not seen them since the start. They seemed to be all fired up and were determined to overtake those ahead of them. That got Graham even more anxious.

"Come on people. We are in the running for third if we try," he urged. "Only check four letters. If it isn't turning into a word by then change the method."

To speed things up, he set to work on the 'random' letters method. By crossing out every second letter he quickly established that that was the method used. "Kirsty, you do this part of it, Roger, you do the next line Halyday, you do the last line. Dianne, you copy it out neatly as we do it," he ordered.

The teamwork did it and they had the answer in two minutes. Graham checked his watch and noted with dismay it was coming up to 1100hrs. He knew that the exercise had to be all over by 1200hrs.

There are probably only two or three legs left, he thought.

By then Stephen had his section moving. Gallagher's also stood up and started off at the same time as Graham's. There was a scramble down into the dry creek and up onto the wide grassy ridge between the two creeks. CUO Grey ended this by yelling at them to stay in section groups. That slowed both Graham and Gallagher because Andrews and Lucy were straggling behind and Gallagher had two cadets trailing as well.

Checkpoint 11 was on the power pole which had been a checkpoint on both the day and night Navexes. It was in numbers and at that Graham almost jumped with relief. It could only be from the one-page double-digit code sheet or from the numerical place of the letters of the Alphabet. He told Roger to try the code sheet with Dianne while he asked Kirsty to help him. As he had already numbered the letters on one of his notebook pages, he was able to read the letters almost as fast as he wrote them down. It was the method and within four minutes he had his section moving, leaving a glum faced Gallagher behind. Graham found himself moving neck and neck with Stephen.

As they moved off, Rankin's and Bannister's sections came hurrying up and Graham glimpsed at least two more sections back at the gate on the other ridge. Graham wasn't sure how many sections were ahead of them, but he was feeling a lot better.

We are well up in the front half of the company at least, he thought.

It was only when they reached a jerrycan with a message taped on it at the point where the ridge reached the Scrubby Creek track near 4 Platoon's bivouac site that he realised there were only two sections ahead of them: Gwen's and Peter's. He was unsure which was leading as both were clustered up near the officer's camp on the crest of Sandy Ridge.

It now became a feverish race against Stephen's section, the two friends exchanging glances and urging their cadets on. It was the Trigram code sheet and Kirsty had it within a minute. By the time she had it written out, Rankin's section had come puffing and sweating up the ridge at the run with Bannister's hot on their heels. To Graham's chagrin, Stephen's section suddenly set off. As quickly as they could, he got the message finished and shown to Sgt Yeldham. Sgt Yeldham scowled but nodded.

"Come on, run!" Graham cried. He looked back and saw Andrews and Lucy were only walking. Before he could yell again, he was surprised to hear Halyday yell at them.

"Oh, run please! Look, it is only just up to the officers. Come on, help us. We might come third or second if you do."

Roger and Kirsty both moved to trot beside Andrews and Lucy to encourage them and the section hurried across the grassy flat. Stephen's section saw them coming and broke into a run to try to maintain their lead. Both sections arrived at the last clue gasping and sweating but together. Graham saw that Capt Conkey was standing watching with Lt Standish and that spurred him on to a last effort.

It was numbers again, and Halyday snatched the codesheet off Dianne and quickly began to read out words and letters. He was right. As they wrote down the message Graham was in a fever of impatience as he could hear Stephen's section doing the same thing. Rankin's section came running in then, followed by Bannister's and Gallagher's.

In the end it was a frantic dash with the final message to Capt Conkey. Graham beat Stephen by a couple of running paces. Capt Conkey looked at the message and nodded.

"Good, third place. Well done, Cpl Kirk."

At that Graham glowed with achievement. He grinned at his cadets and said loudly, "Well done 4 Section. Great team effort."

They smiled back and he led them over to the big tree where Gwen's and Peter's sections sat. "Who won?" he asked Peter as they arrived.

"Who do you think? Headquarters of course," Peter replied.

Gwen poked her tongue and laughed. "Not by much!"

Stephen's section joined them, and the friends sat and yarned. To Graham's relief, Stephen did not seem to resent being beaten and they talked happily. After a while Peter stood up and excused himself.

"I just want to check that the radio piquet has worked okay," he explained. He went over to the CP, which Graham saw was still manned by Carnes and Rundle. A few minutes later Peter came back. "The Hutchie Men have located St Michael's. They are on their way back now."

"Where are St Michael's?" Graham asked.

"At an airfield over beyond the army camp," Peter replied. Graham had seen the airfield on the map but had never been to it. He knew that 4 Platoon and some members of HQ were setting out after lunch to sneak up and do a recon, ready for a night raid and he was aware that he was very jealous. It was exactly the sort of thing he burned to do.

The other sections straggled in over the next half hour and were seated in the shade. Graham allowed the girls to go to the toilet and emptied the last of his four water bottles and still felt thirsty. It was now very hot, the temperature in the mid-thirties, the tropical sun blazing down from a clear sky.

To almost universal surprise Dimbo's section was neither lost, not last. They came in second last but made it. The unfortunate last was Cpl Griffin's section from 4 Platoon. Graham overheard Sgt Grenfell, who had been with them as DS, describe them to CUO Masters as, 'a real pack of noddies!' That made Graham feel even better.

When all were present CSM Cleland checked with the sergeants that no-one was missing, then called them to sit to attention. He handed over to Capt Conkey who then presented prizes. Capt Conkey reminded them of the story that the area had once been the stamping ground of a notorious bushranger: Captain Flashlight.

"Capt Flashlight," he said, "used to rob the stagecoaches carrying gold from Charters Towers back in the 19th Century. He liked to camp along the banks of the rivers, and it is along the rivers where the wildlife lives. Very common along the river are frogs. 4 Section did not find the treasure, but they did win the frogs by coming third. Corporal Kirk, come out and collect your prize."

Graham stood up and walked over to Capt Conkey who was handed a packet of Chocolate Frogs by Lt Maclaren. Feeling both proud and embarrassed Graham shook hands with Capt Conkey and accepted the frogs. He then walked back to sit down, aware that half the company was clapping and the other half sneering or jeering.

Capt Conkey then went on: "All those frogs along the river attract snakes, who love to eat fat, juicy frogs. Second prize is to 5 Section, Corporal Copeland."

Gwen went out to receive a large packet of 'Jelly Snakes'. That caused Kirsty to say, "Aw! I'd rather have the snakes."

At that Andrews retorted, "I'll bet you would!"

Graham blushed with guilty shame but also flared with anger, which he knew was jealousy. "None of that sort of talk Cadet Andrews!" he hissed, hoping the officers hadn't heard. He also blushed again, knowing he was being a total hypocrite.

First prize was to Peter's Signal Section. They got a large packet full of gold wrapped chocolate honeycomb 'Crunchie' bars. The win was applauded and obviously did not cause any great jealousy or resentment. Capt Conkey then reminded them that were moving after lunch and that

4 Platoon would get orders as soon as the Hutchie Men had returned to report. Graham noted that even Capt Conkey now called them the Hutchie Men. As though on cue four shapeless, shaggy bundles of camouflage came up out of the gully near 2 Platoon's area.

"Hutchie Men!" Cadet Halyday cried.

The company burst into spontaneous applause. The shaggy camouflaged heaps stopped, then bowed and waved their arms. Capt Conkey let the company cheer for a minute, then called for silence.

"Alright Cpl Forman, get the Hutchie Men to fill out a patrol report, and make sure they mark things accurately on the new map enlargement. CSM, take charge of the others and get ready for lunch. Company Orders Group in one hour, that is all. Carry on."

CSM Cleland ordered the sergeants to move their platoons back to their areas and to get ready for lunch. Graham handed out the Chocolate Frogs but they were almost liquid from the heat, so he just packed his in his basic pouch. Lunch was nothing special, just sandwiches and cordial. During it Peter came and sat with Graham, Roger and Stephen. The talk drifted to discussing the exercise that was about to begin. As Graham understood it, the junior platoons were to move to a new location and Heatley Cadet Unit was to move forward from the army camp and try to find them and then attempt to infiltrate. At the same time 4 Platoon and some of HQ were to carry out a raid on St Michael's at the airfield, hitting Heatley on the way home. Peter was going on the raid.

Graham drained his cup and said, "I wish I was going with you."

"I wish I didn't have to take Carnes with me," Peter replied.

"Carnes! Surely he's not being sent out on something like this?" Graham asked in surprise.

Peter nodded. "Capt Conkey said he was to go. He is a signaller now."

Graham shook his head. "He should have been sent home."

"I agree," Peter replied. "But apparently he can't be."

"Why not?"

"I overheard Capt Conkey say that he had contacted the parents and they are on holiday at Hamilton Island and would not cancel their bookings. So there is no-one at home to take Carnes to and the parents won't come and get him."

"That's a bit bloody unfair!" Roger cried.

Peter nodded. "Capt Conkey thought so. He really blew his stack about it when he was explaining the situation to the officers. 'We aren't a bloody child-minding service!' he said. He was pretty angry. He then said that the father had told him, the boy must stay and it would make a man of him."

"Poor bloody kid!" Graham said, shaking his head sadly.

As he did, he thought of his own parents and those of his friends and he found himself unable to imagine what it might be like to have parents that didn't care. *I am bloody lucky!* he thought.

The conversation was interrupted by CSM Cleland calling on the company Orders Group to assemble. Peter hurried to finish his meal and left them. Sergeants began to urge the platoons to hurry up as well.

"We want to be gone from here before Heatley's patrols arrive," Sgt Grenfell said.

After that it was all rush, rush. Gear was packed, water bottles refilled, and kitbags piled beside the vehicles for transport. Graham was pleasantly surprised to note that his section worked willingly and were all ready first. Even Halyday and Andrews seemed to cheerfully co-operate.

They are developing into a good section, Graham thought.

At 1305 CUO Masters came back. He called the section commanders and Sgt Grenfell in, then told Stephen to post two sentries facing down towards the highway.

"There shouldn't be anything to see yet," CUO Masters added. "The OCs of all units agreed that no-one would move before thirteen hundred."

When Stephen returned from doing that CUO Masters gave the orders for the move and sent them off to explain it to their cadets. As they were doing that, the HQ Group came past. Sgt Gayney was leading them. Graham gave Peter a 'thumbs up' and wished him luck. He then noted Carnes, now carrying a radio as well as his pack.

Poor bugger! He looks really miserable. I hope he doesn't break down on them.

The Hutchie Men moved next, their numbers increased to five by adding the Corporal Storeman, Vince Brookes. They were also carrying their packs, as was 4 Platoon when they set off into the bush towards the highway. Thommo and Krissy Dunstan were sent by the CSM to fill in the latrines. The remaining members of HQ, under command of the CQMS, Sgt Bates, moved to load stores and kit bags onto vehicles. As soon as Thommo and Krissy returned and handed their shovels back to the Q these were loaded. After that was done the vehicles moved off.

CUO Masters stood up and shrugged on his pack. "Time to go. Packs on 2 Platoon."

Excitement now began to grip Graham. He knew he was to lead a patrol that night and his mind was already dwelling on that. The cadets stood in line and adjusted their gear. Sgt Grenfell walked along from the rear counting them, then reported to CUO Masters they were all there. That was a source of some satisfaction as Graham noted two members of 3 Platoon and one from 1 Platoon who were 'too sick' to do the march. These were now sitting with a radio at the otherwise deserted HQ location.

2 Platoon was the first to move. As they marched across the Sandy Ridge track and down into the gullies near where the 4 Platoon latrine had been 1 Platoon were only lining up and 3 Platoon were still milling around in their area with Sgt Yeldham shouting angrily.

The platoon moved on a compass course. Their route took them northwards down past the rocky dyke and through the area where the dry gullies came together, then along beside the dry creek to near the Burdekin Plum Tree which had been a check point for both the day Navex and the treasure hunt.

Halyday, who was walking in the middle of the section, called out to Graham as they crossed the dry creek and began climbing the slope to the cattle grid near the shed. "If we'd known we could have stayed here this morning."

"Or at least brought our packs," Andrews added.

All the way along members of the section had been making little jokes and none had really grumbled, despite the heat. That lifted Graham's spirits even more and he knew he was really starting to enjoy himself. There were problems, however. CUO Masters halted the platoon and walked back to investigate. It transpired that several cadets were having trouble carrying their packs in the heat.

Graham took the opportunity to walk back along his section to check on each one and to get them to drink. "Anyone need a hand?" he asked.

A couple did. Lucy was visibly wilting in the heat, so Graham took her pack and hung it on his front. To his surprise Halyday took Dianne's pack and Roger took Andrews'. CUO Masters came back wearing a second pack as well.

"Let's move it," he said. "Here comes One Platoon and we don't want them to beat us." He then got the line moving.

The steep little slope up to the cattle grid really tested Graham and he found he was puffing and perspiring by the time he reached it. However not for anything would Graham have slowed down or admitted he was having difficulties as he could see Capt Conkey and CSM Cleland were standing there. 1 Platoon was now visible only a hundred paces back.

As the platoon stepped carefully across the steel rails of the cattle grid Capt Conkey congratulated CUO Masters on how well the platoon was doing. But then Graham heard Capt Conkey mutter angrily, "What the devil is 3 Platoon up to! They shouldn't be walking along the road like that! Heatley will see them from miles away if they have a patrol in the area."

Graham glanced over his shoulder and saw what Capt Conkey meant. From the grid he could see well over a kilometre back up the road all the way to Sandy Ridge and 3 Platoon were tramping down the road in clear view.

At the shed twenty metres further on CUO Masters turned left and led the platoon up a rough vehicle track. This ran up a long, open spur. The ground was studded with football sized rocks and almost bare of grass. Only a few scattered ironbarks gave any shade or sign of greenery.

As Graham sweated and puffed up the slope, he caught sight of their objective 300 metres away: Black Knoll.

Chapter 19

BLACK KNOLL

The ridge up which the platoon was trudging was not very steep, but it went on and on. Close on the left was the fence line which ran up from the grid near the shed and vanished over the wide, flat crest ahead. On the right was a rock-studded re-entrant with a similar long ridge running up parallel beyond it. The actual 'knoll', a pile of black coloured rocks and boulders, was at the top end of this second ridge. Between the flat crest ahead and the actual knoll was a gentle saddle across the head of the re-entrant.

By the time they were halfway up Graham was gasping and wondering if he could make it. The sheer weight of the second pack was dragging painfully at his shoulder muscles but he did not want to give up and admit in front of the others that he was too weak to carry it. He glanced back and noted that Halyday had been unable to carry his second pack. It was now being shared with Roger, who was walking beside him.

As they neared the top of the flat crest, Graham saw three vehicles parked there, just over the rise. Lt Hamilton, Lt Maclaren, and Lt Standish were busy unloading a Land Cruiser. A row of water jerrycans and a pile of kitbags stood beside it. Lt Maclaren directed the platoon to turn right. They headed for the main knoll.

As they trudged across the low saddle along a cattle pad, Graham noted that the main knoll was about ten metres higher. The saddle was over a hundred metres wide. A second fence ran north-south over on their left. It came from behind the knoll over on their left and ran to meet the first fence at right angles beyond the parked vehicles.

The climb up past several piles of rocks to the side of the knoll was a final sharp test of Graham's grit. It took an effort of willpower, but he made it, to arrive gasping on a relatively flat area at the top of the second ridge. To Graham's great relief, CUO Masters told them to drop their packs and to sit. Gwen was ordered to post two sentries facing east down the second ridge. The platoon then relaxed and waited.

As they waited, Lt Maclaren's Land Rover and Lt Hamilton's Landcruiser both drove back down the first ridge towards Sandy Ridge. Graham could see where Sandy Ridge was but the trees on its slope hid the ground. Then 1 Platoon came puffing and sweating around the pile of boulders and past 2 Platoon. They dropped their packs on the far side of the flat area along what Graham knew to be the top of a steep drop below which was the Canning River. About a kilometre away, clearly visible over the tops of the trees lining the far bank of the river, was the homestead and outbuildings of 'Canning Park' Station.

Capt Conkey, CSM Cleland and Cadet James, a signaller with a radio, came walking around from the saddle and stopped on a small flat area right below the main boulders. All were wearing packs which they dropped. Capt Conkey then checked his watch and looked impatiently back towards the first ridge. That prompted Graham to glance at his own watch. It was almost 1500hrs and he marvelled that it had taken nearly 40 minutes to walk only 2 kilometres. Because the four friends did hikes almost every month, he was more used to covering a kilometre in about 12 to 15 minutes.

CSM Cleland walked over and spoke to CUO Masters who set off over to where Capt Conkey waited. CSM Cleland then walked on to 1 Platoon and collected CUO McAlistair. The two walked back to join Capt Conkey, who was now looking distinctly grumpy. The reason became obvious when 3 Platoon at last straggled into view.

"CUO Mitrovitch, leave Sgt Yeldham to look after your platoon and come here for orders," Capt Conkey called.

CUO Mitrovitch looked embarrassed and stepped out of line, pointing to the fence line along the western edge of the flat. As she made her way up to join Capt Conkey and the others, Graham saw Lt Maclaren's Land Rover come back up the first ridge. Capt Conkey seated the CUOs and CSM facing him and began giving Verbal Orders. As he did, Lt Maclaren, Lt McEwen, Lt Standish, Sgt Bates and the three 'sick' cadets arrived to join them.

Halyday became restless "What are we doing now?" he asked.

"Waiting for orders," Graham replied. "So don't complain. Just get all the rest you can because we could be awake most of the night. Don't forget we are going out on patrol."

As he said that, Graham's gaze travelled down the slope to where the shed was just visible, then up to the tree-covered crest of Sandy Ridge. A tingle of excitement ran through him and he was amazed at how his imagination could suddenly invest Sandy Ridge with an aura of the unknown and of hostility. But just being told that it was now 'enemy territory' for the exercise had that effect.

This was reinforced when Cadet James called to Capt Conkey that the Hutchie Men had sighted about sixty cadets with yellow shoulder flashes moving up onto Sandy Ridge from the highway.

That will be Heatley, Graham thought.

He found he was looking forward to the inter-unit exercise. Which, he knew, was to be followed by a second exercise in a couple of days' time, but the details had not yet been explained. His attention then wandered back to Kirsty, who had begun talking to him and was quickly recovering from the march. She joked and smiled, and he knew she was teasing and flirting.

She must still like me, he decided.

That both boosted his ego and aroused his interest, but also raised his concerns about having enough self-control not to let things get out of hand. At that moment he was more interested in the 'military' situation. However, he talked to her while they waited. While they chatted, the others lay back and tried to sleep, using their packs as pillows.

There was a stir as the Company Orders Group broke up. Graham expected CUO Masters to call the platoon together but instead he made sure that each section had someone awake and watching 'out', then called the Platoon 'O' Group together: Sgt Grenfell and the three section commanders. For the next twenty minutes CUO Masters explained the orders for a company defence. To Graham this was really interesting, and he wished that he was actually a real soldier on active service somewhere. In his imagination the unit really was preparing to dig in to make a desperate defence of the hill.

At the end of the orders, CUO Masters led the four NCOs around and pointed out exactly where he wanted each section to be, and where the flanking sections were to be placed. He also indicated where each section was to have its night sentry post. Graham noted that his section was astride the ridge leading down towards the causeway. 1 Platoon was to be on his left and 5 Section on his right.

It should be easy enough to defend, he thought, staring hard at the almost bare slope. There was almost no cover for hundreds of metres, just a few clumps of rocks and an occasional tree or bush.

When CUO Masters was finished showing them where to put their troops, the three corporals went back to their sections to pass on the orders. Before he could do this, Graham had to wake up Pat and Roger, both of whom had slipped off to sleep. Then he had to overcome the negative scepticism of Andrews, who just thought the exercise story was a load of bunk.

"It's just those Townsville jerks," he sneered.

"Then let's do this properly so they can't tease us for not being good enough!" Graham snapped back. He had vivid memories of seeing patrols from Heatley during the annual camp at Speed Creek the previous year. "They are good, and we don't want to look like a mob of useless bloody drongos."

The orders complete, Graham led the cadets to their allotted area and placed them in position. This led to a difficult decision. His first idea was to put them in pairs with himself and Roger at the rear in the proper 'depth' position for the section commander. But the uneven number of girls then led to him wondering who to put Kirsty with. For a short while he wrestled with the strong temptation of placing Roger with Pat and having Kirsty with him.

However, prudence decided him to group the three girls together in the centre. His decision making was assisted by knowing that CUO Masters and Sgt Grenfell would be only 20 paces behind him, and that both Capt Conkey and CSM Cleland could clearly see him from their position. That put Pat and Roger on the left and Halyday and Andrews on the right. That meant he would be on his own at the rear.

Having placed the cadets in position Graham went to where 1 Platoon were also deploying on his left. Their right-hand section was 1 Section and Graham was not amused to find that Erika Goltz and Magda were the two cadets on his immediate left flank. 1 Section extended across the remainder of the ridge to the top of the bluffs. From there 2 Section and 3 Section were lined out facing north. While he was there, Graham had a look at the steep slope and at the dry riverbed below. It was about 50 metres down to a tangle of rubber vines and trees. The slope was not exactly a line of cliffs but was still bluffs that were dangerously steep in places so 1 Platoon was placed well back and had a rope tied across their front for safety. 1 Platoon's left flank met up with 3 Platoon.

3 Platoon was lined along the fence facing west. In front of them was a deep re-entrant that was to also to be the latrine area. The left flank of 3 Platoon was on the rocks of the knoll and linked up with 2 Platoon's right (Stephen's section).

Having spoken to Cpl Brown Graham walked back to the other end of his section. Here Gwen had positioned LCpl Bert Lacey and Cadet Dan Russel, so Graham was content that at least that flank was secure. He waved to Barbara and gave her a grin as he spoke to Dan and Bert.

Satisfied with the arrangements, Graham walked back to his pack and sat on it. For the next fifteen minutes he prepared a sentry roster, allowing for the time they would be out on patrol. He did this by drawing a timeline and marking the hours, then writing in the names alternately on either side to give a staggered 2-hour roster.

While he was doing this Halyday walked over to him. "Hey Corp, where do we put up our hutchies?" he asked.

It took a moment for Graham to realize that Halyday did not understand. "We don't," he replied. "We are going to just bivouac here in our defence positions."

Halyday looked appalled. "But... but... but what if it rains?"

Graham gave a wry grin and pointed at the clear blue sky. "It won't rain."

Looking quite unhappy Halyday went back to pass this news on to Andrews. As they did, Dianne and Lucy came over and wanted to know where they could go to the toilet. That annoyed Graham.

"I just told you in the orders. Over in the gully past 3 Platoon. And don't get lost, and don't leave anything unburied. Be back in ten minutes."

Kirsty hurried to join them, and the three girls walked off out of sight. Graham looked to check that Roger and Pat were both still alert then went on with his writing. The next interruption was from Cadet James. "All corporals up to company HQ for orders," he said.

The CUOs were wanted as well. Graham joined the other corporals and Capt Conkey told them to seat themselves in a semi-circle. He then checked that all had a map photocopy before giving them a set of patrol orders for the night. As the details were revealed Graham felt his excitement rise, along with apprehension.

This will be a bit of a challenge, he thought. The patrol was only to the bottom of the hill to provide local security, but Graham was still looking forward to it.

As Capt Conkey explained, "If this was a real operation we would not be swapping patrols over every two hours. One patrol would go out and stay out and they would be supported by mortars and so on." He then went on to explain that what he did not want was for the enemy to follow a patrol back in. That led to some detailed instructions on what to do if the enemy tried to do that. "If you have a real problem then call us on the radio," Capt Conkey said. "But remember the enemy can monitor everything you say on the CB radios."

All of the section commanders and platoon commanders had the small hand-held radios and so did all of the officers but as Graham knew they were only civilian 'Citizen Band' sets so had no security or dedicated frequencies. The few army radios available for patrols were away with the raiding parties over near the airfield.

Capt Conkey went on, "In any case I want you to keep radio silence except for medical emergencies or when an enemy patrol is likely to catch the company by surprise."

The corporals were told that each patrol was only to be four strong, so Graham had to choose who to leave behind. In the end he decided to make a fair split. He decided to take Kirsty, Pat and Halyday.

The next twenty minutes were taken up by giving the patrol orders to those of the section who had been selected to go. The others sat and faced their 'front'. Giving the orders really made Graham feel important and he felt his confidence rising. Next, he briefed the whole section again on their field routine. While he was doing that Andrews asked why they didn't hide.

"We stick out like country dunnies here," he said. "Anyone down along the road or river must be able to see us. This is stupid."

"No, it isn't," Graham retorted, blushing hotly and feeling the need to justify Capt Conkey's plan. "If we were really defending this hill we would have moved here in the dark last night and dug weapon pits and camouflaged them. As it is the enemy are going to find it very hard to sneak up on us, even at night."

Andrews accepted that but shook his head with dismay at the idea of digging trenches in the rocky soil. Graham remembered something Capt

Conkey had said once and repeated it. "If you don't like this then don't ever join the army!"

By then it was 1700hrs. Sgt Grenfell came along and told them to get back into their allotted positions. "I need a work party," he added. It was for rations and water, so Graham looked at Roger who nodded and told Kirsty, Lucy, Pat and Andrews to come with him. They moved off in a grumbling line behind Sgt Grenfell. Graham told Halyday to act as sentry while he amended his sentry roster and made a copy. This he taped to a rock at the tree where the night sentry post was to be.

The work party returned fifteen minutes later with a jerrycan of water and eight, one day Cadet Ration Packs, plus hexamine stoves and hexamine tablets. These were distributed and Sgt Grenfell came along again and told them to eat by 1800hrs to be ready for 'Stand-to'.

The hardest thing Graham had to do for the next half hour was to ensure that every cadet got a chance to cook and eat and that the person on sentry was changed frequently. As the unit had done four bivouacs earlier in the year, they were all experienced at preparing meals for themselves, but they were struck by the novelty of the one man ration packs and were continually reading the packets and digging out the other meals and talking about the choices and contents. Graham ate as quickly as he could and then spent his time urging them to hurry up. Andrews wanted to experiment with cooking a mixture, but Graham argued he didn't have time.

Sgt Grenfell put an end to that. "Get packed up and ready for Stand-to. If you need to go to the toilet go now while it is still light. Hurry up."

Graham had explained the 'Stand-to' procedure, but the cadets had never done it so now he had to walk back and forth along the line chivvying them to pack up, put on their webbing, clean up any litter and then to lie down behind their packs.

"We have to be ready to march or fight," he kept repeating. "Dusk and dawn are favourite times for an enemy to attack."

By 1825hrs he had them all lying down facing their front, with their webbing on. "Now stop talking," he hissed, glancing to see if his section was first ready. To his delight he saw that they were. That gave him a really good feeling.

They are developing into a good section, he thought with satisfaction.

The sun had gone down by this and the whole western sky was

bathed red. The glow of this painted the white trunks of the ghost gums along the riverbank a ruddy-gold colour.

There was some murmuring, but Graham quickly silenced this. He walked along and checked once again that every person had their webbing on and was ready. No sooner had he done this than CUO Masters came to inspect them.

"Very good, Cpl Kirk," he said, nodding with approval.

That gave Graham another warm glow of achievement. This was added to by noting that both 1 and 3 Platoons were having trouble getting settled. Magda and Erika still had a scatter of gear and litter around them and it took five minutes of angry hissing by Sgt Sherry to get them to pack it, and to get into position.

3 Platoon took even longer and several times Graham heard Sgt Yeldham's voice snapping at cadets to stop talking and to stand to. Because he was now lying down behind his pack Graham could not see what the problem was, but he could guess. Movement behind Graham caused him to turn his head. It was Capt Conkey and CSM Cleland heading for 3 Platoon. Even in the gloom Graham could see a look of annoyance on Capt Conkey's face. Slowly silence settled, the last angry voices still coming from 3 Platoon area behind him.

As darkness set in the whole company lay silent, facing out and ready. The night exercise had begun! A prickle of expectancy tingled through Graham and he strained his eyes trying to detect any sign of enemy moving.

Andrews began to fidget and that drew a hiss from Graham. Next, the girls began to whisper and he had to pad down and tell them to be silent. He had only just done this and returned to his own position when he heard movement off to his left. Three figures appeared at Erika and Magda's position. It was Capt Conkey, CUO MacAlistair and CSM Cleland.

They spoke quietly for a minute or so, then CUO MacAlistair went back to his PL HQ. Capt Conkey and CSM Cleland walked across behind Graham and were met by CUO Masters.

"Okay CUO Masters, let's inspect your platoon please," Capt Conkey asked.

The trio walked back past Graham to where Roger and Pat lay. Graham was unsure whether he should get up and be with them while they inspected his section, so he remained still. The inspection party did not linger but walked quickly along past the girls and onto where Halyday and Andrews lay, then kept on going to 5 Section. That reassured Graham that his section had passed muster. He lay quietly as full darkness set in.

A few minutes later CUO Masters returned. He knelt down beside Graham. "Okay Cpl Kirk, stand your section down and then make sure you have your sentries on duty. Then get your patrol moving. Report to the OC before you go out and after you come back. Any questions?"

"No, sir," Graham replied.

He quietly stood up and felt real excitement surge in him. Now he was going to be tested! But with the excitement came fear as well, the fear of failure, of making a mess of the patrol.

Squaring his shoulders, he walked down to get the others.

Chapter 20

IN THE DARK

Graham had led patrols before, most notably during the exercise near Bowen in August, but he still found this one a real challenge. The reason was that the company was acting on the defensive, trying to keep raiders away from the company position and he therefore felt the responsibility more heavily.

If I muck up everyone will know, he thought.

Having collected the other three who were to go he checked that Dianne and Lucy were both awake and on guard. "And don't go to sleep," he warned. "We will look bloody silly if Heatley just walk in."

He then led the patrol over to where CUO Masters and Sgt Grenfell sat. CUO Masters wished him luck and Graham led them on to Company HQ. A small shelter had been rigged with sleeping bags draped over ropes tied between trees to hide the torchlight. There Graham found Capt Conkey bending over a map marking it. He had a radio handset in his hand and Graham gathered that he was in contact with the raiders over near the airfield. Curiosity about the situation made him lean over to look.

Capt Conkey looked up. "Yes, Cpl Kirk?"

"4 Section patrol moving out now, sir," Graham replied.

"Good. Off you go."

Capt Conkey turned back to the map and Graham glanced at it and was unable to see more than a few red marks on their side of the airfield. He turned and led the other three away. His route out was through Stephen's sentry post, so he led the patrol stumbling over the rocks to there. After a quick word to his friend, he continued on. The patrol made its way down on to the low saddle and back towards the parked vehicles. The vehicles were not in the exercise, being needed for safety and administration, so he steered clear of them. Lt Maclaren and Lt Standish were sitting there in the dark, talking quietly.

50 paces past the vehicles the patrol came to the fence that ran down to the grid. After listening for a minute, they rolled under, discovering in

the process that the ground was covered in small two-pronged prickles. They then went on southeast down the rocky slope. Graham took it very slow, stopping every 20 paces. After listening for half a minute, he then walked another 20 paces. It was quite dark by then, but he could still see quite well in the starlight.

Over to his right he knew was the dirt road to Canning Junction, but it was not visible till they were quite close to it. Here he paused again to listen. The side road was his boundary between him and any patrols from 3 Platoon. Likewise, the fence on his left was the boundary between 1 Platoon's patrols and 2 Platoon's.

Fifteen minutes after starting out, the patrol reached the Canning Road just near a small dip mid-way between the cattle grid and the Canning Junction turnoff. During another pause to listen, Graham carefully looked both ways along the Canning Road. In the starlight it appeared as a wide grey clearing. Satisfied there was no-one on the other side Graham signalled the others to follow and walked quietly across, his boots crunching lightly on the loose gravel.

As the other three joined him in the clumps of grass on the other side of the road, Graham heard the sound of people moving. He hissed for silenced and went very tense as he listened. The noises were behind the patrol. The sound of someone cursing and of boots clattering on loose rocks came clearly to him on the still night air. For several minutes he lay and listened. The others lay close, also listening. After a while, the direction of movement became clear.

"That is 3 Platoon's patrol going out," Graham whispered. Mentally he shook his head at the poor fieldcraft and self-discipline.

That will be Crane's section, he thought.

Rising quietly he moved on, the others following. He led the way across a small depression lined with trees and on across a sandy flat 50 paces wide on which grew several small, twisted trees growing in a clump. The patrol continued on another 20 metres to the bank of the sandy creek that led down from Sandy Ridge. The white sand in its bed showed clearly in the starlight. Turning right, Graham led the others to a small ridge about 5 metres high and 25 metres long that protruded into a bend in the creek. A stand of trees and various clumps of bushes provided good cover.

From there they could see back towards the road and both up the creek and out across the flat beyond it. It wasn't a perfect position and, like most military problems, was too big to be adequately covered by the available force.

Six would be a better number, he thought. But he only had four, and the dilemma of who to put where.

At this point he gave in to what he knew was foolish temptation. Kirsty had been following close behind him all the way, so he kept her with him and placed Pat and Halyday ten metres away They faced east and north. Graham then found a spot where he could watch the road, and the creek line to the south. When sat down he could just make out Pat's head among the trees.

The patrol settled to wait. Within a couple of minutes, Kirsty moved so that her sleeve touched Graham's arm. That got him thinking and excited. Slowly, so as not to make a noise, he shifted to press against her.

"Is that alright?" he whispered.

"No, I want you closer," Kirsty whispered back.

Graham eased over and leaned against her. She snuggled against him, her arm resting on his leg. That got him quickly aroused and hopeful. Greatly daring he took her hand and held it. She responded and snuggled even harder. As she did, a curious muttering vibration began to fill the quiet of the night. Kirsty stiffened and looked around.

"What's that noise?" she whispered.

As she asked, the sound changed to a deeper rumble. Graham held her closer and whispered back, "Only a train going across the railway bridge. It's a couple of kilometres away that way." He pointed off to the south.

She nodded and looked into his eyes. He could see hers glistening in the starlight and felt sure she was sending him a message. His heart began to thump with hopeful anticipation, and he licked his lips nervously.

I think she wants a kiss, he thought. It was a real temptation and his mind raced with hopes and fears. *Will I?* he wondered, all the old arguments again flooding through his mind. *But what if she complains?*

But there was also the dilemma of how she would feel if he rejected her fairly obvious advances! Then, just as he was trying to pluck up the courage to ask her, yelling broke out in the distance.

Graham snatched his hand away in fright then felt foolish. The noise was coming from hundreds of metres away over on the other side of the Canning Road. "3 Platoon's patrol bumping into someone," he murmured. He heard Pat and Halyday both move and saw their black shapes as they stood up to look.

The yelling died down after several minutes and Pat and Halyday sat down again. Then the radio spoke. It was so loud Graham jumped in fright and then blushed with shame.

I should have turned the volume down, he berated himself. With fingers that trembled slightly he did that. It was Capt Conkey wanting information. *Not calling me,* Graham thought.

It took Capt Conkey three calls before Cpl Crane replied and reported that his patrol had run into an enemy patrol. From the garbled answer Graham decided that Crane had blundered into the enemy and he certainly wasn't sure how many there had been or which way they had gone.

I hope we don't get sprung like that, he thought.

After looking carefully in all directions and listening intently Graham again turned to Kirsty. She snuggled close and by mutual consent their heads came together, and they kissed.

Then, curiously, his desire started to wane. As each new act was carried out Graham felt the stab of his conscience more strongly. Added to that was his pride in trying to be a good soldier.

We promised to behave, he thought uncomfortably. *And we are supposed to be guarding the company.*

He gave Kirsty another kiss, then whispered, "We shouldn't be doing this."

"Don't you like it?" Kirsty asked.

"I love it, but I promised Capt Conkey I'd behave. And we are on patrol. We are the outpost keeping the company safe."

Kirsty shrugged and gave him an odd look but then nodded. Graham took his arms from around her, sighing with regret as he did. Feeling quite unsure and self-conscious, Graham eased himself away from her. Kirsty turned her head to give him a hurt look.

As she did, Graham stared out across the creek. A movement caught his eye, the merest flicker in the shadows.

Enemy!

He stared hard and saw a dark shape that could only be a person move from one clump of bushes to another. The enemy group was at least a hundred metres away and were crossing his left front heading towards the shed. He gripped Kirsty's arm and pointed.

The sound of leaves rustling penetrated Graham's consciousness. Just in time he took his hand away from Kirsty's arm as Pat came over. Kirsty was still beside him but now moved slightly away. Graham felt shame begin to burn through him. Pat appeared not to notice anything unusual.

"Someone moving out on the flat to the east," he whispered.

Graham nodded. "I know. I've been watching them," he replied.

As he did, the distinct sound of a stick snapping came to them on the still night air. Murmuring voices could then be heard from the enemy patrol. Next, Graham glimpsed another black figure flit from tree to tree about a hundred metres away. For the next minute he watched, gauging their direction of movement. As he did, he moved further away from Kirsty and into a crouch.

"They are going to go past us," he whispered. He calculated they would pass about 100 metres to their north. "Come on. If we are quick, we can cut them off."

He strode over to Halyday, trying not to make any noise as he did. Pat and Kirsty both followed. With a gesture to follow him Graham went past Halyday and slithered down into the dry creek bed. The others followed.

Down in the narrow, sandy creek bed Graham knew they were out of sight of the enemy so he broke into a run, hoping they wouldn't hear the thudding of their boots or webbing. The creek ran straight for about 50 paces, then curved left and then right and then left again before running straight for another ten metres. At that point, an old road to the North Gravel Scrape crossed it, the actual road being washed away. The creek bank was chest high and steep enough to be an awkward climb.

By then Graham was panting for breath, the running on the soft sand having been harder than he had expected. The others halted beside him, also puffing and gasping. A mist of fine dust, stirred up by their boots, enveloped them and tickled at Graham's throat. As he struggled to stop himself coughing or sneezing, he strained his eyes in the darkness, afraid that the run might have been heard.

Then, only 20 paces away, appeared a person. He came out of the clumps of lantana up on the bank and went to cross the clear lane of the old road only 10 paces in front of the patrol. Immediately behind the leader appeared four more cadets, all bunched closely together. For a frozen second Graham stood there staring at them. Fear of doing the wrong thing combined with fear of starting a battle and of being beaten.

By then there were six enemy and the first was almost at the top of the creek bank about 15 paces to Graham's left front. *I must open fire,* he thought in a near panic, knowing that his group could just crouch there safely and not be seen. *But if we let them pass they might find the company position,* he thought unhappily. The realisation that the whole reason for his patrol being there was to contact enemy patrols made his mind up.

With beating heart, he screamed, "Open fire! Bang! Bang!"

The other members of his patrol joined in immediately. By then Graham was running along the creek bed to intercept the enemy leader. The effect was astonishing. The enemy cadets stopped, then scattered. A couple fired back. One went to ground and two ran back the way they had come. The enemy leader saw Graham coming and fled, running off along the old road as fast as he could go.

"After them!" Graham shouted, scrambling up out of the creek bed.

That decided the other enemy. They took to their heels as well. The one who had taken cover sprang up and ran. He was almost grabbed by Halyday but managed to get away. After 20 paces Graham called on his patrol to stop. The enemy went on running, scattering off across the flat.

Graham stood with chest heaving, exhilarated by the ease of their victory. In the distance he heard the enemy calling to each other as they tried to regroup.

"Nearly had a prisoner then," Halyday grumbled. He was dancing with excitement.

"Just as well you didn't catch one," Graham replied. "We don't need a prisoner to clutter us up right now."

As he spoke, he looked around to check that there were no more enemy. It occurred to him that the patrol might be only the vanguard of a whole company. *We can't see much from down here in the creek,* he thought. The notion that he had somehow abandoned his post made him blush with shame.

Hoping the others had not noticed his indecision, he said, "We'd better get back in position."

"Won't they know where we are?" Pat asked.

"They will know we are somewhere here but not our exact position," Graham replied. He set off back along the top of the bank. As he did, he used his radio to call Coy HQ. Capt Conkey answered and Graham gave him a quick summary of what had happened.

"The enemy have withdrawn to the east, over," he concluded.

Capt Conkey replied, "Well done. Stay in position, over."

Knowing that every CUO and section commander must have heard that made Graham glow with pride. Smiling with satisfaction he kept on moving, his eyes and ears alert for more enemy. The others followed and three minutes later they were back in their original position. After a big drink of water, Graham stood and looked carefully in all directions before sitting down.

Kirsty sat beside him but he shook his head. "We'd better behave," he whispered.

Kirsty pouted but nodded.

Time began to drag slowly. Once Graham thought he heard sounds across the Canning Road in the area they had crossed when getting into position, but he saw nothing. However, his suspicions were confirmed five minutes later when a burst of yelling came from up the hill behind them.

"Sounds like our vehicles just got annihilated," he murmured.

"They will find the company then," Pat added.

As if to confirm this, there was more yelling and banging up the hill but muffled and further away. Graham thought that was either Stephen's section or the section of 3 Platoon between the knoll and the north-south fence.

Kirsty looked anxious and whispered, "Are there enemy behind us?"

"Yes," Graham replied.

"But we might get cut off and be captured," she said anxiously.

Graham felt a spasm of fear at that idea but then shook his head and grinned. "Or they are the ones who might be cut off and trapped," he replied.

Kirsty looked doubtful but Graham suddenly felt confident and he knew he was starting to enjoy the experience of leading a patrol. They settled down to watch.

The next action however came from down the creek the other side of the fence. A spirited mock battle raged for five minutes somewhere near where the two creeks joined below the North Gravel Pit. Obviously, the enemy had run into the patrol from 1 Platoon.

"They are probably the same mob of enemy who ran into us," Pat suggested.

Graham agreed. He now stood and focused on different directions for a minute at a time. He also checked the time. They were due to be relieved by 5 Section at 2100hrs and he saw with surprise that it was already 2035hrs. A feeling of regret made him realise that now he was out on patrol and had actually met the enemy that he was really enjoying himself.

I wish we could stay out longer, he thought.

His desire for more 'action' was soon gratified. Ten minutes later a group of seven enemy came along the dry creek bed from the direction of Sandy Ridge. Graham saw them coming when they were still a hundred metres away. In the starlight they looked like black figure targets as they were silhouetted against the pale sand. By the time they reached the creek bend he had the other members of the patrol spread across thirty metres of front.

At his shout they opened fire. This group of enemy was more alert and much better led. They deployed and pretended to return fire. Then they made several attempts to advance. That got Graham very 'heart-in-mouth' anxious and for few moments he contemplated retreating. Then his stubborn pride helped him to decide to stay. He shouted encouragement and kept moving rapidly from side to side to try to confuse the enemy as to his intentions and numbers. After a while, the enemy pulled back, then turned and went west across the Canning Road near the turn-off.

Graham contemplated following them but reluctantly decided he must stay where he was.

They will get behind us now, he thought.

They did. From time to time he heard them moving in the dip and then on the rocky slope.

I hope Gwen doesn't run into them, he thought.

To warn her he sent a radio report to Coy HQ informing them of the strength and direction of enemy movement. "Warn Patrol Two Three," he added.

As he said this, a battle erupted across the road behind him. There was a lot of yelling and banging and running around for a few minutes. Then Gwen came on the radio to report to Coy HQ that her section had ambushed an enemy patrol that was now withdrawing southwest. She also warned Graham that her patrol was now moving to his location. Voices and boots moving towards his position indicated to Graham that there were people coming from behind him. Graham thought it was Gwen's patrol but just to be sure he had his patrol redeploy to face back towards Black Knoll and he tensed as dark figures flitted across the road. But it was Gwen's patrol. She called softly and Graham went to meet her.

"Did you get ambushed?" he asked.

"No fear! We heard your warning. Thanks. We hid and really caught them," Gwen replied happily.

"All yours then," Graham replied. "We will get back."

"Quickly please. We have only half a platoon holding our part of the front and I think there is another enemy patrol up there somewhere," Gwen replied.

Just as she said this the sound of distant shouts and screams came from the other direction, from Sandy Ridge. The cadets crouched, tense and ready. Then deep "Hoo! Hoo! Hoo!" bellows told them what was happening. Graham grinned "That's the Hutchie Men attacking Heatley's new patrol base," he said.

This was confirmed by more yells of fear, among which sounded the quavering shriek, "Hutchie Men!"

At that the waiting cadets burst into laughter. The two corporals had to angrily hiss for silence. Gwen nudged Graham. "Go on, get back up the hill. Our side of the company is only held by Steve's section and two half sections."

"That's if they are awake," added Pat.

Graham collected his cadets and regretfully set off home. They crossed the Canning Road and headed across the dip and up the rocky slope near the fence. As they went, Graham kept every sense alert.

It was just as well he did as he heard the chink of rock on rock and then glimpsed movement against the stars. He went to ground and the others did likewise. From his right rear came a group moving up the hill following the fence.

Is that 1 Platoon's patrol or the enemy? he wondered.

Chapter 21

CHALLENGES IN THE NIGHT

Graham lowered himself down till he lay flat on the stony ground. By doing so he was able to skyline the dark figures ahead of him. He also found his hands and knees hurting from the sharp rocks and prickles. But he ignored the discomfort. By now his heart was hammering hard with anxiety and excitement.

Definitely not ours, he decided, noting the way the figures kept stopping to stare up the slope.

It took an effort of willpower, but Graham made himself wait till the rival patrol began moving before rising to his feet. He signalled his own patrol to follow and carefully moved one foot at a time. In doing so he and the others dislodged a few stones but luckily the other people were making so much noise themselves they evidently did not hear them.

There was the barbed wire fence to negotiate and Graham slithered under this, heedless of scratches and prickles. The others muttered a few grumbles but followed his example. Within a minute he had them on their feet advancing side by side up the slope. By then the enemy patrol had almost vanished from sight. Graham began to fret that he had moved too slowly and that they would get away.

They will reach the company position if we don't catch them, he thought.

The desire to avoid being seen as a failure by the OC now spurred him to act. The Heatley patrol had vanished over the crest near the vehicles, angling to their right. That would take them away from the vehicles and across the top of the re-entrant. To Graham's dismay, he found he could no longer see them. He stopped and listened.

The faint chink of rock on rock gave him the direction and he waved his patrol forward. Then he was concerned to find that the Heatley patrol was moving much faster than he had expected. They had drawn 50 metres ahead. Angry with himself for miscalculating, he increased his pace.

As the patrol went down to the lip of the re-entrant, Graham was surprised by a voice hissing at him from close ahead.

"Sssh! You are making too much noise," it said.

His heart thudding in shock, Graham strained his eyes and saw a line of dark figures crouched behind trees and rocks only a few metres ahead.

Damn! he thought in dismay, *stuffed up again!*

Then he heard the same voice ask, "Who's that? Get down."

They think we are part of their patrol, Graham thought.

At almost the same instant he realised he had a fleeting chance, so he took it. "Bang!" he shouted.

"Shit! Enemy!" yelled the startled Heatley patrol commander.

To Graham's relief, his own cadets now joined in, running up on either side of him and yelling loudly. There was a minute's confused screaming and scuttling and the surprised Heatley patrol scattered and ran off to the left. Graham led his patrol after them as far as the top of the saddle. He was so excited he was shouting at the top of his voice and could hear the echoes rolling out over the countryside.

Halyday even ran over and grabbed one member of the other patrol as he scrambled under the north-south fence. The Heatley cadet squealed and struggled free. The remainder of the Heatley patrol now rallied as their leader recovered his wits. A banging match began for a minute. Graham wondered if he should try to push further. He even summoned the courage to dash forward to the fence. However, he could now make out six figures in the other patrol and he knew he was outnumbered.

To his relief, the Heatley patrol kept pulling back into the head of the re-entrant on the west side of the saddle.

"Cease fire! That will do!" he ordered.

A wave of exultation surged through him and he stood for a minute revelling in it. The others stood beside him, talking excitedly and laughing. Then Graham realised that wasn't very military.

We could get caught by surprise just as easily, he thought.

"Stop talking! Silence!" he snapped.

When the others had fallen silent, he pointed across the saddle. "Let's go home," he whispered.

They set off towards the clumps of rocks, just visible in the starlight. As they did, he made a radio report informing Coy HQ which way the enemy patrol had withdrawn and that they were coming in.

A minute later a voice challenged quietly from the darkness, "Halt!"

It was Stephen. He was at his sentry post at the base of the knoll.

Graham gave the countersign for the password and then walked over to where Stephen and one of his cadets crouched behind the boulders.

"You caught that mob a beauty," Stephen said with a hoarse whisper.

"We've had a good night," Graham replied. He was now glowing with the achievements of his patrol.

Movement on the rocky path up beside the knoll attracted his attention. It was CUO Masters. He hissed at them, "Cpl Bell, who is it?"

"Cpl Kirk, sir," Stephen called softly back.

"Send him up, and stop talking. That Heatley patrol is still out there and could come back."

"Yes, sir."

Graham realised he had been sweating and now he shivered. He led his patrol up the rough path to meet CUO Masters then followed him around to where Coy HQ was. Capt Conkey and CSM Cleland sat behind their screen of sleeping bags. Graham reported he was back.

Capt Conkey nodded, then said, "Deploy your people back in their defensive position, then come here and fill out a patrol report."

"Yes, sir," Graham said, and led the others back to where their packs were. He could just see a few dark bumps that indicated other members of the platoon and it reminded him of what Gwen had said.

We are a bit thin on the ground, he thought.

Roger and Andrews were on sentry. Andrews looked up and grumbled, "About bloody time! Can I go to bed now?"

"No. Not till your time on sentry is up," Graham replied. "I will relieve you as soon as I have filled out my report."

The other patrol members had bunched up and Pat asked what they were to do. "Go to bed and get as much rest as you can. The exercise goes on till dawn and it could be a long, hard night."

"Long and hard eh? Is that a promise?" Kirsty commented.

Graham blushed furiously and felt a surge of anger. "That will do Kirsty!" he hissed.

Then he mentally kicked himself for not calling her Cadet Weldon. The snickers of the others did nothing to ease his embarrassment. *They must suspect we are doing things,* he thought unhappily.

"Stop talking and keep quiet," he snapped, louder and more forcefully than he intended. "Now go to bed."

To avoid any further comments, he made his way back up past

platoon HQ to Coy HQ. As he did, there was a sudden outburst of loud shouts and cries of 'Hoo! Hoo! Hoo!' from down at the bottom of the hill near where Graham had left Gwen's patrol.

The Hutchie Men, he thought. *I hope they haven't clashed with Gwen's patrol.*

They hadn't. On arriving at Coy HQ, Graham heard CSM Cleland report to the OC that the Hutchie Men had caught another Heatley patrol by surprise. The Heatley patrol had run and blundered into Gwen's patrol and been hit again. That news made Graham grin and he saw that Capt Conkey was smiling and enjoying himself.

"4 Platoon is back on our side of the highway now," Capt Conkey said. "They'll start probing Heatley's new position on Sandy Ridge soon."

"Did they raid the airfield sir?" Graham asked. He craned forward to study the map board in the faint light of the small torch which hung from a cord above it.

"Yes, they did. They even took some prisoners and only had one patrol in trouble. Now, here is a Patrol Report. Fill it in and get back to your section as quickly as you can."

Graham took off his webbing and sat to one side, took out his pocket torch and a pencil, then turned the torch on and held it in his mouth. For the next ten minutes he was busy filling out the report.

He was just finishing when the scuffle and thud of approaching boots sounded. Both Capt Conkey and CSM Cleland looked up expectantly. It was the Hutchie Men. Their camouflaged faces grinned in the dim light.

"Back sir," Porno reported. "We have jolly good time."

"Sit down and tell me about it," Capt Conkey replied. As they dumped their webbing and sat down, Capt Conkey turned to Graham. "Have you finished yet, Cpl Kirk? Good. Give me a quick verbal report. I will read the details tomorrow."

That put Graham on the spot. He didn't want to sound as though he was boasting but he did think his patrol had done very well. He also felt self-conscious telling his story in front of the Hutchie Men.

They will have had real adventures, he thought.

As quickly as he could, he described the various actions his patrol had been involved in. Capt Conkey sat listening, nodding thoughtfully. He asked a few questions to check some details, then said, "Sounds like you did a very good job. Now, get back to your section and stay alert."

Graham badly wanted to stay and hear the Hutchie Men's story but could only nod, stand up and slip his torch and pencil back into his pocket. Hoisting his webbing loosely over his shoulders he walked off. As he stumbled over the rocks, he glowed at Capt Conkey's praise. But the words made him feel even more guilty about the memories of cuddling Kirsty, which had been crossing his mind while he had made his report.

I have to get her to stop without putting her nose out of joint, he decided. *But how?*

It was just coming up to 2200hrs by then so he had a drink and then made his way to the sentry post. Andrews was still grumbling and was pleased to be relieved. He moved back a few metres to where his bedding was and lay down beside Halyday. Ten metres to the left were the dark forms of the three girls and the rustle of plastic and mutter of voices told Graham that Kirsty was settling down. Thoughts of her caused him to shake his head with anxiety.

She will get me into trouble and I will never get to be a sergeant, Graham worried. With these gloomy thoughts he seated himself beside Roger.

"How did it go?" Roger asked.

As quietly as he could, Graham whispered the story. As he did, he realised that Roger was jealous. *Poor bugger!* he thought. But he knew he had to leave his 2ic to command the other half of the section.

The two friends settled to watch in silence. As they sat there, Graham's mind roved alternately from his patrol exploits to Kirsty. Memories of those delicious minutes of kissing and of the smell and feel of her caused him to alternately flush with pleasure and guilt. These reveries were interrupted by the sound of another train crossing the rail bridge. It sounded amazingly loud to him and he commented on this to Roger.

"How far is to the bridge?" Roger asked.

"About three kilometres in a straight line," Graham replied, still marvelling on how well noise travelled in the still, night air.

"They are the best kind," Roger answered with a chuckle. "It's never that easy when you try to walk it."

"You are right there!"

The two then sat in companionable silence as the rumble of the train died in the distance. Graham became aware that he could even hear the noise of cars on the highway and occasionally noted the loom of their lights as they went over a hill several kilometres to the east. Then the stillness of the night was shattered by shouts and screams from down at the bottom of the ridge. Graham tensed for a second, then relaxed.

"1 Platoon's patrol has bumped someone," he commented. For a minute or so he debated waking up the remainder of the section just in case but as the yelling died away, he decided not to.

The enemy are going away, he decided. He settled back to watching.

By then it was 2300hrs, so Roger went and woke Pat. Pat got up without a grumble and quickly came over to take his turn on sentry. He was obviously still half asleep but Graham was still wide awake so there was no problem. Roger took himself to bed. Graham liked Pat.

It's a pity he is only in Year 8, he thought. He knew that Capt Conkey preferred not to send Year 8s on the Corporals Course because they were too young to command cadets the same age. *I will recommend him for promotion to lance corporal though,* he decided.

That got him thinking about his own promotion chances and he decided that he was actually doing reasonably well. *I might be in the top half of the corporals,* he thought hopefully. But he knew that he had to resist Kirsty or he would never make sergeant.

Twenty minutes slid by, the silence broken only by the hoot of an owl and the distant howl of a dingo. There wasn't even a breeze to rustle the leaves. Then a scream from behind Graham made him sit up in alarm. It was a girl's scream, but it was drowned by other shouts and yells. It came from just back over the crest.

"3 Platoon in trouble," Graham said.

He stood up, ready to wake the others. Back towards HQ he saw figures stirring and moving: CUO Masters and Sgt Grenfell. They hurried over to the crest and joined in the mock battle. Graham quickly woke Halyday and Andrews and was about to wake the girls when Roger joined him to report he had done that.

"Keep watching our own front," he ordered.

By now the yells and jeering laughter were receding. It was obvious that a Heatley patrol had managed to infiltrate and was now withdrawing. Graham saw dark figures running and stumbling across the bottom of the knoll from Coy HQ and heard Capt Conkey's voice calling for a report.

"Those noddies from 3 Platoon have let an enemy patrol in," Pat said.

They had too. A few minutes later CUO Masters appeared to check that 4 Section was awake and alert. When he found they were all awake and ready he grunted "well done" and whispered to Graham the story as he knew it.

"Apparently 8 Section's sentries went to sleep: Franks and Bycroft. The Heatley patrol snuck through and marked them all with red felt pen to show that their throats were cut. They were just doing that to the platoon HQ when CUO Mitrovitch woke up and screamed."

Pat chuckled and said, "She probably thought it was you sir,"

"Don't be cheeky Cadet Sheehan!" CUO Masters snapped, but then he chuckled too. "Poor old 3 Platoon. The OC is really peeved. So make sure you lot stay alert so it doesn't happen to us."

"Yes sir," Graham replied.

8 Section, he thought. *Poor old Harriet Harris.*

Then he was ashamed of himself for thinking that it would help his chances of promotion if she had blotted her copybook.

The section was stood down and Andrews grumbled some more about being woken up. It was so close to midnight that Graham told Halyday to stay awake as it was his turn on duty next. He then sat with them till his time was up before thankfully making his way back to his pack. Even then he did not feel tired and really wanted more action. From past experience he knew that he could go for several nights without sleep and be still able to function efficiently, so he was not worried about becoming too tired as he lay on his unrolled bedding staring at the stars.

What he did worry about was Kirsty and his own lack of self-control. The sound of another train crossing the rail bridge diverted these thoughts for a few minutes but then he went back to brooding. To his annoyance the thoughts of Kirsty got him aroused and he found himself hungering for more physical contact with her.

Eventually he dozed off, still thinking about Kirsty. Then he dreamed about her, waking up to the sound of her voice. For a minute he lay wondering where he was, staring up at the stars. It was still dark, and he realised that Kirsty must be on sentry and that she was talking to the other sentry. A moment's listening told him it was Lucy.

Grumbling to himself he walked down to the sentry post. The girls heard him coming and stopped talking. He saw the pale blurs of their faces as they turned to look at him.

"Stop talking or the enemy will find us," he hissed.

And I will get a bad report from CUO Masters, he thought.

Feeling groggy and grumpy, he made his way back to his bedroll and lay down. But then he could not go back to sleep. Feeling annoyed and frustrated he lay and fretted over his chances of being promoted to sergeant.

Movement and murmuring down at the sentry post again attracted his attention, but he saw it was only the change of sentry. Two of the three settled down but the third person began making their way up towards him. Graham looked up. It was Kirsty. She knelt down beside him, then stretched out to snuggle up against him.

"Kirsty! You can't sleep here," he hissed.

"But I will be the only girl over where I sleep because both Lucy and Di are on sentry," she whispered back.

"But we will get into trouble," he said, twisting to look around towards platoon HQ.

"Oh please! I am scared on my own," she murmured, putting her arm across him and brushing her hair on his cheek. "Just for a few minutes."

"No," Graham replied.

"Oh please!" she said, snuggling up to him and holding him tight.

As she did, Graham was torn. "Stop that and go back to your bed," he hissed desperately, knowing he was half defeated. But she didn't stop. That raised Graham's anxieties another notch. "Lucy and Di are just down there. They know you are here," he whispered, trying to get her to stop and to obey.

"They won't tell," Kirsty said.

"Yes, they will. They will gossip to all their friends, and then the whole bloody company will know," Graham replied peevishly.

He felt deeply anxious but also feeling impotent. *How can I get her to obey?* he wondered.

To increase the pressure, Kirsty leaned on him and began kissing him. Torn between fear and desire, Graham kissed her in return. As he did, he saw someone walking towards them from the sentry post. But Kirsty had not noticed and was still cuddling him.

"Kirsty!" he croaked in panic.

Chapter 22

UNDER THE OC'S EYE

The moment Graham noticed the person walking towards them from the sentry post he experienced a panicky mixture of sensations. Fear was uppermost. He whipped his arms from around Kirsty, at the same time pushing her hands away. Then he rolled on his side to try to pretend he and Kirsty had not been doing anything. In the starlight he recognised the person as Lucy. Kirsty realised something was wrong and thankfully moved the other way into a sitting position. By then Lucy was only 10 paces away.

"Hey Cpl Kirk, there are people moving down the ridge," Lucy called quietly.

Graham grunted, too caught up by emotions of shame and fear to speak clearly. His body shuddered again as the passion left him. He moved into a sitting position.

"Thanks," he managed to croak, rolling onto his knees.

He grabbed his webbing, then stood up, swinging it on. Kirsty stood up as well and also picked up her webbing. Graham noted a significant exchange of glances between Kirsty and Lucy and that caused another surge of scorching shame to flood through him.

Did she see what we were doing? he wondered fearfully.

He did not dare ask or even hint, so he set off down to the sentry post, buckling his webbing on as he did. When there, he knelt down to whisper to Dianne. Lucy and Kirsty followed him down and also crouched.

"There," Dianne whispered in reply, pointing down the ridge.

Graham stared in the darkness then remembered his training. With a conscious effort of willpower, he looked away from the area and tried to use his peripheral vision. It sort of worked and he detected a flicker among the shadows. Then he saw them clearly; three dark figures. A glance at his watch told him it was not a friendly patrol. They were all supposed to be home by this.

"Wake the boys," he hissed to Kirsty and Lucy, pointing each way. "I will tell CUO Masters."

As quickly and quietly as he could, Graham set off back up the gentle slope. By then his heart had slowed down but he still had a dry throat and was sweating with anxiety.

Oh, bloody hell! I hope Lucy doesn't say anything, he thought. He cursed himself for being a weakling and a bloody fool for not being able to resist Kirsty.

CUO Masters was awake in seconds. Sgt Grenfell also stirred and both got up. As they tugged on webbing and hats Graham whispered his news. CUO Masters turned to Sgt Grenfell, "You wake the other two section commanders and have them stand-to. I will check, then wake the OC."

Graham led CUO Masters back down to his sentry post. When he got there, he found all three girls seated with Andrews and Halyday.

"Back to your packs," he hissed.

"There are six of them," Dianne replied, pointing down the ridge to the right.

Graham strained his eyes and noted dark shapes flitting from rock to rock or from tree to tree. The Heatley patrol had come up out of the re-entrant and was angling across the ridge towards the top of the bluffs along the river.

CUO Masters looked then whispered, "Well done. Just lie still and don't open fire without my orders. I'm going to tell the OC." He turned and ghosted back up the slope towards Coy HQ.

Graham moved with the girls and made sure they were lying down before hurrying on to check Roger and Pat. They were both awake and watching. After repeating the platoon commander's instructions, Graham lay down beside them. He was fairly sure that the enemy had seen all the movement.

If we can see them they must have been able to see us, he reasoned.

By then his heart was beating rapidly and he had all but forgotten his close shave a few minutes earlier. Now he lay tense and quivering with excitement. The Heatley patrol came slowly up the slope, sometimes crawling, sometimes walking slowly. For several minutes at a time they would stop. To right and left Graham heard noises as cadets were roused and a few of the whispered exchanges were loud and angry enough for the enemy to hear.

There was evident confusion on his left and he could hear Cpl

Rankine trying to get Magda and Erika out of their sleeping bags. The enemy must also have noted the noise as they began moving at a fast walk up across the slope towards 1 Platoon. Graham tensed and hoped none of his cadets would fire as the enemy drew closer: 75 metres, 65, 50. It was obvious that the clash must come at any second. It would be just in front of Graham and the next section. Then he heard noises behind him and risked a glance over his shoulder.

Three large, shaggy, black shapes flitted across the crest to the edge of the bluff and out of sight. Just as they did, Cadet Grey, a cheeky little Year 8 in 1 Section, called out, "Halt! Hands up!"

At that the Heatley patrol 'opened fire' with much shouting. In response all of Rankine's section began yelling. To Graham's intense annoyance, he heard Halyday and Andrews join in from over to his right.

"Stop firing 4 Section!" he called angrily.

Dianne had also just started yelling 'Bang! Bang!' but she now stopped. It took another shout from Graham to stop Andrews.

Bloody drongo! Graham thought angrily.

The Heatley patrol changed direction and began working its way directly up the ridge, but they were clearly visible as there was little cover. As the nearest enemy reached a position only about 25 metres away, Graham wondered if he was going to have to order his section to open fire on his own initiative.

As two Heatley cadets scuttled even closer, now angling towards 2 Platoon's centre, Graham was relieved to hear CUO Masters call, "Open fire 4 Section!"

"4 Section, fire!" Graham shouted.

He was further annoyed to hear that Andrews and Halyday hadn't waited for his order. They all began shouting and that stopped the Heatley patrol. They went to ground and yelled back.

Suddenly, the right-hand Heatley cadet sprang up and bolted back across the ridge. "Hutchie Men! Hutchie Men!" he screamed in a panicky voice.

Out of the dead ground on the top of the bluff, about 50 metres down the slope, emerged the Hutchie Men. In the starlight they appeared as huge shaggy monsters and their shouts of "Hoo! Hoo! Hoo!" echoed along the river valley and across to Sandy Ridge. The three Hutchie Men charged the Heatley patrol. They sprang to their feet and fled.

As they ran, the Heatley cadets yelled in fear, "Hutchie Men! Hutchie Men!"

Graham counted eight in the Heatley patrol and their panicked flight before three Hutchie Men looked so funny to him that he started to laugh. Others joined in and soon a barrage of jeers and mocking laughter pursued the enemy patrol down the slope. One of the Heatley cadets was too slow and was caught by a Hutchie Man. The unfortunate captive uttered a terror-stricken shriek which caused renewed laughter from the defenders. A second Heatley cadet tripped on the rocks and cried out in pain.

Capt Conkey's voice now bellowed out above the uproar, "Hutchie Men! Stop there! Stop there!"

He came hurrying past, ordering the platoon commanders to silence their troops as he did. It took some effort to stop the chattering and laughter. Because Andrews kept snickering and talking Graham got up and hurried along, arriving at his position at the same time as Sgt Grenfell.

Relative silence settled. Graham crouched beside Halyday and Andrews and listened. Voices indicated that Capt Conkey was talking and a few minutes later the murmur of voices receded down the hill. A shaggy figure came walking back towards them and Graham challenged him. It was Ziggy.

In answer to Graham's query, Ziggy explained, "One of them has sprained his ankle. I have to get the CP to radio Heatley and get them to send a vehicle to get him." He hurried on past up to Coy HQ.

"Can we go back to bed now?" whined Andrews.

Graham checked his watch. It was 0330hrs and he was rostered back on sentry at 0400hrs. "No," he said. "We wait till the platoon commander orders it."

Andrews grumbled and muttered under his breath, but Graham ignored him. He had really enjoyed the little battle but now anxiety about Kirsty was seeping back in, along with the early morning chill.

A few minutes later, Sgt Grenfell came along with the order to stand down. Graham walked along and organised this. Lucy and Dianne were still rostered on duty, so he paused and said well done to them. They made their way back to the sentry post. Kirsty gave him a look but then lay down on her own bedding.

"Thanks," he whispered before moving quickly on.

She made a face in reply, but he could not tell what she meant by it. That increased his anxiety, and he went back to his own bedding and sat with it wrapped around him while he brooded over the events of the night.

While he sat there, he heard a vehicle start up on Sandy Ridge. It drove down along the road past the shed to the causeway across the Canning. A few minutes later it went back the same way. Five minutes after that the noise of boots on rocks indicated people coming up the ridge. Just in case, Graham moved down to the sentry post. It was Capt Conkey and the other two Hutchie Men.

As Porno went past, Graham asked, "What happened to your prisoner?"

"Captain, he make me let him go. Spoil sport I tink," Porno replied with an evil grin.

By then it was almost 0400hrs so Graham told Lucy to go to bed. As she walked over to where her bedding was, Graham experienced another bout of anxiety over what she might have seen and what she might say. He knew he was thoroughly ashamed of himself for giving in to Kirsty. But, to his disgust, he also knew he had a driving urge to be with her (or with any girl, the truth be known!).

The next hour crawled slowly by. The bright sickle of a new moon rose above the trees to the east, making it quite hard to see down the ridge but all remained silent. Just once a dog barked and some animal went grunting among the bushes down in the riverbed. Dianne said nothing and Graham did not want to talk to her anyway. Instead, he worried whether Lucy had told her about him and Kirsty. It became cooler but still not cold enough to really need a pullover or jacket. At about 0500hrs a gentle breeze began, blowing from the south.

It was time for the sentries to change so Dianne went and woke Roger then went to bed. Roger joined Graham and sat down and rubbed his eyes, then had a drink from his water bottle. The two friends sat in silence. Shame again scourged Graham as he thought of how he had let down his own friend, and his section.

I must stop misbehaving, he vowed.

The new moon rose above the far ridge and a faint streak of lightness appeared below it. That told Graham that dawn was not far off. A check of his watch told him they were to start getting ready to 'stand-to' in five minutes.

It took twenty minutes of cajoling and persuading to get the section awake and packed up. Andrews was his usual self but, to Graham's dismay, Kirsty was also surly and uncooperative.

"What's wrong?" he asked anxiously.

"I'm just tired, that's all," she replied shortly.

Not at all re-assured Graham moved on, his stomach churning with foreboding.

Even so 4 Section was the first ready. CUO Masters came along and checked they were all packed and had their webbing on. Satisfied he said, "Good," and moved along to Gwen's Section, where voices and muttering could still be heard.

As he did, a distant uproar of voices over on Sandy Ridge shattered the dawn calm. For an instant there was alarm, followed by grins. "4 Platoon attacking Heatley," Graham explained. For many kilometres around, the cockatoos and kookaburras broke into alarmed shrieking and squawking and many flew off.

The battle was a source of satisfaction but also a warning and Sgt Grenfell came along telling them to stay alert, just in case. The distant 'battle' died down and silence settled again. The birds changed to their normal dawn chorus. The breeze increased until it could almost be described as a cold wind. Capt Conkey, CSM Cleland, and CUO Masters came along checking every section was ready. Seeing the OC caused Graham severe twinges of guilt. Once again, he vowed to try to behave.

Daylight crept over them, the grey giving place to colours. The word went around to 'stand down'. That meant the exercise was over and they could relax without sentries. Having issued the order to stand down and eat Graham hurried down the ridge to ease his straining bladder. Having found a convenient clump of bushes and rocks a hundred metres down he proceeded to pee, only to discover to his horror that a whole line of cadets was filing into view from down near the road.

Unable to stop, Graham could only turn his back and finish as quickly as he could. Burning with embarrassment, he then hurried back up the slope ahead of the cadets, who he recognised as 4 Platoon. They trudged into the company area through Graham's section and he again experienced a sharp stab of jealousy to see their 'veteran's' swagger. They were all camouflaged and had their packs and webbing and really did look the part.

As they trudged past him, both Pigsy and Waters gave Graham sneering looks but they were too tired to cause any mischief. HQ Platoon followed them and Graham gave Peter a cheerful "G'day" as he passed. Peter smiled and said that it had been great fun. Following behind Peter, bowed down under his pack and an army radio, was Carnes. The sight of his miserable face made Graham wonder how he had got on.

I must ask Pete, he thought.

But he didn't get time. The usual morning routines claimed him. A work party of half the section was called for by Sgt Grenfell and went off over to the vehicles, returning with two Combat Ration Packs (One man 24 hour) for each person. Andrews and Halyday lugged a jerrycan of water back as well. The section settled to eating, washing, and filling water bottles. Graham shaved and brushed his boots, then badgered the others to do likewise.

That gave him a few twinges as he did not want to annoy Kirsty, for fear she might complain or say something. The old army saying for leaders to be, 'fair, firm, friendly, but not familiar' kept flitting through his head.

Serves me bloody right! Graham thought bitterly.

In spite of his misery, Graham pretended to be happy and kept hoping he could somehow retrieve the situation. A few glances by Lucy and Dianne, which might have meant they were discussing him, added to his discomfort. Feelings for despair, guilt and anger, became so strong he had to walk away down the ridge for a while. He used the time to do his morning crap, this time ensuring he wasn't going to be surprised in the middle of it. As he relieved himself, he again noted that there wasn't a cloud in the sky. By the time he finished, the sun was above the trees and shining full in his face.

By 0730hrs Graham was back with the section and quickly packed up everything, ready to march. That done he walked around the section, chivvying them to get ready. To his surprise they quickly did so. They even seemed to be in a good mood and Halyday cracked several jokes. Best of all Kirsty gave Graham a smile and that considerably eased his anxiety.

I might survive, he began to hope.

By then a Company O Group was under way and Sgt Grenfell came along and got Roger to organise the back-loading of rubbish and water jerries. Roger used Kirsty, Lucy, Pat and Andrews for the work. With nothing to do Graham wandered over to where HQ sat. Peter was checking radios and had no time to talk to him so Graham stood watching. Carnes was being made to help Peter change radio batteries. He looked a very tired and unhappy lad.

So did Sgt Yeldham. He was having trouble getting 3 Platoon packed and ready and looked tired and flustered. The remains of a red ink mark around his throat still showed and he obviously resented any comments on it. Inevitably Pigsy and Waters threw a few sarcastic jibes. Graham just shook his head and wasn't sure whether he felt sorry for Yeldham, or whether he despised him.

He's not very organised, he thought, noting that the sergeant's own bedding still wasn't rolled into his pack, and that cadets just seemed to be sitting around talking.

The arrival of an angry CSM Cleland injected energy into the scene. As this meant that the Coy O Group must be over Graham hurried back to his platoon. He was comfortably in time and sat with his notebook and pencil ready till Stephen and Gwen arrived and seated themselves beside him.

CUO Masters knelt in front of them. "The OC is very pleased with 2 Platoon," he said. "Thank you for your good work."

That made Graham both glow with pleasure- and burn with guilt. He hung his head and carefully noted timings and grid references for the day's training. It was fairly simple stuff, a section patrol exercise, so he quickly briefed his own section then had them sit on their packs ready to move. At 0755hrs, CSM Cleland called on the sergeants to move the troops in for a briefing. A couple of minutes later Graham sat in front of his section. By then the breeze had stopped and the full force of the morning sun shone on their backs.

Every platoon except 3 was ready by 0800hrs. Capt Conkey stood waiting, irritation clear on his face. CUO Mitrovitch stood nearby looking embarrassed as Sgt Yeldham tried to get the platoon organised.

As 3 Platoon at last began straggling over Stephen shook his head and muttered, "He's a bloody useless noddy!"

Sgt Yeldham was in a bad temper and shouted angrily at his cadets to hurry. "Get a move on Bragg, you useless little bugger!" he snapped at a straggler.

At that Capt Conkey interrupted. "Please call your cadets by their rank Sergeant Yeldham, and don't abuse them."

Yeldham flamed with embarrassment and could only nod. It was so unusual for the OC to deliver a public rebuke to one of the senior NCOs that Graham shook his head in worry. His anxieties were almost immediately increased when he felt Kirsty's knees press into his back.

Is she too crowded and doesn't have enough room, or? he worried. He looked over his shoulder to check and saw her eyes sparkle and she gave him an impish grin while nudging him again.

That was good news because it meant she wasn't angry with him. But it was bad news too because he realised that Capt Conkey was standing only a few paces away and was looking at him.

Breaking into a sweat, Graham thought, *I hope he can't see that Kirsty is touching me!*

It was still ten past 8 before CSM Cleland handed over to Capt Conkey. Capt Conkey then de-briefed them on the night's events. He was lavish in his praise of the 'airfield raiders' who had managed to outwit the defenders from St Michaels. Then he went on to explain the plan for the day's training. "We are moving along the bed of the Canning to the junction with the Bunyip. Along the way we will revise a few infantry minor tactics. After that a patrol incident course is to be set up. Each section will move along it to our new night position. That will be a few kilometres away from here, because I think we have stirred up Heatley and St Michaels and hurt their pride. They may try to get back at us."

There was a short pause as a burst of murmuring broke out and cadets grinned at each other. Capt Conkey held up his hand to silence them. "For that reason, 4 Platoon will deploy as a screen to cover us and will then move last through the course. There will also be a few other special patrols and I will be giving orders to their commanders later."

On hearing that Graham's hopes leapt. *Special patrols! I hope I get to lead one,* he thought.

But his anxiety was sent up by Capt Conkey's next words. "One of the things I will be particularly watching for on this patrol incident course is who might make potential leaders. I will be watching cadets to see if they are good team members, and watching section commanders to see if they have good control over their cadets."

That sent a chill of dread through Graham and he imagined Andrews mucking up, or Halyday rushing off, or, worse still, Kirsty disobeying him or flirting. He broke into a cold sweat and started to really fret. His ambition to be picked as one of the next year's sergeants seemed to be melting in the tropical sun.

The briefing over the company began to move. HQ and the Hutchie Men went first, leading the way down the back of the knoll and through the fence. 4 Platoon split up to deploy one patrol on the knoll, and others further south to watch the two vehicle tracks leading to the Bunyip Junction. That roused Graham's jealousy again as he was sure he could do a better job than Griffin or Dimbo. Then it was 2 Platoon's turn to move and he stood up and told the cadets to carry their packs by their top straps till they were through the fence.

As the filed down to the fence Sgt Yeldham was again in trouble because there was litter in 3 Platoon's area and four jerrycans still stood there. Graham glanced at Capt Conkey's angry face and hoped his mood would improve.

From the fence, the route wound steeply down around clumps of thorn bush and rubber vine until it became a narrow track cut through the thick tangle of vines. This led them through a tunnel of overhanging branches and out onto the dry, sandy bed of the Canning. Graham loved that. The idea of the company sneaking off along a secret track really appealed to his imagination. Then his thoughts were shifted back to Kirsty. Her pack got tangled in the vines and he had to go back and help free her. She gave him another mischievous grin as he did so.

Down in the riverbed they halted and were seated on their packs in the shade of the trees lining the bank. There was another delay of ten minutes till 3 Platoon arrived. An even grumpier Capt Conkey emerged from the trees after them and called out his CUOs, CSM and sergeants. There followed a talk-through revision of patrol techniques and what to do when they encountered a patrol from an opposing unit during a field exercise. The sections were then sent to do three quick practices out on the open sand: a talk through and two practices on the run. Because it was now very sweaty in the still air of the riverbed Graham had been anticipating some grumbling from his cadets, but they got up as soon as he called them and seemed to enter keenly into the revision.

Halyday and Pat both tried really hard. Even the girls threw themselves into the practice, only grumbling about the sand which stuck to their sweaty wrists. Kirsty even laughed once. Graham loved it, throwing himself down on the soft sand with relish, imagining he was fighting a real battle against some tough enemy.

After twenty minutes they were called in and told to get ready to move. The cadets hoisted on their packs and trudged west along the bed of the river. That was hard going and soon had them really sweating. Several times Graham licked dry lips and glanced up to see if any clouds had appeared. He also remembered to keep looking at his cadets to detect any heat problems. Knowing they could refill their water bottles at lunch time he made sure they kept drinking.

After ten minutes walking, during which they moved away from the knoll but were still hemmed in on two sides by the dense vegetation on the high banks, and by a growth of young suckers in the actual riverbed, they halted again. This time Capt Conkey had the CUOs and sergeants gave a demo of a Counter Ambush Drill. The sections were then sent to do a 'talk though', a 'walk through' and a running practice.

That really got them sweating but Graham felt confident he could cope with such an incident. *The section is really working well as a team,* he decided.

That was a comfort, as was the fact that Capt Conkey seemed to have relaxed and was smiling again. As the section stood talking after a practice, Kirsty came up to Graham and offered him a drink from her water bottle. He could not resist smiling back, mostly from relief that she wasn't liable to complain. Then he realised that Capt Conkey was looking towards them and he experienced a wave of anxiety.

'Packs on,' was ordered. Kirsty tried to swing hers on and then appealed to Graham to help. He half-suspected she was doing it just to get attention, but he moved over and helped her. In the process they touched elbows and hands a few times and she gave him another 'significant' look and a smile. That caused Graham a spurt of guilt and he glanced around, to find to his horror that Capt Conkey was again watching. The worrying idea that the OC might be deliberately observing them caused him to sweat even more.

Maybe he has been told about us and is watching to see if we misbehave, he thought. *I had better be more careful.*

The company trudged west for another ten minutes, then had another lesson, this time on 'Setting an Immediate Ambush'. As before the sections then did three quick practices in the trees and sand of the riverbed. Half an hour later they moved again, this time for only five minutes before halting at a point where the unit vehicles stood at the end of a dirt track which led down the bank. Another demo-lesson followed. This was on how to cope with the 'Body and the Sniper'.

No practices followed as they were now running short of time. Capt Conkey called over the CUOs and CSM and gave quick orders, then sent HQ to fill their water bottles from a line of jerrycans that Lt MacLaren had organised on the bank. It was 1045 by then and Graham felt hot and tired. So did his cadets who looked worn out. Kirsty looked very pale and had dark rings under her eyes. Even so she smiled.

Capt Conkey gave a briefing on the patrol incident course while Lt McEwen led away the CUOs, sergeants, and HQ platoon. Packs were placed in platoon lots beside the vehicle track and then it was time for 1 Section to move. The other sections were given their start time, 15 minutes apart, and were told to rest, have lunch and make sure their water bottles were full. Capt Conkey and CSM Cleland then walked off across the riverbed and vanished into the trees. That got Graham worried again.

The OC will be watching at the worst possible moment, he thought gloomily.

Chapter 23

UNDER PRESSURE

4 Section was not due to move until 1230hrs so Graham told them to have their lunch, go to the toilet, and to rest. He sat with his cadets in the shade on the soft, white river sand and munched ration pack biscuits coated with apricot jam. Normally he would have been extremely happy in such an environment but now he felt very stressed. Anxiety about how he would handle the coming incident course mixed with doubts about himself.

I'm a bloody weakling, he thought unhappily.

Dozens of incidents where he should have shown greater courage or will power flitted across his mind to mock him and to scorch his self-esteem. All he could do was pretend he was happy and relaxed, while wondering unhappily how he might do better. What really bothered him was the idea that he actually might be a coward, and that he was too scared to really put things to the test when his courage was challenged.

Kirsty was no help. She sat next to him and chattered away as though she didn't have a care in the world. She gave him frequent 'loving' looks and that caused Graham to worry because Lt Maclaren and Lt McEwen were both sitting nearby. The best he could do was pretend he was tired and then lie down with his hat over his eyes. But even that made him feel weak.

I'm just hiding, not solving the problem, he told himself. Inside he knew that he was scared of being firm with Kirsty in case she rejected him. Or worse, that out of spite, she might tell on him. *Reject their advances at your peril!* he brooded. The problem was compounded by the fact that he really did like her, as well as being driven by strong desires.

Hearing the distant shouts and yells of unseen actions in the undergrowth did nothing to ease the tension. After 3 Section filed off to start the exercise, Graham's stomach tightened into a hard knot. As the time to move drew closer he became increasingly restless. A nervous pee did not seem to help at all, merely added to his feelings of inadequacy. He had heard many mocking comments about people wetting themselves when afraid and he wondered if he might be one of them. However, there did not seem to be any alternative but to go on.

I can't just say I'm sick or something, he thought.

The best he could manage was to tell jokes with Stephen, then to drink and refill his water bottles. At 1225hrs he stood up and began putting on his webbing. By then he did feel sick in the stomach.

"Up you get 4 Section," he croaked.

"Who goes where in the patrol?" Andrews asked as he reluctantly got up.

Graham had been thinking hard about that. "Pat, you and Halyday go scouts."

"Aw! I wanted to be a scout," Andrews whined.

"Shut up and do as you are told!" Graham snapped. He was so stressed he had no time for argument. He turned and said, "Roger, you and Kirsty are the gun group, Group 1, Di and Lucy and Ando are the rifle group, Group 2."

To his relief the others accepted this and he was able to line them up without further trouble. Then they stood and waited. It was very hot and sweat trickled down into their eyes and soaked their shirts. Graham wiped his face, looked at his watch for the tenth time then noted it was time to go. He glanced at Lt Maclaren who nodded.

As he gave the signal to move, Graham felt his stomach churn with queasiness. For a moment he felt dizzy and he wondered if he really was going to be sick. But he made himself walk and went trudging across the dry sand behind Halyday.

After wading the ankle-deep flow of water, the section threaded through a stand of young trees. They came out on a smaller dry river channel. This had the small trees on the left and the high bank covered with large, overhanging trees and rubber vines on the right. The boot prints went left so Graham directed the scouts that way. Now that they were pretending to patrol, they spread out so that there were 10 paces between people- or at least there was at the front. Graham found he had to keep turning round to signal or hiss at the three girls and Andrews to spread out. "Stop bunching up!" he whispered loudly at them.

"Bang!" shouted a voice from the trees on the left.

It was an ambush left. After the initial moments of flustered panic Graham got Roger, Andrews and the three girls in line on his left and counter attacked. By the time he had swept through the ambushers, he was sweating profusely and his heart was pounding furiously but he thought he had coped alright. He had managed to keep control of the people with him while Pat and Halyday had done the right thing.

The ambush party comprised CUO McAlistair, Sgt Sherry and Cadet Lyle from the medics. CUO McAlistair pointed to where a small, dry gully led into the riverbed.

"That was well done Cpl Kirk. Now take your section up that gully there. It is Dingo Creek."

Graham gulped down a big drink and wiped sweat from his face as he eyed Dingo Creek. Overhanging trees hid the entrance, which had a large, muddy pool almost closing it off. Beyond that the creek bed was sand and dry mud in a deep gully five metres wide. Both banks appeared to be an impenetrable tangle of rubber vines and thorn bushes. The sides were 5 to 10 metres high and almost vertical in places. A few large trees topped the bank, amidst clumps of vine and long grass. Thistles and some sort of waist-high purple weed grew thickly in places along the creek bed.

Bloody hell! Graham thought gloomily. *This looks a bit grim.*

Nervously they entered Dingo Creek one at a time, their eyes anxiously scanning the thick undergrowth for signs of lurking enemy. About 50 paces on they had to skirt a sludge filled pool under a small tree. The creek then curved left. No breeze penetrated into the deep cleft and the midday sun blazed down directly into it so that a heat wave shimmered off the sand. Graham noted a snake track, pig tracks and wallaby droppings but found his eyes seemed to go fuzzy when he tried to search for hidden enemy.

Then Pat signalled and Graham put them all under cover while he went forward to look. It was a rope tied across the creek bed with a sign hanging on it reading: MINES. Another 20 paces on was a second rope, presumably to show the far side of the minefield. A few tins were just visible in the sand. They coped by Graham deploying two groups to cover while the scouts prodded a path across. Then he followed, half-expecting the enemy to open fire as he did. Then he had each of the other groups join him one at a time.

Around the next bend in the creek was a log which they had to crawl under. Beyond that the creek ran straight for nearly a hundred paces.

Both banks were high and covered in thick weeds or vine scrub. Near the far end of the straight was another large log across the creek and beyond that the creek curved to the right. Worse still, Capt Conkey and CSM Cleland were standing watching near the second log.

"Oh bugger!" Graham muttered.

Seeing the OC and CSM made him sure there was going to be a difficult problem to cope with. He hesitated, trying to pick what the problem might be, or where the enemy might be waiting.

I'd like time to scout along the top of both banks, he thought. He also decided that if he was really on patrol he wouldn't even be in the bed of the gully. *It's just a bloody death trap. I'd cut my way through that vine scrub instead.*

But he wasn't given that option. Capt Conkey called on him to get a move on. Reluctantly, knowing he was walking into disaster, Graham signalled for the scouts to move. Pat and Halyday at least did it well, moving alternately from cover to cover, one on each side of the 5-metre-wide creek bed.

It happened about when Graham was sure it would, and even from where he thought it would; from the top of the bank above the bend directly ahead of him. Voices began yelling "Bang! Bang!"

"Contact Front!" Graham screamed.

He dashed three paces left to the nearest cover, rolling in under the long grass, hoping there were no snakes there. As he did, he tried to decide which bank was the higher so he could order his fire support group to go there. He decided that the left bank was the same height and easier to get up and began screaming to Roger, then saw that Roger and Kirsty were already trying to claw their way up the other bank.

Knowing that Capt Conkey and the CSM were watching added to Graham's feelings of losing control, of failure and of fear. He became flustered and shouted to Roger to come back, then changed his mind as they were already halfway up. That bank was so steep that in places it had been eroded and undermined to expose bare grey earth. His throat hot and dry with shouting, Graham tried to come up with a plan and, at the same time, control his section. He yelled for Lucy and Di to move forward to join him.

"Climb the bank on the left Group Two!" he shouted.

As he did, he signalled frantically with his arm. That was all he could manage before the dust and dry grass caused him to have a fit of coughing. He gasped and spat and tried again. There were muffled cries in reply, over-ridden by screaming from in front. Graham began clawing his way up through the long grass and vines, getting snagged and tangled at every step. Completely snared and now desperate he stopped, chest heaving, to try to work out what to do. He then saw what the shouting in front was. Halyday had raced on along the creek bed, dashing from cover to cover, on a one-man suicide attack. Pat was trying to give him 'covering fire' while yelling at him to stop.

Halyday didn't. He dashed on past the OC and CSM, rolled under the log and launched himself up the steep slope directly into the front of the enemy.

"Oh bloody hell!" Graham cried in despair. *We've made a real stuff-up of this!* he thought miserably.

As Halyday scrabbled up the slope Graham groaned with anguish. But then he heard voices up on the bank above him. It was Lucy, Di, and Andrews. "We found an animal track," Lucy called.

Graham looked around and saw that Roger and Kirsty had managed to get to the top of the other bank and were crawling forward through long grass to a big tree.

That would make a good fire support position, he thought. *Maybe...*

By then Halyday had climbed the bank and Graham heard Sgt Yeldham screaming, "You are… *dead*, you idiot! Lie down and shut up!"

"Stop using that sort of language, Sgt Yeldham!" Capt Conkey bellowed.

Graham took heart. *If I can get up to the top we might do it yet.*

But when he tried he just tripped and became entangled in the vines again. Almost frantic to try to do well while Capt Conkey was watching, Graham struggled till he thought his heart would burst. It was no good. He was only halfway up the bank but was ensnared.

"Lucy! Di! Keep going along the top of the bank to attack. I will try to get up to join you," he shouted.

Knowing that Capt Conkey would hear that Graham burned with humiliation. *What will he think of me!* he thought unhappily. *The section commander who leads from the rear!*

But it was better than doing nothing, so he repeated the order. When he was sure the others were moving, he stopped and took stock of his own predicament. Slowly, one limb at a time, he disentangled himself. Then he was able to slide down beneath the vines and crawl. Dirt and leaves fell on him and went down the back of his collar to aggravate and irritate but he was so upset he ignored them. Wriggling as fast as he could and still hoping there were no snakes, he struggled up the slope.

By the time he arrived on a narrow animal pad on top he could hear that the battle was joined. A glance across the gully showed Kirsty and Roger 'firing' from behind two big trees. Heedless of scratches, Graham dashed along the animal pad, wrenching himself free from any snagging vines by brute force. His heart hammered and his breath came in hot gasps, but he was driven to catch up and lead.

In this he was not successful but only by a few paces. He glimpsed Capt Conkey down in the bed of the gully just as he caught up with Andrews. By then the two girls were standing facing CUO Mitrovitch and Sgt Yeldham. Halyday sat under a bush looking grumpy.

"That will do, Cpl Kirk," Capt Conkey called. "Bring your section down and keep going with the exercise."

Graham stood and gasped air, then gestured to go down the slope along another animal pad. By the time he had slithered down in a cloud of dust he was sweating so much he was coated in grime and had trouble seeing. While he waited for Roger and Kirsty to descend, he had a big drink and washed some of the dirt and sweat off his face.

"Well done gang," he croaked.

He made them all drink, then swapped Andrews and Kirsty to be scouts and got them moving. He was quite unsure how he had performed in the OC's estimation but felt very anxious. This was increased when he noted that Capt Conkey and CSM Cleland were walking along behind the section as they continued on.

Oh no! There must be more, he thought.

A feeling of something close to despair swept through him. Dingo Creek curved right and then ran straight for another hundred metres. It looked awfully like the same scenario and Graham gritted his teeth and prepared to face whatever it was. Then he found himself grinning at Roger.

Bugger it! he thought. *I have probably cashed my chips so I may as well enjoy myself.*

Over the next 20 paces he calmed down. His breathing slowed and he found he could see clearly. He noted animal tracks going up either bank, and that a clump of large trees grew in the bed of the creek at the next bend.

It will be there, he decided.

He acted on that instinct and signalled to Andrews. He was right. Andrews angled up onto the bank to where he could get a better view. Almost at once he went into a crouch, giving the thumb down 'enemy' sign.

Graham moved the section over against the bank and crept forward to look. By now the rubber vine was giving way to grass and trees and he had to move slowly on a thick carpet of leaf litter and dead sticks. From behind a tree he looked around the bend and saw a small 'enemy camp': a couple of hutchies and a smoky fire. Peter was there, with Carnes, LCpl Kate O'Brien, and Cpl Forman. Their red shoulder flashes indicated they were 'enemy'.

A plan formed itself and Graham had to make himself pause to check it wasn't the wrong one. After a minute's thought he decided it was a good plan. With that confidence he slid back and called in Roger. With a stick he drew a sketch map in the sand and explained what he wanted to happen. He was aware that Capt Conkey and CSM Cleland were standing listening but now it did not bother him.

Roger went up to place Andrews and Lucy in position on the side of the bank as the 'fire support' while Graham led the others back 25 metres, then up a cattle pad on the right that he had noticed earlier. This brought them out in fairly open, flat country on top. After another quick explanation he led them along the top of the bank, keeping well back and using the clumps of rubber vines and thorn bushes as cover. When he was opposite the clump of big trees Graham lined his group up in extended line facing the creek and signalled them to walk forward.

The attack began. As Graham's assault reached the top of the bank, Roger's group opened fire. The assault was able to slither down the bank side by side, the slope being suitable for this and free of vines. In a minute Peter's group were all pretending to be dead.

That went well, Graham thought, returning Kirsty's grin as they stopped on the other bank. He began to detail people to search in pairs but was stopped by Capt Conkey.

"That was good, Cpl Kirk. Now, take you patrol up this track here towards the river," he said, pointing up another animal pad on the other bank.

Graham nodded and changed the scouts to Di and Kirsty. He smiled at Peter. "Got you that time mate," he said.

Peter laughed. "You did better than the last mob of drongos. They just charged along the creek bed in a bunch."

"See you later then," Graham replied, signalling to the scouts to move.

Peter shook his head. "Not till tomorrow. I have to do a recon patrol for the big exercise," he answered.

At that Graham again experienced a wave of envy. "Lucky bugger," he said. He then turned to Cadet Carnes who was sitting looking miserable. "Cheer up. We didn't really shoot you then."

"I wish you had!" Carnes blurted out.

Graham was shocked and shook his head as Carnes began to cry. *Bloody hell!* he thought. *He's a mess this kid.* After giving Peter a frown of sympathy, he followed the scouts up the bank towards the river.

To his relief, Graham saw that Capt Conkey and CSM Cleland were not following. They walked back down Dingo Creek. Graham breathed more easily and settled down to enjoy himself. The next incident was a 'body and sniper' at a clearing amid thick clumps of rubber vines in a dense forest of big trees. The 'body' was CUO Masters and Graham guessed that Sgt Grenfell would be the sniper. That made him extra careful and he deployed his cadets under cover. He then directed the scouts where to search and they found Sgt Grenfell without getting caught in the open.

CUO Masters stood up, dusting himself down as he did. "That was good work 4 Section, the best one yet. Now follow the track to the riverbank."

Graham glowed at the praise and smiled happily at the section. They looked pleased with themselves too and Graham had an urge to give Kirsty a hug when she grinned at him. Resisting the urge, he signalled move, sending Halyday and Roger as the scouts.

The next section of track was cut through 200 metres of dense rubber vines among very tall trees. The whole thing formed a gloomy forest and Graham hoped they would not have to battle though it. They didn't. They came out on the bank of the Bunyip above a lovely little island of rocks and grass. The island had a few trees growing on it and looked very inviting. The water either side of the island was crystal clear and looked to be about waist deep. Beyond that was a wide stretch of white sand and pebbles about 500 metres across. This terminated in a line of steep, red soil bluffs which marked the far bank.

Lt Standish sat in the shade of a tree with a radio and First Aid kit. She directed them on along a faint track on top of the bank to their right. For 300 metres nothing happened. Then they had a battle with the Hutchie Men, who suddenly sprang up in their yowie suits.

"Make you crap in pants then eh Kirky?" Porno said after the battle.

Graham denied this heatedly, although he had got a fright. The Hutchie Men all laughed and sent the section on along the top of the bank. The trail was hard to follow, just a few vines or branches snipped clear, but Graham was now enjoying himself.

About 500 metres upstream, they halted where a dry 'anabranch' (flood overflow channel) joined the main river. The water in the main channel flowed cool and clear close under the trees and the section stopped by mutual consent to have a drink.

"A swim would be nice," Kirsty said.

"We aren't allowed," Graham said.

"And I didn't bring my bathers," Roger added.

"We could go skinny dipping," Kirsty replied with a mischievous glint in her eye.

That really got Graham speculating and he met her challenging gaze. Then he shook his head. and whispered to her: "That would be great, but no way. I don't want to get chucked out of Cadets thank you. If you want to do that, we can have a picnic at Kamerunga or Freshwater Creek when we get home."

"Oh spoilsport!" Kirsty replied, but she laughed and Graham knew she was daring him.

That got his heart beating fast with hopeful lust but also reminded him of his problems. *Don't be weak!* he told himself. *You are your own worst enemy Kirk,* he added, as his mind began to speculate on what it might be like to swim naked with Kirsty.

To end the discussion, he directed them on along the dry bed of the flood channel. The flood channel was ten to twenty metres wide with sand dunes on both sides. The sand dunes were about five metres high and were thickly covered in bushes and rubber vines. Every hundred metres or so a clump of trees blocked off vision along the line of grassy flats. Graham found it a very interesting environment and enjoyed the battles they had. There was plenty of cover and the sandy soil and grass were 'soft' when crawling or rolling.

They dealt with two 'lost navigators' and then had to set an immediate ambush to catch two HQ cadets. One last battle was fought at a large open area covered in grass so that it looked like a lawn. This was against the CQMS and Cpl Brookes. As they re-organised afterwards, Sgt Gayney pointed over the grassy dune towards the high bank.

"Go up to the top of the bank and collect your packs and a jerrycan, then come back and go over there and wait," she said, turning to point over a low grassy dune towards the river.

"Is the exercise over?" Roger asked.

She nodded. *Whew! Thank God!* Graham thought, even though he had really started to enjoy himself.

He checked the time and saw it was just coming up to 1500hrs. A cattle pad led over the dune through a belt of lantana and rubber vine. It dipped through a second, narrower flood channel before climbing steeply up the line of ten metre high, sandy bluffs that marked the actual banks of the river. The track up was steep and composed of fine red dust which rose in a cloud to tickle their nostrils and throats.

On top of the bank was flat, open country and they found the unit vehicles parked there and lines of packs on the grass. Lt Maclaren showed them 2 Platoon's packs and also reminded them to take a jerrycan of water. Once he had put on his pack, Graham picked up the full jerrycan and lugged it down the steep slope. At the bottom he handed it to Andrews and led them on across the second flood channel and dune to the wide, grassy area and over the low dune. From there they walked out across a hundred metres of sand to several lines of paperbark trees growing out of small grassy mounds. Graham led the section across to them and found Lt McEwen sitting there. She pointed along the sandy 'avenue' under the trees and indicated 2 Platoon's bivouac area.

Chapter 24

BESIDE THE BUNYIP

The new bivouac area was about a hundred metres long and consisted of two lines of overhanging paperbark trees, each about 10 metres apart. On one side was the water of the river and on the other the wide area of sand. To Graham it looked like a lovely spot and he was happy to dump his pack and flop down on the clean, white sand. The others joined him, Kirsty making sure she was next to him.

That got Graham worried again. After what he saw as the debacle on the patrol course, he did not want further problems from Kirsty.

Not if I ever want to be a sergeant!

But how to tactfully put her off until after the camp?

That kept him puzzling for the next ten minutes before 5 Section arrived. They were neatly lined up on the other side of the 'avenue' by Gwen. Graham found himself looking into Barbara's green eyes and she gave him a friendly smile.

"How did it go?" he asked.

Barbara made a face and laughed. "A few little problems, I think."

"Problems!" Gwen cried. "Disasters you mean! And with the OC watching."

They discussed the patrol course until the arrival of 6 Section. Stephen plonked himself down next to Roger and Graham and began to bewail how his section had been annihilated along the way.

"Bloody Hutchie Men! They scared the crap out of me!" Stephen said. "My bloody glasses were fogged up in the heat and then these huge things jumped up from behind the bushes right next to me. I thought they were wild pigs and nearly shat myself."

They all laughed and talked about the Hutchie Men. The first section of 3 Platoon arrived looking all hot and bothered. Soon afterwards CSM Cleland came along. He at once instructed them to start collecting firewood.

"Two lots, one for your platoon fire, which will be here, and one for the company fire back there where Lt McEwen is sitting."

There was no shortage of driftwood brought down by the floods and Graham enjoyed walking around on the sand without his webbing. Kirsty and Roger both walked with him, Kirsty chatting away happily the whole time and continually meeting his eye.

"What do we do tonight?" she asked.

In his anxiety Graham nearly snapped 'read your bloody program!' but managed to hide his irritation and bite this back. Instead, he said, "It is down as reserved, but I think we are getting a free night."

"Ooh! Goody!" Kirsty cried, flashing him a 'come-hither' look.

That set Graham sweating again as CSM Cleland had just emerged from the trees nearby and was watching them. "Just the people I need," he said. "Dunny digging details. Round up your section Cpl Kirk and go up to the vehicle to get two shovels, two washbasins and two more jerrycans."

"Oh bummer!" Roger cried.

They dumped their loads of firewood and Graham called to Andrews and Halyday to join them. Pat and the other two girls appeared with more wood and were told to follow. Graham then led the others back along the cattle pad across the flood channels and up to the top of the bank. On their return they were met by CSM Cleland at the main grassy flood channel and he took the three girls upstream to dig the girls' latrine and then came back to site the boys' latrine. This was in among the bushes on the ridge between the two grassy flood channels.

The digging was easy enough in the sandy soil and the work only took twenty minutes. Graham walked from one site to the other to ensure they were dug correctly, not wanting CSM Cleland to find his section at fault. He actually enjoyed that. By then the heat had gone out of the afternoon sun and a cool breeze had begun blowing along the river.

This is a really pleasant spot, he thought, pausing to look out over the riverbed to the trees lining the far bank.

He was also pleased with the section. Even Andrews worked without too much grumbling. *They have developed into a real team,* he thought. The only fly in the ointment, he decided, was his relationship with Kirsty. *And that is my own stupid fault for giving in when she started flirting.*

The remainder of 3 Platoon had come in by the time they finished and the area under the trees was now quite crowded and busy. Not uncomfortably crowded though, as there was plenty of room to walk along between the people and lines of packs. Each platoon was separated by about ten metres of sand from its neighbour.

As 4 Section returned to their area, Lucy asked, “Where do we put up our hutchies?”

Graham looked around then shook his head. “Under one of these trees I suppose, but I don’t think that is the plan.”

“You mean we just sleep out in the open again?” Dianne asked.

Graham nodded. “I’d say we just sleep here on the sand under the trees. They will keep the dew off us.”

“What if there is a flood?” Andrews asked.

Graham groaned inwardly at the looks of concern that crossed the other’s faces. He shook his head in exasperation. “It is September. There hasn’t been any rain for weeks. I’m sure Capt Conkey has thought about that. If he didn’t think it was safe, he wouldn’t let us camp here.”

Andrews looked doubtful. “I hope so,” he said.

“You can go and camp up on the bank if you like,” Graham replied. “But I am sleeping here. I reckon it is a great spot to camp.”

Their discussion was ended by the arrival of the CUOs and sergeants. That meant that the exercise was over. In the distance Graham saw 4 Platoon filing in under the trees down past where the officers were standing. CUO Masters was with them but Sgt Grenfell came along to join the platoon. He dumped his pack and said, “Swim time.”

“But I haven’t got any bathers!” wailed Halyday.

“Swim in your dirty uniform and wash it at the same time,” Sgt Grenfell replied.

“But I’ve only got one uniform,” Halyday replied.

“All the more reason to wash it, you grub! Where is your second uniform?” Sgt Grenfell asked.

“In my kitbag,” Halyday replied.

“Too bad,” Sgt Grenfell replied unsympathetically. “You were told to have it packed.”

Graham sighed. He had warned them there would be a swim as it was on the printed camp program they had all been issued. For that reason, he had stuffed a pair of old shorts in his pack, along with his second uniform.

Andrews looked anxiously around. “There are no change rooms,” he said. “Where do we change?”

Graham straightened up from rummaging in his pack and looked at him to see if he was making a joke. When he realised Andrews wasn't, he was astounded. With a disbelieving shake of the head, he gestured downstream to the trees.

"There are hundreds of kilometres of trees and bushes Ando. Hop behind one and change."

"But what if someone comes along?"

Again, Graham shook his head. Stephen answered for him, "It's not that bloody big! No-one will notice. Stop being ridiculous."

The girls all giggled. Andrews sniffed with injured pride and stalked off with his bathers. Graham shook his head and dug out his shorts. The girls went off across the open sand towards their latrine area to change. Stephen, Roger, and Graham walked down past 3 Platoon and HQ and then across into the bushes on the nearby dune.

Leaving his shirt on Graham pulled off trousers and underpants and then went to pull on his shorts. As he did, three people came around the bushes: Pigsy, Waters, and Moynihan.

Pigsy sneered and pointed. "Hello! We've caught the three poofs at it."

The other bullies laughed, and Graham felt anger surge in his blood. Stephen hauled up his own bathers and turned to them, "Is that what you jokers do, sneak around to watch other boys change?"

"Listen four-eyes!" Pigsy snarled. He raised his fists and scowled.

Graham hauled up his shorts and quickly zipped them up, then turned to face Pigsy and his mates. He was angry now. "Piss off Pike! Why don't you go and join your porky mates?"

For a second Graham thought he had gone too far and Pigsy would attack. But all he did was sneer and scowl, while Moynihan laughed. To Graham's relief, the bullies moved on, Waters saying, "Let's find a place where these faggots can't perve on us."

As they went out of sight, Graham heaved a sigh of relief. He scooped up his clothing and boots, then stood watch till Roger and Stephen were changed. The three friends walked back together. By then dozens of cadets were splashing in the water. Capt Conkey and CSM Cleland stood on a small sandy island in midstream and the other officers sat or stood on the bank. The depth varied from ankle deep to knee deep. Only in a few small gutters did it reach waist deep. The water was cool and very refreshing. There was just enough current to make it pleasant.

Graham lay down and then sat to wash his shirt and trousers. Having thoroughly rinsed them he walked to the bank and returned to the platoon area to drape them across the branches of a tree. As he did, Barbara and Gwen came along in their bathers. Graham badly wanted to look as both appeared to be very attractive, but he didn't want them to think he was leering at them, so he concentrated on spreading the wet clothes.

Kirsty, Di, and Lucy appeared, also in bathers, and Graham felt another surge of interest. Kirsty wore a white one-piece which made her look very nice, although it did emphasise that she had small breasts.

Lovely hips and thighs though, Graham conceded.

They all waded in and Halyday and Andrews started a splashing game. Predictably all the girls shrieked as the drops of cold water hit them and there was a lot of laughter and running around for a few minutes. After that they lay in the shallow water and talked. Much to Graham's annoyance Kirsty stayed close beside him, frequently touching him. That got him quite aroused as well as anxious as Capt Conkey and CSM Cleland were still watching.

To hide his condition, Graham lay on his front. Kirsty lay beside him. She nudged his arm and gave an impish grin. "I thought we were going to go skinny dipping?" she whispered.

"Not now. After camp," Graham replied with rising excitement.

"We could go upstream behind those rocks," Kirsty suggested, indicating some clumps of rocks and bushes a hundred metres away.

Graham shook his head. "No, we have to stay here."

"You just aren't game," Kirsty replied.

That annoyed Graham. "I am. I just don't want to get into trouble."

Kirsty gave him a curious look. "I heard you have been skinny dipping with girls before."

Graham blushed and grunted. Heated memories of these occasions flooded through his mind. Mostly they were of him with Margaret. That caused him twinges of guilt because he knew Margaret really loved him.

"Not at cadets," he replied.

"I heard about some cadets swimming in the nuddy at a bivouac earlier this year," Kirsty answered.

Graham glanced sideways to see if Stephen was within hearing. He shook his head. "It wasn't us. It was some other corporals."

"What happened?"

"Ask Gwen. She was there," Graham replied.

He thought Kirsty would drop the subject but to his surprise she called to Gwen. Both Gwen and Barbara paddled over. Kirsty put the question and Gwen looked serious. She also glanced to see if Stephen was watching.

"The girl was Stephen's girlfriend," she explained. "A girl named Elli. We were on a navigation exercise at a place called Bridle Creek."

As Gwen told the story, Graham experienced sharp flashbacks to the event. The images aroused him but also filled him with concern for Stephen. Stephen had been devastated to find his girl swimming nude with Brooks, Crane, and Costigan. It had been a bad time for both of them. Elli had then left cadets.

The story was interrupted by shouts and splashing. A group of boys came running through the shallow water. It was Pigsy and Co. They pushed Roger over then ducked Halyday before running over to Graham. Before Graham could get up Pigsy ran over and jumped on top of him, placing a foot in the middle of his back and forcing him under. Other feet kicked and pushed. A moment's panic turned to anger.

As soon as the pressure was removed, Graham surfaced and sprang to his feet. He found Pigsy being confronted by Barbara. She had her hand ready to slap.

"You touch me buster and you will regret it!" she snapped.

Pigsy sneered and said, "Big talk, bitch!" but he turned away and kept on running.

The group of bullies ran over to duck several more boys then descended on a couple of First Years with shouts and jeering laughter. There was a flurry of foam and Graham glimpsed Moynihan running off holding a pair of bathers. More cruel laughter echoed along the river.

"Stop that nonsense!" bellowed Capt Conkey. "Sergeant Yeldham, keep those people under control."

Pigsy and his mates stopped running and flopped down in the shallow water, but they kept on snickering and glancing at the boy they had just ducked. Graham saw that it was young Bragg and that he was looking anxiously around.

"I think they just dacked Braggy," he said. "Took his bathers."

Gwen looked and shook her head. "Sgt Yeldham is there."

"I think he was involved," Graham added.

Gwen and Barbara both stood up and began wading towards Bragg. Bragg saw them coming and paddled off away from him. They sped up and so did he. Suddenly Bragg curled up, his hands holding himself. He had no bathers on alright. It was obvious he was fiercely embarrassed and afraid.

Gwen called loudly, "Are you alright, Cadet Bragg?"

Graham saw Bragg shake his head, but he did not hear his reply. Whatever he said incensed Gwen as she turned and snapped at Moynihan, "Give Cadet Bragg back his bathers."

Moynihan scowled but did as he was told. Bragg squirmed and struggled to get his bathers back on while keeping himself hidden in the shallow water. Then he floundered to the shore and went scuttling up into the trees, followed by jeers and mocking laughter. Gwen turned her back on him and directed a withering glance across to where Sgt Yeldham and a dozen others were kneeling or standing in a group.

"You should have controlled that," she said.

Yeldham scowled back. "Mind your own business," he snapped. He was red with anger and shame.

Gwen turned on him in righteous fury. "You! Call yourself a sergeant! You make me sick!"

At that moment, Capt Conkey's voice called from the bank, "What's going on now?"

They all turned to look. Graham saw Yeldham's face drain of colour. Gwen began wading to the shore, followed by Barbara. "Cadet Bragg has been assaulted sir," she said.

That got Capt Conkey's attention and he and CSM Cleland turned and hurried to meet the two girls. Pigsy and Co looked worried and began dispersing quietly among the crowd.

Poor bloody kid! Graham thought.

A touch on his thigh caused him to jump in fright. It was Kirsty and she had her fingers on the big scar on his left thigh. "Is that a scar?" she asked.

"Yes," he replied, subsiding back into the water. His eyes met Stephen's and Stephen frowned.

"How did you get it?" Kirsty asked.

Again, Graham's eyes met Stephen's and this time a look of intense distress crossed his face. "In a knife fight," Graham mumbled.

He was assailed by sharp images of those moments of sheer terror on the dark mountain road above Cairns back in March. He had been stabbed and left to bleed to death by a man who had just cut the throat of a young boy. Only Stephen's courageous night walk had saved him.

That led to further images, of how he and Stephen had marched all night to cross the Lamb Range then crept up to the paedophiles secret camp at a gravel quarry. More nightmare images came to him: of his own fear as he had tried to escape from the same man and of his terror while he scrambled desperately to escape from the front-end loader the man was driving. The memories threw into his consciousness the whole question of courage.

I was game to go with Stephen but I was really scared, he thought. Other images of fear and weakness came to shake his self-confidence.

He gave Kirsty a brief account of how he got the wound, being helped by Stephen. Kirsty then said, "Show me your scar again."

Stephen gave a smirk, and said, "Are you sure it's his scar you want to see?"

Kirsty poked her tongue at him. Roger frowned and shook his head. Graham flamed with embarrassment. The situation was ended by the return of Gwen and Barbara.

"Bloody Yeldham," Gwen said. "He was there and did nothing to stop that."

"I think we should get out," Roger suggested.

By common consent they made their way to the bank and collected their clothes. As they made their way up through the trees Graham glimpsed a very unhappy looking Sgt Yeldham wading towards Capt Conkey and Lt Standish.

The boys made their way off into the bushes to change. Graham put on a clean, dry uniform and felt much better. They made their way back to the platoon area to find that the incident was the main topic of conversation. The consensus was that Yeldham was a bully and a drongo.

Sgt Grenfell came along and told them to have their tea. He also said they could remain barefoot while in the trees. Graham sat on his pack and began cooking. Roger, Stephen, Gwen and Barbara all sat in a circle with him. Graham noted Kirsty looking for a place in the circle and hoped she wouldn't try to push in. To his annoyance she did, right next to him. Roger grudgingly made room for her. Stephen smirked and Gwen and

Barbara both gave him questioning looks. All Graham could do was try not to blush and pretend nothing had happened.

The fate of the bullies was still the main topic of conversation. As the friends talked, they cooked and ate the tinned rations, using their hexamine stoves. Kirsty kept whispering to Graham, which annoyed him as the others were obviously aware of it.

"I enjoyed that swim," she said.

"Yes," he replied unhelpfully.

"When are we going swimming on our own?"

That got Graham's attention. *She really does want to go swimming with me,* he thought. The thought of Kirsty nude caused his heart rate to shoot up and he began to fantasise.

"During the holidays after camp I suppose," he said. Then he shook his head. "Oh! No. Sorry. I can't do that. I am going hiking with Peter, Stephen, and Roger."

"Oh poo! I would be more fun than them," Kirsty said with a pout. "Where are you going?"

You would be too! Graham thought, but alarm bells were ringing. *She is under age; jail bait,* he warned himself. *Stay out of the water if it is too deep, or too hot, or full of bloody sharks!*

He took a deep breath and replied, "A place called Stannary Hills. It's in the mountains west of Herberton."

"What are you going there for?" she asked.

They were actually going to do research on the old mining railways so they could build more of their own model railway layout. However, Graham did not want Kirsty to think he was a little boy who still played with trains, so he said, "To look at the old mines and ghost towns."

"Ghost towns! Oooh! Tell me more," Kirsty cried.

As Graham described the outline history of Stannary Hills and what they hoped to find, he saw a very chastened Sgt Yeldham rejoin 3 Platoon. Bragg appeared with Lt Standish. It was obvious he had been weeping and still looked upset. CUO Masters and CUO Mitrovitch came along with an angry looking Capt Conkey and they stood with Bragg while he collected his gear. Then they walked on towards 2 Platoon.

"Hello, what gives?" Stephen murmured.

Capt Conkey and Lt Standish stopped to talk to CUO Mitrovitch, who looked most unhappy. CUO Masters walked on with Bragg. Sgt

Grenfell went to meet them. After a few minutes talk, during which they glanced several times in Graham's direction, they continued on. As they got closer, Graham hoped that he was wrong. He hoped that it was Gwen or Stephen they were making for.

It wasn't. Graham was called out. He stood up and moved to join the group. "Yes, sir?"

"Cadet Bragg is now in your section. He has been given a hard time so look after him," CUO Masters explained.

"Yes, sir," Graham replied.

He met Bragg's eyes and managed a smile, but he wasn't amused. Bragg was a Year 8 with a reputation for being both cheeky and very dumb. His one saving attribute, so it was said around the school, was his good-looking sister in Year 10. Having no choice, Graham led Bragg around to the other side of the circle and moved his own gear back to make space for him between him and Kirsty.

She pouted at that but said nothing. Tea was resumed. Graham tried to relax and enjoy himself. The setting of the bivouac he relished: the shady trees, clean sand, cool breeze and evening shadows. The field cooking he always enjoyed. Also he was with his friends and knew he had just been paid a huge compliment by having Cadet Bragg added to his section. He decided that he was enjoying the camp and hoped he was doing well enough to be selected for sergeant.

The only real worry was that it was getting dark and he was getting signals from Kirsty, which indicated that she was going to mount another attack on his will power during the night.

Chapter 25

ON THE SAND

When he had eaten his dinner, Graham stood up and made his way through the screen of bent trees to the water. There he was alone, even though a hundred others were within metres of him. He crouched to wash his mess tins and to scour them with sand. Having done that, he rinsed his face and sat back on the sand to study the sunset.

"This is a really great place!" he murmured. "It is beautiful."

For several minutes he just sat and soaked up the atmosphere of serenity. Overhead the sky was still blue, but off to the west it was a great swathe of orange melding into red. The flood-twisted paperbarks held a ruddy tinge for a few minutes before succumbing to the lengthening evening shadows. A gentle, cool breeze ruffled the water and brought with it the scent of eucalypts and she oaks.

Graham felt the tension easing out of him. He breathed deeply and felt very content. Several ducks flew by with a whirr of wings and a couple of pelicans drifted down on the current. In the distance some cockatoos screeched. Silence settled, or at least relative silence, with the mutter and chatter of a hundred or so cadets.

"Graham?" It was Kirsty. She stepped around a tree and moved to sit beside him. "Are you alright?"

Graham nodded. "Yes, just enjoying the sunset," he replied.

She sat quietly for a minute then said, "Are you mad at me?"

"A bit."

"Why?"

"You know why. I want to do well in cadets. I want to get to be a sergeant. Breaking my promise to be with you isn't helping," he said.

"Don't you like me?" she asked.

That exasperated him. "Yes, I do! I've told you that. But our relationship, whatever it is, must wait till after camp."

She remained silent but he could tell she wasn't convinced. He opened his mouth to try to reason with her, but Sgt Grenfell spoke from just behind them. "What are you two doing?" he asked.

"Watching the sunset sergeant," Graham replied.

It was now twilight and the sky had changed to indigo and dark blue. Sgt Grenfell replied in a voice heavy with sarcasm, "Well, as long as you are just talking! Now come back and join the others."

Flushing with indignation at not being believed, Graham stood up and made his way back through the trees. Kirsty followed. They were greeted by the welcome flicker of a fire. Half the platoon sat around it. Others sat in small groups off in the shadows. Graham found his pack and webbing and placed them beside Stephen to one side of the fire. He found it very pleasant to walk around in bare feet, the movement of the dry sand between his toes having a massaging effect after so many days encased in army boots.

After unrolling his sleeping bag, Graham sat down on it and leaned back on his pack. Roger came and sat on his other side and Bragg sat next to him. Kirsty seated herself opposite, next to Lucy and Barbara. In the firelight her eyes glistened and for a moment he thought she might be crying. That she was watching him was obvious and he felt quite uncomfortable because of it.

The topic of conversation was the extra duties Pigsy and Co had been awarded. They had been set to digging another latrine and carrying full jerrycans down and empty ones up.

"What happened to Yeldham?" Graham asked Stephen.

Stephen made a face. "He got a real tongue lashing from Capt Conkey, but I think that is all. I suspect that Capt Conkey doesn't know the full story."

"No, I'll bet he doesn't," Graham replied. But he felt very sorry for Bragg.

The poor kid is pathetic. He obviously has some real problems. With a shrug he dismissed the topic and turned to listen to Andrews trying to tell a joke.

The presence of CUO Masters at the fire kept the jokes within the bounds of decency and the 'threat' of Kirsty kept Graham at the fire. Even when his friends got up and wandered off to visit other platoons, Graham stayed there. He lay back and pretended to sleep but in realty his mind was working fast. What exasperated him was that when he tried to think up a strategy to get Kirsty to ease off till after camp, he kept having memories that roused his passions.

Stephen and Roger returned half an hour later. Graham sat up and found Bragg lying close beside him. *Like a bloody dog that's been whipped!* he thought. Then he modified his contempt to compassion. *Poor little bugger!*

Stephen sat down. "I went looking for Pete. Couldn't find him," he explained.

"He's away on a recon patrol for tomorrow's big exercise," Graham answered.

Curiosity and envy both stirred in him at the idea of Peter being away from the unit overnight. It was so unusual and such a mark of trust that it made him sure that Peter must have been selected to be a sergeant next year.

And he deserves it, he decided.

"What is this exercise, do you know?" Stephen asked.

Graham shook his head. "No idea, but it must be a good one." He was now starting to look forward to the exercise and hoped the section would do well.

The friends speculated what the exercise might be about for a while then joined in some singing. Graham noted with relief that Kirsty and her friends had gone, and he was able to relax and enjoy himself. She came back half an hour later and made a point of pushing in to sit beside him. Stephen moved aside to make room for her and gave Graham a knowing smirk which irritated him intensely.

Over the next hour, Kirsty moved closer until she was touching Graham. Then she leaned on him put her head on his shoulder. Her right hand ended up on his thigh. He was caught by surprise and so had no time to object or shift. As he wondered if he should move, or ask her to stop it, he had to admit it felt nice. He also found himself becoming aroused.

What bothered him most was that others were watching, including Gwen and Barbara. They didn't say anything, but Graham could tell by the way their eyes moved that they were aware of what was going on.

Damn! She will get me into trouble, he thought.

And she did.

Capt Conkey came out of the darkness and said hello while he looked around. Graham saw his eyes settle on Kirsty, then a frown form on his face. "You had better stop that," he said. It was said mildly but to Graham it was like a thunderclap.

Oh, you bloody weak fool! he castigated himself. *Why weren't you strong enough to make her stop it?*

Kirsty sat up with a sulky look on her face. Graham sighed with frustration and relief and Gwen shook her head and gave him an 'I-told-you-so' look. Capt Conkey chatted away to the others as though nothing had happened, but he ignored Graham and Kirsty after that.

When he had gone Gwen stood up and said, "Half an hour to bedtime. All you girls move your bedding over to this side of the area."

There was some rebellious muttering but the girls did what they were told. Graham gave Gwen a thankful look for that and moved to straighten his own bedding out. As part of his preparation, he scooped out a hip-hole and then lay down and squirmed until he had formed a body shape in the sand. Then he lay down and stretched out, luxuriating in the comfort and bare feet.

Gwen took the girls away to the toilet as a group. Kirsty looked rebellious and sulky but went with her, but only after flashing Graham a 'significant' look. Graham sat up and had a drink, noted that Bragg was lying between him and Roger, then lay back and composed himself to sleep.

In this he was soon successful. The long days and nights had tired him out and the evening around the fire had relaxed him so that he slid into a deep, trouble-free sleep.

* * *

Several times during the night Graham stirred almost to wakefulness. He became conscious enough to note that it was getting chilly, so he struggled into his sleeping bag. He also noted the soft gurgle of the river and shivering rustle of the leaves. The fire had died down to a mound of glowing embers and he was aware that it was one of those situations he would remember with pleasure for the rest of his life.

* * *

The next time he woke it was with the insistent need to do a pee. He sat up, tugged on his boots and stumped out onto the sand in the darkness. When he was well away from the camp he stopped and relieved himself.

Afterwards, he stood and stared up at the millions of stars and breathed deeply the cool, moist night air. With a feeling of great inner peace, he walked back towards the sleeping cadets.

As he made his way in among the lines of trees, light and movement along at HQ attracted his attention. He saw that Capt Conkey was awake, as were a signaller and three people in bulky yowie suits.

The Hutchie Men. I wonder where they are off to at this time of morning? Graham thought.

A glance at his watch told him it was just coming up to 0500hrs. Settling himself on his bed he watched as the Hutchie Men did a radio check. Then they flitted away from the HQ fire into the darkness.

Something for the big exercise perhaps? he wondered.

Or was it just a security precaution to make sure Heatley didn't get their revenge with a surprise attack at dawn? For a minute or two he speculated on where Peter's patrol might be, and what it was they were doing a reconnaissance of. He decided it must be a fair way away to require an overnight patrol.

He lay back and snuggled into his sleeping bag but found he could not sleep. Instead, he pondered the problem of Kirsty. While thinking about her he became very aroused and frustrated. With all the people around he could not ease the problem and he did not feel like going out into the night again, particularly with the Hutchie Men and heaven only knew what other patrols on the prowl!

At 0545hrs CSM Cleland came along and quietly woke Sgt Grenfell. Graham pretended to be asleep. At 0600hrs the cadets were roused and called out onto the sand for check parade. It was just cold enough for Graham to wish he had a pullover on, but he was too lazy to dig it out of his pack. Instead, he opted for shivering, knowing it would warm up quickly enough when the sun rose.

The first person he really noted was Kirsty. She gave him several anxious and wistful looks and then stood and hugged herself as she also shivered. That got Graham worried as he could not tell what she was thinking. It also annoyed him.

I wish she would ease up for while, he thought. He knew that the big exercise was scheduled to start that afternoon and he had a feeling that it could be important to him. *I really need to do well if I am to retrieve myself in Capt Conkey's estimation,* he decided.

Morning routine was the most relaxed and pleasant so far. Bedding was rolled up and they sat on their packs or on the sand and did their cooking, eating and shaving. To Graham's surprise the river water was warmer than the air and he felt wonderfully refreshed after shaving with warm water from his mess tins, then washing in the river. Kirsty left him alone and only gave him a few looks.

Good! he thought. *She might be getting the message at last!*

The only unpleasant episode during the morning was when Graham encountered Pigsy and Waters at the latrine. He was doing his morning crap, with Stephen and Roger standing guard while waiting their turn, when he heard them arrive.

"Who's using the latrine?" Pigsy asked.

"Graham," Stephen replied.

"Huh!" Pigsy called out. "Hey Kirk! Make sure you put your hat on when you come back so we know which shit is which!"

Graham flushed with embarrassment and tensed, feeling very vulnerable. However, Pigsy and Waters wandered on along the flood channel to dig their own holes and he was left to finish in peace.

After packing up, the company was paraded on the sand. Capt Conkey spoke to them and he seemed to be in a good mood. He particularly thanked them for their good behaviour during the night. Then he had them moved to sit in the shade. As they sat down, Graham noted that Kirsty had moved back to near Roger and that Bragg was the one to sit directly behind him.

For the next hour, the company did walk-through/talk-through platoon attack practices. These were carried out on the sand dunes and among the trees a few hundred metres upstream. Each platoon took turns, with the others sitting watching. HQ provided the 'enemy'. During the first practice Graham's section was one of the two 'assault' sections and he enjoyed that, even though they were specifically forbidden to do any of the actual fighting skills. In his own mind he could picture himself taking part in a desperate attack against impossible odds in some real war.

During the second practice 4 Section was the 'fire support' and had to make their way around to one flank The section carried out the task to Graham's satisfaction and without complaint. They all seemed to be happy and keen, even Bragg and Andrews.

They have developed into a bloody good section, Graham thought.

His pride increased when they were the assault section for a 'one-up' attack on a camp a few hundred metres further upstream. The camp was in a clearing where two flood channels branched. It was overlooked by the line of steep, earth banks and had a guard post on top. This was 'taken out' by Stephen's section, who then provided flank protection and cut-off while Gwen's section became fire support from on top of the bank. Graham's section attacked along the flood channel at right angles to her fire. He loved every minute of it: the creeping forward along a narrow track, the lining up among the rubber vines and weeds, and the charge. CUO Masters came along behind and said it was very well done.

After that, the platoon moved back to sit in the shade of some overhanging trees at the point where a dry, sandy creek named Quilp Creek came in to join the flood channels. As the platoon manoeuvred and then waited, Graham kept looking around. The more he saw of the area the more he loved it.

It is not only very pretty, he thought. *It is ideal for having cadet exercises. All these clumps of trees and sand dunes make it great to sneak around.*

The company had lunch back at their packs, after walking back along the flood channels and across the sand. Graham knew that they were leaving the area after lunch and that made him sad. He liked the place so much he wanted to stay for several more days. Little did he know just how important the area was to be to him in the years to come!

Kirsty hardly spoke to Graham all morning and she sat with Lucy and Di during lunch. That was a relief to Graham, although he suspected he might have done his dash with her.

Oh well, plenty more fish in the sea! he told himself.

At 1230hrs the company began moving in platoon groups. 4 Platoon went first, lugging all the empty jerrycans up to the vehicles, then moving along the top of the high bank. The three junior platoons and HQ moved back along the flood channels and through the rubber vines to Dingo Creek. Graham enjoyed that too, even the dust they stirred up as they trudged along. He had read about armies marching in dust and it gave his imagination another chance to build a story. Even though he knew it was selfish and immoral he really wanted to be in a safe 'little' war with a lot of romance.

I could be rescuing a princess, he thought. That fantasy kept him happily walking along all the way back to the junction with the Canning.

It was hot in Dingo Creek and the dust made them cough, but he didn't mind at all. It was all just more 'hardship' to add to the sense of adventure. The only things that really bothered him were his memories as he walked through the areas where his section had tried to cope with the incidents on the patrol course.

I didn't do very well at some of those, he thought.

When they reached the junction of Dingo Creek and the Canning, they turned left. A hundred paces up the sandy bed of the Canning, CSM Cleland directed them to sit in the shade under the massive overhanging branches of the paperbarks lining that bank. The thicket of small trees in the riverbed screened them for the other side.

1 Platoon was already seated on their packs or on the sand. Sgt Grenfell directed 2 Platoon to sit in section lines in their own 25 metre square area of sand while CUO masters walked up to where Capt Conkey and Lt McEwen were talking. Further along were more cadets but Graham could not see clearly who they were because of the intervening branches and leaves. 3 Platoon was directed into an area next to them. Tired and sweating cadets were glad to flop down on the sand. HQ trudged past to sit beyond 1 Platoon.

Graham knew that the exercise had now begun and looked anxiously around. *We are a sitting target here,* he thought.

When CUO Masters came back he put this to him. "Should we have sentries sir?" he asked.

CUO Masters grinned and shook his head. "Have a bit of faith in Capt Conkey's military ability Cpl Kirk. He has 4 Platoon deployed to cover us in seven sentry posts; two up the Canning, two down the Bunyip, and three more up on the bank opposite here."

That made Graham blush for being foolish. He was about to ask what happened next when the three Hutchie Men appeared from behind them. As they came into view some cadets in 3 Platoon began to call out, teasing and cheering.

Capt Conkey at once called in an angry hiss, "Platoon sergeants! Stop that noise! Keep the troops quiet. We don't want an enemy patrol to find us."

Graham turned to glower at Andrews and Bragg, both of whom

had been calling out. *Damn!* he thought. *I hope we didn't give ourselves away.*

The Hutchie Men went past looking hot and dirty but immensely pleased with themselves. They carried a radio and certainly looked very military. Seeing them roused Graham's envy again.

I wish I was a section commander in 4 Platoon, he thought. Then another more sobering thought came to him. *If I don't get promoted and if I stay in cadets, I will be part of the Control Group next year.*

CUO Masters told the platoon there would be a briefing and company orders at 1500hrs. Graham looked at his watch and saw that it was 1440hrs. With nothing else to do he had a drink and lay back on the sand to rest.

Sgt Gayney came along and called on the sergeants to send work parties for water. Roger was sent, along with Pat and Anderson. The girls were allowed to go back down the river towards the junction with the Bunyip to go to the toilet.

Halyday called after them, "Watch out the enemy don't catch you with your pants down!" Their response was to curl their lips and then ignore him.

Graham told him to keep quiet then returned to daydreaming about rescuing the princess. To begin with he imagined her as looking like Kirsty, but then he changed the image to look more like Gwen. To do that, he surreptitiously studied Gwen several times. Once while he was doing so, he met Barbara's eye and she raised an eyebrow. Graham blushed and shook his head.

No, not Gwen. She is too much of a classy lady for me, he thought.

Next, he turned his thoughts to Barbara but, much as he admired her and liked her, he sensed she wasn't his type either. That moved his thoughts back to Kirsty.

His pleasant fantasies were interrupted by LCpl Kate O'Brien from HQ. "Cpl Kirk, the OC wants to see you," she said.

That was so unusual that Graham at once broke into a guilty sweat. *He must have found out about Kirsty and me,* he thought.

Fearing the worst, he stood up and followed Kate along the sandy riverbed past 1 Platoon and HQ. With every step his mind dredged up another crime or misdemeanour that he might have been found out on. His stomach began to churn with apprehension.

As he walked past HQ Graham saw that the officers were standing in a group near some cadets who were working on a huge sand model in an area of muddy riverbed. Further along, the Hutchie Men were seated near some rocks talking to Lt Maclaren. The sight of the model at once attracted Graham's interest and he tried to work out what it was of. What he did detect was that Peter was the person directing its construction. With him were Cpl Forman and Cadet Carnes.

Pete is back from his patrol, he thought. Then he realised what the model was of. It was a section of the riverbed with two bridges across it. *We are going to raid one of the bridges, I'll bet,* he thought, his interest quickening.

Then he stopped near where a frowning Capt Conkey, Lt Standish, CUO Masters, CUO Grey and CSM Cleland were all deep in conversation. Capt Conkey glanced at Graham and held up his hand to tell him to wait.

That was even worse. *They are talking about me!* Graham realised. *Oh no! I must be in deep trouble!*

All his worst fears swirled through his mind: being demoted, never being a sergeant, being sent home in disgrace, being chucked out of cadets, having to endure shameful interviews with hurt and angry parents.

And Kirsty is under-age, he remembered. Images of the police now entered his tortured imagination. He felt so upset that he became nauseous.

Roger went puffing past with his work party, lugging full jerrycans. He gave Graham a quizzical look, but all Graham could do was give him a sickly grin and shake his head. The agony of uncertainty went on for another five minutes. Then the general nodding of heads and glances told Graham that a decision had been reached. Graham swallowed and braced himself for the worst.

Capt Conkey beckoned him over. "Cpl Kirk, we are taking your section off you," he said.

Chapter 26

ORDERS

For a second Graham stood stunned. His mouth opened and then he shook his head in shocked disbelief.

"My section sir?" he managed to croak.

Capt Conkey nodded. "Well, not all of them. You are keeping a couple, and you are having a couple added to make up the numbers again."

"But... but... I don't understand, sir," Graham said. He was still trying to make sense of what he had heard, to relate it to his fears.

"We are doing a bit of regrouping for this exercise," Capt Conkey replied. "Lance Corporal Lucas is sick, so we are putting Lance Corporal Dunning in 6 Section in his place."

Roger! Graham thought in dismay. *My best friend!* He groped in his mind for some argument to have the decision reversed.

"But sir, we are working well together as a team," he managed to croak out.

Capt Conkey consulted his notebook. "Maybe, but this is the plan. Cadet Weldon and Cadet Sheehan are going to 5 Section, and Cadets Williams and Hind are going to 6 Section."

The girls! Graham thought. A wave of shame coursed through him. *Capt Conkey is moving the girls out of my section. He has heard and doesn't trust me.* As the implications flamed in sharp pulsations of shame, Graham also realised that it must mean that he had not been found out. *He can't have any real proof, or he would be demoting me or chucking me out,* he thought. It was small comfort to his battered feelings.

Capt Conkey then said, "You keep the others. That is Andrews, Halyday and Bragg."

Oh bloody hell! Graham thought, *The three noddies!* Then he modified that. *No, that's not fair. Halyday has turned into quite a good cadet.*

He was just comforting himself with this when Capt Conkey again stunned him. "You are getting four people from 4 Platoon to replace the ones transferred. Lance Corporal Franks will be your new 2ic, and you will be getting Cadets Pike, Waters, and Moynihan."

Pigsy and his mates! Graham thought with dismay. It was so astounding that he felt mentally punch-drunk. "But. but..." he muttered.

"No buts," Capt Conkey said grimly. "They have outlived their welcome in their own platoon and are joining your section. Now don't argue about it and go and tell them. Do it now, and have those people I named with their new sections by the time I start giving orders in ten minutes."

For a few seconds Graham stood facing Capt Conkey. His mind and emotions were now in turmoil. Despair and resentment fuelled feelings of rebellion, but he knew he deserved to have the girls taken away. But to lose Roger! And Pat! And to get his worst enemies in their place! Then Graham bit down on his protests as he recognised what was really bothering him.

I'm afraid! he told himself. *I'm scared of Pigsy and Co.*

Shame at admitting he was a coward, even to himself, mingled with bitter and desperate thoughts as he tried to think of some honourable way out of the mess. None came to mind and he again despised himself when he found he could not open his mouth to argue with Capt Conkey.

"Yes, sir," he heard himself say, and it all tasted sour.

I haven't even got the guts to stand up for myself! he thought bitterly. With self-loathing and contempt surging in his heart he turned and went walking back towards his section. *Or what was my section!* he thought.

CUO Masters walked back with him. Neither spoke and Graham had to struggle not to burst into tears as self-pity welled to the top of his feelings. As he approached the section, he could see their faces looking at him, some curious and some expectant, but all unsuspecting. Determined to salvage a few scraps of pride he gritted his teeth and tried to act calm. But all the while rising panic at how he would cope with Pigsy and Co kept building until he felt nauseous.

To Graham's relief, CUO Masters called Sgt Grenfell over and explained the changes, then told the cadets. That gave Graham a minute to master his despair. He was then gratified at the way the cadets all cried out in protest.

"It's not fair, sir!" Kirsty cried. "We are a team. Now is not the time to break us up."

"Don't argue, Cadet Weldon. You go to 5 Section," CUO Masters said.

Seeing the dismay and resentment on Roger's face added to Graham's feelings of inadequacy. Likewise, hearing the others arguing vehemently against the change made him feel he was a weakling for not having done so himself. He saw Stephen and Gwen looking at him sympathetically, but they only looked a bit unhappy.

The arguments were cut short by CSM Cleland coming along and telling them to move to the briefing area at the model. Graham met Roger's eyes and gave a wry grin. He was now feeling shattered. Some of Capt Conkey's words about Pigsy and Co were starting to hammer in his brain.

They have outlived their welcome, he had said. *Does that mean I am on the outer too?* he wondered.

But Capt Conkey had not said anything about him leaving 2 Platoon and CUO Grenfell acted as though he was still a section commander in his platoon.

The others continued grumbling and muttering about how unfair it was, but their discontent was lost in the general chatter as the platoon stood up and began filing along to the briefing area. Sgt Grenfell pointed and ordered Roger, Lucy and Di to go and join Stephen's section. As Gwen's section stood up, he told Kirsty and Pat to join it. Gwen obviously had mixed feelings but added her weight to Sgt Grenfell's to get them to obey. They did this reluctantly and Kirsty gave Graham an aggrieved and angry look.

He was left with Andrews, Halyday, and Bragg, who all seemed unsure but not unhappy. "Come on!" he snapped.

They walked along the riverbed to where Peter and his patrol had constructed the huge 'mud map'. Capt Conkey directed each section where to sit and Graham found it was not in the usual order of 1 Section, 1 Platoon, etc., in numerical sequence. To his surprise he was seated on the very right-hand end of the company. The cadets were seated in under the overhanging branches around three sides of the model. The model was orientated and the company mostly sat facing south. Capt Conkey stood with his back to the open riverbed and waited while 4 Platoon came trekking in.

I hope we still have some sentries, Graham thought. *We will look really silly if Heatley or St Michaels attack us now!*

He looked around, filled with something approaching despair and wondered what to do. His feelings were pushed lower when he saw Pigsy come into sight. It made him feel even sicker when he saw the reaction of Pigsy and Co when CUO Grey pointed to him and told them to join him. Their sneering disbelief and open contempt savaged Graham's frail hold on his facade of confidence.

As the four 'new' cadets walked towards him Graham forced himself to meet their eyes. Inside his stomach churned and he had to swallow. *Don't let them see you are scared!* he told himself in desperation. He stood up and pointed to the sand behind Andrews.

"Sit there," he said, his voice sounding peculiar and false to him.

"Oh, bloody hell!" muttered Pigsy, but he was glancing towards Capt Conkey, who only stood a few paces away.

The four sat down, their faces masks of anger and rebellion but they said nothing. *That's only because Capt Conkey is there,* Graham thought. He felt sick just imagining how he would control them once he was off on his own.

Then Sgt Yeldham came over, leading Cadet Milson. As they approached Graham had a sense of more bad news. Yeldham gave him a hostile and derisive look and said, "Here's another one for you."

Graham glanced at Capt Conkey, who nodded. *Oh, bloody hell!* Graham thought. *What have I done to deserve this!*

Milson he only knew as a fat little troublemaker with a loudmouth. Graham pointed to the rear of the section. "Sit in front of Lance Corporal Franks, Cadet Milson," he said.

Franks scowled but moved himself back to make room. To Graham he looked to be a long way back and he did a quick head count. *Nine,* he counted. He had to admit he was doing alright there. Some sections only had six or seven. Gwen's now had eight and so did Stephen's. *That must make them happier,* he thought.

Capt Conkey now called for silence. The officers and remaining HQ personnel were moved to sit at the back. CSM Cleland seated himself on Graham's right, with the Hutchie Men. Unusually, the CUO's were seated at the very front, forward of their corporals. Graham sat down and only now turned his attention to the sand model.

I was really looking forward to this exercise, he thought bitterly. *Now it is going to be a real trial.*

Capt Conkey picked up a long stick to use as a pointer and moved forward to stand on the model. Graham opened his notebook, took out a pencil and smoothed his map copy on his knee in readiness. As fully half the NCOs had not yet done this gave him some small satisfaction when Capt Conkey told them to do so. He noted Capt Conkey give him a faint nod of approval as his gaze swept along the front row of corporals.

The sand model was 10 metres wide and 15 long. From one end to the other a ditch 20 centimetres or so deep and 2 metres wide had been dug. This obviously represented the riverbed. A ribbon of blue 'streamer' paper along one side represented the actual water. Two bridges had been constructed out of soft drink cans and pieces of packing case and ration pack cartons. A red streamer ran across one and was the Flinders Highway. A green streamer ran across the other and Graham guessed that was the railway. Various side roads were shown by orange streamers and the hills and gullies were decorated in places with leaves. Rocks and small boxes stood for other features.

Capt Conkey checked his watch then began. "Okay troops, these are the orders for the big exercise. We are taking the opportunity to brief the entire company in one go. I will be mostly directing my orders to the platoon commanders but HQ and the section commanders need to copy down what is important to them. Platoon sergeants obviously need a copy in case their platoon commander becomes sick or gets captured."

Graham followed Capt Conkey's gaze and saw that Sgt Yeldham did not have his notebook out. Watching Yeldham's flustered and embarrassed groping in his pockets gave him a small spurt of malicious satisfaction.

Capt Conkey went on, "This exercise is to be the culmination of the challenges by Heatley and St Michaels. In August, most of you took part in the exercise against Mackay near Bowen. I hope this one isn't as memorable."

There was a ripple of murmuring and Graham glanced over his shoulder and met Barbara's eye. She made a wry face and blushed. Then Cpl Parnell called out, "Don't get lost this time, Dimbo!"

That resulted in an eruption of laughter. Capt Conkey held up his hand. "Keep it down. We think there is a Heatley patrol up on the other bank somewhere." Most of the company glanced that way. Capt Conkey reassured them. "Don't worry, we have some sentries over there. Now, let's get through these orders. First the situation."

He paused while the leaders all wrote 'SIT.' Then he said, "Topography." Then using his pointer, Capt Conkey moved to the model. "We have this very accurate model courtesy of Corporal Peter Bronsky, Corporal Forman, LCpl O'Brien, and Cadet Carnes. They carried out a twenty-four-hour recon patrol to map the whole area. They have done very well. Thank you, HQ."

Lucky Pete, Graham thought. *He is certain to be a sergeant now.* He knew he was jealous of his friend and felt guilty about it. *I wish I'd been given a chance like that!*

Capt Conkey had them refer first to their maps. Graham noted that they were only two hundred metres from the point where the Canning River joined the much bigger Bunyip. The Bunyip came around from the west in a huge sweeping curve of several kilometres. After joining up with the Canning it straightened out and flowed due south for the next ten. Opposite the junction of the two rivers Graham noted a half-moon shaped 'island' which was separated from the far bank by a series of flood overflow channels or 'anabranches'. This was nicknamed 'Ruin Island' because the remains of an old farm stood in the middle of it.

"I am going to call them the Anabranches," Capt Conkey said. "This is so we do not confuse them with the flood channels in the bed of the main river."

The Anabranches split off about a kilometre and a half upstream of the junction, and ran diagonally across the 'chord' of the river's huge curve to re-join close to the western end of the highway bridge. In the main riverbed were clumps of trees, some growing beside the water and others on sand dunes that had built up around their roots.

The topographical briefing lasted for twenty minutes and covered minute details. The bit that interested Graham most was about the railway bridge itself. He knew, from having seen it in the distance, that it was a steel 'through truss' girder bridge. He now learned it was held up on 7 huge concrete pylons.

"The bridge was built in the eighteen eighties," Capt Conkey said. "The cement and steel were all imported from England. Because it is an old bridge, they have just begun replacing it with a new structure about fifty metres downstream of it. This will be finished in a year or two. The bridge is about a thousand metres long and the railway is fifty metres above the riverbed. For the purposes of this exercise the railway is the main supply route of the enemy army. If we can destroy, or even damage, both the road and rail bridges, our army will win the battle which is being fought near Townsville at this moment."

He paused to ensure they understood then went on, "For this exercise we are a company of elite paratroopers who have been dropped in to try to blow the bridge. The enemy knows it is vital to him, so he is guarding it with at least two companies of troops. So, Two, Enemy."

Graham wrote this. By this time he had calmed down a bit and was becoming absorbed in the idea of the exercise. Being an elite paratrooper really appealed to his romantic streak. He was also very interested in the exercise enemy.

"Thanks to two patrols, one by Cpl Bronsky and HQ, and the other by the Hutchie Men, we know a fair bit about the enemy deployment," Capt Conkey said.

There were muted cheers of, "Hutchie Men!" which made most of them smile. Capt Conkey went on to explain, "We think they have deployed in two main defence lines with Heatley closest along the line of the highway, and St Michael's at the rear, guarding the actual railway bridge."

At that Sgt Yeldham commented, "That'd be St Michael's, hiding at the back!"

It raised a few snickers but Capt Conkey was not amused. "That will be enough of those sorts of comments thank you! Don't interrupt," he snapped, flashing an angry glance at Sgt Yeldham. Then he went on, "We know Heatley have been patrolling this area and we suspect they may be watching us even now. They certainly have patrols forward so we can expect contact as soon as we leave this location. There are also sections guarding the ends of each bridge and the bottoms of all the pylons."

He held up a map board with the known 'enemy' patrols and guard posts shown in red. To Graham it made a formidable array. *They don't mean to lose this time,* he thought.

Capt Conkey emphasised the same point. "We have badly dented their pride with our raids on the airfield and the actions at Sandy Ridge and Black Knoll the other night. They want their revenge. It is going to take our very best efforts to get past them to the target. As well, there are umpires from the army staff and from Fifteen A.C.U. They will have white armbands and are supposed to be impartial."

He then went on to talk about civilians and not to annoy or frighten them, to keep out of private property. A new map was handed around to all NCOs and CUOs showing the 'out-of-bounds' areas shaded in. Luckily there didn't seem to be many.

"Meteorology, weather will be fine. Temperatures forecast at a twenty-degree minimum. Moon is not up till nearly zero four hundred tomorrow morning, which is good. However, we suspect that both Heatley and St Michael's have several night vision devices, 'Ninox' and the like, on loan from the army. So good fieldcraft is essential."

That was sobering news and Graham wondered how on earth he could hide from a Ninox night sight on a bright starry night.

Capt Conkey paused for a drink of water, then said, "Mission. Our mission is to destroy the Bunyip River rail and road bridges."

He repeated this and Graham felt a thrill of excitement. This was exactly the sort of exercise he had been hoping it would be. *I am going to enjoy this,* he thought, until he remembered who was in his section.

Next came the 'Execution' paragraphs. In the 'Scheme of Manoeuvre' Capt Conkey explained that there were to be six raiding parties. That got Graham's interest. Capt Conkey showed their routes and targets on the model. Having done this quickly he went over it again in detail when he covered 'Groupings and tasks.' "First are the Hutchie Men. Their grouping is the CSM, the Hutchie men, plus one signaller from HQ. They are to go upstream to the right and come around the end of the enemy via the railway from Bunyip Bend. Their target is the steel power pylon on the west bank near the rail bridge. Next is to be 4 Section. Grouping is 4 Section, plus one medic and one signaller from HQ. They are to go upstream to the Anabranches and then south via the ruins of the old meat works, then attack the western end of the rail bridge, the concrete abutments or Pylon Number Seven."

When he heard this, Graham at first did not comprehend. It was only when he heard what the others were going to do that he realised he was not to operate with his own platoon. 2 Platoon (minus) was to move down the west side of Ruin Island and attack the road and rail bridges. Their main targets were Pylons 5 and 6. 4 Platoon, plus Peter as a guide and signaller, plus a medic, was to do a wide detour back over Sandy Ridge and around to the south of the rail bridge to attack from the south against Pylons 3 and 4. 1 Platoon was to go cross-country between the river and Bare Ridge to attack the eastern end of the rail bridge, Pylons 1 and 2. 3 Platoon was to advance south along the eastern bank of the river to attack the highway bridge, and the enemy HQ near a picnic area toilet block.

"3 Platoon is to move ahead of 2 Platoon and 1 Platoon and is to break up the pattern of the enemy defences at the highway," Capt Conkey explained.

When he was sure that each group knew their objectives, he went on to the 'Co-ordinating Instructions'. During that Graham learnt that his section was moving with the remainder of 2 Platoon at 1700hrs, along with the Hutchie Men and 4 Platoon. Once across the open sand of the riverbed, they were to split up and 4 Platoon was to do a big circle of three kilometres back to their previous night's bivouac area. They would then march back to this location.

"This is our deception plan," Capt Conkey explained. "I am sure that Heatley will have a patrol watching the riverbed and I hope they will see lots of troops go across the river to the west bank. As most of company will actually be raiding down the east bank, I am hoping that will decoy a lot of their patrols over that way. Sorry 4 Platoon, but you are going to have to demonstrate that you are big and tough and can march those extra kilometres. I want you back here by eighteen hundred."

Other timings were given. The raiders were to try to pass the highway at about 2030hrs and to hit the railway bridge at about 2100hrs. They were all to be home by midnight, or were to report to the nearest unit for a safety check. The routes were then covered again in detail, with map references. Graham was satisfied he would have no navigational problems.

Boundaries were made clear, rendezvous allocated then the 'Action on Contact' was explained in detail. Capt Conkey held up two red cloth strips and two yellow cloth flashes.

"The red flashes are being worn by St Michael's and the yellow ones by Heatley. We are to wear two green ones."

He held one of these up. It was a bright green colour. Then he explained: "If you are captured, or if an umpire says you have lost the battle, you are to hand over one of your flashes to the enemy. When you have lost both you become a prisoner and stay with them. If you win you get their flashes. If you get their last one then they are out of the exercise and must go to their HQ and take no further part in the battle. Is that clear? Yes Cpl Bell?"

Stephen had his hand up. "Sir, if we capture a set of enemy flashes can we wear them to trick them?"

There was a ripple of applause and laughter. Capt Conkey shook his head. "No, Cpl Bell. We are using skill and fair play, not trickery. The CSM has already suggested this afternoon we whip into Charters Towers and buy the right coloured cloth to make full sets of enemy flashes."

Graham met Stephen's eye and he grinned. *Trust Steve to think of that!* he thought with a mixture of admiration and disapproval.

Capt Conkey then went on to remind them of the standard safety rules. "No physical contact. No hitting. No throwing. No running in the dark. Safety first!" To back this up he gave detailed information on the locations of safety vehicles and the medics. Graham learned that each platoon, plus his own section, each had a medic attacked.

I wonder who that will be? he thought, gloomily running through the HQ roll in his head.

The action at the objective he found fascinating. Capt Conkey explained that, in reality, it would take tons of explosives placed in exactly the right place by skilled engineers or demolition experts to knock down such huge bridges.

"We are lucky," he said. "We have the latest technology bombs, 'Supersemtex'. A tiny amount causes enormous damage."

He bent down and picked up a plastic container out of the ration pack boxes and held it up. It had BOMB written on it in felt pen, plus the unit name. "All you have to do is get one of these to the base of a pylon, or the end of a bridge and leave it. If you do we have won."

"What's inside it, sir?" Cpl Griffin asked.

"These are formal orders Cpl Griffin. Questions at the end. But the answer is nothing. They are just empty boxes. You can put a piece of paper saying 'Bang!' and your names if you like," Capt Conkey replied.

"But, sir," Dimbo called out, "What if the other mob hide it and deny we put it there?"

"We have to hope they will be fair," Capt Conkey replied.

"But they could lie, sir!" Dimbo persisted.

"Maybe, but we won't. So you can add your names in felt pen on the concrete, just to be sure. They won't be able to remove that in time."

That satisfied them. Capt Conkey had a bomb issued to every section commander, each sergeant and each CUO. He then covered 'action if lost' and went on to Administration and Logistics and then Command and Signals. During that Graham learned that his section would be given a signaller. He noted that the Coy Radio Net had ten army radio sets on it: one at the CP, one with the OC, six with the raiding parties, and two with safety vehicles. Capt Conkey would be moving with the other OOCs, except Lt McEwen, to be at the exercise HQ. Lt McEwen was to stay with five sick cadets at this location and would man the unit CP and base radio station. The platoon nets were still the small hand-held CB radios. They were then given the password and countersign- SANDY-SAHARA.

Capt Conkey then did as time check and said, "Any questions?"

There were plenty but Graham had none. He sat and mulled over his part in the exercise and knew it was going to be the biggest test of his cadet career.

Chapter 27

THE NEW SECTION

As soon as Capt Conkey finished his briefing, Sgt Gayney and Cpl Parnell issued the green flashes to each platoon sergeant. These were then handed to the section commanders for distribution to cadets. Tying them onto his webbing made Graham feel quite special and he was torn by a mixture of emotions. He knew he was looking forward to the exercise as an event, yet afraid of failing as a leader. There were also the glimmerings of satisfaction that his section would be operating on its own.

At least no-one else will see me when things go wrong, he thought; for he was sure that things would go wrong. Already he could hear the discontented mutterings from behind him as the initial shock of transfer wore off among his new members.

Capt Conkey called, "Platoon commanders, get your people moving. Get ready."

CUO Masters stood up and called out, "Up you get, 2 Platoon. Section commanders move your sections back to the platoon area and have tea."

Graham had no choice but to stand up and face his new section. The first small test was thrust upon him. "Stand up 4 Section."

To his relief they did, although there were hostile and rebellious looks from the four ex-4 Platoon members. Graham made himself face them. "You blokes go and collect your gear and join us," he instructed, trying to sound at least neutral.

"Gawd! Bloody hell!" Pigsy muttered.

"Just do it!" Graham snapped, his own emotions so jangled he was on the edge of losing his temper.

"But we are senior cadets," Waters challenged. "Why should we be with a junior platoon?"

"Ask CUO Grey, not me!" Graham replied. "Or ask Capt Conkey. Now either do what you are told or take yourselves to the CSM."

The four scowled but LCpl Franks turned and started walking away towards where 4 Platoon had left their gear. *He is the weakest,* Graham thought as he watched the others reluctantly follow.

He was amazed to find his heart was beating as rapidly as if he had run a race and he knew he was deeply angry. But at least they had obeyed.

"Come on!" he snapped at the others and led them back to where their packs were. Once there he sat down on his pack and dug out his stove and food. By then he was so upset he did not feel like eating but made himself.

As he lit his hexamine, Graham saw that Kristy was looking at him. For a moment their eyes met and she looked quite wistful. All Graham could do was shrug and look down.

I don't understand either, he told himself, although he thought he had a pretty good idea. *I've been given all the rejects so I must be one too!*

The four ex-4 Platoon cadets returned while Graham was stirring his food in his mess tins. They were still scowling and grumbling but had obviously not complained to either CUO Grey or Capt Conkey. They sat to one side and in a way that signalled they did not want to be part of the section. Turning their backs on the platoon they began preparing their evening meal. It all made Graham feel quite stressed, but he forced himself to pretend he was relaxed and happy. To that end he boiled water for coffee and ate his food with apparent enjoyment.

All the while he kept glancing at his watch. There was no time to be wasted. The platoon was due to move at 1700hrs and the minutes seemed to fly. There was so much to do that Graham became quite anxious. As quickly as he could he washed up, packed away his stove and mess gear, added a tin of food and the 'bomb' to his webbing, then refilled his water bottles. He even made a point of brushing his teeth. All the while he chivvied the others to hurry, avoiding a direct confrontation with 'The Four' as he did.

The 'raiders' were leaving their packs in a row back against the bank and were doing the raid in 'Patrol Order', which meant basic webbing. Graham badgered the cadets to hurry, to make sure they had full water bottles; that they had a spare meal; that they had been to the toilet, and that they had their torches and matches in case of an accident or becoming lost. It all took time and the minutes sped by.

CUO Masters and Sgt Grenfell added to the sense of nervousness by walking around and urging the section commanders to get their people ready. Graham saw that Gwen's section had all finished and were starting to apply camouflage and that made him even more anxious. He told his own section to do likewise. In none of this was he helped by Franks, his nominal 2ic. All Graham could do was shrug and do the work himself. His 'original' cadets were willing enough and quickly cammed up. Even Bragg was keen and helped Milson.

As Graham began applying his own camouflage cream to his face, a group of cadets came along the riverbed and reported to CUO Masters. Graham glanced up and saw that they were the 'attached' personnel from HQ Platoon: two medics and two signallers. But when he saw who were being sent to his section his heart plummeted in dismay. The signaller was Cadet Carnes, and the medic was 'Slim' Lyle, so called because he was big and fat.

Oh, bloody hell! he groaned. *What have I done to deserve this pair of slugs?* That opinion he instantly revised. *No, Slim is okay,* he told himself.

Slim looked like a big, docile child. He had a baby face and was thought to be a 'bit of a sook'. His face split into a friendly grin as he approached, and Graham could not help smiling back. Carnes on the other hand just looked miserable and said nothing. He dumped the army radio on the sand and slumped down next to it.

More rejects! Graham thought unhappily. He studied Carnes' face and then had an idea. *He was on two patrols with Pete. Maybe he isn't as bad as he looks. I'll ask Pete.*

Seeing that he still had 15 minutes before they were due to move, Graham went in search of Peter. He found him swinging on his webbing, preparatory to moving over to join 4 Platoon. Peter was grinning happily and was clearly enjoying himself and looking forward to the exercise.

Graham was so miserable and down that he was sorely tempted to unburden his sorrows to his friend, but instead he managed a smile and said, "I've been given Carnes as my sig. Who decided that?"

"He asked to go to your section," Peter replied.

That was a surprise, and it must have showed. Graham shook his head and said, "You had him in your patrol. What's he like?"

Peter looked thoughtful, then answered, "Most of the time he is no trouble. He just mopes along, and he does what you tell him without argument. But he is a real loner and keeps to himself."

"Is he a good sig?"

Peter made a face. "No. Poor to average."

"So he didn't give you any problems, even at night?" Graham asked.

"Well, not really," Peter replied. For a moment he looked thoughtful again, then said, "There was just one incident. At the rail bridge."

"What did he do?" Graham asked.

"Something quite odd," Peter replied. "We spent half a day studying the rail bridge from a hide a few hundred metres away. We couldn't go closer because the officers from Heatley and St Michael's were there planning their defence. So we waited till the middle of the night before crossing the bed of the river under the bridge. It was about three in the morning and I stopped the patrol while I measured the circumference of one of the concrete pylons. It was weird."

Peter paused and Graham felt a distinct sense of apprehension. "In what way?" he asked.

"When I finished, I found Carnes just standing there, staring up at the bridge. You could see it clearly enough in the starlight. I spoke to him, but he didn't move, just kept staring up as though he hadn't heard me," Peter explained.

Graham shivered. "What happened?"

Peter shrugged. "I spoke to him again and he just looked at me, then seemed to snap out of a trance. After that he just followed along with no problems."

"Oh bugger! Is he an epileptic or something?" Graham asked.

"Don't know. You'd have to ask the officers that," Peter said.

A call from CUO Grey ended the conversation. Peter put out his hand and patted Graham's sleeve. "Don't worry. You will manage. He must like you. Anyway, I gotta go. Have fun! See you later."

Not at all reassured Graham hurried back to where 2 Platoon was now pulling on webbing and preparing to move. There was no time for any further discussions, so Graham swung on his own webbing and did it up, then ordered the section to line up. Most of them did this readily enough but 'The Four' made it plain by their deliberately slow moves that they weren't going to just roll over and give up.

As he walked along the line checking they were all there and ready to go Graham felt his stomach churn with anxiety. The looks in the eyes of The Four told him that they were sure to give trouble the moment there was no CUO or sergeant around. The thought of miserable failure reduced Graham to near panic and he wondered how he could possibly get out of the situation.

No escape offered itself and his hopes were ended by CSM Cleland giving the signal to move. Graham gulped and felt the bile rise in his throat to sour the moment. The Hutchie Men filed off behind the CSM, then 4 Platoon. As Peter went past he gave Graham a 'thumbs up' and Graham managed a 'good luck' in return.

"We don't need it," Peter quipped, "We depend on skill!"

Graham snorted and had to smile. Then CUO Masters tacked on behind 4 Platoon, followed by his attached signaller, Cadet James. Graham had no option but to start walking behind James. By now he was feeling so agitated that it seemed he could not contain his restlessness. He had to force himself to think about something else so as not to break into fits of trembling or tears.

Graham glanced anxiously back along the line, partly to check that the section really was following, but also to get a glimpse of Kristy. He did, but she looked a long way back and he wasn't sure if she had seen him. For a few seconds, his feelings were pushed aside by the impression of sheer military purpose in the long line of camouflaged cadets snaking along under the trees.

That looks really good! he thought.

For a few minutes he recaptured the old thrill and excitement that he had experienced on previous exercises. It had begun! They were on their way! The elite paratroop raiders about to strike!

CSM Cleland led them along under the overhanging trees until they came out into the open, sandy bed of the Canning just near where it joined the Bunyip. After that they clambered from rock to rock to get across the narrow strip of water between the bank of the Bunyip and the downstream end of the small, tree-covered island. All the while Graham kept looking around, noting where they were, checking for any sign of the enemy, looking back along the line of camouflaged raiders.

We look bloody good! he thought. The camouflage, webbing, radios, and the green flashes all formed an image that lifted his spirits and helped stiffen his resolve.

The island was only ten metres wide and then there were more rocks to step across, and even a few paces of wading in knee deep water. The water seeping into his boots didn't bother Graham, but he heard loud moans and complaints from The Four. He glared back at him, but they ignored him, only relapsing into silence when CUO Masters called back angrily. That scorched Graham's pride too.

He will think I can't control my section, he thought unhappily.

The rocks littered the riverbed for a hundred metres. From his rudimentary knowledge of geography Graham decided it was a rock bar which extended most of the way across the river. Most were only boulders but there were several extensive sheets of smooth, water-polished granite. This was slippery to walk on and most of Graham's attention was taken up with keeping his footing.

Beyond that was sand- hundreds of metres of sand. As they trudged across this Graham looked downstream to his left and his mouth fell open in surprise. *There are the bridges!* he noted with astonishment.

He knew from the map that the highway bridge was only one and a half kilometres downstream, and the railway bridge another kilometre beyond that but he had not expected to see them so soon. The highway bridge was a grey bar half hidden by clumps of trees growing in the bed of the river. The railway bridge just showed as a criss-cross of spidery lines against the sky beyond.

Seeing the objective moved Graham's thoughts to the defenders and he looked first over his left shoulder at the line of trees along the riverbank.

I wonder if Heatley does have a patrol watching us? he thought.

Ahead and to the left front was the line of steep sand bluffs which marked the outside edge of Ruin Island. Graham scanned the crest but there were so many trees and bushes and clumps of grass that an enemy patrol would have no trouble staying hidden. Then he remembered what Capt Conkey had said during the briefing: 4 Platoon was to double back later on and go the other way. Marching openly across the sand in daylight was all part of the deception plan.

We are the decoys, he told himself. *I hope they are watching!*

Loud muttering, curses and grumbles from behind caused him to amend this to 'listening'. The Four were making so much noise that any enemy patrol on either bank of the river for hundreds of metres would be able to hear them. Once again, he glared at them and then hissed angrily, "Stop making so much noise back there!"

"Stick it up..." he heard muttered back but was not sure who had said it. However, the noise did tone down for a while.

What The Four were complaining about was walking along the sandy riverbed. It was hard on the leg muscles, particularly the upper thigh muscles. Graham began to pant and perspire. He kept looking back and noted Carnes plodding along, head down and the corners of his mouth down as well.

Oh, I hope he doesn't give me any dramas, he worried.

Pigsy's voice carried clearly to him. "This is bloody stupid! We must stick out like a country dunny walking up the middle of the bloody river like this. Why don't we try to sneak up on the enemy?"

Graham stepped out of line and waved Halyday on. When Pigsy and Co came up to him he started walking level with them. "If you'd listened to the orders, you'd know that was the idea," he hissed. "Capt Conkey wants the enemy to see us so they will move more patrols to our side of the river."

"Oh, that's bloody great! That makes it even harder for us!" Moynihan replied with a sneer.

Graham felt all his anxieties well up again, but he kept his voice level. "And you four aren't helping by making so much noise. Every enemy for miles must be able to hear you. So keep quiet."

"Up ya bum, ya sniveller," Waters replied.

By then Graham had turned and was striding along to regain his place at the front of the section. *Do I make an issue of that?* he wondered. He decided to ignore it, but that caused another bout of mental self-flagellation. All his fears about being a weak leader and a coward swirled round in his head. *I should stand up to him straight away,* he thought. But he didn't, instead continuing to feed his worries.

These were exacerbated by the fact that every step brought them closer to the far bank; and to the moment when his section would move off on their own.

Then I will have to sink or swim, he thought unhappily.

All too soon that moment arrived. The long line of cadets, about sixty in number, at last reached the base of the sand cliffs. Close up these still looked steep but not as high. About ten metres Graham calculated. Along the bottom ran a dirt vehicle rack, just two wheel ruts in grass. CSM Cleland turned right and followed these for about 200 metres.

When the track went in among head-high weeds, some sort of prickly burr, he halted.

"2 Platoon rest," CUO Masters ordered.

He went forward to consult with CUO Grey and CSM Cleland. Graham had a drink and took out his map to study it. He was still looking at it when CUO Masters came back.

"We are here, just near the northern end of the Anabranches," CUO Masters said, pointing at the map.

That confirmed what Graham had thought. He could see how the sand cliffs had become steadily lower and were giving way to rocks and trees. CUO Masters said, "Do a radio check and then follow 4 Platoon for a hundred metres. That will bring you to the other side of the Anabranches. There is a gate in this fence beside us and the vehicle track goes up the bank. You follow that."

Graham nodded and felt his stomach churn.

This is it! he thought.

Chapter 28

MOMENT OF TRUTH

A surge of something close to panic welled up in Graham's emotions. It took all his mental effort not to let it show as he forced a smile to CUO Masters. To help hide it Graham turned away and beckoned Carnes to come to him.

"Do a radio check Cadet Carnes," he said.

While Carnes did this Graham called CUO Masters on his own hand held radio and it worked 'loud and clear'. When Carnes reported that his radio check was carried out there was no excuse for delaying any longer. 4 Platoon was already moving.

"Right Cpl Kirk, off you go, and good luck," CUO Masters said.

Graham could only nod in reply, he felt so choked up. He signalled to the section and began walking along the dusty track. The others followed, Carnes walking directly behind Graham. A glance back showed him the others were following but also confirmed that he was now on his own. Already 2 Platoon was pushing through the weeds towards Ruin Island.

A hundred metres further along, the track divided. CSM Cleland and the Hutchie Men were standing there at a gate on the left, while the last members of 4 Platoon were vanishing among the trees off to the right. They would be heading over to recross the river and then to circle back to the Canning Junction through the rubber vines and Dingo Creek.

CSM Cleland pointed up through the now open gate. "Up this way, then go left, Cpl Kirk," he said.

That nettled Graham. "I know sir," he replied shortly. His pride was badly enough dented without anyone assuming he couldn't navigate!

Porno held the wire gate open and offered rude and cheeky advice as the section filed through. "Don't you get captured by dem St Michael's fellas or you get sore bum," he warned.

As there were no female cadets in either patrol, CSM Cleland made no comment to the crude repartee. Pigsy and Co all made smart remarks back, and Andrews said, "How do you know, Porno? Did they catch you?"

"You be careful with smart-arse talk little boy or you get sore bum now from my boot!" Porno retorted.

And then Graham really was on his own. Porno closed the gate and CSM Cleland and the Hutchie Men walked off to the right along the line of the fence. They were soon lost to sight behind the numerous large thorn trees which grew on the higher ground. Graham swallowed a mouthful of water to calm his jumping insides, then checked his watch.

1745hrs, we are going alright, he thought. *About three quarters of an hour to dark.*

They had over a kilometre to cover to the highway and he did not want to cross in daylight. Graham decided he would move along just above the swampy depression that formed one of the Anabranches. There were plenty of thorn trees and clumps of grass. He motioned Halyday and Andrews up and whispered to them what he wanted.

"You two are the scouts. Head across that way but take your time, move from bush to bush. There is no hurry."

Just as they began to move the pack radio suddenly crackled and began talking. Graham spun round and snapped angrily at Carnes, "Put the bloody earphones on and turn that thing down. Don't let that happen again!"

Carnes looked shocked and for a moment Graham thought he was going to burst into tears. Carnes did as he was told, his face a sulky mask. *Damn!* Graham thought. *I didn't handle that very well!* Flitting across his mind was the imagined comment on his own Personal Qualities Report: Reaction under stress. *Poor!* he thought.

The patrol began moving, the two scouts creeping one at a time from cover to cover. Their efforts were then set at nought by Pigsy and Co starting to talk. Graham gulped and knew he had to act.

If I can't shut them up, we will get caught for sure, he thought. Images of failure spurred him to move. He stalked back along the line and glared at The Four.

"Stop talking. We don't want the enemy to hear us."

"You are making more noise than we were," Pigsy pointed out.

"Just shut and co-operate!" Graham snapped back, his temper rising. "Be fair to the others in the patrol."

Pigsy curled his lip. "This mob! I couldn't give a rat's arse about them. We didn't ask to be stuck with little first year toads like them."

That really nettled Graham. "Well, your last platoon didn't want you, and I can see why. Now shut up and do your job properly."

The barb went home and Pigsy gave him a venomous look but made no reply. Graham turned and made his way back to his place in the line. He found his heart was hammering in what felt like erratic palpitations and he was glad the battle of wills had not come to a head. He nodded and Halyday moved forward another ten metres.

The route they followed was across the side of a very gentle slope. Down to the left the bright green of the swampy anabranch was visible. Beyond that was a real tangle of thorn trees and rubber vines which hid the other flood channels and Ruin Island. Graham knew that the remainder of the platoon would be moving along parallel to his patrol over there but he could not hear anything.

The area was thickly dotted with the thorn trees but there was almost no grass. The numerous cow pats explained why; it was heavily grazed by cattle. A few of these became visible in the distance and Graham signalled halt while he considered what to do.

If we frighten those cattle and they stampede off ahead of us it will warn any enemy we are coming, he thought.

Before he could decide on a plan the issue was settled for him. A harsh laugh sounded from the back of the patrol: Pigsy! The cattle stopped eating and lifted their heads to look, before bolting off away from them.

Oh, bugger it! Graham thought. The laughing and talking continued. By then the evening hush had set in and Graham knew that the sounds must travel for a long way on the still air. *I have to shut them up or we fail!*

In his heart he knew that he faced one of those crucial tests in life. *If I don't face this now, no matter what, I will despise myself for the rest of my life,* he thought.

The sheer starkness of his choice made him pause. Even now he groped in his mind for some strategy to put off the confrontation he that knew he must force if he was to retain both his self-respect and the control of the patrol.

This is a test of manhood, and of leadership, he told himself.

He just wished it was not so, that the problem would somehow resolve itself, but from some fundamental part of his being he understood he had no choice.

I either settle this, or I go under, he told himself.

For over a minute he stood, trembling with apprehension, his imagination conjuring up dark pictures of what The Four might do. These were counter-balanced by other images; telling Peter and Stephen how his patrol had gone on the exercise, and knowing he would have to lie to make it sound as though they had done well. The very thought of it made him feel sick.

Moynihan called out and Pigsy snickered. Graham flamed with shame. *They are so loud CUO Masters must be able to hear them. He will think I am a useless bloody section commander!* That thought was followed instantly by an even gloomier one. *He must already, seeing I have been split off with the rejects!*

That made him angry. *Bugger it! I'll show him!* He started walking back along the line. *The worst Pigsy and Co can do is bash me,* he reasoned, but he wasn't sure what strategy to adopt. As he passed the other cadets he could tell by their faces that they understood very clearly that the showdown had arrived.

As he approached The Four, they kept joking and talking but he knew they were watching him. He suspected that they were deliberately baiting him and testing how he would react. They were at the back of the section, with Slim, Milson, and Bragg ahead of them. Graham gritted his teeth as he tried to think up a plan to solve the problem. He saw LCpl Franks glance at him and that cheered him up.

Franks is scared! he realised. *So it is not four, only three.*

Then more advice from his father helped clarify his plan of attack. Graham's father had been a ship's captain for twenty years and was obviously a tough customer. *If there is a mutiny,* he had said one day to his sons, *you single out the ringleader and deal with him. The others won't interfere. They are just spineless curs.*

Pigsy is the ringleader, Graham thought as he approached them.

With that in mind, he forced himself to stride across to confront Pigsy. For a moment the two stood facing each other. Graham spoke quietly but clearly, "I told you people to keep quiet. If you don't, then I will have to take some action to make you."

Pigsy sneered. "Haw! You and what army? You can go and get stuffed."

"I told you to be quiet," Graham said with desperation.

To add to his feeling of stress he was aware that the other members of the section were all watching and listening. *If I lose this, they will all despise me. I will be finished as a section commander,* he thought. That helped stiffen his resolve.

"You are just a boot licker!" Pigsy said, spitting at Graham's feet to emphasise his defiance.

"I'm the corporal," Graham said, gesturing to his two stripes. Even as he did it, he had a sinking feeling that he had made a mistake by saying that.

Pigsy jeered and laughed. Waters and Moynihan laughed as well and moved to take up threatening positions behind him. Pigsy said, "You've only got two stripes because you crawl to the officers. You're just a gutless weakling."

Graham felt his stomach turn over and he knew he was really scared. But he was also desperate and knew instinctively that this was a battle of wills he had to win, or at least go down fighting. He put his hands on his hips and said, "Either turn down the noise and do what you are told, or I will take you back to the camp now."

Pigsy turned to his mates and laughed. "Big man! He will take us back!" He turned back to Graham and bunched his fists onto his hips. "How will you do that you gutless jerk? All you can do is dob us in later, and that will just prove you are weak."

That was what Graham thought too and he now tensed, ready for open conflict. Among his options was the one frequently used by American 'heroes' in movies of beating Pigsy in a fight. To his own surprise he found he wasn't afraid of fighting him, but it went so much against all he had been taught about leadership that he rejected it as an option.

That is not the way the Australian Army does things, and it is sinking to his level, he thought. But he was still stumped for a workable plan.

After a moment's tense silence, he shrugged and said, "Then you can walk back to camp now, and explain why when you get there. That way you can put your version in with the officers before I do."

"Make us!" Pigsy retorted, curling his lip.

Graham looked him straight in the eye. Noting the flickering in the irises he suddenly thought, *He's scared!* That emboldened him. *I've come this far. I can't just let this fizzle out now or it will just fester and resurface. I have to settle it.*

Having resolved that, he said, "Either agree to do the right thing or get going."

"Get stuffed!"

"You are finished, Pigsy. Do as you are told."

"Oh yeah! What'll you do? Dob us in the officers?"

At that Graham smiled. "Of course. That's how the army system works. It has to work that way or the bullies like you will win. You think I haven't got the guts to report you because you will tease me for being a dobber. And you think you can frighten me with threats. Well, you are wrong on both counts. You are the one who hasn't got the guts. You aren't even game to do your own dirty work. You have to get other people to tease little kids like Braggy."

At that Pigsy lost his temper. Graham saw his eyes, already suffused with a reddish tinge, narrow. He sensed what was coming and braced himself for it. Suddenly he knew that he was winning. But the battle wasn't over, and it hurt. Pigsy lashed out. The punch took Graham full in the face, knocking him back several steps.

There was shocked gasp from the watching cadets. Graham's head spun and he had trouble keeping his feet, but he managed to keep his own hands by his sides. With a disdainful sneer he taunted Pigsy.

"That's the end of you, Pigsy. Criminal assault in front of witnesses. Now we can involve the police as well as the officers."

"You gutless shit! You aren't even game to fight," Pigsy snarled. He jumped forward and punched again.

It took a real effort of willpower, but Graham stood and wore it. The blow knocked him to his knees. Shaking his head to stay conscious and to fight off the dizziness he straightened up.

"Striking a superior officer, eh?" he commented. "You are finished, Pigsy. Cadet Carnes, give me that radio so I can call the OC."

For a second Graham thought he had provoked Pigsy into completely losing control, but he saw the eyes flickering and the raised fist and knew it was almost over. Neither of Pigsy's mates made any move to help. The only person who tried to interfere was Slim.

He cried, "Hey! Stop it!"

"Stay out of this, Cadet Lyle," Graham replied.

He had trouble speaking clearly because his lips were going numb and he could taste blood. Pigsy stood glaring at him but looking baffled.

When he did not punch again, Graham said, “Right, Cadet Pike. This is the deal, and it isn’t open to negotiation. Co-operate and make this patrol work and we will forget that you lost control. If you don’t want that, then we move directly to the highway bridge and call in the officers. Take it or leave it.”

Pigsy glared at him but looked unsure. He glanced at his friends, but they had now edged away, clearly not wanting to get involved. Graham breathed out and set his jaw. There was blood trickling down his face, but he resisted the urge to wipe it off. He sensed he had the upper hand but now had to turn it into complete victory. He stepped closer to Pigsy and looked him straight in the eyes.

“Well? What is it to be? Make your mind up, and fast.”

Pigsy licked his lips and again looked to his cronies for support but Graham noted Moynihan shaking his head. Rather than give Pigsy any time to think of some new tactic, Graham said, “Right, to the highway,” and spun on his heel.

“Wait!” Pigsy cried.

Graham paused. “No negotiations,” he called over his shoulder. “You either obey orders or you are in deep legal trouble.”

“Bastard!” Pigsy snarled.

“Abusing me will just make it worse,” Graham said. He turned to the other members of the patrol. “Come on, let’s get this over with, then we might be allowed to go on with the exercise.”

As Graham started walking, Pigsy gave a strangled cry. For a moment Graham tensed, thinking Pigsy was going to attack him from behind. Instead, Pigsy cried out, “Alright! I’m sorry. I didn’t mean it.”

Graham turned to face him and said levelly, “I did. So, are you saying you will obey orders?”

“Yes,” Pigsy replied.

Inside Graham heaved a massive mental sigh of relief. With an effort he kept his voice level and his face stern.

“Then let’s get on with the patrol.”

Chapter 29

DECOYS

As Graham walked back to his place in the line, he felt that something fundamental had changed. To be sure he was shaking with relief and his heart was hammering but deep inside he felt a new sense of certainty.

I can do this, he thought. It was as though he saw the world through new eyes. *Pigsy and his type are just weak bullies,* he realised. *Even if it comes to a confrontation it is better to stand up to them than to give in.*

None of the others said anything and Graham did not want further discussion. He nodded to Halyday and Andrews and pointed the way he wanted them to go. They turned and resumed their scouting. A quick glance behind showed that the whole patrol was following. Pigsy and his mates all looked angry, but there was something else. At first Graham thought they were subdued, but then he decided they were scared.

They know they overstepped the mark and that I have called their bluff, he told himself.

The tactical problems of avoiding patrols from the 'enemy' now absorbed Graham's thoughts and he scanned carefully in every direction, hoping to spot any enemy before they saw his people. When he glanced back every few seconds to check that the others were following, he was continually surprised at how many people there seemed to be. For much of the time the last few cadets in the patrol were out of sight behind bushes as they snaked across the slope.

It was only then that it really dawned on Graham just how big his patrol was. He had known it intellectually from the moment he had been briefed but now it really struck him emotionally.

I've got eleven in my patrol, counting me, he realised. For a while he mulled over this, then shook his head in puzzled wonder. *That is nearly half a platoon in size,* he thought. Most of the platoons only had about 20 in them; a HQ of two and three sections of six or seven.

That got him thinking. *We are the decoys, but why so many? And why not give the command to a sergeant or the CSM?* There were at least two possible answers. One was profoundly depressing. *We are all the rejects, so it doesn't matter if we get wiped out. That is why we are the decoys.* The other thought only came later, that maybe Capt Conkey had enough faith in him to trust him to do a good job. After considering this, Graham shook his head. *No, he wouldn't have broken up my good section in that case. This mob will be no loss to the company.*

The role of decoy made him angry. *We are the expendable pawns,* he thought, using a term Capt Conkey had employed during a history lesson. *While we draw the flak the good troops get through.*

Looking at the route he had been told to take, and the ground he was actually crossing, seemed to reinforce this. The thorn bushes were becoming more scattered and he was getting long views of several hundred metres through the gaps.

Any enemy at the highway will see us, he decided.

That caused him to signal a halt. They had moved about 700 metres across the gentle slope, and he knew the highway should be only a short distance ahead. It was twilight by this time, but visibility was still quite good. Overhead the sky was darkening and the first stars were twinkling.

We had better find a hide till it is fully dark, Graham thought.

There looked to be a slight dip off down to the left about 50 metres away, so he moved them that way. The dip turned out to be a shallow depression that deepened very slowly as it ran off down towards the Anabranches. After following if down for another 50 paces Graham decided it was the best he would get. A small thicket of thorn trees offered some cover from the direction of the highway.

He moved the patrol in and sat them in a circle facing out. When all had arrived, he said to them, "We will wait here till we hear some action before we cross the highway. No talking, no lights and no fires. Just rest."

Even as he said this Halyday hissed and pointed up the slope to the west. Graham looked, and in the gloom he saw a line of cadets walking northwards across the slope a hundred metres away. Instantly, he dropped to a crouch and peeked through a bush.

"Down! Enemy patrol," he whispered.

The others lay flat and Andrew felt a surge of excitement that left his heart hammering and his throat dry. His mind raced as he worried about what to do if the enemy had seen them. But the way they were walking quickly indicated that the enemy were unaware of their presence.

They are walking along the vehicle track heading towards the gate we came through, Graham decided. That caused him a grim smile. *If we had been a few minutes later, they would have spotted us moving.*

Waters poked his head up to watch and then croaked, "They are getting behind us. We will be trapped!"

"Rot! We know they are there and we will just detour around them," Graham replied. "Anyway, we will worry about them on the way back. First we need to get to our objective."

He waited until the enemy patrol had vanished towards the river then said, "I will do a recce with Cadet Halyday to find the best place to cross the highway."

The others looked at him in the dusk and no-one argued or disagreed. Graham was careful not to provoke another incident with The Four by not referring to the previous crisis. Once he was sure they understood he left Franks in charge with Bragg as sentry then set off towards the highway.

While moving up the gentle slope from the dip Graham went at a crouch but closer to the crest he went down on all fours. That was a mistake he soon learned. The ground was littered with small, sharp stones and thousands of burrs. Most were the tiny twin pronged 'bindis', but some were the viciously sharp, three-pronged 'goat heads'. After suffering several in his hands and one in his knee, he gave up crawling and went back to crouching.

Little by little the other side of the slope became visible as he moved cautiously from tree to bush. That he was close to the highway was plain from the frequent passing of motor vehicles. Then he was able to see over the crest and stopped to observe. Halyday ghosted up to settle under cover beside him. The ground sloped away in two directions at such a gentle angle he could not see most of it. Only a few clues to the location of the highway were visible: a fence line and the flicker of passing vehicles, most of which now had their headlights on.

Away in the distance, across a wide, grassy plain was the railway bridge. A massive earth embankment led out of the distant hillside across the plain, ending in the huge concrete abutments which were his objective. From his study of the map Graham knew that from somewhere up to his right a dirt road led down from the highway across the grassy plain to the end of the rail bridge. In the twilight Graham was unable to make out any details and could not see any sign of the defenders.

They must be in position by now? he thought.

Even as he did, he tensed. From about a hundred metres in front of him a voice had spoken. Another answered and a third laughed. Yet another voice called angrily, “Keep your voices down. We don’t want that Cairns mob to hear us.”

With a shock Graham realised there was an enemy patrol sitting along the fence. *If we'd kept going we would have walked right into their arms!*

That was a rude shock. He breathed out then wondered where other defenders might be, and how to get across the highway. According to the map he was about 300 metres from the end of the highway bridge.

There will be guards there for sure, he decided. The map also showed that the highway curved south towards the tiny settlement of Bunyip Bend. *Might be more at the bend,* he reasoned. That was where the dirt road to the end of the railway bridge branched off and it seemed a logical place to put a guard post.

Then the hair on the back of his neck stood on end. Distinctly on the night air he heard voices muttering- and it was coming from behind him! *Bloody idiots!* he thought. An urgent desire to not get caught was mixed with anger at The Four (He was sure it was them!).

“Come on Halyday,” Graham hissed.

Keeping the bush between him and the enemy patrol he hurried back across the bare, open ground. It was light enough to see where he was putting his feet, yet not dark enough to hide them from any watcher. But the noise was more of a threat.

Bloody selfish fools! he fumed. *Why did I have to be lumbered with them?*

Then the idea came to him. *We are the decoys for the company. Why don't I use them as the decoys for the patrol? That way I get rid of them and they perform a useful function at the same time!*

It had such elegant appeal, tied as it was to concepts like ‘poetic justice’, that he decided to use it. But first the talking had to be stopped! Moving almost at a trot he hurried back to the dip. As he rounded the bushes Graham saw that The Four were sitting in a group to one side. The other cadets still lay facing out in pairs, as he had positioned them. Standing over The Four, fists on hips, he glared down at them. In the gloom he could just see their faces.

"There is an enemy patrol just over at the highway," he said quietly but coldly. "You people should not be talking. It will give the game away."

"Huh, that's all it is, a stupid bloody game!" Waters replied.

Graham was about to snap angrily back that it wasn't a game, but then he realised that the real issue was that his own future and promotion were bound up in succeeding. Instead, he changed tack. "I don't care what you think it is, except that our unit's reputation is involved. We don't want those Heatley people jeering at us for being so useless that they can hear us coming from a kilometre away. So stop talking and don't let your mates down."

Pigsy gave him a resentful look but said nothing. Franks looked embarrassed and Moynihan just sat in surly silence.

"So what do we do now?" Waters asked, his voice tinged with rebellion.

"We wait till it is time to cross the highway, so we co-ordinate our move with everyone else's," Graham replied. He then crouched down and took out his pocket torch. Crouching so that the front of the tiny torch was only a centimetre above his map he turned it on. Speaking to Franks, he pointed to the map. "See this vehicle track here, the one up to our right that leads down to the gate we came through? When I tell you to move I want you and these three to go up there, then along it to the highway. Cross the highway and follow this other road down to the bridge."

"Why us? Are you trying to get rid of us?" Waters asked.

Graham met his eyes. "No. I am trying to give the patrol a better chance of winning by splitting into two groups. One of us should make it to the railway bridge."

"There's only one bomb," Waters pointed out.

"So write your name on the concrete with felt pen," Graham replied. He knew they had them because they used them to mark people's faces while they were asleep.

"What if we run into the enemy?" Franks asked nervously.

"You probably will. I reckon there will be a guard post at the road junction. Avoid them and fight any others you bump into," Graham replied.

"They might catch us," Moynihan said accusingly.

"You are senior cadets, aren't you?" Graham retorted. "So give them a good run for their money and get away."

"What do we do after we get to the bridge?" Waters asked.

On hearing that Graham heaved a mental sigh of relief, as he knew it meant they had accepted the plan. "Look for trouble. Stir the defenders up, then withdraw back to the gate at the river and wait till we arrive," Graham replied.

He then gave Franks timings to work to and again told them to spread out and be quiet. To his relief, they did so without argument. Silence settled, broken only by the passing of cars or trucks.

It was coming up to 1900hrs by then and the last streaks of red had faded from the western sky. The patrol lay in the darkness in silence. With an hour to wait Graham fretted that someone would give them away but there were only a few quiet murmurs. Then distant shouting reached them on the still night air. Graham raised his head and listened.

"That's a long way away," Halyday whispered.

"Yes, over on Bare Ridge I think," Graham replied.

After a few minutes the faint yelling died away. Next the radio called and Graham asked Carnes what was said. "4 Platoon have just reported being ambushed by a Heatley patrol on Sandy Ridge," he said.

"4 Platoon eh? That will hurt their pride," he said.

To himself he thought, *Not a good start!*

Silence again settled and he tried to rest. The sound of a train crossing the bridge carried loudly to them. Graham marvelled at how noisy it was, and how far the sound travelled. After it had gone over the next rise in the direction of Townsville relative silence again settled. This was broken at 1940 by more shouting. It was closer but still a long way away.

"That is on the other side of the river too I reckon," Halyday said.

It was. Carnes passed on a radio report from 1 Platoon saying they had run into enemy on the road to Canning Junction near Black Knoll. That worried Graham and he wondered if Capt Conkey's decoy plan had failed.

They are certainly hitting us a long way out, he thought. That got him reconsidering his own plan. After thinking it over he shook his head. It still seemed like a good idea. *A smaller group is easier to control and has more chance of success,* he reasoned.

At 2000hrs he called the whole patrol in and went over the plan a second time. They then had a drink and prepared to move. Just as Graham was about to tell Franks to take his party away there was more yelling, closer again, but still a fair way off. The shouting and 'bang! bang!' yells went on for a good ten minutes.

It was 3 Platoon. They had encountered a Heatley patrol at the stop butts to an old rifle range on the flat between Bare Ridge and the river. As that 'battle' died down another began, much closer and obviously in the riverbed.

That must be our platoon, Graham thought.

He was right. A radio report to Coy HQ confirmed that 2 Platoon were running into a line of enemy across the sandy riverbed two hundred metres upstream from the highway bridge.

This is not looking good, Graham told himself. *Every platoon has run into enemy a long way from their objectives, and we have enemy both in front of us and behind us.*

That got him worrying that they would not be able to cross the highway undetected. Suddenly the decoy idea looked even better. "Off you go Lance Corporal Franks," he said.

Franks swallowed and nodded, then signalled to Pigsy and Co to move. Muttering with discontent they stood up and vanished among the thorn trees further up the slope. Graham did not wait. He got his own group up and moving, but angled down to the left, following the dip. After moving 50 paces he stopped then moved along the line to check that everyone who should be with him was. Then he got them moving again.

As they walked slowly down the slope towards the highway, Graham felt his spirits lift. Without the presence of The Four he felt much happier. Then he heard a stumbling sound and a curse from behind him. It came from The Four and it made Graham grin with malicious pleasure.

Good! he thought. *They must be a hundred metres away now, and if they are making that much noise they are sure to attract the enemy's attention.*

Once Graham's patrol had gone a 150 paces down the slope, and he was sure they were clear of the waiting enemy patrol, he had the scouts angle out of the dip and across towards the highway. They moved one at a time from bush to bush, pausing to listen frequently. About 50 metres from the road, they went down into a deep, grassy depression, which ran down towards the tangle of dark bushes that marked the end of the Anabranches. Beyond that was a fence and then the highway.

Graham stopped the patrol and crawled forward to join the scouts at the fence. The fence was a typical three-strand cattle fence and had long grass growing between it and a deep drainage ditch beside the highway. As Graham slithered under the bottom strand, he realised he had miscalculated and that they were closer to the bridge than he had wished. He lay in the grass on top of a low cutting and studied the layout. Now he was starting to really enjoy himself and his heart beat faster with excitement.

Two cars and a semi-trailer roared past. Graham and Halyday lay flat and closed their eyes until they were past. As the last one went past towards the bridge Halyday touched Graham's arm.

"There!" he hissed.

Three strange cadets were lit up by the passing vehicle's headlights. It was an enemy guard post near the end of the bridge and right where Graham had expected it to be.

We will have to back off and go further up the road, he decided. That got him anxious as it was almost 2130hrs and he wanted to try to cross the highway at the same time as the other raiding parties. *Do we have time?* he wondered.

Halyday touched him again. "One of those guys down there has a night sight," he whispered.

Graham looked and noted the faint green glow on the enemy cadet's right eye. It indicated he was using one of the old-style night vision devices.

That settles it, Graham thought. *We will never get across unseen if he looks this way.* A look up to his right showed the highway stretching up to a starry backdrop a few hundred metres away. That didn't help. *If we go far enough up the road to get out of sight of the bridge, we will run into that first patrol we just missed earlier.*

What to do? Time was pressing. Graham nudged Halyday and slid back under the fence. As soon as he was in the depression behind, he signalled the patrol to follow and set off at a fast walk up the dip, staying parallel to the fence.

He had only gone 50 paces when a hullabaloo of yelling broke out at the top of the slope ahead of them. *The Four have walked into something,* he thought. Once again he felt a spurt of malicious glee. *Good! Now, will the decoy plan work?*

He moved to the fence and slid under. Up to the right he could hear voices calling out and a person talking on a radio. Then another radio began down near the bridge.

The decoys have got them going alright, he thought. *We had better make the most of it.* He could hear the distant shouting moving away and deduced that The Four must have crossed the highway *They are running towards the railway bridge,* he told himself.

Time to go, Graham decided.

He signalled and slid forward, down into the deep grassy drainage ditch beside the bitumen. Halyday followed, then Andrews. As each reached him Graham whispered, "Line up side by side and we will all cross at the same time."

Carnes joined him, his eyes looking very large in the starlight, then Milson, Bragg and Slim. Satisfied that all of his patrol were there Graham looked both ways along the highway to pick the right moment to cross. As he did, he saw the headlights of three vehicles pull onto the highway over on the far bank. The vehicles drove onto the bridge towards him.

"After these vehicles go past," he hissed. "Then just stand up and walk quickly across."

He saw nods and eyes flicking nervously in the rapidly increasing light from the approaching vehicles. So as not to be seen they all pressed themselves flat in the bottom of the ditch. The first vehicle raced past, its headlights illuminating several cadets standing beside the road a hundred metres up the slope. *The guard post we dodged,* Graham noted.

Then he looked up in alarm. The next two vehicles were slowing down. To Graham's annoyance they braked to a halt directly opposite where the patrol lay. The nearest was only five metres away. Then his annoyance turned to dismay. They were army trucks and he saw that the back of the one he could see into was crammed with cadets. In the truck headlights he could see yellow flashes.

Heatley! The enemy! he thought.

Worse still, it was obvious they were about to debus!

Chapter 30

UNRAVELLED

Graham stared up at the cadets in the back of the truck in horror. *Oh no! Sprung!* he thought.

To his relief the truck's headlights were then switched off but the side lights were left on. Doors opened and the army drivers and two Officers of Cadets came around to the backs of the trucks. They undid the tailgates and let them down.

One of the officers pointed and bellowed at the cadets sitting in the back of the nearest truck, "Out you get! Line up over against the bank on the left off the road."

Cadets began climbing down off the trucks and milling around, ignoring the officer's calls to move away, while they fumbled with webbing or waited for friends. Graham watched them anxiously, his heart beating rapidly.

Any moment now one of them is going to walk over to this side of the road and see us, he thought. There were at least thirty cadets he estimated, and they had radios. *The mobile reserve deploying,* he decided.

Then another idea came to him, a flash from something he had read once. *Now is our chance,* he thought.

Knowing that the opportunity would be gone within a minute or so he leaned over to Andrews and said, "Get up and cross the road, wait at the fence on the other side. Just walk, don't try to sneak. Tell Halyday. Go!"

He saw Andrews' mouth open in surprise and Graham wondered if he would muck it up by being too slow on the uptake to grasp the plan. Without waiting to see, he stood up and waved to the others beside him.

"Get up! Follow me!" he called, hoping his voice would be lost in the yelling of the Heatley sergeants and corporals as they tried to sort out their sections.

Graham then clambered up the bank to stand near the back of the first truck. His heart was now hammering so fast he seemed to have trouble hearing and his vision was blurred.

Looking back, he was relieved to see Carnes and Bragg climbing up to join him. Then others rose and scrambled up the bank too. Graham waited till he was sure they were all up out of the ditch and then turned and walked through between the trucks. By now most of the Heatley cadets had moved to the far side and were forming up at the side of the road. In the darkness there seemed to be cadets everywhere, creating just the confusion he was now depending on.

Graham made his way past a CUO or sergeant who had a night vision device in his hand. The person was ordering a section to get in line. Graham went left around the end of the group and then climbed straight up the grassy bank beyond. At the top he paused and glanced around, noting that Carnes was still close behind him. A line of dark figures came bobbing through the faint light from the truck's taillight, which was luckily still shielded by the lowered tailgate.

His patrol seemed to be following and that gave Graham hope. He heard an NCO call for 9 Section to follow him and saw a line of figures start moving along the side of the road past the front truck in the direction of the crest. Carnes joined Graham, who now turned and walked into the long grass on top of the cutting. Bragg and Milson scrambled up the bank to join them and he saw others were following. At that moment, the tailgate of the front truck was slammed up into position and Graham glimpsed Slim as he hurried past it, right beside a Heatley officer who was helping to do the tailgate clips up.

For a second the Heatley officer glanced at Slim. A puzzled look crossed his face, but he said nothing and turned to talk to the driver. Graham led the way the 10 paces to the fence. As he stood up after crawling under it he saw a line of cadets climbing up the bank and moving across to the fence ten metres to his right. Not knowing the enemy plan, he could only hope they would continue to think his patrol was one of theirs.

One by one his cadets crawled under the fence. Halyday and Andrews appeared at his elbow, both chuckling with excitement. Graham did a quick count and noted they were all still with him. "Get going, that way," he said, pointing into the overgrown field beyond. This was full of long grass and thorn bushes and seemed to offer good cover. Halyday at once set off.

By then the Heatley section off to their right was also through the fence and seemed to be walking parallel to them. *Blast!* Graham thought. *This could get awkward.*

He decided to slowly edge away on a diverging course and pointed further left to guide Halyday. At that moment there was another outburst of yelling up at the crest of the hill. The Heatley cadets broke into an excited babble and their leaders urged them to hurry. They went trampling off into the darkness in that direction.

That was the Decoys, Graham thought. That made him smile. *We've done it!* he told himself.

Jubilation welled up and he chuckled. The others were also very excited and began whispering and murmuring so he had to hiss at them to keep quiet.

Screams and shouts broke out down in the riverbed a few hundred metres to the left. *2 Platoon trying to break through,* Graham told himself.

He heard urgent commands near the trucks and a group of Heatley cadets went trotting off down towards the bridge. Then the trucks started up and went driving off up the hill. Graham kept his patrol moving, ignoring the long grass, uneven ground, and small thorn bushes.

Only when he was at least a hundred metres from the highway did he stop for a check. By then he was sure they could not be seen from the road. The headlights of a passing car showed up as no more than a few flickers of light through the thorn bushes.

"Have a drink and get your breath back," he ordered.

"Boy! That was fun! I was sure we were caught then," Andrews said loudly.

"Sssh! Shut up! Save the war stories for after the exercise," Graham cautioned. But he was pleased. So, obviously, were the members of the patrol.

Except Carnes, who pointed and said, "What's that?"

Graham turned to look. It was a whitish wall with dark doorways and windows. "Just the ruins of the old meat works," he replied.

"Ruin?"

"Yeah, a ruin. Come on, let's get moving," Graham replied.

They began to move to the left of the ruin, which turned out to be much bigger than Graham had thought it was. The whole place was overgrown with weeds and thorn bushes. The buildings had no roofs and most of the walls were half-tumbled down. A few still stood, with the windows and doors making spooky looking blocks of shadow. Underfoot the cadets began to encounter blocks of concrete, loose bricks, broken glass and sheets of rusty corrugated iron.

When Halyday walked onto a sheet of iron it sounded very loud and they all froze in fright. Graham had another thought. Until now his greatest fear, snakes, had not crossed his mind, but he knew that they loved to nest under old iron in ruins. "Back off and we will detour further from the ruins," he said, but he didn't mention snakes for fear of spooking his cadets.

Andrews achieved that instead. "Do yer reckon this place is haunted?"

"No," Graham replied, but he still felt a thrill of fear and his heart rate increased.

"Ghosts you mean?" Carnes gasped. He stared at the shadowy ruins with wide, fear-filled eyes.

"Oh rot! Get moving Halyday," Graham snapped angrily, but he could not stop the shiver of goose bumps which went over him.

They hurried away through the thorn bushes, banging their shins on more blocks of broken bricks and walking across another sheet of old iron in their haste. Graham found Carnes so close behind him that he kept bumping into him.

More battles in the riverbed and beyond slowed them and returned their thoughts to the exercise. Graham stopped the patrol to listen and to check his watch. His radio was turned right down but he could hear snatches of orders and reports.

2 Platoon alright, he thought, recognising Stephen's voice as he reported to CUO Masters that he was past the highway bridge but had enemy chasing him. That made Graham feel bad as his friend was just down to his left somewhere in the riverbed. *But my orders aren't to help in their battle,* he reasoned.

So he kept his patrol moving slowly forward. He didn't want to reach the rail bridge ahead of time and he knew they had an hour to go one kilometre. From the sound it seemed there were several battles going on across the river.

"That big battle sounds like it is right back near Bare Ridge," Halyday suggested, as a distant outburst of shouting broke out.

"Yes, it does," Graham agreed. He turned to Carnes. "Are there any reports on the radio?"

Carnes just looked at him. Graham leaned closer. "Cadet Carnes, are there any reports on the radio?"

Carnes shook his head. At first Graham thought he just meant no but then he realised Carnes did not have the radio. "Carnes! Where is the bloody radio?" he cried. Not only was the radio important for safety but Graham knew they cost a lot of money and he didn't want to get into trouble for losing one.

Carnes suddenly burst into tears. Only after a couple of minutes of sobbing did Carnes calm down enough so that Graham could get the gist of what he was trying to say. "I left it back at the road," Carnes said.

"Bloody hell!" Graham groaned in vexation.

But what to do? Go back and get it, or go on without it? He knew he could call on his hand-held radio but also knew that because it was a 'CB' the enemy would almost certainly detect the transmission. After some anguished thinking he decided to go on.

"We will get it on the way back," he said.

Carnes kept sobbing and that wore Graham's patience thin.

"Oh shut up, for Christ's sake! We don't want the enemy to find us because you are making a noise."

Carnes lapsed into shuddering, wracking sniffles. Graham noted the looks of astonished disgust and contempt on the faces of the cadets near him as they stared at Carnes. He felt that way himself but tried to hide it. He gestured to Halyday to keep moving.

Then Graham realised he had miscalculated again. *We are right on top of the riverbank,* he noted.

He had meant to keep a hundred metres or so from it but now found they were following a fence only 10 paces from the edge of the steep bank. Worse still, the ground on the right opened out to a bare, grassy field. The best option seemed to be to move among the thorn bushes on top of the bank.

To that end he had the patrol roll under the fence then begin moving slowly from bush to bush. The whole area seemed to be devoid of undergrowth and the grass had been cropped to stubble. For 200 metres they crept slowly along.

Then Graham heard what he had been dreading: movement coming the other way. He gestured them to get down but Halyday and Andrews had already done so, crawling in under thorn bushes. Graham slithered in under another thorn bush, although it seemed to be pitiful cover; too high and with bare ground under it. And goat dung! Then Carnes huddled in against him.

Ignoring Carnes Graham began to consider the options: over the bank into the thick growth of vines and thorn bushes, out into the open field, or lie still and hope. Then he realised it was too late and he was committed to the 'lie still and hope' option. Into view about thirty metres away had come two cadets. They were walking along beside the fence. Three more appeared behind them. They were moving slowly and obviously searching.

They will see us for sure, Graham thought despairingly. He tensed ready to 'open fire'.

Suddenly, a small battle erupted a few hundred metres to the right, on the other side of the open paddock. *Either the decoys or the Hutchie Men,* Graham thought. The enemy patrol, now almost beside Halyday, went into a crouch and stared towards the sounds.

Then their commander said, "Let's get them!"

To Graham's relief, the enemy patrol stood up and ran off across the open field. Only then did Graham realise they had been on the other side of the fence. He crawled out and gestured to Halyday. "Move!" he hissed.

There won't be another patrol in this area for a while, he thought, as Halyday and Anderson got up and began moving at a quick walk.

After checking the remainder of the patrol were following Graham hurried after the scouts. By then the 'battle' to the right had died down but there were still people yelling, apparently co-ordinating a pursuit.

Out in the darkness one of the enemy yelled, "We've caught one!"

Drat! Graham thought. *I hope whoever it is doesn't blab his big mouth off and let the enemy know we are here somewhere.* He tried to visualise Pigsy or Waters standing up to questioning. *No, it will be Franks who is the weak link,* he decided.

Not knowing who had been captured did not help. Nor did the knowledge that he had lost one of his patrol to the enemy. That hurt his pride.

Another much larger battle erupted on the other bank of the river, almost directly opposite them. Graham stopped to study the situation. He could see torches flashing and a powerful spotlight came on and swept the riverbank and then the trees and sand in its bed.

That is the enemy HQ, he deduced when a vehicle's headlights were added to the illumination. He saw tiny figures running and heard them yelling but could not tell which side they belonged to.

If they are ours, they are in trouble, he considered. Then he looked around and breathed out with satisfaction. There was the rail bridge! He could see the massive concrete pylons in the sandy bed of the river and the criss-cross steel girders against the stars. *Not far now,* he thought. Perhaps 300 metres he decided.

He checked his watch and saw that it was 2110. *Only twenty minutes to H Hour. We had better get a wriggle on,* he thought.

He got the patrol moving, walking at a steady pace along the top of the steep bank. Down behind to his left fierce skirmishing broke out in the riverbed. *That must be our platoon,* he thought. It did not sound good. There was a lot of yelling and arguments and he glimpsed torches from time to time. *It sounds like our people aren't even getting close to the rail bridge,* he thought.

More running battles across the river and along the top of the opposite bank confirmed this. The most hopeful thing was there did not seem to be any more patrols in front of him. His patrol moved steadily closer to the bridge. Graham kept counting down the distance: 250 metres, 200 metres, 150 metres.

At that he stopped the scouts and went forward to them. "There are sure to be guards at the bridge so start creeping really carefully," he whispered.

They nodded and went down into a monkey run. Graham copied them, relieved to find there did not seem to be many burrs. The other cadets followed. The scouts moved one at a time, crawling from bush to bush and Graham was very pleased with how well they did it.

Halyday has turned into a really good scout, he told himself.

They came to an area where the thorn bushes thinned out. A few cattle pads went down through the thicket towards the riverbed. For a moment he considered going down one, in the hope that the cover might be better. He decided not to.

We might clash with our own platoon if we do, he thought, and hurried the patrol across the open areas.

After that, the thorn bushes grew in a real thicket and were hard to get around or even under. The most annoying thing was that Carnes kept glued to him like a shadow, bumping him frequently. Graham hissed at him to spread out several times, but Carnes ignored him. Then Graham paused to listen. Above the yelling and banging in the riverbed sounded a vibrating, rumbling noise. It took Graham a minute to realise what it was: the sound of a train. It was a big freight train, coming from the direction of Charters Towers. He saw the locomotive's headlight come onto the long embankment out to his right. That sent them all to cover as it bathed the whole area in light.

As the engine went onto the actual bridge the noises were all magnified enormously, the throbbing roar of the huge diesels and the rattling, shrieking, clanging thunder of hundreds of steel wheels and couplings. The train's headlight flickered among the steel girders and threw weird moving shadows into the sand of the riverbed.

Just what we need to cover our movement, Graham thought.

He gestured to Halyday and Andrews to move, then quickly rose and hurried across to the next bush himself. Confident that the terrific roar of the-kilometre-long train crossing bridge would cover any noises they made, he urged the scouts to hurry. They quickly scuttled to the next couple of bushes. Graham hurried on to join them, then glanced back to check the others were following.

But there was no-one behind him!

Where the hell is Carnes? Graham wondered.

He paused and kept looking back in hope. After a minute no-one had appeared and the scouts were now nearly out of sight. They would have been except for Halyday looking back and stopping Andrews. Graham hurried forward to them. He was anxious now because the H Hour, the time set for all the raiding parties to attack at once, was now only about ten minutes away.

"The patrol has broken in half," he whispered. "Wait here while I go back and find out what has gone wrong."

Halyday nodded. Graham turned and walked quickly back the way he had come, and 30 metres back he found the problem: Carnes had not moved when he did and all the cadets behind were waiting for him to go. Anger boiled in Graham and he crouched next to Carnes.

"Come on, Cadet Carnes, get moving," he hissed.

Carnes made no move, remaining crouched on all fours, his head up and eyes staring. Being disobeyed set Graham's temper flaring.

"Carnes! I said get moving!" he hissed.

Carnes made no move of any sort, did not even turn his eyes, never mind his head. A peculiar sensation, a mixture of fear and astonishment swept over Graham. "Did you hear me?" he asked.

No response. Graham bent and looked closer. Carnes had his eyes open and seeing them scared Graham. In the light of the spotlight across the river he noted that they were wide and not moving. Carnes seemed to be staring at the rail bridge, which was now close enough to tower over them. Anger gave way to anxiety.

"Carnes, are you alright?" Graham asked.

No answer. Not even a flicker. Graham reached under the thorn bush and touched him. Carnes did not react. Graham shook the boy's shoulder and again asked if he was alright. To his surprise Carnes' muscles were all tense. The boy was rigid. Graham felt another prickle of anxiety.

Is he having some sort of seizure? he wondered, remembering Peter's story about the bridge. To test this idea Graham moved his hand close to Carnes' eyes.

Not a blink. Graham was both astonished and afraid. *I wonder if I should get him medical aid,* he thought.

That at least started him moving. He signalled to Cadet Milson, who scurried over. "Get the medic," Graham instructed.

Milson nodded and went back to call up Slim. While he waited for him Graham fretted about the lost time and about what to do. He tried to remember what he had been taught on his First Aid course about epileptic fits. To be sure he checked that Carnes was breathing normally and put his fingers on his throat to check his pulse. Even at that Carnes made no move. The pulse was rapid but strong.

Slim arrived and Graham explained the problem. Slim looked very worried and said, "I think we should just leave him to come out of it naturally Kirky, then get the officers."

Graham bit his lip in indecision. He wanted to get on with the exercise. At the same time, he was feeling really stressed in case something serious was wrong.

Why me? he thought, then shook his head, *This is what would happen in a real battle, unexpected casualties. But what should I do?* For a moment he fingered his hand-held radio, thinking to call CUO Masters. *He should be just down in the riverbed a few hundred metres away.*

But he did not want to call if it was not serious, so he hooked the radio back on to his shirt. His frustration moved him to act. He shook Carnes firmly by the shoulder. "Carnes! Snap out of it!"

To his enormous relief Carnes gasped, blinked and turned his wildly staring eyes on Graham who thought, *Bloody hell! He's gone bonkers!*

"Wh... what....what?" Carnes gasped. He broke into a bout of shivering and Graham saw sweat beading his face. "Are you alright?" he asked.

Carnes nodded, then sobbed. "Ye... ye... yes. I'm j... ju... just sc... sc... scared."

Carnes had great difficulty speaking because his teeth were clacking and chattering together as he shivered. Graham had heard about people's teeth chattering when they were frightened but actually seeing it made him come out on goose bumps.

"What are you scared of?" he asked in astonishment.

"G... g... gh... ghosts, and d... d... death!" Carnes croaked.

Graham was astonished, and annoyed. "Bloody hell! It's only a cadet exercise. It's not as though anyone is shooting at us!"

"And the b... br... bridge," Carnes added.

Graham had no idea what he was talking about. "Yes, the bridge," he agreed. "That is our objective. So, if you are alright, we will get moving."

He made to go but Carnes shook his head and stared at the bridge. Graham was really agitated now. He bent and hissed, "I said, let's go."

"No," Carnes replied.

He is scared stiff! Graham observed. He found it hard to believe. He was also aware that the minutes were ticking by.

"Listen Cadet Carnes, I gave you an order. Get moving."

Carnes shook his head. "No! I won't go."

Oh no! Graham thought. *Not another disciplinary battle of wills!*

He bent close and pointed to his rank badge. "See these stripes? They say I can give you orders. Now get up and move!"

Carnes refused. Being defied really sparked Graham's anger. He shook his fist in Carnes' face. "Oh, get bloody moving before I thump you!" he cried.

Even as he said it, he knew he was in the wrong. In desperation he groped in his mind for a strategy to deal with the situation. Carnes now crouched in a shivering ball and burst into tears.

Then a great outburst of shouting in the middle of the riverbed, but downstream of the bridge, indicated 4 Platoon must be attacking. At once the other platoons began their attacks, although most seemed to be still a long way from the bridge.

Oh bugger! Graham thought. *We are late.*

That decided him. "Okay Slim, you stay here with him while we raid the bridge," he said. Slim looked distinctly nervous and licked his lips. Graham pointed to the embankment, now only about a hundred metres away. "We will be just there. There is a safety vehicle there too. If there is a problem, you can just yell out and we will bring help."

Slim nodded at that and agreed. Graham took another good look at Carnes, saw that he was still crying and shivering, then waved the others to follow him. He didn't feel good about it but reasoned he could tell the St Michael's officers as soon as they reached the bridge. Hurrying to make up for lost time he led the tail end of the patrol forward to where Halyday and Andrews waited.

By then the battles all seemed to have fizzled out. "Sounds like our people have been driven back," Halyday suggested.

It sounded that way to Graham too and fuelled his desire to succeed. "Keep going, but be careful," he instructed.

It was only then that Milson touched his sleeve. "I don't know where Braggy is," he said.

Graham looked around and did a quick count. Halyday and Andrews, Milson and then Slim with Carnes, plus The Four.

Count yourself, he reminded himself. Then he swore quietly but vehemently. One missing: Bragg. *Oh, bugger it!* he thought. *My patrol has unravelled on me at the crucial moment!*

Chapter 31

UNDER THE BRIDGE

Graham felt sick. Then his anxiety level rose almost to panic. *Oh bloody hell! I started with eleven and there are only four left! And we've lost one, and had another captured, and we have lost the army radio. What will Capt Conkey think?*

For a minute or so he was gripped by black despair. *I'm a failure as a patrol leader,* he thought miserably.

Then the battle flared up across at the other end of the bridge. Hearing it got his blood up. *Beaten without firing a shot!* he thought. Then he shook his head. *No! Like bloody hell! We are almost there. We will do our bit then look for Bragg.*

Gritting his teeth with determination, he turned his back on Halyday. "Get the bomb out of my combat pack," he ordered. Halyday did so, handing it to him. "Now keep going," he said.

Halyday grinned and set off. Graham gestured Andrews to go behind him. With such a small patrol he reasoned he did not need two scouts. *And I don't want Andrews stuffing things up either,* he thought. Having made the decision to go on, he was determined to see it through.

Just 20 metres further on they came to the base of a huge steel power pylon. Graham carefully studied the bushes on the other side of the clearing till he was sure there were no guards then sent Halyday across. This time they went down on their stomachs in the short grass, leopard crawling.

There were a few prickles and burrs, but Graham ignored them, hissing angrily at Andrews when he yelped with pain. They reached the thorn trees on the other side and kept crawling on hands and knees. Under the thorn trees there was no grass, only a deadfall of leaves and twigs-thorny twigs. By this time, they were within 50 metres of the massive concrete bridge abutments and the whole gigantic structure loomed above them.

They came to a dirt vehicle track which went off down to the riverbed. Halyday crossed by crawling. Graham edged up, ready to follow.

We are really close now, he thought *Where are the guards?*

As though in answer to his question, voices spoke along the track to his right. Graham stretched out flat, his heart beating rapidly. Two enemy cadets came into view only ten metres away. They were walking slowly along the track, peering into the shadows under the thorn trees. Graham was only three metres back from the edge of the track and knew he had no real cover. He lay flat, hardly daring to breathe. Across the track he could see the dark, lumpy shape that was Halyday.

They will spot us for sure, Graham thought.

In his mind he rehearsed racing for the end of the bridge while the others fought the defenders. The two enemy cadets came closer and closer, until they were almost directly between Graham and Halyday. One of them bent to peer more closely at Graham. Graham tensed, ready to shout and run.

Suddenly Bragg's voice sounded clearly from down in the riverbed to the left.

"Cpl Kirk! Cpl Kirk! Where are you?"

Bloody Bragg! Graham thought. *They were right! The only thing he has going for him is his sister!*

The two St Michael's cadets stared down the track towards the voice. Bragg called again, his voice quavering with fear.

"Cpl Kirk, where are you?"

"Up here!" called one of the St Michael's cadets.

He was a big lad. Graham thought he recognised him from the promotion course; did he do the sergeants course? The lad snickered and said to his mate, "That smart-arse, know-all Kirk must be somewhere around here."

The other St Michael's cadet laughed and replied, "Him! He thinks he's just too good. Let's catch him."

Hearing such an unflattering description of himself caused Graham to burn. Knowing that his cadets had heard it as well made it even worse. But there was relief too. The two St Michael's cadets went hurrying off down the track.

Now is our chance, Graham thought. He got up, waved Milson and Andrews to follow then walked quickly across the track.

As he moved in under the thorn bushes near Halyday, Graham heard Bragg say loudly, "Is that you, Cpl Kirk?"

"Yes," replied the St Michael's cadet. Then there was a loud shout of 'Bang!' and the St Michael's cadet yelled, "Gotcha!"

Bragg cried in fright. Graham shook his head and gestured Halyday to keep crawling. As they moved into the next thicket, he heard the St Michael's cadet ask Bragg, "Where is Cpl Kirk? Where is your patrol?"

Graham tensed, ready to hear the worst, but Bragg replied, "I don't know. I lost them back at some ruins near the highway."

Graham had the good grace to feel ashamed, and to upgrade his assessment of Bragg. He heard the two St Michael's cadets questioning him as they brought him back up the vehicle track. By then Graham and the remnant of his patrol were 20 metres further on and had reached the other side of the clump of the thorn bushes. There was nothing ahead of them but bare ground and then the bridge.

Graham lay in the grass under a thorn bush and strained his eyes in the darkness to study the situation. Directly in front of him was another dirt vehicle track leading steeply down the bank. Beyond it on his right front, underneath the actual bridge, was a level area of bare earth and short grass with a couple of small erosion rills leading off down the slope towards the next pylon. This was clearly visible and had at least two cadets standing guard at its base. Coming from beyond the bridge and passing underneath it, right against the concrete wall of the abutment, was another dirt road. This went past Graham's right shoulder to where it joined the first dirt track on which Braggy was even now being questioned. Parked there was a Land Rover.

From there the road turned left, to run off inland away from the river. *That is the road which comes down from the highway,* Graham remembered.

He carefully raised his head to check where the defenders were. There were four or five at the Land Rover and two at the gate where they could see along the road beside the embankment, but there did not seem to be any right in under the bridge.

So what to do? Graham was strongly tempted to play the hero and just stroll nonchalantly across and place the bomb in position.

I could do it before they could stop me, he thought. Then he told himself that was childish. *That would only work if this was a suicide attack. In reality we would place the bomb and set a time delay fuse so we could get safely away.*

So, which was the best way to creep forward; and what to do if he was seen?

While he was thinking this he could hear the St Michael's officers questioning Bragg. They were only about ten metres away. There was also a radio crackling there. From the sound of the voices the defenders had high morale and thought they were winning. Then Graham saw movement in the shadows at the other side of the bridge.

There are two guards there, he noted. *A section, plus a HQ.*

Suddenly there was an outburst of yelling inland near the railway embankment. The interrogation of Bragg was ended, and Graham heard an officer calling on a radio to Four Bravo, wanting to know what was going on. Graham deduced the battle must be either the Hutchie Men, or The Four. *Hutchie Men more likely,* he told himself.

The officer on the radio suddenly called. "Cpl Snodgrass, your sentry post at the bend has captured two Cairns cadets. They might be from the same section as this bloke and might be able to tell us where the rest of that section is. Take a cadet and go and bring the prisoners here, quickly."

Snodgrass! Graham remembered: a tall, lanky, red-faced cadet who had been on the Corporals Course with him. *He was the cadet we helped rescue last year at Speed Creek when he got bitten by a snake.* Vivid memeoires of the incident flashed across his mind and helped boost his determination.[1]

Cpl Snodgrass replied, "Yes, sir! Come with me, Cadet Pottinger. Let's go."

Graham heard the thud of boots as the pair ran off along the dusty road. *There must be only four of five left,* he thought.

He began toying with the idea of a diversionary attack while the bomb was placed. That gave him a difficult choice. As the leader he wanted to play the hero and place the bomb but he also knew Capt Conkey was very strong on section commanders being with their troops when they did an attack. 'Follow me!' was how Capt Conkey had drummed into his corporals the right sort of leadership in a crisis.

Graham wrestled with his desires, versus his duty, for a full minute, aware that he had only a short period of time to exploit the opportunity. Reluctantly he bent down next to Halyday. "Here, you take the bomb. I want you to crawl across to the wall there and plant it."

---

[1] Read *Fourteen* by C. R. Cummings

"Okay," Halyday replied, obviously delighted.

"There are guards at the other side there," Graham cautioned.

"I've seen 'em," Halyday replied. He began shrugging off his webbing.

"We will cover you. If you are seen we will attack and you run over with the bomb," Graham explained.

Halyday nodded and grinned. Graham then said, "Have you got a felt pen to write on the wall?"

Halyday dug one out of his map pocket and held it up. Graham smiled and said, "Off you go."

Halyday grinned again, then lowered himself flat. With only a faint rustle he slid out of the grass and onto the bare track. Graham moved into a crouch, ready to act, his heart now speeding up with anticipation and excitement. Halyday slid on, worming forward in a 'hunger crawl' on his stomach. He went across the bare earth beyond and looked to be only a black lumpy shape that slowly moved.

An outburst of shouting down in the riverbed near the next pylon made Graham jump he was so tensed. He could hear CUO Masters yelling and knew it was 2 Platoon. They were obviously having trouble reaching the pylon and Graham experienced a strong twinge of conscience for not joining in the battle to help them.

His anxieties shot right up when the St Michael's guards down at the next pylon started shouting for help. The people at the Land Rover also began calling out. Graham heard the officer say, "Quick Sergeant Burns, you and Carter move to cover their flank on the slope."

Two cadets came running from the Land Rover. They went past in front of Graham only two paces away, then spread out and went down the slope, almost stepping on Halyday as they did. Graham held his breath but saw that Halyday had flattened himself into a tiny washout. The two St Michael's cadets began shouting, 'Bang! Bang!' as they joined in the battle at the bottom. Graham could just see them. They went about halfway down the slope. He also saw the two guards at the other side of the bridge move across the road to the top of the bank. They also joined in, but did not go over the crest.

Halyday raised his head, noted this, and began slithering forward, across the road and into the darkness right at the base of the wall. Someone down the slope was flashing a powerful torch about and its flickering light allowed Graham glimpses of Halyday as he inched across the road on his stomach.

More St Michael's defenders could be heard joining in the battle down in the riverbed. It was obvious 2 Platoon had not made it and Graham felt quite guilty. He heard Stephen yelling for 6 Section to pull back and that twisted the knife in his conscience.

But Halyday was there! He had rolled across flat against the base of the wall. In the darkness Graham could hardly see him. He was moving but only slightly. *Come on Halyday! Plant the bomb and get out of there,* he urged silently. He began chewing his knuckles and fingernails.

By then the battle down in the riverbed was dying down; 2 Platoon was clearly withdrawing. Graham raised his head to watch the two St Michael's cadets on the slope and was relieved to see that they had gone even further down and were joining in a loud, laughing conversation with the guards at the base of the pylon. They were gloating over their victory.

Halyday was on his way back by this time. He moved faster coming back, still crawling and hugging the shadows, but not being as careful. Graham held his breath with excitement and silently cheered and urged him on. He kept casting anxious glances at the two guards twenty metres further on, but they were also still looking down the slope.

Then Halyday was back. He was chuckling to himself and his eyes danced with excitement. Graham thrust his webbing into his hands and whispered, "Let's get out of here!"

Without waiting for Halyday, he began crawling back the way they had come. Milson and Andrews were still lying under cover. Graham gave a 'thumbs up' and told them to follow. As he did, he heard voices at the Land Rover. It was Cpl Snodgrass returning.

The officer said to him, "Get Sergeant Burns back up here in case the section these prisoners came from try to sneak in."

Cpl Snodgrass came running past along the track behind Graham and he heard him calling down to the two.

Whew! Just in time! he thought.

The hard thing now was not to hurry and thereby spoil things by making a noise. The raiding party had to creep back through the thicket within metres of the Land Rover to reach the first dirt track. They were helped in this by Pigsy and Waters. Graham identified their voices as they made cheeky and insulting answers to their captors.

I'll have to apologise to them, Graham thought, while he silently congratulated himself on the success of his decoy plan.

A minute later, the patrol was back across the first track and moving through the thicket of thorn bushes. Two minutes later they reached the power pylon. Here Graham stopped them to check they were still with him, and to have a drink. He found his throat was dry and his temperature high. The battle seemed to have died down right across the area and all Graham could now hear was the murmur of voices back at the Land Rover, and a few defenders calling out down in the riverbed.

By his watch Graham saw it was 2210hrs. The cadets with him started to tell each other about what they had done. "Shut up!" Graham hissed. "We have to get away now. We still have to get back across the highway."

"Yeah, but we did it!" Halyday replied.

"What took you so long?" Graham asked.

"I buried the bomb in the sand so they wouldn't see it, then I wrote 4 Section, Cairns, on the concrete with my felt pen," Halyday replied.

"Well done! You are a bloody great scout," Graham told him.

"Bloody great crawler alright," Andrews added, his voice tinged with jealousy.

"Quiet. Let's go and collect Slim and Carnes," Graham said.

"I'd leave the useless bastard," Andrews commented.

"Shut up or you can go back on your own," Graham threatened.

He set off along the top of the bank, his eyes and ears still alert for defending patrols. *We will look silly if we just blunder into a patrol on the way home,* he thought.

What was really nagging at him was the problem of how to get back over the highway. That problem was brought home by the sounds of a series of battles ahead of them as the other raiding parties ran into lines of defenders at the highway bridge and up along the highway past Bare Ridge.

Anxiety continued to grow in Graham's chest. Now he was worrying about Carnes. However, he found him sitting quietly with a very relieved Slim under the same thorn bush.

"You okay, Cadet Carnes? Do you need to go to the doctor or anything?" Graham asked.

"I'm alright," Carnes replied.

"Bloody sook!" Andrews teased.

"Shut up, Cadet Andrews. Now, no talking. Let's go back and find that radio," Graham said. He led off along the fence, walking quickly now, but still alert. The others followed.

Five minutes walking had them at the junction of a fence that went off west and enclosed the patch of overgrown thorn scrub that contained the ruins of the meat works. For simplicity of navigation to retrace his steps to find the radio Graham wanted to go back through that paddock, but concern over Carnes having another fit about ghosts if he went past the ruins caused him to vary the route. This time they went left through the fence which ran along the top of the bank, then followed around the outside of the ruins along another fence, staying just back in the edge of the scrub.

This brought them to the highway about a hundred metres up from where Graham thought they had crossed it on the way in. By then the night was quite silent, except for an occasional car. He stopped the patrol under cover and crept forward to the edge of the road to look. Lying on his stomach amid the grass and burrs, he strained his eyes and ears to try to locate the defenders.

By this time, he was becoming depressed as the exhilaration of reaching the bridge wore off. Not only did he still have to get back across the highway, but he had to find that radio. Then he had to get what was left of his patrol back to camp by midnight and that only gave him about one hour to move at least 3 kilometres.

Then I have to explain to Capt Conkey how I lost half my patrol, he thought unhappily.

Chapter 32

REPORT

As Graham lay alone in the darkness, depression began to grip him as he thought about how he would report to Capt Conkey.

Lost a radio sir. Lost half my patrol sir. What will he say? Graham agonised.

After a couple of minutes of gloomy contemplation Graham stirred himself into activity. *Oh well, no point in putting it off. We had better get back,* he told himself.

The thought of adding to his problems by being late got him moving. He had been unable to detect any sound or sign of defenders so decided the best tactic was to line his section up and all cross at once, then depend on speed to get away from any pursuit.

Then we will have to try to dodge that patrol on the other side, he thought.

He made his way back to where the patrol waited and quickly briefed them on what to do. Andrews then annoyed him by moaning, "I've got sore feet. Do we have to walk all the way back across that sand?"

It was on the tip of Graham's tongue to tell him that if that was how he felt he could walk down to the bridge and surrender, but he bit the comment back. "Just get up and follow me quietly," he hissed.

Andrews muttered something about being tired and cold, but he got up and began walking. Graham led them to the highway and personally spaced them out three paces apart along the fence and told them to crawl to the edge of the bitumen. This led to more grumbles about prickles, but he was in such a bad mood that they obeyed.

As Graham reached the verge of the highway, he heard voices calling out a hundred metres or so up to his left. Quite clearly on the cool night air he heard a voice shout, "Sit down and shut up so we can count you!"

They are pulling in their guards or a patrol has returned, and they are checking they haven't lost anyone, he deduced. For a moment he was tempted to just wait till they were gone. A glance at his watch dispelled that idea. *We will be late if we don't get a move on.*

A car was coming from his right. He hissed to the others to lie flat but risked a look as it came across the bridge. As he had expected, there were still cadets standing on guard there.

As the car went past, Graham put his head up and used the vehicle's headlights to show him if there were any defenders up the road. A group of cadets was illuminated at the bend a hundred metres away.

Now is the time to cross, while their eyes are dazzled, he thought.

At that he stood up and called quietly, "Cross now. No running. Go!"

To his relief, the cadets on either side of him rose from the grass and padded quickly across the road. On the other side they waded through the long grass to the fence then crawled under. Andrews got snagged and did some swearing and grumbling till Graham snapped at him to shut up.

Graham checked that Carnes was still with them then told them to wait.

"Where are you going?" Andrews asked.

"To give myself up to the enemy, what do you think!" Graham retorted.

"You aren't!" Andrews cried anxiously.

"Oh, shut up! Have some sense. I'm just going to find the radio you bloody drongo!" Graham snapped.

As soon as he said it, he regretted it, knowing that he shouldn't have called Andrews that but was now feeling very anxious and depressed. Guilt at all the mistakes he thought he had made had given him a very short temper.

Leaving the others sitting in the grass behind the fence he hurried down towards the bridge, moving at a crouch. He was very worried about finding the radio, even though part of his mind told him it would be easy to locate in daylight. At that image he shook his head.

I don't want that sort of humiliation. I've stuffed up too much as it is.

And there it was, just lying amid some trampled grass. With a shake of his head and a sigh of relief Graham scooped the radio up and hurried back to the others.

"Did you find it?" Andrews asked as Graham handed the radio to Carnes.

"No Ando, I snuck up and cut an enemy sentries throat and took his," Graham retorted sarcastically. "Okay, let's move."

Graham did not bother taking out his compass. He just walked north using his instinct for direction and the fall of the ground to guide him. Nor did he bother much with scouting, reasoning that any defending patrols would have been pulled back to the highway by this.

If we run into one we will just fight them, he thought.

At that moment he felt in the mood for a fight. He angled across the slope until he found a cattle pad running the right way just up from the dark tangle of the Anabranches. It was easy enough going as the stars gave enough light to avoid the thorn bushes. Despite mumbles from Andrews, Graham had them back near the gate leading down to the Bunyip by 2310hrs.

He had only just noted the grey ribbons of the wheel ruts on his left when he heard a noise. It came from the left rear. Signalling urgently, he got the others to crouch under cover. Moving behind a bush Graham peered up the vehicle track, then felt a thrill of anxiety. A dark figure was hurrying down it, almost at a run. That puzzled Graham. Just one person? He strained his eyes in the night but could not make out any others. The approaching person was a cadet. Even in the starlight his hat, camouflage uniform and webbing were visible.

Lost maybe? Graham wondered. He waited until the person was only a few paces away then quietly called, "Halt!"

The cadet let out a loud cry of fright and sprang back as Graham stood up. It was LCpl Franks. "Oh shit! You bloody scared me then," Franks gasped. "I thought you was a big pig. I seen one earlier."

"What are you doing? Where are the others?" Graham asked, casting anxious glances in all directions. The mention of pigs made him worry and he found the Anabranches a spooky place to be in the middle of the night.

"They all got captured, but I got away," Franks replied.

Ran away more like, Graham thought, but then he remembered just how useful the decoys had been and decided to believe. *I have to weld this section together so I'd better not make it harder by accusing people of lying.* he told himself.

"That's great," he said. "You blokes did a really great job at drawing away the enemy patrols."

"Did you reach the bridge?" Franks asked.

"Yes, we did. Halyday planted the bomb," Graham replied.

Halyday came forward and wanted to describe in detail how he had done it but Graham stopped him. "We have to get back," he said. "Save it for later. Cadet Carnes, call HQ and tell them we are at the north end of the Anabranches."

While Graham opened the wire gate Carnes tried calling. There was no reply. "They aren't answering," Carnes replied.

"Is it turned on?" Halyday asked, making Graham blush for not thinking of it himself.

Graham moved to the radio and looked, then reached across and turned the on-off switch. At once the radio crackled. "Okay try again," he said.

As the patrol filed through the gate, Carnes called HQ. Graham closed the gate behind them and was relieved to hear HQ answering.

"Where are we?" Carnes asked.

Graham took the handset and told HQ, then gave ETA 15 minutes. He was feeling much better now. Not only had he recovered the radio and another missing patrol member, but they should make it back by midnight.

Even if we don't get back in time HQ know we are alright and won't be worrying, he told himself. *Now it is just a walk.*

It wasn't quite that simple though. The walk was a kilometre on the soft sand and that took the 15 minutes. Andrews grumbled all the way, either about sore muscles or the cold. It was getting cool but the exercise was enough to make them perspire. The sweat chilled on the skin as a cool breeze was blowing up the riverbed. Then Graham miscalculated and went too far to the right. In the starlight he did not notice the break which indicated the mouth of the Canning in the black line of trees which lined the far bank. That brought them to a deep, wide pool of water.

Graham stared at it, wondering how deep it was. He could see the stars reflected on its surface and thought it was the pool at the mouth of the Canning. Telling the others to wait he dropped his webbing and waded in to check how deep it was. He was now so anxious to get back he did not care if he got a bit wet. In the end he got more than a bit wet. The bed of the river was soft sand and the slope suddenly increased sharply. Unable to stop himself he slithered and floundered, then slipped right in.

The water was well over his head and he had to swim. With a lot of splashing, and feeling really foolish, he floundered back to the shallows.

"How's the water Kirky?" Halyday asked with a chuckle.

"Corporal Kirk to you Cadet Halyday," Graham snapped, his frail ego burning at the mistake.

"Yes Kirky."

Andrews then whined, "I ain't going ter cross there!"

"None of us is!" Graham snapped. He was dripping wet and worrying about his torch, map and notebook. He emptied his pockets, the placed the sodden contents in a plastic bag which he pushed into his webbing.

Then Milson said, "There aren't any crocodiles are there?"

"No!" Graham snapped, but he wasn't sure and it must have sounded in his voice as they all stared anxiously at the brooding, dark water.

"What about bunyips?" Milson asked.

Oh, for heaven's sake! Graham thought as he noted the scared looks on the faces of the cadets. "There are no such things as bunyips," he said.

"So why is this called the Bunyip River?" Milson queried.

Graham was unable to answer that. He just shook his head in exasperation. "If it was dangerous Capt Conkey wouldn't do an exercise here," he said. All he now wanted to do was get back to camp. The water had been warmer than the air but now it began to chill him and he shivered. "Let's go!"

He led them left until he was sure he had located the mouth of the Canning and the small island. Then, what had been simple in daylight, was difficult in the dark. While crossing the rocks and wading the narrow channel both Franks and Carnes slipped and fell. Carnes let out a cry of fear and went right in with a loud splash.

Bloody hell, the radio! Graham thought in dismay as Carnes floundered around.

He at once jumped in and grabbed hold of the radio and heaved Carnes upright. Carnes began to sob and had obviously received a real shock. Graham snatched the handset and squeezed the pressel switch, "Four, this is Four Bravo, radio check, over."

There was no answer, and he didn't think the radio was transmitting. That got him all depressed and upset again. He snapped testily at Carnes, "Oh shut up! It was only bloody water. You swam in it yesterday. Now get moving!"

The patrol stumbled, slithered and splashed its way across to the island, then waded across to the far bank. After that it was easy but tiring.

As they trudged up the bed of the Canning in the dark it seemed very spooky as the overhanging trees cast weird shadows. The scuttle of small animals up the bank and the mournful hooting of curlews added to this feeling. Then an instinct stopped Graham and he froze.

Straining his eyes, he moved back a pace. "Halyday, have you got your torch?" he asked.

"Yeah, why?"

"Shine it here," Graham said.

Halyday did and Graham felt a chill of fear. He had been right. Sliding slowly across the sand in front of him was a snake. It was only about a metre long, but it was a brown of some sort.

"Bloody hell! I nearly trod on him," he croaked through a mouth that had suddenly gone dry.

"He's not moving very fast," Franks observed.

"Probably too cold," Graham said, staring in fascination at the repulsive thing. He loathed and feared snakes and the sight of it made him shudder.

"So am I," Halyday added.

The snake had been apparently ignoring them up till then, but Andrews now threw a stick at it, causing it to curl swiftly into the 'S' shape ready to strike. The cadets all backed hastily away, Graham almost tripping over Carnes as he did.

"You bloody idiot Andrews!" he snapped.

To Graham's relief, the snake now slid off into the flood debris against the base of a nearby tree. It was only then that Graham realised there were several other snake tracks showing clearly in the sand. He had to struggle with the urge to have Halyday lead with his torch versus the military sense of doing things correctly with no lights. Pride finally won and he told Halyday to turn the torch off.

No sooner had they started walking again than a pig went snuffling off up the bank into the rubber vines 50 paces ahead of them. Graham's hair stood on end with fright and Franks cried out in fear. They stood listening, ready to run. The pig snorted and snuffled and crashed off over the top of the bank. Silence settled, to be broken by the eerie wail of a curlew close by.

"What's that?" Carnes asked, his voice quavering with fear.

"Only a bloody curlew," Graham snapped.

All he now wanted to do was get back to the bivouac area, but it seemed further than he remembered.

Milson didn't help by saying, "I was told they are the ghosts of dead Aborigines calling out."

Remembering Carnes' earlier mention of ghosts Graham groaned inwardly and said, "Rubbish! Now stop talking and let's go home."

"That's where I want to go, home," Milson agreed.

Graham ignored him and tramped on along the sandy bed under the trees. By then his leg muscles were feeling really strained and his feet felt hot. To hear voices ahead was an enormous relief and then a sentry challenged. It was a cadet from 3 Platoon.

Thank God! Made it! Graham thought.

After giving the password he trudged on past where 3 Platoon's packs were but there was no sign of the platoon. At 2 Platoon's area there were voices and movement and Graham was met by Sgt Grenfell.

"Ah, Cpl Kirk. Good! Your patrol can stop here and you report to Capt Conkey."

"I've lost a few," Graham replied, wishing to get it over quickly.

"Lost them! How many? Where? Who?" Sgt Grenfell cried.

"Captured. They aren't out in the bush," Graham answered.

"Phew! That's okay. Off you go," Sgt Grenfell replied.

Graham told Carnes and Slim to go back to HQ and the others to stop and go to bed, then he walked on along past where 1 Platoon was settling down for the night, lying in their sleeping bags under the overhanging branches. Ahead he saw the glow of a fire and smelt the wood smoke. In the flickering firelight he saw some of the officers and CSM Cleland sitting there. Swallowing with anxiety, Graham trudged wearily over the sand to make his report to Capt Conkey.

Judging by his face, Capt Conkey was obviously not happy; and as Graham drew closer, he heard him say, "A whole platoon captured twice! How humiliating! If Sgt Yeldham had stayed with them, they might have had a bit of leadership."

"Might have," Lt Hamilton replied doubtfully.

By then Graham had reached the edge of the circle and he noted that CUO Masters was there, busily writing. Lt Standish and CUO McAlistair were there as well. Capt Conkey opened his mouth to answer then saw Graham.

"Yes, Cpl Kirk, what do you want?"

"I am reporting back, sir. My patrol has returned," Graham answered.

"How did you go?" Capt Conkey asked.

A dozen perceived mistakes flashed through Graham's mind. He opted to get the worst out straight away. "I lost four of my patrol, sir. They were captured."

"I know that," Capt Conkey replied with a scowl. "I was at the defender's HQ and they delighted in rubbing it in every time some of our cadets were captured. They are on their way back now. But did you make it to the bridge?"

"Yes, sir," Graham answered hastily, wishing to redeem himself.

Capt Conkey's face turned to a smile. "You did? Can you prove it?"

Graham nodded. "Yes, sir. Cadet Halyday said he wrote our names in felt pen on the concrete wall at the end of the bridge, just above where he buried the bomb."

"Good! That is something at least." Capt Conkey replied, his tone much more friendly. Then he gestured at Graham's clothes. "What happened to you? Did you fall in the river?"

"Yes, sir. I slipped getting back across," explained Graham. As he did, he felt very foolish. Also, his mind raced, *Do I mention the radio or not?* Carnes had gone off back to HQ carrying it. He decided to wait and find out if the radio still worked before reporting that.

Capt Conkey grunted, then dug in his brief case and held up a printed form. "Here is a Patrol Report. Fill it in and then tell us about it."

Graham moved over and took the form, then seated himself to one side. CUO Masters gave him a smile and nodded, then returned to writing his own report. Graham took out a pen and held the paper so that he could see what he was writing by the light of the fire. Filling out the first part of the report was easy. The headings told him quite clearly what information was required. He found there was insufficient space to describe in detail the route he had followed and even less when he had to cover comments on the enemy and on the results of clashes with them.

For a while he puzzled over how to explain why he had split his patrol but then just kept it brief. That made him give a wry smile, remembering a history lesson with Mr Conkey in which the teacher had explained how people wrote history by leaving out the bits that made them look bad.

He will understand, Graham thought.

All he wrote was: 'After leaving the Bunyip I sent a party under the 2ic in a decoy role. They played a major part in the success of the raid by drawing away defenders at critical moments. Unfortunately, four of this group were captured during these encounters.'

He had a few qualms about that because it suggested that Bragg had been with the decoys. *I hope Capt Conkey doesn't ask for details,* he thought anxiously. Then he worried over whether to mention Carnes and his odd behaviour or not. In the end he did not. *I will just explain that,* he decided.

However, when Capt Conkey read the report and then questioned him, Graham made no mention of Carnes, thinking to tell him at the right moment. Somehow this did not seem to come up and then 4 Platoon came tramping along the bed of the Canning and the moment was lost.

To Graham's relief, Capt Conkey said, "That will be all Cpl Kirk. You can go and get out of those wet clothes and go to bed thank you."

Reluctantly Graham stood up. Tired as he was he really wanted to stay and hear how the other platoons had got on. He lingered, watching as the line of dark figures went tramping past. CUO Grey and Peter came into the firelight and Graham noted that both were minus one of their green flashes.

"How did it go, CUO Grey?" Capt Conkey asked.

"Not too well, sir," CUO Grey replied. "We got ambushed twice on the way there and then got held off and trapped by some sort of mobile reserve when we tried to cross the railway. A platoon arrived in trucks and surrounded us."

"They were probably the same platoon that nearly caught us," Graham said.

Capt Conkey and CUO Grey both looked at him. Capt Conkey frowned and said, "Thank you, Cpl Kirk. You can go now."

"Yes sir," Graham replied.

Idiot! he called himself. *If you had kept your mouth shut you might have learned more.*

He caught Peter's eye but then shrugged and turned to walk away. As he did, he heard Capt Conkey ask, "Did you reach the bridge?"

CUO Grey replied, "No, sir. We got blocked down in the riverbed by a platoon, then taken from behind by another that had been hiding among the trees."

That was all Graham heard. As he made his way slowly along the riverbed past the remains of the sand model where 4 Platoon were now unpacking bedding, he thought about what he had heard.

It looks like the defenders really had their act together alright. It sounds like we haven't done very well as a unit.

That was galling to the pride and he wished he had done better. *We didn't even fight the enemy, just snuck in and away,* he mused.

As he walked back in the darkness to where 2 Platoon was now settling down his spirits began to slump again. True Capt Conkey had said a qualified 'good' but he had not seemed very happy.

And I didn't do very well, Graham thought unhappily.

By the time he reached his pack almost everyone else had settled down and he had to find a patch of bare sand to unroll his sleeping bag on. Next, he washed his face and wiped off as much of the camouflage cream as he could. In the process he winced with pain. The memory of Pigsy punching him flooded back but that gave Graham a sharp feeling of success. Ignoring the pain, he kept wiping.

That done, he unlaced his boots and tugged off the boots and wet socks, then dug out a dry shirt from his pack. He didn't have a spare pair of trousers so he could only shrug and leave them on. After changing his shirt he slid into his sleeping bag and lay back, staring at the dapple of leaves and stars overhead.

For some time he lay awake brooding over the exercise and how he might have done better. Thoughts of what might happen when Capt Conkey found out about all the things he had done wrong swirled round in his head, depressing and tormenting him.

Chapter 33

LEADERSHIP EVALUATION

What really depressed Graham and gnawed at his self-esteem was the thought that he had been given a section of troublemakers who were the rejects of their own platoons.

Does that mean I am a reject too? Is that what CUO Masters thinks of me? he worried. *And we were the decoys and didn't even manage to do that properly!*

The mournful dirges of the curlews fitted right into his mood of gloomy introspection. Then another thought crossed his mind. *And there were no girls in my patrol either. Does that mean Capt Conkey knows about Kirsty?*

And where was Kirsty? She was one of the dark forms sleeping on the sand around him, but he suddenly didn't care. He was too tired and down to be interested in girls. He went back to minutely analysing every part of the patrol. The only incident that gave him any satisfaction was how he had stood up to Pigsy. That gave him a good feeling, a sort of glow of certainty deep inside. Instinctively he knew he had passed some sort of fundamental test of character and that he would never be afraid of such people again.

Better to take the bashing, he told himself, gingerly pressing at his sore cheek as he did. *Dad was right. Physical pain only lasts for a little while but mental pain lasts a lot longer.* He knew he would have despised himself if he had backed down and now he hugged that success to himself.

There were noises and talking and then more people came tramping past in the night. By his watch Graham saw that it was nearly 0100hrs. The new arrivals were a very disgruntled 3 Platoon. They settled down to camp but with a lot of grumbling and bickering. It was plain that they had not reached their objectives, and had been captured as well.

A whole platoon taken prisoner! Graham marvelled. *How did that happen?* The Great Raid on the rail bridge certainly looked less like a success all the time.

Then more people came trudging into the area. Graham groaned and tried to block the noises out so he could get to sleep. That idea was banished when he identified the voices: Pigsy and Co. Bragg was with them.

"Where's my bloody pack!" snarled Pigsy.

Graham sat up, groped in his webbing for his torch then stood up with it. "Your packs are over here," he said, shining the beam on them. "Get to bed quietly so you don't wake everyone else up."

"Stuff everyone else!" Waters muttered.

Graham chose to ignore that. Instead, he said quietly, "You blokes did a really good job as decoys. You drew their patrols and guards away at exactly the right times. Thanks for that."

He wasn't sure about that, suspecting the Hutchie Men may have done some of the work but reasoned it would do more good than harm to praise their efforts.

"Huh!" Moynihan grunted. "Did youse get to the bridge?"

"Yes, we did, now go to bed. We will talk about it in the morning."

By then the four 'prisoners' had found their packs and were looking for patches of bare sand. To Graham's surprise they did as he said and were soon lying down in their sleeping bags. He switched off his torch and returned to his own bed. This time he just went off to sleep within minutes.

* * *

The murmur of voices roused Graham from a deep sleep. He returned to wakefulness in slow stages, his mind registering that it was daylight. The talking was coming from 1 Platoon area. A check of his watch showed him it was 0640hrs. For a moment he thought his watch must be wrong until he remembered the exercise orders about check parade being at 0700hrs. The extra hour was to compensate for the late finish of the night exercise. Thinking to get up and go to the toilet before parade he went to sit up. That dragged a groan from him as stiff muscles protested.

After that he spent a few minutes massaging his leg muscles and stretching. He pulled on socks and boots and laced them up, then walked off past the sleeping cadets and into the bushes. Having relieved himself he walked back, enjoying the cool morning air in spite of a feeling of anxiety about how things had turned out.

Back at 2 Platoon he saw that Sgt Grenfell was sitting up and lacing his boots. He gave Graham a smile and a nod which did something to restore his morale. On returning to his gear, Graham noted his damp shirt hanging over a branch. He was about to move the shirt out to where the sun might catch it as it rose when the green flashes on it caught his eye. For a moment he rejected the idea that came to him as being too much of a deliberate showing off, but then he took the green flashes off the wet shirt and slid them onto the one he was wearing.

Check parade followed. Graham stood and woke all the members of his section and urged them to get out of bed. To his own mild surprise, he did not hesitate to walk over to nudge Pigsy with his boot.

"Get up, Pikey," he said, deliberately using a new nickname.

"Go to buggery!" Pigsy grumbled, but he still sat up and began pulling on his boots.

Moynihan scowled and grumbled until Waters did a thunderous fart. That helped ease the tension as the others teased him. Graham smiled and looked away, to find himself looking into Kirsty's eyes. That made him blush, but she giggled.

With the section assembled Graham led them out across the dry river channel to where CSM Cleland was calling out. They had to splash through the shallow flow and that caused some muttering and grumbling but Graham didn't care. 4 Section was first out in 2 Platoon.

The company formed up in line along the open sandy bed of the river. It took ten minutes before all the platoons were present, 3 Platoon again being last. As they stood there, Graham chatted to Stephen about the night's battles. He noted that both Stephen's and Gwen's sections had only one green flash.

"What happened to you lot?" Stephen asked, indicating the two green flashes Graham wore. "Did you get lost and miss the battle altogether?"

"No. We made it to the bridge. Did you?" Graham replied.

"No," Stephen conceded. "Too many guards. We had to battle all the way."

Further conversation was ended by CSM Cleland calling them to attention and then right dressing them. After the sergeants had marked the roll and reported to him CSM Cleland told them to be packed up, ready to march, by 0900hrs. Sgt Grenfell led 2 Platoon back to their area. Once there, Graham ordered the section to roll up their bedding first.

Pigsy and Co muttered about doing it but obeyed. Then Graham told the section to move slightly further away.

"Sit in a circle on your packs," he added.

"Why should we?" Waters demanded.

"Because I said so," Graham replied firmly. "And because we are the best section in the company, even if we are only the decoys."

"What's a decoy?" Bragg asked.

"What you were last night when you got captured," Graham replied.

In the resulting laughter and explanations, The Four obeyed, though with surly expressions on their faces. Breakfast began. As he sat on his pack getting his stove out, Graham saw Kirsty looking at him from nearby. For a moment he thought she might come over to sit next to him, but he gave a little shake of his head. Her response was to pout, shrug, and then turn to talk to Stephen.

During breakfast, stories were swapped and Graham learned that the decoys had indeed been the ones to draw away the guards at the critical moment. Halyday took centre stage, telling and retelling how he had crept over to the end of the bridge past the guards. He was even able to relate to Pigsy what questions the guards had been asking him as the section crept past.

Other stories filtered in. Two really surprised Graham. One was about the Hutchie Men. It seemed they had gone into the wrong farm and been shot at by an angry farmer who had bailed them up behind his pig sty, then held them prisoner until the police had phoned the army. The OC and another OOC from Heatley had arrived by vehicle to remove them. The Hutchie Men had been allowed to continue but had run out of time so missed the exercise altogether.

As Porno explained it, "I fair crap myself when spotlight come on and shotgun go bang! Hutchie Men not so brave when bullets real!"

The second story was about 3 Platoon. They had been surrounded and lost one flash while trying to cross the highway at the eastern end of the bridge. Then they had blundered into the defender's HQ which was well defended. After extracting themselves from that CUO Mitrovitch had left them hiding among the trees on the riverbank while she and Cpl Gallagher had gone ahead to reconnoitre a route. Sgt Yeldham had been left in command, but he and Cpl Crane had gone off to try to catch two defenders they could see on the skyline. While they were away a patrol from St Michael's had come along and found the platoon. The platoon had surrendered.

"Bloody sixteen captured by five!" Roger had exclaimed as he told Graham about it.

"And by St Michael's," Stephen added.

That was worse. To have been captured by Heatley would have been bad enough, but by St Michael's! That really scorched their pride. To cap it off CUO Mitrovitch and Cpl Gallagher had been captured near the rail bridge, and Sgt Yelhdam and Cpl Crane were also captured when it turned out they were not taking on two but six! It was obvious from their body language, faces and voices, that 3 Platoon were not a happy band.

After eating, scrubbing his face clean, shaving and washing up, Graham went over to talk to Stephen and Roger about the exercise. While doing so Kirsty came and sat down next to him, placing her hand on his knee as she sat.

"Hello Graham. How are you?" she asked.

"Good," Graham replied, but he could see that Sgt Grenfell was watching. "Kirsty, take your hand off my knee please," he said quietly.

"Why? Don't you like it?" she asked.

"I love it, but I don't want either of us to get into trouble," he replied.

"Oh poo! Don't you love me?" Kirsty whispered.

A spurt of annoyance surged through Graham. "No. I like you. And today is the leadership evaluation exercise and I don't want to fail it. So, if you really like me, then help by not causing problems please," he replied.

"Oh fine! If that's how you feel!" Kirsty snapped. She flashed him an angry look, then stood up and flounced away.

That gave Graham some mixed feelings. *Hell hath no fury, eh?* he thought. He noted Gwen giving him an approving look but he didn't feel like that sort of treatment either, so he also stood up and wandered off.

While he was walking around chatting Graham was stopped by CUO Masters. "What happened to your face Cpl Kirk?" he asked.

"Just a little problem during the exercise sir," Graham replied.

For a moment the two stood facing each other and CUO Masters raised a quizzical eyebrow. "Well?"

Graham simply replied, "It was resolved at the time sir."

There was a silence as CUO Masters waited for more information.

However, Graham kept silent and just gave a slight smile. CUO Masters glanced across to where 4 Section sat. For a moment he eyed Pigsy and Co, then looked back at Graham and gave a wry smile.

"And you aren't going to say?"

"No, sir. It is dealt with," Graham replied.

CUO Masters nodded and walked off, looking thoughtful. That got Graham anxious and he hoped there would be no further enquiries. It also spurred him to get the section moving. "Hurry up and get that mess gear packed away. Andrews, wash your face. Waters, brush that mud off your boots. You too Cadet Moynihan. Pick up that rubbish Cadet Milson."

He was in no mood for arguments and they did as he ordered. By 0830hrs the section was ready to march, their routine completed and their packs laid out in a neat row. Sgt Grenfell gave Graham a grunt of satisfaction and went on to chivvy Stephen's section, some of whom were still cooking.

By 0900hrs the unit was standing out on the riverbed in three ranks. CSM Cleland called them to attention and then handed over to Lt Maclaren. The platoon commanders were put on parade and then Lt Maclaren stood them at ease.

"We are just waiting for Capt Conkey and Lt Hamilton to come back," he explained. "While we wait platoon commanders can inspect their platoons for dress and hygiene."

"Oh crap!" Waters muttered.

"Keep quiet!" Graham snapped over his shoulder. As he did, he noted Sgt Grenfell's mouth open. He had been about to reprimand Waters, but Graham had beaten him to it. Sgt Grenfell met Graham's eye and nodded. That made Graham feel better.

I might be the commander of the rejects, but I will go down fighting, he told himself.

The inspection took 15 minutes and Graham was pleased to note that only Andrews and Waters were spoken to in his section while half of Stephen's section had their names taken for something. Stephen himself had neglected to shave. Gwen's section, as usual, seemed to be perfect. That got Graham worrying again. He knew that the main event on the day's program was the leadership evaluation exercise.

We are all being watched today, he thought.

Once again he did the mathematics: 16 corporals with only 7

sergeants and the CSM's job available for them. *At least half of us must miss out,* he deduced.

Thinking about all his mistakes of the previous week, and of being made commander of the reject section, caused him to become quite despondent. He became so dejected he felt like just giving up and leaving cadets.

What's the use? Everything I do I muck up! he thought unhappily.

A vehicle drove down the bank behind them and a smiling Capt Conkey marched across the sand to take over the parade. After doing so he stood and looked along the line slowly before his eyes found Graham. Graham was sure he was staring straight at him and it made him very uncomfortable.

Capt Conkey then looked away, and said, "When I left the Exercise HQ last night both Heatley and St Michael's were very full of themselves, crowing about how we had totally failed."

He paused. Graham shared the collective shame. Then Capt Conkey went on, "But I have just confirmed that we did not fail. One of our raiding parties made it to the rail bridge and planted their bomb successfully. I have just been to the spot with the OCs of Heatley and St Michael's and confirmed this. It was really good to see their faces when I dug up the bomb and pointed to the names written in felt pen on the concrete."

There was another pause and Graham sensed the rising spirits of those around him. He also prickled with anxiety. *That was us,* he thought, bracing himself for the jealousy and ill-will that such a success might bring.

Capt Conkey now met Graham's eyes again and he said, "We sent out six raiding parties and only one of them made it through. That was 4 Section led by Cpl Kirk. Well done, Cpl Kirk. You have saved the unit's reputation."

Graham blushed fiercely and could only nod at the applause. Capt Conkey went on, "I understand there were a few problems along the way, and that you made good use of the four reinforcements you were given from 4 Platoon. Well done Lance Corporal Franks and your group for the decoy role you carried out so well."

"Franks!" Pigsy hissed indignantly. "It was my plan!"

On hearing that Graham had to smile. He could tell that Pigsy and Co were pleased at the praise.

Capt Conkey then had them moved into the shade of the trees on the south bank. As they were being seated in section lines two more vehicles came down to park on the bank behind them. The OC of Heatley and some of his OOCs got out. They began chatting to the Cairns OOCs. Then a long line of dusty, sweaty cadets carrying packs came into view down the track. They wore yellow shoulder flashes.

Heatley, Graham noted, experiencing a distinct feeling of envy at how military they looked. He remembered having the same feelings on his first annual camp the previous year when he had seen a Heatley recon patrol go past.

The Heatley cadets began filing across the riverbed towards Dingo Creek. As they went past, cadets from both units began making comments. The Heatley cadets were crowing over how good they were and about beating Cairns the night before. The only effective rejoinders were, "Yeah, but we blew up your bridge, so we won!" and by Porno threatening to bring the Hutchie Men to catch them when they were alone at the dunny. That raised a good laugh and left the Cairns cadets thinking they had had the best of the exchange.

As the last of the hundred or so Heatley cadets vanished among the trees on the other bank, Capt Conkey came back and stood in front of the company. He was obviously now in a good mood, but his words caused Graham's anxiety level to shoot up.

"Today is a very important day. Every annual camp we run a Leadership Evaluation Exercise to help select the candidates for the promotion course in December. We have obviously been watching you since you joined but this helps clarify who is best."

He allowed them time to think about that, then reminded them that the officers also depended on the reports filled out on every person by their superiors. "And on our own judgement," he added.

Graham knew about the reports, having seen his report the previous year. He now learned that all the corporals would have a report filled out on them by their platoon sergeant, another by their platoon commander, plus one by the CSM and one by Capt Conkey.

"That is four reports. It will allow us to remove personal bias to some extent and get a fairer result," Capt Conkey explained.

Sixteen corporals, Graham pondered. *And only seven jobs, maybe eight. So who might they be?* In his head he began compiling a list of who he thought would be selected while Capt Conkey went on with the briefing. *Gwen, Peter, Gallagher, Brooks because he is in the Q Store, Parnell in HQ, Stephen- maybe.*

Then he found it harder. A couple he thought he could eliminate: Dimbo and Griffin, but it still left a lot of uncertainty. Brown, Costigan, Harris and Bannister were all ones he disliked and wouldn't have picked but he had to concede he did not really know how well they had performed as section commanders.

It was very worrying. *I'd better put my best foot forward today then,* he thought, hoping he might claw his way back up from the reject pile into the middle.

Capt Conkey explained that each group would move along the same course from incident to incident. At each 'stand' a 'Directing Staff'' (DS) member would note who showed leadership on a form which had been prepared for the purpose. He read them the headings so that they were aware of what was being looked for. Then Capt Conkey explained that the corporals and lance corporals would be removed from every section and grouped to compete against their own rank levels.

The story was the same as the exercise Graham had done the previous year; they were a commando patrol in enemy territory. They had just attacked an enemy HQ and were now trying to escape with secret documents. However, in the battle their corporal and lance corporal had both gone missing. They had the only maps, so the patrol had to follow the route back to the sea where a submarine would pick them up.

"Do we really have to walk all the way back to the sea?" Bragg whispered anxiously.

"No, Braggy, the sub will come up the river," Halyday replied sarcastically.

"Will it?" Bragg cried, glancing towards the Bunyip.

There was a collective groan and Capt Conkey flashed them an angry glance. "Keep your section quiet Cpl Kirk," he snapped.

Oh bummer! Graham thought. *I don't want to be noticed that way!*

After the explanation there was a half hour break while the course was set up. The cadets were allowed to talk and go to the toilet. Graham noted that Kirsty was busy talking to Cpl Gallagher and he was surprised at the intensity of his jealousy. There was regret too, and relief. Instead he talked to Peter about how 4 Platoon had fared on the exercise.

When Capt Conkey returned just before 1000hrs he called the corporals out and handed them blank Personal Qualities Report forms. "As soon as you finish the exercise sit and fill these out, then hand them to me. They are confidential so don't talk to anyone about them, or show them to each other."

He then divided the corporals into two groups. Graham found he had been placed in the group with Gwen, Dimbo, Gallagher, Crane, Costigan, Parnell, and Brookes.

Oh bum! I didn't want to have to compete with Gwen, he thought. *She is too good.*

It was a relief not to have to be against Stephen or Peter, both of whom were in the other group. The group Graham was in was selected to go first.

Capt Conkey then pointed across to the trees near where they had slept. "Go that way until you meet Lt McEwen," he said.

"Do we have to patrol, sir?" Graham asked, remembering the previous year's exercise.

"Not yet," Capt Conkey replied. "Now off you go."

It was hot by then, with the sun blazing down from a clear blue sky. But Graham was sweating with anxiety too. He had a big drink as he walked along with the others. They splashed across the shallow water and made their way through the belt of small trees. In the shade near 3 Platoon's packs they found Lt McEwen.

The first stand was a First Aid dilemma. They were being hunted by enemy patrols with dogs and helicopters. One member of the patrol had been badly wounded and they had to decide what to do, keeping in mind that the injured member knew the whole plan, plus a lot of other secret information. It was a discussion activity and was dominated by Gwen, with some stupid suggestion by Brooks and Dimbo. Graham tried to put in positive and sensible suggestions. Then he made himself useful in constructing an improvised stretcher.

To his annoyance, it was Gwen who took command when it came time to lift the stretcher, which had Dimbo on it.

After that they were told to patrol along Dingo Creek. There was a pause and they looked at each other. Gwen spoke first, "We had better organise ourselves then."

But instead of nominating tasks, she looked at Graham. He saw that the others were also looking at him. Aware that Lt McEwen was watching and taking notes he tried not to get flustered. *Seize the initiative you dummy!* he told himself.

He pointed at Gallagher. "You go first scout. Craney, you be a scout too."

To his relief no-one argued and he took the position of patrol commander, then got them moving. As they entered Dingo Creek he began to really sweat, remembering the patrol course two days earlier.

Oh, I hope we don't get a contact in here! he thought.

They didn't. First, they met CUO Mitrovitch and Sgt Yeldham at a 'minefield'. They had to discuss how to get across quickly and safely, and not leave any tracks. As they talked Graham noted that Yeldham looked really miserable. He was certainly touchy and bad-tempered and snapped angrily back at Costigan when he made a teasing comment about getting captured.

Then it was on along the bed of Dingo Creek. Sgt Bates met them and took their names, then told them to keep walking. That made Graham very anxious and he scanned the steep slopes and rubber vines, trying to have a workable plan ready. At the sharp bend to the right Sgt Gayney suddenly stepped out with her hands up.

"I surrender," she said.

"Bang! Gotcha!" was Brookes' response.

Sgt Bates pointed to some shade just around the bend. "Okay, let's sit and discuss what you would do in this situation."

That led to an animated argument over whether to shoot the prisoner or what else could be done. Graham was quite sure that shooting was wrong and said so heatedly.

"You're just a softie!" Brookes told him.

Gwen and Gallagher supported Graham. They thought the prisoner could be left tied up where he would be found, or taken with them and used as a hostage. At the end Sgt Bates said that either of those options was acceptable. That made Graham feel better.

Capt Conkey is very strong on morality, he told himself.

Further on, at the bend where Peter's group had set up their 'camp', they met CUO Masters. The problem was a deserted camp, with a map clearly visible in the hutchie.

"It's a trap," Graham said. "Let's just by-pass it."

"No. We need the map," Gwen insisted.

There was a short but tense discussion and Gwen's plan was adopted. Graham still seemed to have command so he positioned a group up on the bank to the right, then sent the scouts to search. They duly found Sgt Grenfell and LCpl Telford hiding in ambush.

"Good work," CUO Masters said. "Now go up the bank there along the track to the Bunyip."

As Graham directed the scouts that way, he realised Capt Conkey had been standing at the top of the bank watching. That got him all worried again. He became even more concerned when he noted that Capt Conkey was strolling along at the rear. CUO Grey met them and took their names, then told them to proceed.

Graham's fears were justified when they reached the more open areas of rubber vine on top of the flat tongue of land between Dingo Creek and the Bunyip. Three 'enemy' suddenly appeared and began 'firing' at them. After diving for cover Graham looked anxiously around, his eyes prickling as sweat trickled into them.

I have to do well, he told himself. *Be bold! Be aggressive!*

Then he got all worried lest it become a case of fools rush in. He shouted to get control, then decided a frontal attack was the best option. With that in mind he warned the flank people to watch and then began 'pepper-potting' the groups.

Then it seemed to be easy. He just screamed orders and each group doubled forward 10 paces in turn until they had over-run the 'enemy'. On being told to stop by CUO Masters, Graham stood up, chest heaving and wiped the sweat from his face.

"Okay Cpl Kirk, you have been shot," Capt Conkey said. "You become one of the last in the section."

Does that mean I did well or very badly? Graham wondered.

Capt Conkey did not nominate a new section commander so Gwen stepped up and took control. Nobody disputed this and they were directed on along the track through the rubber vines. To Graham's relief, Capt Conkey turned and went back, presumably to watch the second group of corporals.

There was no incident in the rubber vines. They came out at the bank of the main river at the northern end of the island to find CUO McAlistair and Sgt Sherry sitting in the shade. The corporals were told they had come to a crocodile infested river and that the enemy search patrols were close and catching up. The only way across was a narrow old footbridge but sitting at their end of the bridge cooking a meal was an enemy soldier. He had his rifle leaning on a tree. What were they to do?

While they discussed this Graham stared off across the sand of the riverbed, reliving the exercise of the previous night. In the distance he could see the dark pattern of the railway bridge.

It was certainly a good exercise, he mused. In his heart he knew it had become one of the most important incidents in his life.

The exercise route sent them left along the riverbank back to the mouth of the Canning opposite the other end of the island. Lt Maclaren and Lt Standish were waiting there, and they had the problem of who they would leave behind if the only boat available to take them out to the submarine obviously could not carry them all safely. This was a secret ballot. After discussing it they voted on slips of paper. Graham decided he would leave Costigan behind.

When they had finished Lt Maclaren pointed under the trees 50 paces up the Canning and said, "Go and wait there and have lunch, then fill out your Personal Qualities Reports. Also plan your skit or act for the campfire tonight."

"Aw sir! Do we have to?" Crane grumbled.

"Yes, it is part of the section competition," Lt Maclaren replied. "Now get going. When your section arrives take them back to camp."

As the group walked along the sandy bed of the Canning, Graham thought, *Well, that is that. I hope I did well.*

As he sat down in the shade, he wondered what else he could do to improve his chances of being promoted.

Chapter 34

CAMPFIRE

Graham seated himself a few paces away from the other corporals and began to fill out the Personal Qualities Reports on his cadets. For some this was easy and he did it quickly. For a couple of the others he had to pause and think hard. One of these was Halyday. Over the last few days, Halyday had seemed to blossom and had done a very good job. Graham had to revise his earlier opinions of him but was glad to do so.

While he worked Graham also worried about what might be said about him in the reports that CUO Masters, CSM Cleland and Sgt Grenfell would be filling out. All he could do was hope that he had redeemed himself to some extent. As he thought back over the events of the week, he had quite a few strong regrets. He was also aware that the camp was due to end the next day and that made him sad.

I am really starting to enjoy this, he thought. *I wish it could go on for another week.*

The need to do a pee caused him to stop work and look around. *Where can I go that won't have cadets swarming around in it?* he wondered.

In the bush across the Canning was the obvious place. Placing the reports in his map pocket he stood up and trudged across the hundred metres of sand, splashing his way across the shallow flow of water. Two minutes later he was up among the trees near the junction of the two rivers and out of sight.

While he was relieving himself, Graham heard a vehicle approaching. It was driving slowly down the dirt track from up on the bank. As he finished and zipped up, he saw the vehicle through the foliage. It was an army Land Rover and was heading for near where he was. A vehicle track led to a small clearing just back from the junction of the two rivers.

Assuming the vehicle had nothing to do with him, Graham started making his way back. He had only just emerged from the trees when the Land Rover pulled up 10 metres behind him at the end of the track. A voice suddenly called to him.

"Hoy! You there, cadet!"

Graham turned to see a fat Officer of Cadets with piggy little eyes leaning out of the window of the vehicle. Lt Cain, from St Michael's, he remembered, having seen the man at the promotion course in December.

"Yes, sir?"

"Are you from Cairns?"

"Yes, sir," Graham replied.

Dopey git! he thought, as he was still wearing his green flashes.

"Where is your OC?" Lt Cain asked, getting out of the vehicle.

Graham pointed across the dry bed of the Canning. As he did, several more people climbed out of the Land Rover. To Graham's astonishment one was Cadet Carnes, also still wearing his green flashes.

"Take me to him," Lt Cain ordered. He turned and snapped at Carnes, "Come on boy!"

Followed by Lt Cain, Carnes and another OOC from St Michael's, Graham walked back across to where Lt Maclaren and Lt Standish were. On the way they had to splash through the shallow water, and it gave Graham some sardonic amusement to hear Lt Cain muttering in distaste as he followed. He glanced back to watch and caught a glimpse of Carnes' face. It was a stony mask and he had obviously been crying.

Poor bugger! I wonder what happened? he thought.

To satisfy his curiosity, Graham lingered to listen when Lt Cain met Lt Maclaren and Lt Standish. Lt Cain gestured to Carnes and said, "Found this fellah down at the railway bridge and brought him back."

Lt Maclaren looked surprised and said, "Oh yes? Thank you very much. What happened?"

Lt Cain said, "We went back to look for some gear lost during last night's exercise: hats, water bottles, that sort of thing. Anyway, as we drove down under the railway bridge, we found this lad standing there. He looked very lost and did not seem to know where he was, so we brought him back."

Lt Maclaren looked at Carnes. "What were you doing, Cadet Carnes? Why did you leave here without permission?"

Carnes made no answer, just looked miserable. He stared off into space.

Lt Cain shrugged. "He wouldn't tell us either. Just stood there staring up at the bridge and muttering to himself. He's got a screw loose if you ask me."

Lt Standish reacted to that. "There's no need to talk like that in front of him!" she snapped.

Lt Cain looked at her with a half-sneer on his lips. "Thank you for your gratitude at our efforts. Good afternoon."

At that he turned and began walking back towards his vehicle. The other OOC, a young 2nd Lieutenant, gave Lt Standish an embarrassed smile, then followed.

"Thank you very much," Lt Standish called.

"God, he's an arrogant pig that bastard!" Lt Maclaren muttered. Then he became aware of Graham's presence. "That will be all, Cpl Kirk. You can go."

"Yes, sir," Graham replied. He turned and walked away. As he did, he heard Lt Standish ask, "Why did you go back to the bridge on your own, Cadet Carnes?"

"To look for my watch, Miss," Carnes replied.

Graham did not hear any more, but the answer puzzled him. *Which side of the river was he found on?* he wondered. Then he shrugged, remembering that Carnes had also gone to the bridge with Peter.

Pushing the incident from his mind Graham settled back to writing reports. Soon after that, the second section of corporals arrived and Peter and Stephen came over to join him. As Peter sat down, Graham told him about Carnes.

"I saw him back there with Lt Standish," Peter replied. "I wondered what he was doing there."

Stephen looked that way. "You mean he walked all the way back to the railway bridge on his own?" he asked.

"Must have," Graham replied. "It wouldn't be hard. You can see it from just over there. All he would have needed to do was walk along the riverbank."

"What a dipstick," Stephen commented, siting down and taking out his reports and pen.

Peter did likewise but was thoughtful for a few minutes. Graham continued to write reports and was soon finished. The last one was on LCpl Franks and he wrote the comment: 'Not recommended for promotion.'

The first group of lance corporals arrived soon after. Talking and joking began. Roger joined Graham and bewailed his efforts on the exercise. That got Graham thinking.

Should I also write reports on the people who were in my section earlier I wonder?

Unsure of what to do, he got up and walked back to Lt Maclaren to ask him. Lt Maclaren nodded and said, "Yes, if you have spare reports. Oh, and take Cadet Carnes back with you to Cpl Bronsky."

Carnes stood up and followed Graham. He still looked thoroughly miserable and sniffled several times. Graham looked at him and said, "Cheer up, Cadet Carnes, it is nearly over. The camp ends tomorrow and you can go home then."

"Don't want to go home," Carnes muttered.

"Well, you will be away from cadets anyway," Graham commented.

Carnes just shrugged. "Don't care. Anyway, I'm not going back to my parents. I hate them!"

"Where will you go?" Graham asked.

For a few paces Carnes made no reply, just looked sulky. Then he cried, "I'm not going back to them! They don't want me."

That shocked Graham and he tried to cheer him up. "Sorry you feel that way. Anyway, hang in there. It will be over soon."

"Yes, it will be," Carnes muttered then added something Graham could not hear.

By then they were back with the others and Graham handed responsibility over to Peter. He told Carnes to sit nearby and not to wander away without permission again. Carnes grunted and slumped down on the sand, hiding his face as he did.

With nothing to do, Graham sat and talked to Roger. Mostly they discussed the expedition to Stannary Hills they were due to start on the following Monday. Roger was worried that one day's rest might not be enough and canvassed the idea of cancelling or postponing it. Graham considered the idea, but he had another agenda altogether: Kirsty. He kept this secret, however, knowing from experience how his friends would pour scorn on his romantic notions.

The first section arrived and soon after that CSM Cleland. He collected Cpl Brooks and sent him back to the bivouac area to work for Lt Hamilton. As CSM Cleland went to leave, Graham called to him to settle a question that had been nagging at him.

"Excuse me, CSM, are that mob from Heatley likely to sneak up and raid us?"

CSM Cleland shook his head. "I doubt it. They have gone upriver to the place where we were two nights ago and have their own unit platoon versus platoon exercise to do," he said, then added, "Why do you ask?"

"Just worried in case they caught us by surprise, sir," Graham replied.

CSM Cleland laughed then said, "You let Capt Conkey worry about the unit tactics, Cpl Kirk. Now get on with your reports."

"Finished, Sergeant Major," Graham replied.

"Good," CSM Cleland replied. He walked off up the dry riverbed.

Graham returned to talking with Roger. Another section of 1 Platoon arrived and was led off by its section commander. Ten minutes later 4 Section, plus two from 5 Section arrived. Graham stood up and told them to follow him. He led them back to their packs and told them to get their toilet gear and change of clothes ready for a shower. Already 1 Platoon was moving off under the command of the CSM.

Sgt Gayney arrived to take charge, followed soon after by CUO Mitrovitch. That told Graham that the exercise was ending, the last sections having passed those stands. Ten minutes later CUO Masters and Sgt Grenfell walked in with the remainder of 2 Platoon. They were organised for a shower and then the whole platoon walked across the river carrying towels, clean clothes and toilet bags. As they puffed up the steep, dusty track to the top of the riverbank Graham felt a great sense of sadness. The last exercise of the camp was over and they would be on their way home the next morning. All that really remained was the campfire and he wasn't really looking forward to that. He knew every section was required to put on an act, this being marked as part of the section competition. What bothered him was that he had no idea what act the section could perform.

Puzzling over this helped him push aside his other concern: what to do about Kirsty. He knew that he had to make some move tonight. *If I don't I may as well kiss her goodbye,* he thought.

And what about the following week? He was really torn by the dilemma of having organised to go camping with his friends yet wanting to take Kirsty out. What really added a fine twist of anxiety to the decision was the nagging suspicion that she was not really the right girl for him anyway.

Waiting on top of the bank was an army truck and Lt Hamilton. He loaded the platoon in, climbed in with them and told the driver to get going. Graham recognised the driver as the one who had been driving the first truck the night before. The truck drove up the dusty track past Black Knoll to the Canning Road, then up and over Bare Ridge. As they drove past Sandy Ridge Graham looked at the area and marvelled. It now seemed to have been a long time ago that they had first camped there.

It's been a great camp, he thought, savouring the successes of the raid on the bridge.

As the truck turned left on the highway, he was able to see both the road and rail bridges. Screwing up his eyes against the glare and wind, he studied the distant riverbank, trying to pick out the route his patrol had followed.

Five minutes later they were at the army camp. As the cadets climbed down from the truck CSM Cleland took control, ordering the platoon to place its gear in section lines on the lawn to one side of the shower block. Nearby were lines of kit bags and they were told to collect their own and get ready for a shower. 1 Platoon was nearby, some of the cadets already showered and others lined up at the door waiting to go in.

Across the gravel ring road opposite the last building were dozens of hutchies with cadets standing among them. It was St Michael's and they began to call out jeering comments about which unit was the best. Graham saw Sgt Jones there and pointed him out to the section. "He is the bugger who captured you Braggy," he said.

Andrews and Halyday began calling comments back until told by Sgt Grenfell to stop. To Graham's surprise Pigsy and Co did not join in and seemed quite meek and obedient. While they unlaced boots and waited their turn Graham asked the section if anyone had any ideas for the campfire skit. That started a lively debate. The problem was that no-one seemed able to agree, or that some other section had already claimed particular acts.

Lt McEwen arrived and told the girls to follow her to the showers in the building used by the staff. Kirsty stood up and pouted. "Oh! I wanted to have a shower with the boys," she said.

"Ya can if ya want," Pigsy replied quietly, "But don't complain if we do things to ya."

"That's enough of that sort of talk, Cadet Pike," Graham snapped.

Graham expected a verbal battle but Pigsy just shrugged and said, "Yeah well, what does she expect?"

Kirsty turned her nose up at Pigsy's comment but gave Graham a meaningful look that set his emotions whirling. Then she followed the other girls.

Pigsy spat and said quietly, "Little troll! I hear that Whitey's got her lined up for tonight."

Graham was shocked and hurt. "Who, Sgt White?"

"Yeah, 'course," Pigsy replied.

That hurt! Graham felt ill and cursed himself for a fool. He then wondered if the rumour was true, and if it was, what he should do about it. Deep, gnawing worries about whether Kristy was a 'two-timer' chewed at his insides as he joined the line at the door of the shower. Remembering the conflict with Pigsy and Co on the previous shower, Graham braced himself for trouble. However, Pigsy and Co went through with the others without anything other than a few mildly humorous jibes. They even seemed to be self-conscious when it was their turn.

Graham went through the shower last, going as quickly as he could because the remainder of 2 Platoon were lined up at the door and Sgt Grenfell was urging them to hurry. Back outside and dressed in a clean uniform he sat on his dirty clothes and carefully dried and powdered his feet before pulling on clean socks. That felt very nice. All the while he worried about the campfire.

Then 3 Platoon arrived on the truck and debussed. 1 Platoon climbed aboard and were shuttled back to the bivouac area. That caused a few grumbles from Halyday and Andrews about not eating at the army camp. It was obvious that St Michael's were going to as they began forming up for a mess parade with their 'dixies'.

"They are just a mob of sissies," Pigsy commented.

Graham knew he was supposed to stop any sexist put-downs but he agreed with Pigsy and said nothing.

Then his emotions were snapped into top gear by Kirsty returning. She smiled and sat next to him while she brushed her hair. She seemed so innocent that Graham could not credit Pigsy's allegations. All he could do was be nice in return, while anxiously wondering how to keep the situation under control that night.

It is the last night and she is sure to put on the pressure, he thought. *I must be strong,* he told himself, still clinging to a faint hope that he might be selected for sergeant.

The truck returned with 4 Platoon and 2 Platoon was ordered aboard. As they did, Graham noted that Kirsty had taken the opportunity to go and talk to Sgt White.

Maybe the rumour is true? he thought anxiously. It was very demoralising and hurtful.

Ten minutes drive had the platoon back at the Canning junction. As they made their way down the steep slope past HQ, Graham again raised the question of what act to put on at the campfire. To his surprise Pigsy answered.

"What about 'The ugliest monster in the world'?"

"That's a great idea, Pikey," Graham answered. "What does everyone think?"

The others all enthusiastically adopted the idea and began haggling over who got the jobs. Graham had to intervene and allocate tasks. "It was Pikey's idea so he can pick what job he wants," he said. He was still amazed at how docile and co-operative Pigsy was.

Pike chose to be the 'ringmaster' and narrator. Waters was chosen to be the monster, with Moynihan and Milson as the 'handlers' to control him. Halyday and Graham were picked to be the first 'volunteers' to view the monster. That left Andrews and Bragg without a job, but they seemed happy enough with that.

On arrival back at the bivouac area wet clothes were hung over branches and the section then moved off behind the line of small trees in mid-stream to rehearse for the skit. Andrews and Bragg were posted as sentries to keep others from observing. Even so several other sections saw what they were doing, as they were busy with similar practices. Graham found he was really laughing and enjoying himself. It seemed to him little more than miraculous the way the section was all working together as a team.

One by one the other platoons returned from the shower. The sun sank lower and the evening calm settled on the river. While they waited for the evening meal Graham took the opportunity to walk out along the bed of the Canning to the edge of the water in the Bunyip. He stood on the bank of the deep pool he had fallen into the night before and relaxed, drinking in the beauty of the sunset. To him it was a magical moment to be savoured and remembered for all time: the pinkish tinge on the white river gums and paperbarks; the wide stretch of sand across to the line of ruddy bluffs on Ruin Island; the shadows and cool breeze; the distant highway bridge and beyond that the criss-cross pattern of the rail bridge.

That had now become a symbol to him of something very special, a real achievement, almost a coming of age. For long moments he stood alone, relaxed but pleasantly excited. Romantic thoughts flitted in his mind, but he pushed them aside. One reason was that he found it was not Kirsty's face that he pictured when he did think about love.

She might be more trouble than she is worth, he thought.

There were birds drifting peacefully on the river: swans, pelicans and ducks. It was all very delightful and memorable. He sighed and watched the sky turn red out to the west. Then distant shouted orders ended his reverie. Mess parade. He had to get back. With a sigh of pleasure, he turned and strode back along the sandy riverbed.

It's wonderful to be alive, he decided, and he again wished the camp could go on for another week or two.

The evening meal was fresh rations delivered by 'hot box' from the army camp. Lt Hamilton and his Q team set up the feeding point on the riverbank near the vehicles and the platoons filed past and were given their food. After that they sat in groups on the sand. By then the sun had gone but there was still plenty of light, the sky clear and blue. Graham sat down with his section and felt that they had seemed to meld into a group by some sort of magic. Most amazing was how Pike, Waters, and Moynihan appeared to be happy to be with the section. They even made cheeky comments to tease 4 Platoon.

By the time the washing up had been done it was dark. Light was provided by several lanterns and by the lighting of the campfire. There was a lot of laughing and high-spirited calling out as the cadets began to prepare for the campfire. Graham packed his mess gear away and then found Kirsty next to him.

Uh oh! he thought. *Here comes more pressure*.

"Hi Graham," Kirsty said. "Are you looking forward to the campfire?"

"Yeah, it should be good," Graham replied.

"What about after it?"

"What about it?" Graham asked, his heart sinking.

"You and me. We could sneak off and meet somewhere," Kirsty suggested.

It was that word 'sneak' that finally did it. The idea of breaking his word again and acting deceitfully burned at his conscience. He shook his head, "No. Sorry. I will be happy to go out with you after camp, but I'm not sneaking off anywhere."

Kirsty was silent for a moment while she absorbed this. Then she sniffed and tossed her head. "Oh well, if that's how you feel!" she cried. She spun on her heel and walked away.

Graham made no attempt to call her back. *That's it then,* he told himself, knowing in his heart that was the end of the relationship. To his own surprise there was more relief than regret. He shrugged and went off to round up his section.

By 1930hrs all the cadets were seated in section rows on the sand in a semi-circle facing a large bonfire. This had been lit out in the middle of the sandy riverbed where there was no danger of it causing a bush fire. As he checked that all the members of his section were there, Graham caught Kirsty's eye but she turned her nose up and looked away.

Over alright, he told himself.

The campfire began. Capt Conkey said a few words to thank them for their efforts during the camp then sat to one side to act as the judge for the competition. Lt Hamilton then took over as MC. He told a couple of jokes and then called on 6 Section to put on their act. To a chorus of jeers and laughter Stephen led his section out. They had chosen to do the 'Fortune Teller'. The cadet they picked on to be their victim was Percy. When it came to the punch line and Stephen, acting as the swami, said that he could see from the sole of Percy's boot that he was going on a long walk there was a loud aside.

"He'll be going to jail if he keeps acting the way he has," said CUO Mitrovitch.

This caused such an outburst of laughter that the actual throwing of the boot off into the darkness lost much of its impact. Even so the skit got the show off to a good start. Graham relaxed and laughed with the rest. Lt Hamilton then told a couple of jokes before calling out 7 Section. They did a skit which showed the recon patrol being spotted by Heatley.

More jokes followed then 8 Section got up and sang a song. Many jeered and made unkind comments till the sheer quality of the singing silenced them. Graham was impressed in spite of himself.

I didn't know Fiona could sing that well! he thought in astonishment. *And she is very pretty.*

That got him looking around for Kirsty. At first he could not see her, but then he spotted her sitting beside Sgt White. Jealousy and regret coloured Graham's feelings during the next act; 9 Section doing the trained elephant. They picked on Bragg as their victim and Graham could only shake his head and wonder how any person could be so dumb as to not realize something was going to happen to them; in this case the 'elephant' 'peeing' on them.

When the laughter had subsided and another couple of jokes been told 10 Section got up and did a teasing skit called 'The Lost Patrol' which was obviously at Dimbo's expense. 11 Section followed that with a series of poems about various people on the camp. Some of these lampooned particular characteristics of people like Capt Conkey, however he laughed and seemed to take it well.

12 Section put on a silly joke which was stopped by Lt McEwen when it started to become crude. The section was ordered off and Lt Hamilton went on to tell some more jokes while HQ prepared. While they were doing this Peter came over to Graham, looking quite agitated.

"Have you seen Carnes, Graham?" Peter asked.

"No, why?"

"He's supposed to be part of our act," Peter replied.

He looked around the circle of faces in the firelight, then shrugged as Lt Hamilton called out to the signal section to move on stage. Graham also looked but soon forgot about Carnes as Peter's skit got under way. Peter did 'Bomber over Germany' with a cast from his own section, plus volunteers from the audience. The volunteers provided the four engines. Halyday was talked into being Number Four engine. After much play acting about incidents during the flight a cadet raced in from the darkness pretending to be a German night fighter. There was a lot of stuttering machine gun noises and engine noises.

Peter suddenly looked over his shoulder and shouted, "Number 4 Engine is on fire! Hit the fire extinguishers!"

Whereupon several cadets took out cups of water and thoroughly doused the unfortunate 'Number 4 Engine'. Halyday got angry and chased after Cadet James but then calmed down and sat near Graham looking sulky.

The HQ girls performed next by doing a song and dance act. This was enthusiastically received, with a few suggestions about taking clothes off until Lt McEwen silenced the comments. Graham found it very arousing and wondered briefly if he should try to make it up with Kirsty. A glance at her seated beside Sgt White killed that idea. She was laughing up at him and giving him adoring looks.

Oh well, plenty more fish in the sea, Graham told himself- but it still hurt!

Capt Conkey and Lt Maclaren did a skit about the two retired colonels which put Graham back in a good mood. After that 1 Section had to get up. That got Graham all anxious as he knew it would be his section's turn soon. 1 Section sang a song so poorly they were booed off the 'stage'. 2 Section did a 'David Jones' skit about people wearing various items of clothing they got from David Jones, till the last person came along in a towel and said he was David Jones. Then it was 3 Section's turn and the tension increased.

3 Section did the mime of the bobsled team. Then it was time. Graham moved his section to the rear and checked they had all their stores and that everyone knew their lines. On call they went on. Pigsy made the skit. His style as a raconteur had the audience in stitches and the whole thing went off very well. Feeling immensely relieved, Graham resumed his seat on the sand to watch 5 Section do the fire engine. This time Roger was selected as the victim for a dousing, but he took it well and laughed.

All too soon it seemed the campfire was over. Capt Conkey stood up and thanked them for their good behaviour and ordered them to bed. "Don't forget you have a long day tomorrow," he reminded.

As Graham stood up, he felt a wave of sadness. That was the last real activity of the camp. All that remained was the long drive home and admin. He tramped back to his section area with the others and set about making his bed. It was only 2130hrs and many cadets did not want to go to bed but platoon sergeants came around snapping and ordering them to lie down. Having unrolled his sleeping bag Graham sat on it to unlace his boots.

A person came along and shone a torch on him. Graham shielded his eyes and was about to snarl angrily when the person spoke. It was Peter.

"Graham, have you seen Carnes?"

"No," Graham replied, but he felt a stab of anxiety. "I'll help you look."

Talking his torch he stood up, leaving his hat on his bed. Sgt Grenfell shone his torch on them and demanded to know where they were going. Peter told him and Sgt Grenfell said they could go. The two friends then walked along the line of platoons, shining their torches on the groups of people sitting or lying on the sand. They were sworn at repeatedly but as the minutes went by Graham became more and more anxious.

Having checked the platoon areas, the two friends walked on along the sandy riverbed to the big pool at the junction with the Bunyip.

"Where the hell could he be?" Peter muttered, plainly worried.

Arriving at the water's edge the two friends stopped. Graham shone his torch around and asked where else Peter had looked.

"Just about everywhere," Peter replied, biting his lip with anxiety. "I've searched the HQ area, and up around the vehicles, then around the campfire."

At that moment Graham became aware of the sound of a train crossing the bridge. He looked down the bed of the Bunyip and saw the faint flicker of the train's headlights as it crossed the distant bridge. Then some instinct in him stirred and he felt a wave of uneasiness.

"The bridge," he said. "I'll bet he's gone to the bridge."

"The bridge! Why?" Peter asked in astonishment.

"He's going to commit suicide," Graham replied with certainty.

There was a chilled silence for a moment then Graham turned and began striding back towards the bivouac area.

"Come on, we must tell Capt Conkey!"

Chapter 35

CARNES

As Graham strode anxiously back towards the camp, his feelings firmed to one of certainty. Peter did not argue, having known and trusted him for many years. By the time they reached the bivouac area Graham had become so worried that he felt nauseous. So intense was his concern that he unconsciously walked as fast as he could. Thus the friends arrived back at 2 Platoon panting and starting to perspire.

"We must tell Capt Conkey," Graham said.

"I'll just check if Carnes has arrived back at HQ," Peter replied, adding, "We will look bloody silly if we hit the panic button and he is sound asleep in his bed."

Peter detoured over to where HQ was settling down. While he did that Graham stood waiting. Beyond the stream he could see figures sitting near the remains of the campfire. Among them he recognised Lt Standish and Lt McEwen. Nearby in the darkness was a smaller group.

Peter came striding back. "He's not here," he said.

Graham had guessed that and started walking towards the group at the fire. He splashed across the stream, barely noticing it. Peter hurried after him. As he drew closer to the group at the fire Graham saw that the two female officers were comforting a sobbing female cadet. So pre-occupied was he with worry about Carnes that Graham did not think about intruding. Only when he saw the annoyed looks on the officer's faces did it occur to him that he should have stayed away.

Lt Standish called to him, "Go away, Cpl Kirk."

Only then did Graham see that the sobbing girl was Lucy, and that Gwen Copeland and Barbara were both there comforting her.

Uh oh! he thought. *Trouble here!*

But he was determined and replied, "We need to see Capt Conkey, Miss. It is very urgent."

"He is over there but you should wait. He is busy," Lt Standish replied, shielding Lucy from his gaze as she did.

"Yes, Miss," Graham replied, but so concerned was he that he ignored her advice and headed straight for where a group stood in the darkness near the far bank of the river. Once again Peter followed.

As they approached the group, who were all standing, Graham heard Capt Conkey say in a very angry voice, “So if you didn’t give her the condom how come I have it here? She gave it to Lt Standish and said you gave it to her! How do you explain that?”

To Graham’s surprise, Sgt Yeldham answered, “I didn’t give it to her, sir. She is making it up!”

Hello! Graham thought, *Yeldham has put the hard word on Lucy!*

As this thought crossed his mind a powerful torch came on and shone on him. Lt Hamilton snapped, “Go away!”

Graham stood his ground. “Sir, I need to speak to Capt Conkey.”

“Go away! Come back later,” Lt Hamilton ordered gruffly.

Graham stubbornly stood there and shook his head. “This is very important too, sir.”

Capt Conkey spoke next, his own torch lighting up both Graham and Peter. “Yes, what is it?” he asked irritably.

Peter answered, “Cadet Carnes has gone missing sir.”

“Oh, damn and blast! That’s all I need!” Capt Conkey cried angrily.

Graham said, “I think I know where he has gone, sir.”

“Yes? Where?” Capt Conkey asked, lowering his torch beam.

“To the railway bridge,” Graham replied.

“The railway bridge!” Capt Conkey cried in astonishment. “Why would he go there?”

“I think he is going to commit suicide, sir,” Graham replied.

There was a moment’s silence, broken by Capt Conkey muttering “Oh Christ!” Then he asked, “Suicide? What makes you think that?”

“Just a few things he said, sir,” Graham replied. “He went to the bridge this afternoon.”

“This afternoon! Are you sure?” Capt Conkey asked.

“Yes, sir,” Graham replied. “I saw him brought back by the OOCs from St Michael’s.”

Lt Maclaren spoke from the darkness beyond Capt Conkey. “That’s right. I was there when they did. I meant to tell you about it.”

“Bloody hell!” Capt Conkey cried. He stepped closer to Graham. “What makes you think he is going to commit suicide?”

Graham tried to remember exactly what Carnes had said but could only give a general idea. "He seemed to have an obsession about the bridge sir," he said. He then explained how Carnes had frozen up and said he was afraid during the raid.

Peter agreed with this, describing how Carnes had stood staring up at the rail bridge during his recon patrol. Graham then said, "Carnes told me he hated his parents and that he wasn't going back to them. I don't remember the exact words sir, but I thought they were odd at the time. Now I think he meant he was not going back because he was going to end it all. I am sure he has gone to the bridge."

Capt Conkey ground his teeth and shone his torch on his watch. As he did, so Graham saw the stricken look on his face and he experienced a surge of sympathy for him.

"When was he last seen?" Capt Conkey asked.

CSM Cleland, who had been standing quietly at the back, answered that, "I saw him just after we had everyone seated for the campfire sir. I had the platoon sergeants do a check and he was here then."

Capt Conkey glanced at his watch again. "Twenty past ten. And he was last seen at about 1900hrs. That is nearly four hours!"

"He could certainly walk to the bridge in that time, sir," Graham said. "It is only two and a half kilometres."

Capt Conkey bit his lip, then nodded and said, "We must look for him." He turned to Lt Maclaren, "This business must wait. You take command here. Get the CSM to have the CUOs and sergeants check every person here. Get them all up and on parade. Then organise search parties to look along the riverbed and tracks. Look up Dingo Creek too."

He then turned to Lt Hamilton. "Hamish, get going and drive all the roads, then come back to check within half an hour. Go both ways along the highway for ten minutes. Check at the army camp and warn Major Ross. If you haven't found him drive to the bridge and contact me. I will take the other Rover and go to the bridge."

The group dispersed. As Capt Conkey made his way up the bank Graham followed. He did not wait for orders or ask. He just felt he had to be there. Once again Peter came with him. Capt Conkey glanced at them as he reached the Land Rover but made no comment. Graham climbed into the passenger seat, while Peter clambered into the back. The engine was switched on, then the lights. A moment later they were grinding up the steep, dusty track to the top of the bank.

As they accelerated along the better track up on the flat, Capt Conkey said, "Tell me more, Cpl Kirk. Tell me everything you can remember."

Graham did so. Capt Conkey drove fast, the vehicle bouncing and rattling over the bumps and corrugations. In their trail of dust the headlights of Lt Hamilton's vehicle followed. As he talked, Graham leaned forward, craning to see better through the windscreen. The Rover's headlights lit up a shifting cone of road and bush. At every second he hoped to catch a glimpse of Carnes. His main worry was that Carnes might try to hide.

At the junction of the Canning Road, Capt Conkey turned right. Lt Hamilton went left, back towards the Canning Causeway. As they drove up onto Sandy Ridge and then along Bare Ridge, Graham recounted the bullying and misery that Carnes had experienced; and as he did, he became more and more certain Carnes was going to try to do away with himself. He began to berate himself for not doing more to help.

"Not your fault," Capt Conkey replied gruffly. "It is mine. I should have taken more notice of the warning signs."

With every passing second Graham became more and more anxious. He kept hoping to glimpse Carnes in the headlights, but they reached the highway with no sign of him. There was no other traffic so Capt Conkey turned right onto the highway, accelerated, braked, turned left and then drove as fast as he dared along the gravel road leading to the railway bridge. Ignoring the bumps and shuddering he drove across the flat through the scattered thorn trees to where the road divided on top of the riverbank.

Ahead through the windscreen Graham could see the black outline of the bridge girders. He stared hard at them, biting his lip in anxiety and unknowingly drawing blood as they hit several potholes very hard. The road went along the top of the bank for 200 metres before dipping down to end on a grassy shelf fifty metres wide right under the bridge. Capt Conkey drove down onto the flat and braked to a stop with the headlights facing out across the riverbed. The beams lit up the huge concrete pylons, making them look like a row of stark monoliths.

As soon as the vehicle stopped, they jumped out. To Graham's great concern, there was no sign of Carnes. Graham ran to the edge of the grassy flat and looked down. The bank dropped down through a thin belt of trees to where the stream of shallow water flowed under the bridge.

I wonder if he has drowned himself? Graham thought. Then he shook his head. That didn't make sense. *He could have done that back at the camp easily. If he came here he means to jump.* With that he looked up.

The gigantic steel structure stood out starkly against the stars. It was so high above his head he had to crick his neck back to see it. Even where he stood it was a good thirty metres above him and he knew it was at least ten metres higher out over the sandy riverbed. He scanned the dark lattice work anxiously but could see nothing.

Capt Conkey turned on his powerful 'Big Jim' torch and swept the beam along the actual bridge. Graham caught a glimpse of white.

"There he is!" Peter cried.

Graham stared upwards in dismay. High above his head, leaning over the side of the railway line, was a tiny white face. It was Carnes staring back down at them. Carnes was out on the next section of the bridge, over the sand and at the place where the drop was longest.

As Graham watched, Carnes moved. Graham gasped, fearing Carnes was jumping. "Carnes! It's me, Cpl Kirk! Don't do it!" he shouted.

"He's going to jump!" Peter cried.

"No, he's not," Capt Conkey said, his voice torn with anguish. "He's trying to tie a noose on to the rail. He means to hang himself."

Before he realised what he was doing, Graham started running across the flat towards the end of the bridge. Peter ran with him, the friends arriving at the base of the slope together. A washed-out and overgrown vehicle track went up the slope. Graham ran up this, stumbling frequently. He skinned his hands and collected a dozen burs but ignored the pain and ran on, brushing at them. Once on top, he and Peter still had to run 50 metres to the embankment that carried the railway out across the flood plain.

The end of the bridge was built up on a steep sided embankment overgrown with long grass and prickly weeds. There was a barbed wire fence across the base of this. Graham hurled himself flat to wriggle under but in his haste snagged his shirt. Peter scrambled under the bottom strand of the next panel beside him and went on climbing the slope.

Graham swore and struggled then felt the barbs dig into his flesh. He swore again and eased back to try to unhook himself. Peter heard him swear and paused to look back.

Seeing Peter hesitate, Graham shouted, "Keep going Pete! I'll get myself free. Go!"

Peter continued climbing, his feet scrabbling in loose gravel. Graham swore again, his mind noting that Capt Conkey was shining his torch on him to help. In its beam he saw he was caught because the bottom strand was very close to the ground. He slid back and this time did it the way he had been taught: diagonally on his back. Quickly he lowered himself and tried again, using his hands to hold the barbed wire away. Again, the barbs snagged him, this time in the knees. This time his anxiety and sense of dread made him keep going forward. Heedless of the pain and ripping of cloth he tore free and scrambled up the slope after Peter.

By then Peter was up on the top of the embankment and Graham heard him shouting to Carnes as he raced off along the railway. His back stinging from the scratches, Graham dug his boots in to get a grip on the slithering gravel and forced his way up. A few seconds later he arrived at the top, gasping from the effort but all but oblivious to his own condition. Without hesitation he turned right and dashed along the railway.

The first 50 metres of bridge had high steel sides but it was still dangerous as the actual rail bridge consisted of the wooden sleepers bolted to the steel girders underneath, then the two steel rails fastened to the sleepers. Between the rails were two planks, each about 20 centimetres wide. A miscalculation on this section would mean a leg down between the sleepers, or between the girders.

It was the next section that mattered. Here the rails were still bolted to steel girders underneath, but the girders had no sides close to it. Every 5 metres or so a steel crossbeam led out to the crisscross of the 'through-truss' girders. In between these crossbeams was just thin air. Below was an ever-increasing drop. Ahead of him, Graham could see Peter running along the two planks. He did likewise, his heart pounding with fear. That a slip could be fatal was all too obvious. The height was only too apparent as he got glimpses of Capt Conkey and the Land Rover's lights below.

"You boys take care!" Capt Conkey shouted anxiously.

Graham ignored him and so did Peter. After a single glance which showed Capt Conkey talking on his mobile phone Graham hurried on. It was so obviously dangerous that he knew it was best to run and not think about what might happen if he stumbled or slipped. What really made it hard was the sense of being trapped by a prison of girders. The bridge was so long it seemed to vanish into the darkness. Their boots thudded on the boards with a hollow, thumping sound.

By the time Graham was halfway across the first main section Peter was past the first pylon and still running. Then Peter stumbled, causing Graham to gasp in fright, but he recovered and ran on, yelling to Carnes not to jump. Graham could not see Carnes at all because Peter was in the way. Then Capt Conkey's torch beam found them and Graham glimpsed Carnes leaning over the side. His face was towards Peter and he was calling something which Graham could not hear because his own laboured breathing and thumping heart interfered.

As Peter got closer Carnes, who had been kneeling and looking down, turned his head and put up his hand. He screamed, "Keep away! Don't come near me!"

Peter slowed and called back, "Don't be silly! It will be alright. Don't jump."

In the torch beam Graham glimpsed Carnes' frantic resolve. To Graham's dismay, Carnes had the rope tied around his neck. The other end of the rope was tied around the steel railway line. As Peter walked forward, Carnes shouted again, "Don't come near me!"

Peter stopped and tried to reason with him, but Carnes just shook his head and looked down. In the torchlight Graham clearly saw him swallow. His eyes looked very large and glistened in the light. He opened his mouth to say something to Peter, then stepped back and stumbled. For a second Carnes tried frantically to regain his footing, then he fell.

Carnes screamed and so did Graham, who was still 20 metres away. Carnes dropped straight down but then came to an abrupt stop, his body still above the railway line.

His foot has slipped through between the sleepers, Graham thought.

His own heart hammered frantically with anxiety as he hurried on forward. Fear had now slowed his progress as he could clearly see what a huge drop lay below. Now he was out past the shallow water and was over the sand of the main riverbed.

Peter called, "Wait, Carnes! Don't move! I'll help you." He began walking towards Carnes.

"No! Get away!" Carnes screamed. He began to struggle frantically to haul his leg free. In the process he squirmed so that he was hanging out over the edge.

Peter kept moving and reached Carnes. "Stop moving so I can help you," he cried.

Instead, Carnes began hysterical shouting and struck at Peter. "Leave me alone! Leave me alone! I want to die!"

There was a smack and Graham saw Peter stagger, then heard him cry out. To Graham's horror Peter suddenly toppled sideways and fell off the bridge. One second he was there, the next he was gone. There was a thud and the bridge shuddered. A metallic clang sounded and Graham saw that Peter had landed across one of the crossbeams. Then he slid over the side, his hands clawing desperately for a grip.

Unaware that he was screaming in despair, Graham dashed forward and looked down, seeing only the struggling black shape that was Peter. Far below was the sand, floodlit by the Land Rover's headlights. Somehow Peter had grabbed on, but he was hanging by one hand from the bottom flange of the cross girder and could slip and plummet to his death at any second. And in Graham's way was Carnes. He had managed to get his leg free and was crouching on the sleepers staring down at Peter in shocked dismay.

"Help him Carnes! Don't just sit there!" Graham shouted.

Carnes shook himself and stared at Graham. "I didn't mean to! I just wanted him to keep away," he wailed.

Graham clenched his fists and grated his teeth. "I don't care what you meant! Grab hold of him! Quick!"

But Carnes just knelt there babbling it wasn't his fault.

"Help me!" Peter gasped. "Hurry! I can't hold on much longer!"

"Hang on Pete! Hang on!" Graham cried as he hurried the last few steps.

It was only then, as he knelt down to reach for Peter that he realised what the distant glow and the growing vibration meant.

A train was coming!

Chapter 36

HANG ON!

"Hang on!" Graham shouted to Peter.

Peter had managed to get his other hand up to grab hold of the crossbeam, but it was a poor grip as only the fingers were over the lip of the steel girder.

"Help!" Peter gasped. "I can't hold on much longer."

Graham dithered for a second, looking frantically around to try to work out the best way to help his friend. Carnes was in his way, so Graham stood up and moved around to his other side. Then he took hold of the rail and lowered one boot down over the end of the sleepers till it reached the crossbeam. With his heart hammering from fear, he turned himself around and slid backwards down, ignoring the scraping on his chest and stomach from the ends of the rough wooden sleepers. Trembling and sweating and on the brink of paralysing terror, he reached down and grabbed the top of the beam. Carefully, he stood side on and then lowered himself until he was sitting astride the crossbeam with his back to the railway.

As he sat down, the vibration through the rail told Graham that the train was now on the bridge. It was coming from the far end and he hoped he had time. By now the headlight of the approaching locomotive was lighting everything up in brilliant black and white. That helped Graham as he looked in under the sleepers.

The main beam was about half a metre deep, with flanges 20 centimetres wide. The cross girder he was sitting on was similar in size. There were huge bolt heads but nothing to actually hang onto. Far below was the riverbed. Graham broke into a sweat of fear and trembled, feeling very insecure.

One slip and I am a goner, he told himself.

For a few seconds he was paralysed by vivid flashbacks of when he had clung to the slippery face of Stoney Creek Falls. Then he shook his head and gritted his teeth.

There was nothing for it but to take a risk. Shaking with fear he lay down and locked his legs together around the girder. The hard steel edges cut painfully into his flesh, but he ignored this. Holding on with his left hand he leaned out and down and grasped Peter's left wrist. To his dismay, both his hand and Peter's skin were slick with sweat. Above him, Carnes was still leaning over and crying that he hadn't meant it.

Suddenly, Carnes became aware of the train and began to scream and jibber, "A train! A train!"

In his agitation he began clawing at Graham, almost pulling him off balance. Graham knew that there were small safety projections for bridge maintenance workers to use, so he pointed to one and screamed, "Get onto that!"

Carnes either did not hear him or did not understand as he kept screaming. He leaned over and grabbed at Graham. Graham swore and tried to ignore him. What was taking up most of his consciousness was Peter's terror-filled face as he dangled by his hands below him. By now the roar of the approaching train had become a deafening thunder. This was drowned out as the engine sounded its air horn, the blast seeming to shake the whole structure.

This is not going to work! Graham thought as he felt Peter slipping from his grip. But did he dare let go for a moment while trying to get a better grip? *I have to take the risk,* he thought.

Desperation made him act. Judging he was safe from the train, Graham tried to ignore it. He let go of the crossbeam with his left hand and reached down with it and grabbed hold of Peter's shirt sleeve, twisting the cloth into his grip. The action drove some of the burs deeply into his palm but he ignored the pain and tightened his grip. In doing so Graham had to lean over the side of the beam, depending on his legs to keep a grip.

"Swing your legs up Pete!" Graham shouted, his voice all but drowned out by the massive roar of the train.

Peter tried to but was obviously scared to swing much lest his fingers slip off the rim of the girder. Graham tightened his grip with his left hand and then let go of Peter's wrist with his right. Leaning even further over Graham reached down and seized Peter's shirt with his right hand. At that moment the locomotive's horn blared deafeningly again and then the thunder of its approach changed note and Graham knew it had roared onto the section of bridge they were on.

Suddenly, boots struck at Graham and he felt Carnes grabbing at him. Terror-stricken, Carnes came scrabbling down on top of him, grabbing frantically at his clothes for a hold. Graham felt pure terror surge in his veins as he began to slip sideways off the beam. He screamed at Carnes to stop it but was ignored. With an ear-shattering roar, the engine raced past a few centimetres above his head. The noise was so loud and terrifying that Graham found it all but paralysing. All he could do was hang on.

To prevent himself being dragged sideways off the beam, Graham braced his boots under the main girder and clung on, literally for grim death. Above him sounded an even more ear-splitting screech as hundreds of brake shoes came on, to scrape at hundreds of steel wheels. The din was absolutely stunning. The whole bridge seemed to thunder and shake.

By this time, Graham was almost frantic with fear as he could feel himself being slowly dragged off the beam by Carnes, who now grabbed him around the neck and upper body. Carnes' boots hammered at the steel girder and then beat at Peter, who clenched his teeth and clung grimly on.

This can't go on, Graham thought. He could feel his strength giving out.

"Climb up over me Pete!" Graham screamed, at the same time using all his strength to haul Peter upwards.

Peter's shirt stretched, then ripped, but it was enough. With a desperate lunge Peter let go of the rim with his right hand and managed to get it up over the top of Graham's back. He grabbed at Graham's trousers and hung on, his boots flailing at thin air as he tried to swing them up to get a grip.

Carnes was in the way. Worse still, he was slowly dragging Graham off the beam. Something began pressing sharply into Graham's neck and back and he realised it was the rope Carnes had around his neck. Suddenly the rope went slack, and Carnes slid even further over until he was dangling beside Peter. In the process he clung frantically to Graham who could feel himself being pulled over as well. Knowing that he was doomed if he allowed this to happen, Graham used all the strength in his leg muscles to brace his boots under the main girder.

For over a minute all he could do was hang on with all his might. On one side was Peter, pulling at him as he tried to get a foothold. On the other was Carnes, who was now screaming in Graham's ear as he clung desperately on.

Then the last wagon of the train rolled past and the fearful metallic screeching, clashing, and banging began to recede. Graham was quite unable to move his head and feared that Carnes was going to break his neck as he clung to him. His cheek was pressed hard down onto the cold steel of the crossbeam.

Suddenly, the weights shifted, almost causing Graham to slip over under the beam. Peter had got a boot up onto one of the diagonal crossbeams and now reached up over him to grip the sleepers. Then Peter was above him and sitting astride him, his boots placed on the lower flange of the crossbeam. It hurt but Graham guessed that Peter knew what he was doing.

"Hang on, Graham," Peter yelled in his ear.

Graham did, with Carnes still hanging from him. But it was not a stable situation. Carnes was squirming and struggling so much that he kept upsetting Graham's grip and balance. By now his thigh and calf muscles were starting to quiver and feel white hot.

"Stop moving, Carnes, and we will get you up," Peter yelled.

But Carnes was beyond reason. He clawed at Graham, gripping his shirt. This ripped right across the back where it had already been torn. Carnes screamed and dropped. For a moment Graham thought he had fallen, but then the rope went tight across his back and shoulders and he knew that Carnes was dangling on the end of it. To the extent that he was himself being strangled by its pressure across the back of his neck, Graham half-wished Carnes would fall off.

"Pete! Do something!" Graham gasped. "I'm being choked."

"Wait. Just hold on," Peter replied.

There was movement and Peter said, "Have you got hold of him?"

"Yes," Graham called back, grabbing hold of Carnes' sleeve.

"Try to lift him and hang on for a minute while I get back on to the bridge," Peter replied.

"Let the bloody rope hold him," Graham gasped. *It's what he wanted*, he thought, but didn't say.

"I can't," Peter replied. "The train has cut the knot and I've got the end around my wrist. You'll have to take the weight so I can get up."

Graham shouted to Peter he had the weight and clung on grimly. The rope suddenly went slack and Peter put a boot in the middle of Graham's back. Then the pressure was gone. Graham was able to turn his head and breathe. He looked over the side into Carnes' terror-stricken eyes. Carnes was screaming and babbling for them to save him. As he did, he jerked and squirmed, his legs flailing at thin air.

"Stop moving, bugger you!" Graham yelled. He could hardly hold on himself and could feel Carnes slipping through his grasp.

Carnes ignored him and kept frantically trying to climb back up to him. Suddenly the rope went tight, and Carnes began to choke. His eyes bulged and his tongue stuck out. With his left hand he clawed at the noose around his neck. Graham stared in horrified fascination.

Peter shouted in Graham's ear, "Grab him and lift!"

Graham realised that Peter was leaning over the side of the bridge next to him and was reaching down with both hands. Peter shouted again, "Quick! I've tied the rope on to stop him dropping. Help me!"

Seeing Carnes choking to death before his very eyes galvanised Graham for a last big effort. He reached down, grabbed Carnes' hair and heaved up. Peter was able to reach Carnes' shirt and he took over the hauling while Graham transferred his grip to Carnes' trousers. Then it was relatively easy. Peter used all his strength to drag Carnes up over the end of the sleepers onto the rails.

Graham lay astride the girder, shuddering with exertion and fear for a moment, then opened his mouth to call to Peter to help him. He had no need. Peter had already acted and reached down to grab his clothes.

"Okay Graham. Up you come. Take it slow."

Graham did. He was shaking so much he feared he would slip or lose his grip, so he moved one limb at a time, only moving another when he was sure he had a tight grip. The hardest part was twisting around to get a grip behind him, then turning to reach up for the rail. Once he had the rail in his grasp it was easy. He placed a boot on the crossbeam and pushed himself up so that he slid forward on his front across the rails.

Peter held him while he did this but once he was up both boys just lay down across the track. For several minutes all they could do was lie there. Graham was so shaken and sore that he felt as though elephants had trampled him and tried to pull him apart.

Suddenly, a ghastly thought crossed his mind: was Carnes being strangled by his noose?

"Pete, check that Carnes isn't being choked to death by his noose," he called.

Peter did so then lay back. "It's okay, he's breathing," he said. "He didn't tie a proper noose, so the knot didn't tighten up."

Poor old Carnes, Graham thought. *Couldn't even hang himself properly!*

Then he lay back and began to sob as the reaction set in.

It was the lights and shouting which roused Graham. He turned his head and saw the headlights of another vehicle parking below them. Then the thud of boots sounded on the bridge and a minute later a desperately anxious Capt Conkey arrived to join them.

As he swept the beam of his torch over the three boys, he cried aloud, "Oh, thank God! All safe!"

Capt Conkey made them lie still while he made more phone calls. As he did, Graham roused himself. "Sir, call the railways and tell them to stop any trains."

"The police are doing that, and that train that just crossed is stopped a little way up the line," Capt Conkey replied. Then he sat down and shook his head, then sobbed, "Oh my word, that was bloody close!"

"You are telling me!" agreed Peter.

He sat up and Graham tried to do so as well but found all his muscles quivering. Capt Conkey insisted they lie there till they had recovered and more help had arrived. Lt Hamilton was the first, then the very anxious train crew. They were mightily relieved to learn that no-one had been injured or killed. Next to arrive were two army officers and an army medic from the camp.

Between them they assisted the boys to walk safely back off the bridge. As he made his way along with Capt Conkey walking behind him and holding his arm, Graham felt quite dizzy and shuddered at the risks he and Peter had taken running out in the dark along the two planks. When he at last reached the embankment at the end of the bridge, he sighed with relief and offered a silent prayer.

By the time they had slithered down the embankment and negotiated the barbed wire fence, two more vehicles had arrived: a police car and an ambulance from Charters Towers. The boys were at once taken to the ambulance. Graham's scratches were cleaned and daubed with antiseptic and he was asked if he wanted to go to the hospital to see a doctor.

"No thanks," he replied. "I am alright, just a little shaken up."

Peter gave the same reply and both he and Graham were taken to one side while Carnes was placed in the ambulance. After a discussion between the adults, a policeman climbed in the back of the ambulance and it drove off. Graham and Peter were both then questioned by the officers and the police. That was something Graham found a bit of an ordeal as he was hurting by then. His scratches smarted and his over-stretched muscles continued to tremble. He found he was shaking and felt flushed.

Both he and Peter were then driven to the army camp. Here the army medic again washed the cuts and scratches and they were fed with hot Milo. A spare shirt was found for Graham and he gingerly pulled it on. During a break in the questioning, Graham gave Peter a wry smile and said, "I reckoned you were history when you were dangling by just one hand."

Peter made a face. "So did I!" he replied. "Now I know how you felt that time you were thrown over the cliff beside the Kuranda Railway last year." With that he put his head down and sobbed, then broke into a fit of shivering.

Graham waited till he had recovered and then asked if he was alright. Peter nodded and then said, "Thanks mate."

Which made Graham all embarrassed. Even so he shuddered every time he thought of that ghastly drop and what might have been.

It was well after midnight before Capt Conkey drove them back to the bivouac area, both having declined to spend the night in the RAP. Back at the campsite they found the officers all still awake but were told to get straight to bed. They were also told not to discuss the incident with anyone until given permission.

"We need to protect Cadet Carnes," Capt Conkey explained. "It is personal in confidence stuff."

By this time Graham was feeling very stiff and he hobbled off into the darkness to find his bed.

In the platoon area all was quiet. Everyone was asleep. Graham found his bedding and gently eased himself down onto it. His muscles protested but it was such a relief that he sighed and then slowly stretched out. He was sure he would not sleep but after giving thanks in another prayer he slipped quickly into a deep sleep.

When Graham was shaken awake, he was dreaming he was teetering on a huge steel bridge and was in danger of falling off. As he woke, he experienced a spasm of panic till he realised it was only a dream. Only when he tried to sit up did the memory really hit him, brought on by the pain of stiff muscles and aching scratches. With a groan he sat up and gently eased himself to his feet.

Sgt Grenfell was standing there. "Time for check parade," he said, giving him a quizzical look.

This was the first of many, but Graham just shook his head and said he couldn't say anything. The platoon formed up with the others for check parade. After it was over, they straggled back to their bivouac area to pack up.

While he was rolling up his bedding Kirsty came and stood next to him. "What happened last night?" she asked.

"I'm not allowed to say," Graham replied.

As he looked up, he noted that she had several bruises on her neck. *Love bites!* he thought. He found that immensely saddening and knew he was jealous, yet glad he had been strong enough to resist her.

At that moment, CSM Cleland came along. He gave them both a hard look, then said, "Cpl Kirk, come with me. Capt Conkey wants to speak to you."

That got Graham all anxious again and while he walked to Company HQ he examined his guilty conscience, wondering why. Capt Conkey was sitting with all the other officers but he stood up and walked over to meet them as Graham and the CSM approached. For a few moments he looked hard at Graham, who found it difficult to meet his eyes.

Then Capt Conkey asked, "Cpl Kirk, were you planning to stay in cadets next year?"

Here it comes, Graham thought. *He has found out about Kirsty and is going to chuck me out!*

He swallowed and nodded. "Yes sir, I wanted to."

"Good. How would you like to be CSM?" Capt Conkey asked.

For a moment Graham did not comprehend. Then it dawned on him he was not in trouble. He again swallowed and nodded, then said, "Yes, sir. I'd like that."

"Good. I have been very impressed with your leadership and determination during the camp. And after the last few nights I am really impressed by your courage. If you can resist the wrong sort of temptations you will do very well," Capt Conkey said.

Graham simultaneously glowed with pleasure at the praise and shame over Kirsty. *He has noticed,* he thought, *and he is warning me.* Deeply moved, he silently vowed to do the very best he could.

"Yes, sir," he managed to say.

"Good, now I have a less pleasant task for you," Capt Conkey said.

"Sir?"

"Sergeant Yeldham has been relieved of his duties and 3 Platoon needs a platoon sergeant. Are you willing to be an acting sergeant for the remainder of the year?"

"Yes, sir."

"Good," Capt Conkey said. He dug into his pocket and took out a brassard with sergeant's chevrons on it. "Then put this on and go and get them packed up ready to march. CSM, give Sgt Kirk their roll book."

CSM Cleland handed Graham the 3 Platoon roll book and said, "Get going sergeant."

"Yes, sir!"

Author's Note

This is a story about the problems of leadership. Its characters are teenage army cadets on their annual camp. The story deals with a wide range of problems and situations, all of which may be encountered by young leaders to test their character and training. Because some of the situations involve the issue of 'fraternisation' there are, of necessity, some sexual references.

Because most of the incidents involve teenage boys there is some coarse language (Strongly modified for the book and not nearly as colourful or objectionable as they tend to use in reality). There is also some discussion about maleness- as seen through the eyes of teenagers.

This places the author in a difficult situation. If reality is included some people may be offended or object- but if reality is not included how then does one advise and help people to cope with the world they actually live in?

So this is a watered down but 'warts and all' story describing the sorts of things young leaders may encounter and offering helpful hints on how to deal with them. The author commanded an army cadet unit for 34 years and can assure the reader that all of the situations described have actually happened- with minor changes for the sake of the story- but thankfully not all to one poor cadet corporal.

The book was written in North Queensland in the days before combined camps with 'Tier' Training and the style of camp described is, in this author's opinion, a much better way of achieving the character building and leadership training objectives of the AAC.

Enjoy more C.R. Cummings stories

The Air Cadets

The Navy Cadets

The Army Cadets

www.ingramcontent.com/pod-product-compliance
Lightning Source LLC
LaVergne TN
LVHW030908080826
845145LV00010B/2810

* 9 7 8 0 6 4 5 0 6 5 6 6 4 *